"Eric Clapton's Lover"
and Other Stories from the
*Virginia Quarterly Review*

# "Eric Clapton's Lover" and Other Stories from the *Virginia Quarterly Review*

Edited by
SHEILA MCMILLEN AND GEORGE GARRETT

With an Introduction by George Garrett

UNIVERSITY PRESS OF VIRGINIA
*Charlottesville and London*

THE UNIVERSITY PRESS OF VIRGINIA
Copyright © 1990 by the Rector and Visitors
of the University of Virginia

*Second printing 1991*

Library of Congress Cataloging-in-Publication Data

"Eric Clapton's lover" and other stories from the Virginia quarterly review / edited by Sheila McMillen and George Garrett ; with an introduction by George Garrett.
    p.  cm.
  ISBN 0-8139-1269-5. — ISBN 0-8139-1285-7 (pbk.)
  1. Short stories, American. 2. Short stories, American—Virginia.
3. American fiction—20th century. I. McMillen, Sheila.
II. Garrett, George P., 1929–   . III. Virginia quarterly review.
PS648.S5E75 1990
813'.0108—dc20                                                89-48258
                                                                  CIP

Printed in the United States of America

*This book is dedicated to Charlotte Kohler,*
*Staige D. Blackford, and Barbara Murphy.*
*And to the memory of Nancy Hale.*

# CONTENTS

"Eric Clapton's Lover"
and Other Stories from the
*Virginia Quarterly Review*

# *Introduction*

*Probably creative people have no more respect
for critics and collectors than a chemist
has for litmus paper.*

David Stacton, "A Visit to the Master"

The *Virginia Quarterly Review* can fool you. I have to admit that it has pretty well fooled me over most of my adult lifetime, the somewhat more than forty years that, as a writer and a teacher (among some other things), I have regularly been watching and reading and sometimes even writing for the *VQR*. During all that time, and from the magazine's beginnings in 1925, the outward and visible changes have been, to say the least, subtle ones. Some years ago Staige Blackford, the current editor, changed the page numbers in the front section of the magazine from Roman to Arabic; and there have been some slight changes in typeface and changes in the texture and color of the cover, from the dark blue of the earliest days on up through several shades of orange, and, most recently, the first use of photographs to enhance the otherwise austere front cover. This latter surprise shocked us oldtimers about as much as a hand grenade going off in the reading room of some club or library.

You get the idea.

This is a pretty quiet place. Kind of subdued even when it's being busy and noisy. During a brief riot in 1970, the rioting (protesting) students suddenly discovered that they were tearing up the turf and sod of Mr. Jefferson's famous Lawn and, rather than continuing that kind of ill-mannered, outrageous desecration, they quickly moved their riot around to the other side, the street side, of the Rotunda. The University of Virginia is a quiet and beautiful place with a rich patina of tradition. So you wouldn't expect the *VQR*, housed at the impeccable address of One West Range on the original Grounds (now a National Landmark), housed in a cluster of spacious, high-ceilinged eighteenth century rooms, with wide waxed and stained floorboards and elegant fireplaces (the editor and his staff have to use the bathrooms over in Alderman Library, across a street and fifty yards away; but you can't have authenticity and all the modern comforts and conveniences, can you?), to be anything less than part and parcel of the general ambiance: traditional, then, if not purely and simply conservative. Maybe even vaguely reactionary, if studied and judged from some popular contemporary points of view. After all, in more than one interview Staige Blackford has elected (half in irony) to stress the traditional character of the *VQR*: "There is a sense of trying to carry on a tradition here," he has said. "This is such a TV age. But I think there is a future. We are trying to keep an ideal alive."

Blackford is not being ironic when he expresses his debt and obligation to Charlotte Kohler, who edited the *VQR* for thirty-three years before he came on board. "I inherited from Charlotte one of our foremost intellectual beacons," he says. "And my job is to keep that beacon shining." Charlotte Kohler, who edited the Quarterly from 1942 to 1975 (the other editors, from 1925 to 1942 were James Southall Wilson, Stringfellow Barr, and Lambert Davis), before retiring and turning it over to Staige Blackford, developed the tone and style and range of concerns which characterize the contemporary *VQR* as we know it. This prominent and influential female editor, whose contributions to the mainstream of the modern American intellectual climate are significant and deserve honorable recognition, now lives in retirement in Charlottesville close by the University.

If, on account of the gently sly outward and visible changes, over more than sixty years, at the *VQR* and because of its place at the University, an institution which seems to emphasize traditions, you snapped to the judgment that the *VQR* is simply old-fashioned, you would be mostly wrong. First, because the heart of the Jeffersonian tradition was and is revolutionary, at once innovative and radical. The statues and monuments, of which there are a gracious plenty at this, his university, no matter how accurate and aesthetically well made, are boring when set against his words and deeds. Some of

Thomas Jefferson's words are proudly placed above an entrance to Cabell Hall and are as rare and radical and outrageous to this day as they were when he uttered them: "Here we are not afraid to follow Truth wherever it may lead nor to tolerate any error so long as reason is left free to combat it." The subtitle of the *VQR* is "A National Journal of Literature and Discussion." That is, as it has always been, the context of the magazine, its critical and cultural purpose. Its literary credentials, of course, are impeccable. In addition to full-scale literary essays and essay reviews of current books, the *VQR* offers, under the rubric of its "Notes On Current Books," more book reviews than any other literary magazine or quarterly in the nation. But because the editors have taken seriously the second part of the subtitle, "Discussion," the *VQR*, unlike most of the other literary magazines and quarterlies, has a wide spread of interests in more general topics. There are general essays on history, politics, economics, and, indeed, all the arts and sciences. Blackford is pleased to point out that he likewise regularly publishes essays and articles on a variety of less academic subjects, "including sports and sex, neither of which you'll ever find in *The Sewanee Review*." And Blackford likes to include at least one "personal" essay in each issue. He sees the *VQR*, together with a very few of the other major quarterlies and even fewer among the commercial magazines, as "the last repositories in America for what I call the 'elegant essay,' one that requires length to develop itself and the use of language somewhat above a seventh grade level."

Poetry and fiction have an assured place in this context. Each issue presents a selection of poems culled from the work of the more than one thousand poets who submit to the *VQR* each year. Something like two thousand short stories, give or take a few, also come in with the mail each year, jostling and elbowing each other for attention and an average of three places per issue (twelve stories a year). No wonder that Blackford allows: "The most difficult thing is that we get so much short fiction (good and bad) that it is very difficult to separate the wheat from the chaff." Some of this separation and winnowing is accomplished by one or more trusted readers. At present the *VQR*'s first readers of fiction are local novelist Philip Gould and co-editor of this anthology, story-writer Sheila McMillen. In the recent past Blackford has had the good services of Nancy

Hale and Ann Beattie and Alyson Hagy (all three represented in this volume) and others. "I have been very lucky with my readers," Blackford says.

When Sheila and I had the idea of putting together a representative gathering of the best fiction from the pages of the *VQR*, we agreed that the fiction of the *VQR* was and is not as well known as it deserves to be, in spite of the fact that stories from it have frequently been selected for annual prize anthologies like *Best American Short Stories, Prize Stories: The O'Henry Awards,* and the new kid on the block, *New Stories From the South.* When Sheila and I set out seeking and finding the best stories we could find from among, roughly, twenty-five years of already strictly chosen and carefully edited examples, we were in for some surprises. We soon discovered that we had been more than just a little deceived by our own casual illusions and easy expectations. This is a serious admission; because, as I have already indicated, neither one of us was or is exactly a stranger to the magazine. We had read it, have done some different kinds of work for it; and we really ought to have known better than we did. For example, we both assumed that the fiction would be much more uniformly "regional" than, in fact, it is or ever was. Truth turned out to be that, at least for all the years we carefully examined, the fiction of the *VQR* has been *less* regional in setting and orientation than that of almost any other quarterly or institutional literary magazine we know of. In part, this is a matter of the editorial policy firmly stated in the subtitle—that the *VQR* is "A *National* Journal of Literature and Discussion" [italics mine]. But we also noticed right away something you will likewise notice in reading these stories—how, thus accurately reflecting our national interests and point of view, any number of the stories have an international setting or concern. Blackford explained the situation this way: "The tradition of the *VQR* has been to be national and yet regional, also, since it found itself located in the South. But the truth is that in fiction and nonfiction we have taken the best of what is. And that does not preclude anything." We didn't look for stories with global interests and concerns. They were there. And they are here in this book. For instance, Lawrence Dunning's "A Walk to Shinabaru" is set in Japan; Alyson Hagy's "Where Men Go to Cry" takes place in part in Ouagadougou, Upper Volta; Ward Just's "Journalism" follows the Third World wars of our own time; Clayton Lewis's "Children of Esau" centers on the Vietnam War; poet William Meredith places his story, "The Dolly Varden," in the Aleutians, where he served in World War II; David Stacton's "A Visit to the Master" summons up the art gallery scene of Western Europe; Ted Walker's "The Peace Rose" evokes the shabby ambiance of England in the 1970s. And even when a story is precisely southern in setting—William Hoffman's "Sweet Armageddon," for example, which takes place an hour away from Charlottesville, in contemporary Richmond—there is a strong sense of the impingement of other distant, alien worlds. Here Amos, the retired minister and former missionary, summons up a memory to make an analogy: "During the summer glossy blue lizards had crept from crumbled mortar to sun themselves and made him think of Brazil and his years among Indians at the jungle's edge—quiet, dark-eyed people whose aroused savagery was like the wrath of terrible children."

Place is important, then, and so is time. Not surprisingly these stories, which first appeared in a "surround" of historical, political, and social essays, tend to emphasize rather precisely the time of their happening. Thus Kelly Cherry's "Where She Was" ("This is a portrait of the girl who became my father's wife"), is set in the Louisiana of Huey Long, of 1933. "A Walk to Shinabaru" is the Japan of the American Occupation. Joann Kobin's "The Lost Glove" calls up the 1950s, specifically the end of 1953 and the early months of 1954. "The Dolly Varden" could only have happened when it did, during World War II. Peter Taylor's celebrated "Dean of Men" covers an American lifetime from the early days of the Depression onward. Steve Yarbrough's Poland is only a year or two behind us, during the days of Martial Law. And it is hard to imagine a more exact indication of specific time than Ann Beattie demonstrates ("'Interested in Nixon's phlebitis?' he called from the T.V. room.") in our title story.

Clearly in the context of spent and recovered time, memory is vitally important. Not all the characters would, by any means, agree with the full sense of the wistful observation from Ellen Wilbur's haunting story "Faith": "The older the memory, the more beautiful it has become." But a goodly number of stories in the VQR and in this book take the form of a first-person memoir. Among the latter: Hal Bennett's "Virginia in the Window," Kelly Cherry's

"Where She Was," Anne Hobson Freeman's "Hugh," William Peden's "Hurricane," Deborah Seabrooke's "Secrets," Peter Taylor's "Dean of Men," and Ted Walker's "The Peace Rose."

Similarly, we did not anticipate finding much, if any, "experimental" fiction, early or late. And no question that there has never been much high-stepping, off-the-wall-and-all-over-the-page short fiction in the *VQR*. If that, taken with a dose of pure obscurity and a large dollop of absolute inaccessibility, is your definition of the "experimental." Truth is, we found plenty of examples of writers working within straightforward narrative conventions who subtly pushed these conventions towards their vague limits, who have routinely invented new dances to the old tunes. The modestly self-reflexive form of Joann Kobin in "The Last Glove" is unusual for the *VQR*. But there are some other sly and idiosyncratic gestures. For example, at the time of its publication (1964), the present-tense narration of "A Walk To Shinabaru" was still rare enough to have the shine of novelty. William Hoffman's apt use of biblical fragments in "Sweet Armageddon," is at once surprising and appropriate. William Peden's gear shift, from third- to first-person point of view, following the first paragraph of "Hurricane," is so well executed (as might be expected from a master teacher of story technique) that you might miss it. And in "Dean of Men" Peter Taylor reanimates an old-fashioned form, rare enough nowadays to qualify as "experimental," by having the reader eavesdrop on a private monologue addressed to a specific character.

You will notice, first to last, from Beattie to Yarbrough, that each of these writers has a strongly distinct voice. They do not sound very much like one another. Sometimes it is the voice of a speaker, as in this woman attending her twenty-fifth reunion at Bryn Mawr in Anne Hobson Freeman's "Hugh": "I'm 46 years old and I have this premonition—if I can give myself a little time this summer, I just may be about to grow up." Or the sad pomposity of the narrator in "Dead of Men": "It is important to broaden one's humanity, but it is important to remain a mere man, too." There are superbly effective examples of third-person narration which is carried so close to the vernacular first-person tale telling as to be virtually indistinguishable from it. As, for example, in Jack Matthew's powerful funny/sad and more than somewhat gothic, bucolic tale, "On the Shore of Chad Creek." Or, in appropriate places, in Clayton Lewis's

"Children of Esau": "One night in Subic Bay he and Layton had raised hell. Like he was in a lousy war movie, Layton took the O Club singer back to his hotel room." Or this, from Kent Nelson's gritty story of New York City losers and street people: "One time the Chinese restaurant next door caught fire and the firemen had called for the tenants of his building to evacuate, but Blumenthal stayed in his room pretending he wasn't home." Strict third-person storytelling is exploited fully in Ward Just's remarkable story of the career of a woman journalist going to pieces with our times— "Journalism." Here he shows and tells us why she usually went in company with male reporters to the front in the wars: "She believed she could not discover the truth about men at war unless she saw them with their own kind, at a distance; when she was alone with them, she was the living proof of the Heisenberg Principle."

Incidentally, Just's wonderful portrayal of a woman's being and Alyson Carol Hagy's extraordinary realization of the *physicality* of maleness, in "Where Men Go to Cry," render irrelevant the debate as to whether or not imaginative writers can escape the limitations and habits of gender. Note, too, the wide range of *ages* in these stories, sometimes, as in Taylor's "Dean of Men," within the same story.

On more than one occasion Blackford has pointed out something else, another quality of the fiction published in the *VQR* which is almost rare enough to be called "experimental." Speaking to a reporter on the occasion when Gail Godwin picked two of the *VQR* stories for the 1985 edition of *Best American Short Stories* (one of them, Deborah Seabrooke's "Secrets," is included here), Blackford insisted: "Both the stories happen to contain one of the missing ingredients in most American short fiction today—*humor*." Ann Beattie's fiction has often been singled out by critics for its inextricable coupling of irony and pity. One of the reasons we elected to title this anthology after her story is that, though every story gathered here is essentially different from every other, all of them share that quality of linking irony and pity, tiptoing close around the choice of laughter and of tears. Maintaining this kind of delicate, perilous balance is one proof of the excellence of these stories.

Another expectation which was soon to be modified, if not entirely diminished, was a little more complicated (though brutally simple at heart). We knew from experience that many prominent writers, "name " fiction writers, were a regular feature of the VQR. With so few publications offering a home for any serious fiction, with the "market" shrinking steadily to near invisibility in the years since the Second World War, how could it be otherwise? And with only about twelve stories a year to be ruthlessly culled from the roughly two thousand submitted for consideration, it would seem that at the VQR, as everywhere else in short fiction's major leagues, the better-known writers would lay claim to most of the space and steal the show. After all, the editor has to sell magazines and subscriptions. Big Names help. And Big Names (even in the little literary world) carry weight and significance "in house," locally. English professors, for example, are nowdays a major source of strength for the literary status quo. They know and can keep up, somewhat, with the Big Names; but they leave the risks and pleasures of discovery to others, anybody else, in fact, with the time and stomach for it. You don't often become a chaired professor of anything, except maybe nuclear physics, by taking a lot of chances. Magazines affiliated one way or another with institutions which, one way or another, support them, tend to keep this always in mind. Because they have to.

Well, then. The VQR has published its share of well-known writers from its beginnings until now. In the early days there were regulars like Robert Frost and Conrad Aiken, H. L. Mencken and Bertrand Russell, D. H. Lawrence and Katherine Anne Porter. Sheila and I expected to encounter good work by undeniably prominent literary figures published in the VQR over the past twenty-five years. And we did. A few, a fair proportion of them, are represented in this anthology. Probably anybody's literary scorecard would list Ann Beattie, Nancy Hale, William Hoffman, Ward Just, Hilary Masters, Jack Matthews, and Peter Taylor. A few, too few, would render full honors of fame to David Stacton. And, if the publication of prominent writers had been our goal, we could have filled all these pages with the good work of some very well-known people. But if we had done so, it would not have been a just representation of its original source—the VQR. The VQR has always been actively dedicated to the purpose of the discovery of new talent quite as much as to the support of established artists. Excellence is the primary quality demanded; but about half of the stories accepted and published in the *VQR* are by relative newcomers or writers who have not yet earned the recognition they merit.

Blackford has said flatly and simply that the *VQR*'s role is "nurturing and encouraging writers known and unknown." Which is another perilous balance not unlike the equipoise maintained between the innovative and the traditional. Discovery is important to Blackford, who is fully aware that, under the circumstances and the system, "I just might miss some mute, inglorious Milton." But it is the ones who didn't get away who please him most. The *VQR* must be and is a home for many of the best of the established writers of short fiction, but it also is and must be a stage for the introduction of new voices. The reader will find that our contents assert this primary characteristic of the magazine.

What we have done here, then, with pleasure and with admiration for the magazine and for all of the writers involved, is to pick and choose, from among several hundred available first-rate stories, a good and representative group, the earliest of which, as it happens, was published in 1964, the most recent being from 1989. There are stories from each decade, though, as a matter of fact, the eighties tend to predominate, mainly because so many of the earlier stories have already had a full and active public life in individual collections and prize anthologies. We know you will find excellent stories here. We think that you will find real pleasure, choosing, yourself, among the rich variety of the voices and modes of contemporary fiction. These are first-rate stories by first-rate writers. And it is a good book, if I do say so myself.

We hope that you enjoy it.

# *Eric Clapton's Lover*

$F$ranklin Fisher and his wife, Beth, were born on the same day of March, two years apart. Franklin was 39 years old, and Beth was 41. Beth liked *chiles relenos*, Bass ale, gazpacho; Franklin liked mild foods: soufflés, quiche, pea soup. How could she drink Bass ale? And it was beginning to show on her figure. It wasn't just beginning to show—it was showing in more places, bulging actually, so that now she had big, fat hips and strongman arms. Her disposition had changed, too; as she got larger, she got more vehement, less willing to compromise. Now she cooked two dinners and ate spicy lamb shish-kebob, smacking her lips, shaking on more salt, while Franklin, across from her, lifted a forkful of unseasoned spinach soufflé.

Things got worse between Franklin and Beth after Franklin Junior ("Linny" to his mother) got married and moved to San Bernardino. Their son's bride was "learning to drive a rig." She demonstrated how to turn a truck wheel coming down an incline by leaning forward on their sofa, spreading her legs, and moving her arms in what seemed to be two separate circles. Neither Franklin nor Beth knew what to talk to her about. Franklin Junior said, "Yes, sir!" as his bride-to-be simulated steering the truck. She talked about her rig, drank a shot of scotch, declining water or an ice cube, and left after half an hour.

"You're sorry they're moving so far away, aren't you?" Franklin said to Beth.

"No," Beth said. "She gives me the creeps."

"Maybe she was putting us on," Franklin said.

"What for?" Beth asked.

"Maybe she was high."

" 'High,' Franklin?"

"It could be," Franklin said.

"You don't understand anything," Beth said.

"What do you think it meant?" Franklin asked.

"She was learning to drive a truck."

"Why would she want to be a truck driver?" Franklin asked.

"It's better than being a mother," Beth said. "Then your kids grow up and marry truck drivers."

"There's nothing really *wrong* with driving a truck," Franklin said.

"You don't understand anything," Beth said.

It was one of the last times Beth spoke to him at any length. The following morning she turned her head on the pillow to face him and said, "I must have a day of silence" and wouldn't talk all day. He tried a lot of questions, but nothing provoked a reaction. "Did you know that a silver teaspoon inserted in a bottle of Coke will keep it fizzy for two days after it's opened?" he asked. Nothing.

The next morning she turned her head and said, "Another day of it."

"Want to hear why Avon is losing business?" he asked at breakfast.

"Interested in Nixon's phlebitis?" he called from the T.V. room.

"Would you like to adopt a Vietnamese child?" he whispered just before she dropped off.

On Monday Franklin went to work. He had worked on a magazine called *Canning Quarterly* and had just been promoted to editor of this magazine and another, *Horizontal World,* when his secretary said, "Congratulations, Mr. Fisher." He smiled, then realized that there was nothing to smile about. Her first and last official duty was to type his letter of resignation. Now he had a new job, selling tickets at the movies. It was always very quiet on the job; people filing past with puckered lips: "Two, two, two . . ." the tickets snapping through the metal slot on the counter top. When the movie started Franklin got an orangeade and sat on his stool reading Dear Abby, hoping that she would deal with a problem similar to his own. She did not. She helped a daughter-in-law whose mother-in-law's seeing-eye dog snapped at her ankles, a teenager who wanted to know how to peel her own face to get rid of acne, and a waiter whose restaurant did not take BankAmericard. There was also a "confidential" to T.S. in Portland, Oregon saying that yes, many unwanted babies were eventually loved.

Franklin usually called Beth after the second show began, just to say hello, but tonight he kept flipping through the papers, looking for guidance: a picture of Teddy Kennedy behind a podium, his cheeks stuffed with nuts that he intended to store for the winter; a picture of a cat—Mr. Tom Cat—and below that, "Please Save Me"; a warning about contaminated canned lima beans; two packs of pencils for the price of one. A teenage girl came up to the counter. She wanted a Coke.

"The girl will be right back," Franklin said.

"Couldn't you get it for me?" the girl asked.

"Go to the bathroom and get the girl," Franklin said pleasantly.

Franklin smiled as the girl returned and got the teenager the Coke. The week before, when he was there early in the morning to look for his lost watch, he had seen the exterminators laughing at a mouse that was swimming inside the Coke tank.

Franklin hopped off the stool and lifted the phone off the hook. He expected at least a hello from Beth, but the phone rang once and then there was silence.

"Beth?" he said.

"I can hardly wait to get home to you, darling," he said.

"Do you miss your beloved?" he asked.

He put the phone back on the hook. The girl behind the candy counter looked away just before their eyes met.

"There are mice in the Coke machine," Franklin said.

The girl picked up a box of chocolate covered raisins and moved to the far side of the counter.

"Mice. Swimming in there," Franklin said.

"There are not," she said. She moved farther away.

Instead of going to work, Franklin went to the race track. He stared at the horses, at their small heads, their straight ears, their big bodies, their delicate legs. How could such animals do anything? He bet on number one in the first race, "Fine'N'Fancy," and lost. In the next race he bet on number two, "Daddy's Delight," and lost again. He won in the next race by betting on number three, "Golden Gospel." He stuffed his winnings into his trouser pockets and went out into the parking lot, where he had left his car. The aerial had been bent into an arc. Franklin got into the car and tried the radio. Static. Franklin got out, kicked the side of the car below the aerial, got back in and drove away. He drove until he got to the seamy part of town. He locked his doors and drove slowly down the main street, looking for—or thinking about looking for—a woman. At a McDonald's he double-parked and got out. A young black woman was twisting a mulatto child's arm behind its back, yelling, "Do you understand?"

"Sir?" the boy behind the counter said as Franklin approached.

"I don't want any of this awful shit," Franklin said and started away. He patted the head of the child whose arm was being twisted on the way out.

A Puerto Rican girl was sitting on the hood of his car, swinging her legs. She had on bright blue platform shoes with blue plastic bows on the ankle straps.

"Your car?" she said, hopping down.

"Want to get inside?" Franklin asked, drawing the money out of his pocket.

"No," the girl said.

"Were you going to eat at McDonald's?"

"No," she said.

"Because if you were, I could take you some place nicer for dinner."

"What for?" she laughed. She had a broken front tooth. She had on orange lipstick.

"Company," he said.

"You're not that bad," she said. "Don't you have a girlfriend?"

"You're right," Franklin said. "I'm not that bad. I just don't have my girlfriend with me at the moment, so I thought you might want to go to dinner with me."

The girl was laughing harder. Franklin looked in back of him and saw a policeman. The girl continued to laugh, walking away.

"Wait a minute," the cop called. "He bothering you?"

"No," the girl said.

"Wait a minute," the cop said to Franklin. "I've got a present for you, big spender." It was a ten-dollar ticket.

"Give me a break," Franklin said.

"If I heard you just then, I'd take you in for harassing an officer and creating a disturbance," the cop said. "Did I hear you say anything?"

Franklin shook his head.

"Am I watching you drive away?" the cop asked.

The cop waved as Franklin drove away, shaking.


"Hello, sonny," Franklin said. He was very drunk.

"Who's this?" Franklin Junior asked.

"Your daddy," Franklin said. Perhaps he was not as drunk as he thought; he was keeping up his end of the conversation pretty well.

"Pop?" Franklin Junior said.

"It is I," Franklin said.

"What's the matter with you, Pop?"

"It's what's the matter with your mother."

"What *is* wrong with her?" Franklin Junior asked quickly.

"It must remain a rhetorical question," Franklin said.

A muted conversation.

"Pop?"

"Yes, sonny?"

"Are you all right? Is Mom there?"

"Which question do you care most about?"

"Pop?"

"How are you doing in your new life?" Franklin asked.

"Let me speak to Mom, Pop."

"She's not here, sonny. You'll have to speak to me."

"Okay. What is it, Pop? Are you sick?"

"You didn't answer my question," Franklin said.

"Three minutes. Please signal when through," the operator said.

"Operator?" Franklin Junior said. "Pop?"

Both were gone. Franklin had dropped the phone so he could pick up a glass he had dropped.


Beth Fisher did not know where Franklin was, and she didn't care. What a mess that man was! He had convinced her that they should marry because it was in the stars: they had been born on the same day of March. He mentioned that first when he introduced her to his friends. Even Franklin had not been able to see anything more in the relationship to talk about. All those wasted years! She had called her daughter-in-law, lamenting her marriage to Franklin. The girl had told her that there was nothing as exhilarating as driving a rig. It was all she could talk about. And Linny—he was so full of questions about Franklin that he wouldn't listen to her.

Beth got a job in the lingerie department of a store and prayed that Franklin wouldn't come back. Women came into the department all day, holding up fluffy nylon nightgowns and admiring themselves in the mirror, buying matching satin slippers, wanting to appear beautiful for their husbands. Beth thought they were silly. She believed that she was becoming a feminist. She joined N.O.W. She ate what she wanted and thought that she looked healthier when she was heavy. By December she was quite fat; she often spoke in favor of abortions to the ladies buying the frilliest nightgowns. In January she was moved to the drapery department.

She went out a few times with a salesman from the drapery department, who said that the other women were spiteful. They went to a bar and ate pizza and drank Bass ale, and after that he took her home and didn't kiss her. The salesman thought that she should file for legal separation. He said that men could be spiteful creatures. He gave her a kitten for Christmas. "This is Hildegard," he said as he handed the small white kitten to her. When he wasn't there she called the cat Snowflake.

Shortly after Christmas, Beth came home and found Franklin in the living room. He was reading a novel. A shark, more teeth than body, lunged across the cover; to the side, a man was being slugged in the face. She had time to consider the book because Franklin didn't put it down when she came in. His shoes were by the chair. His toes had broken through the sock of the right foot; they protruded in a tiny fan.

"I'm not exactly clear on what happened between us," he said.

She went into the kitchen and got a beer. She came back to the living room.

"I realized that there was nothing I wanted to say to you and there was nothing I wanted to hear," she said.

Franklin nodded.

"The movie theatre manager keeps calling," Beth says. "He sees great significance in the fact that you disappeared after seeing *Dirty Harry*."

"Maybe I could get the job back," Franklin said. The kitten hopped onto the footstool and bit at Franklin's toes.

"What have you been doing?" Franklin asked.

"Working. In a store."

"I've been living off a Puerto Rican woman I picked up outside a McDonald's. She was making plans to go to Puerto Rico. When she went to work today I left."

"I don't believe you," Beth said.

Franklin looked at the shark's teeth.

Franklin and Beth were snowed in. He had spent the night (the cliché would be "on the couch"; he was sprawled in the Eames chair with his feet on a pile of magazines on top of the telephone book), intending to leave in the morning, but by morning he couldn't have opened the front door if he had wanted to. Leave like Santa Claus? He looked up the chimney, full of soot, then made a fire and sat cross-legged, trying to think—he thought this was a position people got into to meditate—when Beth came downstairs, excited and surprised by the snow. They had celery and beans for lunch. Beth wore a thin blue bathrobe that made her hips look even more enormous. He thought of the horses,the racetrack. . . . He wanted flan, he wanted his Puerto Rican lover back, to kiss her orange lips. The orange lipstick was flavored with oranges. His Puerto Rican lover wanted to go to Florida and eat oranges. More than that, she wanted to go to Puerto Rico: her sister the nun, her brother the blacksmith, the grave of her youngest sister, the other sister a cook for wealthy people, another brother—wasn't there another one, or was that the one who was born dead? Born with the measles. He told her that that wasn't possible. But a doctor had been there! Then he hadn't known what he was talking about. Those big bright lips. He tickled them with a feather once when she was asleep. He pulled it out of his pillow and brushed it across her lips and she drew them together, sat up scratching herself. She wanted to be Eric Clapton's lover. He had never heard of Eric Clapton. She said that Eric Clapton was addicted to heroin. She agreed with Franklin that his son was addicted to drugs; otherwise he would love his parents. She wanted him to call his son. What for? For reconciliation! But there had been no fight. Nothing ever came entirely apart.

He had had to hound her and hound her to be his lover. For almost a week after first seeing her he sat in his car, parked outside McDonald's, and waited, and then he hounded her, offered his car, which was all he had with him. She refused. She was not a whore, she was a clerk. He didn't want a whore, he wanted a clerk. This made her eyes big, like her mouth. She wore such high heels. She was as tall as he was in those shoes, and without them she was just a tiny woman. He offered his belt or shirt, if she would not take the money or the car. "Okay," she said. "Which?" he asked, "The belt or the shirt?" wondering where he would get a belt to keep his pants up late at night after she put him out. She had a girlfriend who walked into her apartment in the morning and beat his head with the pillow when she saw him sleeping there. What an odd person the friend was, and his lover—what a strange woman, comparing him to Eric Clapton, saying that she never had a chance in hell with Eric Clapton anyway.

Beth said that they would have to feed the birds. Feed the birds? He lived in suburbia. In the grocery stores there were little bells of suet and bird seed that women brought home and hung in trees. Beth didn't have one of those; she wanted him to tear up bread, put it in a pan, take it to the birds. He told her that he couldn't get out the front door because the snow had drifted. She said that the birds would die. He climbed out the bathroom window. The bread crumbs were blown out of the pie tin, mixed with the snow, disappeared. He climbed back in through the window. He wrapped a towel around his head and sat in front of the fire.

"Being born on the same day seemed a very good thing to go on," he said.

He examined his wife. He thought the bathrobe peculiar, had no idea that she had gotten it very cheaply: marked down to seven dollars by the buyer after Beth jabbed a pen through the back of it. From 45 dollars to 25 (small hole) to 15.50 (large hole, two runs) to seven dollars (hole, runs, hem coming loose.)

"It's hard to imagine that somewhere in the world it's warm today," Beth said, forehead against the foggy window. She was chewing celery, heavily sprinkled with chili powder.

HAL BENNETT

# *Virginia in the Window*

Looking back, I realize that my mother was always at her very best during snow, although she was always exquisite all of the time. My mother—our mother, really, for there were six of us depending upon her for life support, our father long ago having deserted the fold—but I suppose that being the youngest, at 12 going on 13, gave me a special sense of ownership about my mother for which I was always being slapped down gently and politely behind her back by others of the family who also thought that they owned her.

But all of us were wrong in that respect, for my mother was nobody's property, although she had long ago given herself to gentleness, good manners, and extraordinary common sense. She was a poor woman from Virginia, which meant that here in Cousinsville, N.J., and anywhere else in even a semicivilized world, she would be considered a lady of excellent good breeding if not of solid means. For even Virginia's "worst"—if such a thing existed in the Old Dominion—would always be thought to be at least a cut above everybody else's very best.

So my mother thought, so we all thought and acted in the way we treated each other and our neighbors, our friends, and our guests. Even the bullying of my brothers and sisters against me carried a warmth and gentility about it that made the torture somewhat easier to bear. If we had been from some place like South Carolina or Georgia, then blood would have been flowing like rivers through all of our eight rooms on Decatur Street in Cousinsville. But because we came from Virginia, we treated everybody with consideration and respect, even if they didn't deserve it; to have done less would have been as unspeakable as boisterously breaking wind at the Sunday dinner table and especially in the presence of guests.

As for children at the dinner table, we were orchestrated by the eyes of grownups, like instruments guided by the conductor's baton, eyes always on us to approve, chide, or subdue, with not a single word spoken to us as we worked our way through the dazzling labyrinths of a Virginia dinner—that most splendid of all events—where the cook for the occasion usually lurked in a tizzy in the kitchen to slit her throat if the meal was not judged to be excellent in all respects.

Even Virginia's colored people, like Germany's Jews long before the Hitler era, considered themselves to be the *crème de la crème* among colored people everywhere, and subject to a more benign malignancy when it came to the matter of "separation," as the thing was nicely called in the Commonwealth in those days. Politeness and pleasantness were everything, with something as picayune as replacing a burned-out light bulb falling within the purview of good taste and requiring the services of at least two Virginians: one to screw in the new bulb, and one to lay the dead bulb to rest by talking about how "good" it had been, how truly long it had served and lasted.

Of course, none of this code was ever put into words—that would have been tacky—but I suppose it came to all of us, and to generations of Virginians ever since the first permanent English settlement at Jamestown in 1607—by a kind of not always pleasant osmosis, passing through the semipermeable membrane of custom and usage, race and status, as quietly as the body goes about digesting a blob of homemade peach preserves dissolving around quietly excited taste buds on a happily erect tongue.

Which brings me to the girl who sat in the window sometimes on the first floor of the house directly across Decatur Street from us. Her name was Rita Mae Brown, and her family had come to live in Cousinsville from Virginia only last summer. Mr. Brown, an invalid, was wrapped in blankets in a wheelchair on the porch that late November afternoon in the 1930's when my mother was baking a cake, and before the season's first snow began trickling down. Mr.

Brown was said to have been wounded in the last war, requiring the amputation of both legs just above the knee, and received a pension for that. His wife, who attended him, was a tall, thin, sour-looking, and rusty black woman who had the reputation of being stuck up.

But it was Rita Mae Brown who brought the Virginia sunshine with them from Burnside to Cousinsville. She was around my age and nearly as tall and thin as her mother. But she was certainly not stuck up, with large velvety brown eyes and shiny black hair that she wore in corn rows, and lovely lips that formed a beautiful smile in her oval-shaped face. If I had known then what love was, I would have realized that I had loved Rita Mae Brown right from the first minute I saw her early last summer.

And I watched her now as she fussed over her father's blankets where he scrunched down in the wheelchair on the porch. Mr. Brown was fussing at her, calling her all those dreadful names that murders something in children before it is ever fully grown. "You're dumb, you're stupid, you ain't fit for a damned thing!" Mr. Brown shouted that, showing that absolutely nothing at all was wrong with his tongue. We all had known at once that he wasn't a native Virginian, even before word got round that he'd been born in South Carolina, which explained everything.

Still, he was probably in great pain from having lost both legs and most of his youth fighting some war somewhere for his country that gave him as little love as he gave Rita Mae. I could hear his abuse from all the way across the street. But, of course, he *was* from South Carolina—geechies, they were called; they ate rice and fish heads, like Chinese coolies do—and I probably would have gone over and given him a piece of my mind, if I'd been older. "Now listen here, Mr. Brown. You're hurting that girl, can't you see?"

But of course he could not see, for she had taken refuge behind him. And when I looked at her, she was already looking at me, eyes bright and shiny, as though seething with tears underneath the soft surface. She had been looking at me that way ever since she came to Cousinsville; and it was too much to see. I left the gray outdoors, the threatening sky, and went into our house, where my mother, on her day off, was putting the finishing touches to a golden layer cake with chocolate icing.

My mother was a sleep-in maid in East Orange for an Irish family, with Thursdays off; and her appearance among us that single day a week brought us all together in the house on Decatur Street and away from whatever other tasks or ramblings we might have been involved in, just to be in the presence of my mother's eyes, her warmth and smile, and the unyielding excellence of her Virginia gentility.

She had married young and would die young, leaving the six of us to brood about the wrongs we might have unknowingly done her. And, for my own part, believing in a heaven against my better judgment, where I might fly into her angel's arms and confess all the sins that I had wrought against her in the name of love and in the name of jealousy, which is love's uglier twin.

I suppose that all of this came to me as things usually did—in a series of quick flashes, like lightning streaks—just before Mr. John Nabors came to our door that day. By then, my mother was almost finished putting icing on the cake; outside, it had turned cold and dreary, with a light snow falling on Decatur Street. Everything outdoors seemed to be drawn down and huddling inside itself, an aspect of misery that was cold and gray, and that my mother seemed to want to undo by baking a cake which we could hardly afford. In those days, everything cost only a few pennies, a few dollars at the most; but it was during the Depression and money was hard to come by. Although our house was warm and comfortable with the coal stove burning, our mother there, and the smell of cake creeping like a delicious but invisible fog through all the rooms.

So when Mr. John Nabors came—he of the enormous feet and the absolutely staggering appetite—and knocked on the door, nobody especially wanted to open it. There was a starched white curtain covering the top part of the door, which was made of glass; and we could make out the unmistakable silhouette of Mr. Nabors with his old slouch hat, his glutton's lips, and the stub of a pipe that he gnawed on between forever hungry teeth.

When he knocked again, my mother looked at us all with a clear admonition in her eyes. "Somebody let Mr. Nabors in," she said softly, spinning the cake in a platter held in her left hand as she laid the chocolate on. I looked at the delicate serenity of her features as Jesse dragged over to the door as though he had been told to let a wolf in. My mother's lips parted in the faintest of smiles.

None of us children especially liked Mr. Nabors, who came to visit us almost every Thursday probably because there was always something good to eat, along with my mother's pleasant laugh, her gentle conversation, and a sense about her that she could forgive even John Nabors' terrible hunger and his awkward ungainliness even if no one else in our town could.

He was a very tall, powerfully built black man in a black overcoat, a gray felt hat, and long, large brown shoes that fitted his feet like boats. He always made himself comfortable at once when he came to our house, for it was his nature to do so as well as the nature of our home to encourage his comfort.

"How good of you to drop by, John Nabors," my mother said, extending her hand. "Do come in. It's indeed a pleasure to see you again." And John Nabors' outsize lips slid into a pleased grin. So we were taught by example, our mother's own special way of welcoming a guest, and the guest responding with a sense of easiness and amplitude that her welcome was as genuine as it was warm.

"The very strangest thing happened to me today," Mr. Nabors said, once he was out of his coat and galoshes, and had settled down to watching my mother go back to work on the cake. We were all watching my mother, in fact, as she balanced the platter aloft on the tips of her fingers now and designed the last intricate sworls and patterns in chocolate on the double-layered cake that perfumed the kitchen like a hot sachet.

"There," my mother said. "That'll be ready to serve soon." Taking off her apron and folding it away, she sat at the table with Mr. Nabors. "What did happen to you, John? I'm sure we're all just dying to know."

The prospect that we might really be near suspenseful death seemed to agree with Mr. Nabors. "Well, I was on my way here," he said, grinning around the stub of his pipe to all of us, but especially to my mother, "when I stepped off the curbstone over in front of the tavern and there was this old T-Model Ford coming around the corner. Well, you know that I'm not a small man and those T-Models don't weigh all that much. And I didn't feel like stepping back up on the curb. So I just reared back and the car ran over my feet."

He laughed lazily at his own stupidity, heisting up those vessels he called feet for everybody to laugh at. By evening, he would be in Memorial Hospital with both feet in plaster casts from being broken

because of his little adventure. But none of us knew that then; and I
for one was not really amused, although I went along with the
general laughter.

For I had seen the really darker other side of Mr. John Nabors,
that big, dumb looking clown, which he had made me promise
absolutely never to tell about. Although I recalled it vividly as
everybody laughed at Mr. John Nabors and waited for the cake to
cool. My mother's laughter was like the rippling of clear creek
water, and she laughed until tears came to her lovely brown eyes.

I had found Mr. Nabors lying in an empty lot early last spring
where he had fallen asleep among weeds, assorted trash, and the
wrecks of cars. But he had probably gone there for the same reasons
that I had, which shocked me once I considered it. How did Mr.
Nabors know that people went to the empty lot at night to make love
in the abandoned cars? Cousinsville was my private domain, or so I
thought then, where only I saw everything while all others went
around in dumb depression, looking for what they surely thought
were the essentials of life. My own ramblings had to do with my
own essentials, and I especially looked for those acts that people
perform in what could be called a public secrecy.

Like the lanky white men in flamboyantly colored costumes who
came to Cousinsville and sat on flagpoles for days and nights at a
time. Everybody went to see them during the day, as they perched,
aloof as Oriental potentates, on platforms on the tops of poles that
they had shinnied up like lizards. We had all seen them eating as
they sat atop their silly perches; but how did they respond to
nature's other calls? I went late at night and surprised them relieving themselves in gray enamel pots that were raised and lowered to
them on pulleys. After that, they did not seem so extraordinary to
me. I had cracked their code, so to speak, and the mystery had
disappeared.

The empty lot had also lost most of its mystery. I had found a
garter snake there, a multitude of old condoms, and several pairs of
women's discarded underwear, the last items giving me a hint of
what really went on in the lot after dark. So I went there often, and
peeped through broken windows of slowly rocking and creaking
cars with rusty old springs singing unexpected songs of love.

I was the only one who knew of these happenings, or so I

thought; even the people who put on the performances came and went as though they were engaged in some respectable endeavor or enjoyed a special veil of visibility through which only I could see— high-stepping women in tight dresses; greased and shined men in pin-striped suits, adding to the further pollution of the empty lot.

So I was surprised when I found Mr. Nabors there among the garbage. "What you doing here?" Mr. Nabors said thickly. It was obvious that he had stumbled onto this lode because of drunkenness and not from any previous knowledge or an established plan. He was notorious in Cousinsville for the size of his feet; and I sus-pected that he had slipped in the mud and got himself tangled in them.

"I'm going home," I lied, edging away from him as he crawled towards me on all fours. It was grotesque and appropriate, I thought, and I felt like a kind of sovereign with big, ugly, black John Nabors on his knees in front of me. But before I could get away, he recognized me and grabbed. "You Mrs. Hubbard's boy, ain't you? What you doing out here by yourself?"

"I'm going home," I said, trying to get away from his hand. But he held me fast; then, using me for support, he pulled himself up like a scarecrow rising from collapse.

There were wooden tenement buildings around us—what were known as tenements in those days, two and three story apartments piled hideously atop one another—and I could see the rising moon behind them, spattered across the sky like runny egg yolk, even as I heard the exotic song from two or three cars that moved up and down and side to side like the large dislocated lungs of dinosaurs. Men and women were making love in those cars—the night air was rich with subdued sighs and blissful groaning—whiling away the time until World War II should fall upon us, dragging us from these dark caves into the shining bright light of the Atomic Age.

"You come on with me," Mr. Nabors said. "I got something I want to show you." At my hesitation, he slyly defied my own estimation of myself. "You're curious, ain't you? Well, I'm going to show you something you never seen before. Nobody ain't ever seen it before."

It was hardly a challenge that could be refused, since I had long ago grown tired of the singing cars and what went on inside them. My own excitement had more recently turned to small, exasperated

puddles in my hand, and I was hungry for new adventure. So Mr.
Nabors cleaned himself up as best he could, and we slunk like
conspirators down the streets of Cousinsville under a steadily
strengthening moon. We boarded the trolley car on Main Street and
swayed and bumped against each other on the hard seats under the
blinking lights until we got off at the meat packing plant near
Orange Street, and the almost empty trolley took off with a hideous
clanging of bells and grinding of wheels.

There were hardly any people at all on the streets in those nights,
everybody at home usually, huddled around radios listening to
"Amos 'n' Andy," "I Love a Mystery," "The Kate Smith Hour," or
some other popular program that bound families together even
while that other destroyer of families, television, was already in the
experimental stage for its mass onslaught against the social fabric.

My heart was thumping with excitement as Mr. Nabors led me
across the trolley tracks to the back door of the meat packing plant,
where the odor of blood hung in the air like a noxious mist. "What
we going to do here?" I whispered, as though we were walking
through a graveyard. Before Mr. Nabors could answer, a clock in
the Catholic church nearby began to toll; it rang nine times before it
stopped.

And Mr. Nabors sucked on his pipe and allowed his large juicy
lips to curl in a satisfied smile. "I'm on time," he said. "I work
here." Then, with a masterful flourish, he opened his overcoat and
dug into his vest pocket for a large key. "They trust me with this," he
said proudly. "So I don't want nobody to know what I'm going to
show you. You promise?"

"I promise." I was squirming with excitement at so much mystery and decided that I liked Mr. Nabors after all. Terrible stories
had been told about him all through Cousinsville—how his wife
had died of breast cancer without his lifting a finger to help her;
how his son, also named John, had driven stark naked in a Model-T
Ford into James River in Virginia, leaving a condemning note that
was safety-pinned to the flesh of his chest in his first-grade scrawl: *I
done it cause Daddy don't love me.* Everybody knew these things, and
especially my mother, which probably explained why she seemed to
treat Mr. Nabors with a special affection whenever he came to our
house. And he came practically every Thursday because he was
hardly welcome anywhere else, and probably drew strength from

my mother's excellent ability neither to judge nor to be dismayed by the gossip of others.

The smell of blood was stronger and wilder inside the plant, as though some sort of unholy orgy had recently taken place where extraordinarily strong beasts had been gutted and bled, leaving their dried stench as a punishment to survivors. Mr. Nabors walked softly—tipping, actually—on the toes of his large shoes; I did the same, feeling a sense of something ominous in the deeper shadows etched upon the shadows that surrounded us. It was very cold and absolutely quiet, except for the sound of our breathing and walking, as though we had violated an ancient tomb where horror and revenge awaited us. Then, Mr. Nabors stopped; his arm reached out and clicked the light switch; and I was blinded for several moments by the sickly glare.

When I could see, a thousand small pink eyes were looking at me, as though embedded in a maze of white cotton. They were rabbits, hundreds and perhaps thousands of them, like an invasion of Easter bunnies, watching us from absolutely indifferent pink eyes. The sight of them shocked and surprised me, so many of them and yet so silent. Always silent. I have never liked rabbits because they are so silent and weak. Looking at this mass, I felt sickened and drew away. But Mr. Nabors eased me forth. "They always call me whenever there's a shipment in," he said. "Now, you don't go telling anybody, you hear? You know how folks like to run their mouths."

I did not know what there would be to tell people; but after his double admonition, I sensed that something was going to happen that might well be worth the trip. So I waited impatiently while Mr. Nabors went to a locker against the wall, and changed from his street clothes into white coveralls. The unlit pipe was still stuck in his mouth, and his breath came out in little puff balls from the cold.

As for the rabbits, they seemed to have come alive, hopping and bumping among themselves with far more energy than before, as though trying to keep warm. I had seen other animals suddenly come to life at feeding time, and I felt decidedly disappointed. Had Mr. Nabors misjudged me so much that he thought I would be satisfied watching him feed a bunch of rabbits? Grinning, he jumped into the pen with the greatest alacrity and began to cut their throats.

When he jumped into them, it was like watching a large frolicking child leap into a snow bank. Perhaps all the rabbits were not white, but it did not seem to matter as Mr. Nabors yanked them up by the ears and sliced their throats, tossing the still quivering carcasses onto a pile this side of the wire mesh fence that separated me from the slaughter.

The cold in the room intensified, and something in my own throat seemed to close down and go dry. Mr. Nabors was killing and grinning, the pipe somehow still clenched between his teeth; rabbit's blood was all over him and his coveralls, scarlet and dripping, the smell like a warm kind of dreadful disease in my nostrils. I took a step backwards, prepared to flee. But Mr. Nabors sliced another rabbit's throat—so viciously that the head came off in his hands, blood shooting out like a geyser—and paralyzed me with his eyes.

And then the mayhem began in earnest. Throwing the knife away, he grabbed the rabbits by the handsful and broke their necks. I was reminded of the snapping of brittle twigs as you walk through winter woods. But what was perhaps most horrible of all was the incredible silence, except for the stumbling about of Mr. Nabors as he picked up rabbits in great bountiful armsful, like a jolly black giant gone berserk, and broke their necks, or mashed them to death against his chest, pulled their heads off, or reached inside their fluffy breasts to rip their hearts out.

It was more than I could stand. "I'm going home!" I cried; and the words seemed to break the spell.

"Home?" he said. He was bathed in blood and his eyes seemed glazed, like hot, stunned marbles. "Well, it certainly was nice of you to come with me. And you give my regards to your mother, you hear?"

It was like a tremendous slap in the face, that he could remember to be *polite* while he stood in the midst of his slaughter. "You're not from Virginia!" I cried, and it seemed the craziest possible thing to say.

He stared at me in utter amazement through the blood. "I most certainly am from Virginia," he said, with pride and indignation. "Why on earth would you say a thing like that?"

Why, indeed? Somehow, I got the door open and went out into the refreshing air. It had turned cold and the moon was round and seemed stained with blood, that day's miserable afterbirth. Not

having carfare, I walked and ran all the way home to throw up in
our bathroom so as not to dirty the street.

Easter Sunday would be in another two or three weeks, when
everybody on government relief—as welfare was called in those
days—would be given frozen packages of the rabbits Mr. Nabors
had killed. Our family was not on relief; when it was proposed, my
mother had rejected the offer with quiet dignity: "We'd rather
work, sir, if it's all the same to you."

And we all did work, including myself on weekends, when I
delivered groceries for Mr. Mellinger and Mr. Meyer, the two
Jewish grocers, who paid me enough for me to make my small
contribution to the family pot.

So I was thinking about the secret I carried when John Nabors
came to our house that snowy November afternoon and talked
around his stub of a pipe clenched between his teeth while my
mother and the rest of us waited for the cake to cool.

"With that car running over your feet," my mother said, once the
laughing had settled down, "it's a wonder you didn't break them."

And John Nabors slapped his sturdy thighs and glowed. "It'll
take more than a T-Model to break me," he said. I had a momentary's vision of him bloody and heated among the rabbits, how he
had broken them. And I remembered how his knife had sliced the
fluffy throats and my own throat felt vulnerable, dry.

Did he remember? He never gave me any indication that he did;
and his very indifference towards me seemed to increase the men-
ace and the weight of the burden he had laid on me. I had promised
never to tell about the rabbits, which was a worrisome pact between
us; for some Virginians have been known to die before revealing
personal secrets.

I went to the window where cold had fogged the glass, and wiped
a space with the heel of my hand to look out. Rita Mae Brown was
also in her window, looking out. Between us was the narrow street
and the snow falling now in heavy flakes, like large white feathers.
It was still afternoon, but a strange kind of darkness had set in over
the pointed rooftops and formed a gloomy backdrop to the swirling
snow. Yet I knew that Rita Mae's eyes locked with mine, like the
clasping of warm hands, as if we were alone in a world which would

never be the same again beyond this day. The falling snow seemed to hit the street and sizzle, as though a heated white chasm separated and brought Rita Mae Brown and me together at the same time. When my mother called me softly, I turned from the window with an unaccountable sense of sadness. The snow was like a curtain covering over the past; nothing ever would be the same again.

Smiling happily, my mother was holding the cake high for all of us to admire it before the feast; and it seemed to be a creation worthy of Michelangelo himself. I was sure that my mother was smiling especially for me; but probably all of us had that same sensation of being special in her eyes. Looking at that cake, in the comfortable heat of the kitchen, we might have been admiring the crown jewels of England suddenly transported to Cousinsville and exposed to our hungry eyes. Even John Nabors seemed to be more than normally impressed by the goodness he contemplated.

As for my mother's eyes, they seemed to flash out and encompass us all at once—I thought of a lighthouse steering exotically laden ships into the warm arms of piers—but with a mellowness that chipped away any resentment we might have had that Mr. Nabors, as guest, would get the first slice. But above all else, the cake represented the triumph of our family over our father's desertion, and government relief, and the fact that we were still a family together that even had prospered in the face of adversity and the country's worst Depression ever.

But our guest was foremost in our mother's mind as she carved the gem into eight equal parts. "You certainly do deserve cake, John, after all you went through today." And she held out the platter to him.

Which he dutifully took, along with the paper napkins from her hand, and began to eat the whole cake. "That's mighty hospitable of you, Mrs. Hubbard," he said, mouth crammed, knocking off a chunk in two or three bites, already reaching for the next slice.

I was absolutely astonished. We all were. Except my mother, of course. She seemed to undergo a marvelous transformation as her shoulders hunched forward and her eyes flashed out and held us, shooting messages to us like arrows: *He is a guest in this house. If any of you dare say a word or so much as snicker, you'll have me to deal with later on. Is that clear?*

I felt like wetting my pants from excitement and disappointment, but my mother's message was very clear indeed. I had never seen her so intense. Of course, none of us had ever been exposed to the spectacle of John Nabors eating all of our precious cake, making a real pig of himself. But what I most clearly remember was my mother's narrowed eyes commanding us all into silence, and the quick, birdlike jerks of her head as she held us mesmerized while John Nabors finished the cake, then herded the crumbs on the platter together with his fingers, and stuffed them into his mouth as well.

With the cake gone, John Nabors decided to go too. "Well, Mrs. Hubbard, I sure do hate to eat and run. But I don't want to overstay my welcome. And I can't tell you how very much I appreciate the cake. It was just delicious, it most certainty was." He was pulling on his galoshes, letting Jesse help him into his overcoat, arranging his pipe back between those unforgivable lips.

My mother's eyes flashed another warning at us, then settled on him with the sincerest warmth. "It's always a pleasure to have you, John. And we are so pleased that you enjoyed yourself. Do come back and see us real soon, you hear?"

"I'm certainly going to do that, Mrs. Hubbard." He drew his overcoat collar up around his neck, said his final goodbyes, and went out into the snow. A blast of cold air came through the opened door which Jesse quickly closed behind him.

Now certainly we would talk about it, show our indignation. . . . But my mother's eyes still denied us, the control intensified, slender shoulders in a near crouch, eyes blazing, transfixing, magnetizing.

And then, when it was clear that we dared not question the actions of a guest, even in his absence, she reached for her change purse and counted out coins. "You go and buy a pound of sugar," she said to me, examining *my* eyes for any sign of bad manners or a tendency toward gossip about a guest.

Did she see the slaughter of the rabbits in my eyes, framed by John Nabors' sickening grin? Or did she see my disgust at the absurd code that permitted any aggression by people like John Nabors, as long as it was done with politeness?

Apparently not. She folded the coins into my hands with a pressure that seemed to be a promise and a plea: *Trust me; it's not perfect, but it is a way.* She also sent Jesse and Brother out for more ingredients. The storm had worsened; snow kissed my face like sharp cold lips that dissolved into a sensation of warmth.

Looking across the street, I made out the figure of Rita Mae Brown in her window with the light on behind her, for it had suddenly become very dark and the storm was howling now. But I could see that she was smiling; and when I lifted my arm to wave at her, she waved back. It was the very first time we had done that.

I walked on to Mr. Mellinger's. And despite the darkness, the cold and wind and snow, I had a wonderfully clear vision of what my discipline would be: some night soon, I would hold Rita Mae Brown in my arms in the forbidden darkness of the empty lot, and perhaps take her innocence as I gave her mine.

Then, exactly two weeks from today, my mother and the rest of our family, dressed in our very best, would trudge through deep snow on Thanksgiving Day to take a small basket with turkey, fruit, nuts, and cake to Mr. John Nabors in Memorial Hospital to cheer him up. It was what you did when people were alone and you were from Virginia.

# Where She Was

My mother was a child in Lockport, Louisiana, where there were six "good" houses distinguishable from the small row houses, each with a two-seated outhouse in the back yard, in which the unskilled workers, most of whom were Cajun, lived. To the east of the mill were houses for the sawyer and two mill officials; to the west, houses for the mill's bookkeeper, the commissary manager, and the filer, her father. Papa, she called him.

A wide veranda extended across the front of the house. Here my mother spent long hours in the lazy bench swing, saved from the fierce afternoon sun by a Confederate jessamine vine starred with small white fragrant flowers that relentlessly seduced big hairy black-and-yellow bumblebees and long-billed hummingbirds whose rapidly vibrating wings seemed an excessive labor on such days. Beneath the house, which was set high on pillars, was a cool, dark place hidden from view behind a skirt of green lattices, where her papa built shelves to store her mother's Mason jars of mayhaw jelly and mustard pickle and brown paper bags of sugar beets.

Inside the house, in the living room, were the phonograph and the piano, the Morris chair that was "Papa's chair," and several tall glass-enclosed bookcases containing, my mother remembered, illustrated editions of *Paradise Lost* and *Paradise Regained*, *A Child's Garden of Verse*, the family Bible, *Evangeline*, *Girl of the Limberlost*, complete sets of Scott, Hugo, and Dickens, and *The Princess and Curdie*, on the front of which was a picture of the princess in a gown of pale green silk that seemed to glow when she looked at it, like a will-o'-the-wisp.

She was a shy child, my mother, easily embarrassed, a perfectionist at five, but she was also inventive, able to entertain herself happily, and able to abandon herself to her imagination. On rainy days she read the Sears, Roebuck and Montgomery Ward catalogues or the French book her sister, studying library science at Carnegie Tech, sent her, with the nouns depicted in garments that suited their genders (*"la fenêtre"* wore a ruffled frock). She played her autoharp or copied music onto homemade manuscript paper, though she could not yet read the notes. She played with Isaac, the little black boy who helped her mother with her gardening, or Charlie Mattiza, whom she summoned by calling "Charlie Mattiza, Pigtail Squeezer!" from his yard.

The early evenings, the blue-to-lavender time between supper and bedtime, she spent on her papa's lap in the Morris chair, listening to phonograph records. His phonograph was his prize possession. It was the first one in Lockport. He had records of *Scheherazade, Night on Bald Mountain,* Weber's *Invitation to the Dance,* and overture to *Oberon.* (Later, he was to get Stravinsky's *Rites of Spring,* which he listened to over and over, until he felt he understood it.) She was her father's favorite, the two of them drawn powerfully to a world that did not even exist for the people around them, in Lockport, Louisiana, in the century's teens.

By the time my mother was in her seventies, living in England, she had come to believe that human beings were like cancer cells, destroying everything worthwhile—though she had her quarrels with nature too (eating, for example, was an essentially ugly act, whether performed by people or animals), and there were a few human achievements that conceivably validated our presence on earth (Bach's music). I think she felt that the life-processes had been devised purposely to humiliate her. She considered that sex was an invasion of privacy, sleeping was a waste of time, and having children was like signing a death-sentence for your dreams, whatever they might be. She told me these things while we were sitting in front of the television—the telly—flipping through the cable "videopaper" by remote control, to check out the temperature in Wisconsin, the exchange rate for dollars, the headlines. Emphysema and strokes had whittled her life down to the size of the screen. Despite my best intentions, I sometimes became irritated by her. I was at a point in my own life where what I wanted more than anything was to feel connected to other people, and I found it difficult not to feel bitter about a point of view that, I now saw, had to a great extent ghostwritten, as it were, my autobiography. For I was my mother's daughter, as she was her father's, and I had tried to be the reflection of her dreams that she wanted me to be—as she had tried to be her father's.

Sometimes her papa brought scraps of wood home from the sawmill for his youngest daughter to play with. As the saw-filer, it was his important job to keep razor-sharp the teeth of the whirling, circular saw that the sawyer, riding his carriage back and forth, thrust the logs into. Out came boards, and the curls and scraps and shaving he took home to my mother. She laid them out on the front lawn like the floor plan for a schoolhouse, assigning a subject to each "room," and wrote a textbook for each subject, using Calumet Baking Powder memo books that were distributed free at the commissary and elderberry ink. Requiring a pupil, she invited Elise Cheney to her schoolhouse—having decided that Elise, of all her acquaintances, was most in need of an education. After a few sessions of trying to teach Elise how to spell "chrysanthemum," she renounced her teaching career in disgust—my mother was impatient with dullards—and turned her attention to the seven Henderson children, whose names, for some reason, she felt compelled to remember in chronological order. Pumping her tree swing to the top of the great oak in the front yard, she sang loudly and mnemonically, for hours on end,

> Oh the buzzards they fly high down in Mobile
> (Lalla, Lillie, Georgia, Billy, Flossie, Edna, Beth).
> Oh the buzzards they fly high down in Mobile
> (Lalla, Lillie, Georgia, Billy, Flossie, Edna, Beth).
> Oh the buzzards they fly high
> And they puke right out the sky
> (Lalla, Lillie, Georgia, Billy, Flossie, Edna, Beth).

One summer they rented a house on Lake Prien, where her father fished for tarpon by day and was in demand as a dancing partner by night, when the grown-ups paired off to the strains of Strauss waltzes, starlit breezes blowing in through the open win-

dows, billowing the muslin curtains. He was handsome man, serious and loyal, permanently dazzled by his lively wife, a petite
redhead he'd courted for a year in Mobile, wooing her with a bag of
grapes in his bicycle basket.

My mother was going to be a beautfiul woman, a finer version of
the young Katharine Hepburn, but she didn't know it yet. She was
the baby—a tall, skinny baby, she thought, while her mother and
two sisters were visions of stylishness. This was the summer her
middle sister, about to join the flapper generation, launched a
campaign to persuade her parents to let her have her hair cut short.
When tears and tantrums failed, she began to pin it up in large
puffs that stuck out over her ears. These puffs were popular with
her classmates and were called "cootie garages." Each day, the
cootie garages grew a little larger—and finally, when her head
began to look as though it had been screwed on with a gaint
wingnut, her parents said to her, "Please, go get your hair cut!"

My mother was still in her edenic chrysalis, fishing in doodlebug
holes with balls of sand and spit stuck to the ends of broomstraws.
She went fishing with her papa on his boat, the Flick, helping him
to disentangle the propeller when it got caught in water hyacinths.
The dreamy, wavy roots were like cilia or arms, holding up traffic.
They passed the pirogues in which Cajun trappers push-poled their
way through the bayous. Drying on the banks was the Spanish moss
from which the Cajuns made their mattresses. Crawfish crept
along the sandy bottom of the bayou, and water bugs skated on the
surface. Cottonmouth moccasins slithered away in disdain. Hick-
ory and hackberry, willow and cypress shut out the sun. Her papa
pointed out birds that were like lost moments in the landscape,
helping her to see what was almost hidden: white egrets, majestic as
Doric columns, red-winged blackbirds, pelicans, and pink flamin-
gos. This was my mother's world.

She had boyfriends. When she entered the consolidated school
for Calcasieu Parish, at Westlake, which, like her pretend-school,
had a different room and even a different teacher for each subject,
she boarded the school bus at the commissary, always sitting next to
Siebert Gandy, the sawyer's son, who never failed to save one of the
choice end seats for her. From the two end seats, one could dangle

one's legs out the rear of the van. On rainy days, the potholes filled up wonderfully with a red soupy mud that tickled one's toes.

Siebert was two years older than she was. He frequently handed her a five-cent bag of jawbreakers when she got on the bus. To cement their unspoken bond, my mother "published" a weekly newspaper, printed on wrapping paper from the butcher at the commissary. There was only one copy of each edition, which appeared at irregular intervals, and she delivered it surreptitiously to Siebert's front yard. After her family moved to Gulfport—the timber had been used up and oil had been discovered in the swamp and the mill closed down, scattering its employees—she received a letter from Siebert, whose family had moved to California, which began, "My dear little girl." She never got beyond the salutation. She burst into tears and handed the letter to her mother, who carried it off with her and never mentioned it again. So Siebert had loved her—but why had he waited until he was two thousand miles away to tell her? When she was in her seventies, living in England, she told me that she thought she really had loved Siebert. She never forgot him. He had been a part of the world that closed off after she left Lockport.

At first she loved Gulfport. They lived two blocks from the beach. She was growing up, and the freighters in the harbor, the sun flashing on the wide water that rolled across to Mexico, the white sand and palm trees and merchant seamen, all seemed like landmarks in her expanding horizon. But this new world was busy with other minds that had their own ideas about how things were to be done. She could no longer escape into private dreams, a secret music. A clamor began, and so did an unacknowledged rage at it— this infringement, this stupidity, this noise.

She did not let herself know how distressed she was. There was a glassed-in sleeping porch that became her bedroom; her middle sister was away at college, and her library-science sister had gotten a job in Tampa. It was a tiny, cramped porch, overlooking the back garden, and on the side, the alley that separated the lawn from the Everetts'. On the wall above her bed she pasted a picture she'd torn out of a magazine—white daisies, with yellow-button centers like butter in biscuits, on a field of green, a dark gray sky overhead like a monastery.

She was facing a whole new set of problems; worries she had not realized came with growing up: how to make her stockings stay up (garters were not yet available; stockings were rolled at the top, and then the rolls were twisted and turned under; the other girls' stayed up, but hers slid down her thin legs and finished up around her ankles, so that she had to keep ducking behind oleander bushes on her way home to pull them back up); what to do if she met a boy on the way, God forbid; and, most of all, how to avoid being laughed at.

Despite the book of French nouns, she had gotten off to a bad start in French class in Gulfport. When she joined the class, skipping two grades, the students had already learned to answer the roll call by saying "Ici." She thought they were saying "Easy" and so when her name was called, she said "Easy." Everyone laughed. When she prepared her first assignment for English class, she thought her paper would look nice if she lined up the margins on the right side as well as on the left, which necessitated large gaps in the middle. The teacher held her paper up to the class as an example of how not to do homework.

The same English teacher terrified my mother by requiring every student, during Senior year, to make a speech at morning assembly. My mother began to worry about her "Senior Speech" when she was still a sophomore. When senior Dwight Matthews walked out on the stage with his fiddle and said, "I shall let my violin speak for me," and then played "Souvenir," she fell in love with a forerunner of my father, and so my future began to be a possibility, an etiological ruck in the shimmery fabric of the universe.

My mother had inadvertently learned to read music back in Lockport when she'd entertained herself by copying the notes from her sister's piano etude books. The first time she attempted the violin, her fingers found their way by instinct to the right spots. Soon she was studying with Miss Morris at the Beulah Miles Conservatory of Music on East Beach. Miss Morris often carried her violin out to the end of the municipal pier in the evening to let the Gulf breezes play tunes on it. (She also recited poetry to the rising sun.)

My mother's violin was an old box that had belonged to her papa's father. Eventually, by winning the New Orleans *Times-Picayune*'s weekly essay contest, she saved up fifty dollars (though this took some time, as the prize for her essay on the Pascagoula Indians, for example, was fifty pounds of ice) and sent off to Montgomery Ward for a new violin, complete with case, bow, and a cake of genuine rosin (progress over her former sap-scraped-from-pine-bark).

Even with the new violin, there was time for boys. She and her best girl friend, Olive Shaw, used to go cruising, though this activity was not much more sexual than crabbing, which they also did a lot of. Olive had an old Dodge that Mr. Shaw had named Pheidippides, after the Greek athlete who'd run himself to death. Olive was only thirteen, but no one needed a license to drive in Mississippi. They liked to drive out to the Gulf Coast Military Academy to watch the cadets' parade and hear the band play "Oh, the Monkey Wrapped Its Tail around the Flagpole." She cannot have been as backward as she thought she was—when the marching was over, the boys gathered around the car, flirting like crazy.

But she knew nothing of sex, the mystery she and Olive were dying to solve. All the Zane Grey books ended with the hero kissing the heroine on the blue veins of her lily-white neck. My mother's neck was as brown as her cake of rosin, from her hours swimming in salt water and lying on the pier. She was not in danger of having her blue veins kissed—she examined her neck in the bathroom mirror, and not one blue vein showed under the light. Finally one of the cadets kissed her, after a movie date—on the mouth, not her neck. She worried that she might be going to have a baby, but her stomach stayed flat, and after a while she forgot to think about it.

Much social life revolved around church, which my mother nevertheless avoided as much as possible. When she did go— Sunday services were obligatory—she tried to act as if she were not related to her family. Her mother's hymn-singing sounded rather like Miss Morris's violin-playing (off-key), and her own mama, perky in a new bonnet, seemed to become a stranger to her, as if she belonged to other people instead of to her own daughter—busying herself with the flowers at the altar, saying "Good morning!" and "Isn't it just a lovely day!" to all and sundry. My teen-aged mother cringed when her grandmother called across the street to her mama: "Hat-*tee,* when you come to lunch, bring the bowl of mayonnaise and the Book of Exodus!"

She survived these humiliations, and even her "Senior Speech" since she'd been lucky enough to be assigned a role in the school play. She had one line to speak: "I'm your little immortality," and

after weeks of practice, she learned to say it loud enough to be heard
by the audience. It came out "I'm your little immorality," but it
satisfied the English teacher's requirement.

Her mama took her shopping in New Orleans for her graduation
clothes: a green silk dress for Class Day, a white chiffon for graduation, and a pink organdy for the Senior Prom. But when the
morning of the prom arrived, she still did not have a date. Her
mama disappeared into the hallway to whisper into the telephone,
and soon Alfred Purple, whose mother was, like my mother's
mother, a member of the United Daughters of the Confederacy,
called to ask my mother to go to the prom with him.

Alas, that night when Alfred called for my mother he had one
foot done up in a wad of bandage, as if he had the gout. At the
dance, they sat briefly on the sidelines; then my mother asked him
to take her home. She hung the pink organdy prom dress on a satin-
covered hanger. In two years, she would be one of the popular girls
at LSU, dancing to all the latest tunes—but she had no way of
knowing that that night. She was convinced Alfred had returned to
the prom afterward, with both feet in working order. Anyway, she
was done with high school. She was fifteen. This is a portrait of the
girl who became my father's wife.

After my parents were married, and my mother was pregnant
with my brother, they made a trip back from Baton Rouge to
Gulfport. One day my mother and grandmother went for an afternoon outing in the Model-T Ford, my grandmother at the wheel.
They drove past rice paddies and sugar cane fields, and cotton
fields, the cotton bursting out in little white pincushions. As they
scooted along the highway, relishing the breeze the car created for
them, they chatted about love and marriage and impending babies.
They stopped beside a deserted beach to eat the fried chicken wings
and hard-boiled eggs that my grandmother had packed. From the
car, the sparse dune grass seemed almost transparent in the haze of
heat, like strands of blown glass. The gentle waves broke the water
into smooth facets that flashed like the diamond on my grandmother's finger (my mother, a Depression bride, had only an inex-
pensive gold band). The salt in the air was so strong they said to
each other that they could salt their hard-boiled eggs just by holding
them out the window. My mother laughed. She felt so close to her

mother, so free, now that she was grown up, about to have a baby, that she decided to ask her a question about sex. "Mama," she said, "isn't it supposed to be something people enjoy? Is something wrong with me?"

The gulls were diving off shore. My mother was aware of her heart beating like a metronome—she wished she could stop it, that determined, tactless beat. As soon as the question was out, she realized she had gone where you should never go—into your parents' bedroom. She blushed, thinking about the time she'd surprised her papa in the bathroom.

Her mother looked straight ahead, through the windshield, and drummed her fingers on the steering wheel. "Your father and I have always had a wonderful sexual relationship," she said firmly. "I'm sorry if it's not the same for you."

That was all. It was like a nail being driven in, boarding up a dark, hidden place. On Class Day, my mother's "gag" gift had been a hammer—because, as Bill Whittaker, the master of ceremonies, had explained, everyone knew my mother wanted something for her papa. She remembered how happy the little joke had made him as he sat in the school auditorium.

They fed the leftovers to the crying gulls. The sun was dropping in the west like an apple from a tree. On the way home, they talked about other things—her sisters, the apartment in Baton Rouge.

She had dropped out of graduate school to marry my father, at twenty. The apartment was in a building rented to faculty. My father taught violin and theory. In fact, my mother had been responsible for his coming to LSU: as the star violin pupil, she'd been asked to offer her opinion on the *vitae* the department had received. In those days, job applications were routinely accompanied by photographs. My mother instantly chose my father.

She was so pregnant—eight-and-a-half months, and it seemed to her that no one had ever been as pregnant as she. She felt like Alice after she'd bitten into the "Eat me" cake, grown too huge for the room. She thought she would never be pretty again—in less than a year, she'd become an old lady, almost a matron. Her dancing days were over. These were dull days. She had no friends, because any friendship one married woman had with another had to be shallow (you couldn't talk about your husband or your sex life or how much you hated having to cook three meals a day, or how you felt about anything). There was no money for movies or dresses—it was 1933, and only by the grace of Huey Long, who, demagogue though he might be, saw to it that not a single LSU faculty member was laid off, the only university in the country that was true of, did they have any money at all (but often it was scrip). She couldn't have gotten into a new dress anyway, not any dress she'd want to get into.

She couldn't even practice—her stomach didn't give her arms enough mobility. When she did the laundry in the bathtub, scrubbing shorts and socks on a grooved aluminum washboard, she felt so solidly planted on the tile floor that she envisioned getting up again as an uprooting.

In bed, she lay with her back to my father, facing the wall. Such long sticky nights, and then the barest increase in comfort with the coming of winter—but the emotional temperature in the room remained high. My mother did not understand what had happened to her, how just by loving music and my father she'd become enmeshed in misery, in a spartan orange-crate apartment, in a life that was devoid of the beautiful epiphanies of her childhood.

But she was too well trained to inflict her depression on my father. There were no tears—she was not one for self-pity. Even on Christmas morning, which felt as foreign to her as Europe, as exotic as Catholicism or snow, because this was the first Christmas she had not spent with her family, she made the bed and fixed my father's breakfast, no lying in or moping around. The tree reached almost to the ceiling, and the lights, which she had tediously tested one by one, were all shining. On top of the tree stood a gold star that lasted through the years until I got married, and my parents began to dispense, a little bit at a time, with the ceremonies and symbols Christmas had acquired for them.

She and my father were awkward with each other that morning, addressing each other with a formal politeness better suited to guests. It seemed to them that every small choice they made was setting a precedent for Christmases to come—and also represented a rupture from their pasts. They ate pain-du, day-old bread fried in egg yolk and sugar, a Cajun variant of French toast. My mother drank cocoa and my father drank coffee—choices that later became habits and eventually defining characteristics. In the early morning light, which temporarily softened the drab apartment, lending an impressionistic reticence to the sharp edges of the furniture, the scratchy upholstery, they sat self-consciously on the floor by the tree. My father kissed my mother and placed in her hands the present he had bought for her with a kind of desperate good will, searching all over New Orleans for something that would make her happy again, glad to be married to him. When he had bought it, leaning over the glass counter in Maison Blanche on a fall day that was hot even for Louisiana, conferring with the sales clerk while sweat ran down the inside of his shirt sleeves under his suit jacket, he had seen my mother gesturing gracefully with the little evening bag in her left hand like a corsage of sequins, her beautiful smiling face a sonata on a blessedly cool evening.

It was red. It seemed to slide under your fingers, the hundreds of tiny, shiny sequins as tremulous as water. It was as flirtatious as a handkerchief, as reserved as a private home. When my mother took it out of its box, the tears she'd been hiding from my father were released—they fell from her eyes like more sequins, silvery ones. She knew how she was hurting him, but there was nothing she could do about it. She tried to explain how ugly the evening bag made her feel, but the more she tried to explain herself, the more she seemed to be accusing him.

She ran to the bathroom, sobbing, where she could be alone. The red evening bag lay half in its box, half out, like a heart at the center of the burst of white tissue paper. My father's present waited under the tree. He went into the kitchen and sat at the formica table, drinking another cup of coffee. There were tears in his eyes too, behind his glasses. He blew his nose. He was drinking his coffee from a pale green cup with a vee-shape, a brand of kitchenware that was omnipresent at the time. He felt wounded and frustrated and angry, and sad, and confused, and disgusted.

When I was 17, I took a train by myself from Virginia to New Mexico, having transferred for my sophomore year to the New Mexico Institute of Mining and Technology. On the way out there I stopped over in Gulfport to visit with my mother's mother, Grandma Little. She was at the station to hug me hello. She was wearing white open-eyelet shoes and a lavender print and a pale pink straw bonnet, and when she smiled her face turned a pretty shade of rose as if she were a bouquet all by herself. "You may call me Hattie now," she offered, meaning that if I was grown up enough to make a trip like this alone, I was grown up enough to be treated like an equal. She was eighty-two.

She was standing in front of the chest of drawers in the hallway, watching herself in the mirror as she took off the bonnet. Partly because her name was Hattie, she always wore hats—and also because they kept the sun off her face. She showed me where I could put my suitcase.

She still lived in the old house just a couple of blocks from the beach. The house had thick stone walls to keep the heat in in winter and the coolness in in summer. She had made up a bed for me on the sleeping porch, and when I woke up the next morning the first thing I saw was a blue jay in the pecan tree. The second thing was Grandma Little brushing her long white hair. It fell almost to her waist, even pulled over her head from the back as she brushed the underside, and made me think of a bridal veil. She had been a widow for eight years. After she put her hair up, we ate breakfast in the kitchen. I had never been alone with her before. The day in front of us seemed as long as a railroad track.

She drew a map for me, and I walked down to the beach. The sun on the water was as bright and sharp as knife blades. By the time I got back to the house, in the midafternoon, clouds had rolled in— they arrived on time, I learned, like a train, every day at this time of year, and it rained for an hour, and then the sun came out again, as nonchalant as if it had never been supplanted.

Grandma Little had her feet propped on a footstool Grandpa had made for her for Christmas one year. She was sitting in a deep, wide armchair. I sat on the couch, and she told me about my mother. The light in the room grew heavier and slowly sank out of sight. I turned on the floor lamp.

"When we moved to Lockport," she said, "your mother was five. Up until then, we had been living in Lake Charles. Your mother had to leave her rabbits behind, and she was very upset about that. She loved those rabbits. She always preferred animals to people. When she was *very* little, and we had company to dinner, she used to hide under the table, where no one could see her eat. She insisted that I hand her a bowl of oatmeal—that was all she would eat— under the tablecloth. Well, when we first moved to Lockport, she decided she was going to learn how to be sociable, and on her first day of school, she came home with all her classmates. She had told them it was her birthday. My goodness, I don't know how many children there were! I didn't want to embarrass her by telling them that it wasn't her birthday, but of course there was no ice cream or cake in the house. Why would there be? And we made our own ice cream in those days, don'tcha know. So I gave each of them a banana and a glass of lemonade and they all sang 'Happy Birthday' to your mother, and I think she felt very pleased with herself about what a grand occasion it was."

I blinked back tears. I was seventeen and homesick.

"Oh, yes," she said, "your mother was a handful, strong-willed and skittish."

Grandma Little had gotten quite stocky, and she had to work to get out of the enveloping armchair, but she refused to let me help her, saying it was better for her to make the effort. Finally she was standing in front of me, her hands on her hips, head cocked to one side. "Dinner is ready," she announced.

We ate chicken spaghetti off the Spode plates in the dining room. As we ate, it seemed to me that the room filled up with the ghosts of children. The air shimmered with their small shapes. Elise Cheney and Charlie Mattiza stood at the back of the room, and all seven Hendersons (Lalla, Lillie, Georgia, Billy, Flossie, Edna, Beth). Isaac was there with his trowel, almost as big as he was. Siebert Gandy came with a bag of jawbreakers, his birthday present for my mother. Then things got mixed up and others crowded in —Olive Shaw, Dwight Matthews, the cadets. They were all so young that even I felt old. They were almost as young as the century had been. They seemed to be playing, or dancing in slow motion, and laughing—I could almost hear their laughter, as if it were an overtone, the music behind the music. Their faces were as translucent as wind.

I washed the dishes while Grandma Little went on ahead to bed. She got up at four every morning, to do the cleaning and most of the cooking while it was still cool. The hot, soapy water on my hands felt like a reprieve from a disembodied existence I was both tempted by and frightened of. I dried the dishes and returned them to their shelf on the china closet in the dining room. I remembered my mother's saying how she had found a secluded glen on the high ground on the far side of the narrow footbridge that crossed the swamp at the west end of Lockport, near, it seemed to her, where the sun went down. It was a circular clearing completely enclosed by leafy shade trees. Here she could lie on the grass, surrounded by wild violets and forget-me-nots and dandelions, and watch the clouds of yellow butterflies that drifted across the sky above her. As she lay there, she heard a symphony she had never heard before. It was not on any of her papa's records. It seemed to come from inside her head, and yet she didn't know how it could, since she couldn't write music. When she was in her seventies, living in England, she was to say, "I wished I could have written it down, because I wanted so much to remember it. It was the most beautiful symphony I have ever heard. After that first time, I spent many afternoons in the glen. No one ever disturbed me there. Nobody ever knew where I was."

# A Walk to Shinabaru

Corporal Samuel Dirkson, sagging limply inside his mosquito-netted bunk, watches without interest as the only other remaining occupant of the quonset hut prepares for his nightly bout with village morality. Private Tolbert, formerly of Clay City, Mississippi, stands before the solitary cracked mirror at the other end of the narrow room, intent on worrying a recalcitrant hair into his incredibly precise pompadour.

"I always thought you looked bad in khakis," Dirkson moans, flipping one corner of the net up over the T-bar. "I wouldn't wear a shirt like that if I was queen of the May."

Tolbert scowls down an endless row of unmade bunks. He owns, by Dirkson's actual count, at least two dozen tropical print sport shirts and is inordinately fond of every last one of them. "Gawddam, Dirk, " Tolbert drawls, "I do believe you gone rock-happy on us poor boys. You be careful, actin' like that, or they'll be bound to send you on home."

"Rave on, you lunatic," Dirkson snorts, swinging his feet heavily to the floor. "You know damned well we're all permanent residents of this screwed-up island. You die, they bury you in a little tin box down by Osuki. With full military honors, which means the good captain urinates on your grave so the flowers'll grow."

"Relax, man," Tolbert says, rolling his sleeves up to his shoulder blades. "Sure you don't wanta come along? Nice girls, Dirk . . . nice beer."

"Your invitation tempts me, really it does." Dirkson stares at the curved ceiling. "But the spirit's unwilling, and the flesh is very weak. Give my love to Mitsuko."

"Hadako," Tolbert corrects him. "Mitsuko, now, that was last week."

A rusted steel spring bangs the door shut behind him, and Dirkson continues to stare at the ceiling. After a while he pulls himself out of the bunk, opens his footlocker, and with great effort manages to focus his attention on the untidy mound of paperback books inside. He fingers the cracked spines of several books, finally picks one out for a closer look at the cover but almost immediately tosses it back into the pile. Allowing the lid to slam shut of its own weight, he searches the empty room dispiritedly for something other than the naked light bulbs to fix his eyes on. What a time for an inspection, he thinks wryly, delighted by the idea of an entire platoon being sent to the stockade at once. A certain amount of security goes with the thought, however; there never has been an inspection here, and probably never will be.

At last, in desperation, he tucks his uniform shirt into his trousers and wanders outside to the latrine, then down the hill fifty yards to an almost identical quonset hut that serves as battalion headquarters. He pushes through the door and is immediately relieved to find no one inside except the sergeant on CQ duty.

The sergeant, languidly leafing through a picture magazine, looks up without speaking as Dirkson passes his desk. Dirkson finds the sign-out board, scrawls his name, and clamps a moist, somewhat wrinkled overseas cap to his head. The sergeant looks up with more purpose this time, swinging his legs into an adjacent chair so that Dirkson's escape route is partially blocked.

"Where to, Boy Scout?" he says sourly. "Got a hot date?"

"Sure . . . hell yes," Dirkson answers, wishing bitterly that sometime, just once, he will tell whoever is sitting in the seat of authority that it is none of his goddamned business. But of course he never does. "Brigitte Bardot flew over to spend the night with me on our delightful rock."

"Very funny. You young guys kill me with your jokes." The sergeant shifts his legs off the chair. "You don't look so good. You worried about something?"

"Yeah," Dirkson says, "Brigitte's late."

The sergeant flips a page of his magazine. "I'm just going to ignore that, Dirkson. You know, you remind me of my Aunt Flora. She has reason to worry—ugliest woman in the whole state of Pennsylvania."

Dirkson smiles involuntarily. It is strange, the sergeant showing even a passing interest in his well-being. Dirkson cannot remember speaking to him more than once or twice the entire time he has been on the island, even though he sees the sergeant an average of ten times a day. The fact that someone asks you where you are going on a particular night has nothing to do with friendship here, not even casual interest. It is a question asked by one bored soldier of another bored soldier—a ritual perpetuated by loneliness.

"Stay out of trouble," the sergeant is saying. "The MP's are busy enough without having to flush guys like you out of those gonorrhea palaces down in the village. Besides which, you'll go on the old man's list if you get a disease."

The voice of experience, Dirkson thinks. "Don't worry," he says aloud, "I'm just going for a walk."

The sergeant snorts, clearly unable to believe a man walks without a destination. "You take my advice, you'll head for the nearest servicemen's club and get plastered. The climate don't bother you so much that way."

Dirkson adjusts the cap on his head and brushes past the sergeant, stooping at the doorway just in time to avoid scraping his scalp on the metal stripping overhead.

Outside, the lush tropical twilight is rapidly melting into darkness. As Dirkson aims himself down a hilly path toward the intersection of roads below the quonset complex, the air in motion is almost cool against his perspiring face. A mosquito lights on the back of his neck and he slaps at it absently. Down below, toward the bay side of the island, the first few lights of another army camp wink on like timid fireflies against the darkness of the hills.

For the seventh time since the afternoon mail, Dirkson pulls the crumpled envelope from his pocket and begins to half read, half recite from memory the hurt, confused words in Marguerite's letter. He does not yet understand what it is she expects from him, or why she seems to think everything between them has changed; but whatever the difficulty, he recognizes the words she hasn't used as meaning the continuance of their engagement is now more or less impossible. He glances up from the letter and sees that he has passed the intersection, and that he has unconsciously turned onto the old road running south toward the village of Shinabaru. He stuffs the letter back into its pink envelope, tears both to shreds, and lets the bits of paper trickle slowly from his hand as he walks.

The road to Shinabaru winds through the hills and across the open flat land like a drunken snake, bisecting the island for a distance of about five miles. Motor vehicles seldom use this road any more—haven't, in fact, for the three years since the army engineers completed a modern four-lane highway running along the coast from the island's midsection to its southern tip. The old road, constructed sometime in antiquity by hundreds of natives with crooked backs, has become a silent ghost of the island's life before its rebirth as a strategic military stronghold.

The roadbed itself is a hundred million pieces of crushed coral laboriously chipped bit by bit from the huge reefs lying offshore. This particular part of the island is dotted with the crumbling remains of ancient stone tombs, and the whimsical road, in detouring past them, seldom moves in a straight level line for more than a hundred yards. The army engineers refer to it as a monumental masterpiece of poor planning and at one time even tried to regulate it out of existence.

Dirkson discovered the road quite by accident one lazy afternoon. Its careless design immediately appealed to him, for precisely the same reason that the engineers disliked it. The road is quite obviously an extension—almost an integral part—of the islanders who still occasionally use it. Both are still able to laugh, even after Dirkson and thousands of others like him have come to disrupt the quiet harmony of this friendly, backward, rotting Eden.

Now, Dirkson hears almost as an echo in his mind the clicking of the coral beneath his feet as he walks briskly along the road. Attempting for the thousandth time to relate himself to the things around him, he studies the curious patterns made by the hills and the flat-topped trees reflected darkly in the flooded rice paddies on either side of the road. A fresh breeze blowing across his sweating temples momentarily startles him. He turns toward the apparent source of the wind, toward the sea whose silent waves constantly brush a rocky beach. Far away a dog barks forlornly; snatches of some native song push timorously against the thick silence of night and are lost forever.

For a few seconds Dirkson stands perfectly still, sniffing the heavy air and listening intently for the familiar but still alien sounds of the island. It would be pleasant to find some new smell, a new sound, something completely different from all the days and nights that have slowly disappeared since he was a part of the world beyond the island. Sadly, he realizes everything is the same, as of course it has to be. His friend, a battalion cook, said it succinctly: "Here it don't matter if it's noon, Saturday, or Christmas." The cook said it cheerfully enough, but Dirkson cannot accept it that way. To an extent, of course, it is true—the people always look the same, the land always smells the same. Dirkson and the others wear the same sweat they wore yesterday and last month because they never dry off, no matter how many showers they take. And there is always the same routine monotony of doing things they don't much want to do and wondering what good any of it is. Only occasionally does Dirkson realize that he is glad for the routine, because without it his mind would be free to think, and his life would probably become a sort of hopeless grey treadmill.

The endless days on the island continually run headlong into each other, obliterating everything in their path. Even remembering is difficult. Before the army, Dirkson was a junior copywriter in a medium-sized Chicago advertising agency. It seems foolish to him even to think about that now, it is so unreal. But when he does think about it, his memory is colored by a feeling that it was a time of nothing but fabulous parties—Marguerite, of course, and people of all sizes and sexes standing around in a very small apartment, absently spilling cocktails on their evening clothes while they talked about business and the cold war and politics and baseball, all with equal enthusiasm and equal lack of knowledge. The parties always ended, but there was never anything sad about that because with any luck at all he could talk Marguerite into coming to his apartment afterward. And the next morning she would be cooking eggs over his tiny stove in that special way she had, and he would be sitting on the rumpled bed staring at her back, particularly at the spot where her hair folded carelessly around her neck, and he would feel a tightness in his throat because of his love for her.

And then she would turn toward him, because she could feel the warmth of his watching her, and they would laugh together suddenly, sharing a deliciously personal secret. . . .

Now, on the road to Shinabaru, on the pile of coral that forms such an insignificant dot in the southern Pacific Ocean, Dirkson again remembers the people and the parties, and surprises himself with the certain knowledge that he will never again fit in with much that he used to take for granted. Too many things have happened to change his life in the past year, not the least of which is the letter lying in pieces on the road behind him. Thinking suddenly becomes painful, and he concentrates on the dusty road and the sharp pieces of coral that dig into the leather of his shoes, bruising his feet. He has been walking more than a half hour, and in all that time has passed only one old island woman who was not at all reluctant to let Dirkson watch her relieve herself in the traditional way, squatting beside the road. In spite of this essentially vital act, he began to think of it then as a dead island, inhabited only by dead men. Men like himself, dead on arrival and probably deader on departure.

The yellow moon, just rising, dips behind a cloud and leaves the road full of dark shadows. One of the shadows, cast by a low bush beside the road, looks something like a man's face. For no reason he can think of, the shadow calls up in Dirkson's mind the image of Mr. Tanaka. This venerable old gentleman is a popular and influential figure in island politics and, although physically small by American standards, possesses a voice capable of chilling cold steel in two languages. His voice was recently raised to a pitch never heard before after his daughter came home crying and claiming she had been raped by an army supply sergeant from a camp at the northern end of the island. As clerk to the battalion legal officer—a young, likable lieutenant named Harding—Dirkson often comes into contact with a great many unsavory facts not generally known, at least not by the wives, parents, and sweethearts back in the States. The rape case was nothing unusual, except that everyone knew Mr. Tanaka could and probably would give the army a bad time. Even when he has not been personally injured, Mr. Tanaka feels a great responsibility toward his people.

The sergeant involved appeared bewildered at the charge brought against him. He readily admitted having relations with the girl, but insisted that she was quite willing. "I don't care who her old man is," he told the Military Police captain who arrested him, "she's no better'n the rest of these little native whores."

Oddly enough, the captain seemed to agree in principle with the sergeant. "You know how these damned slant-eyed girls are," he told Lieutenant Harding. "They got no more morals than an alley cat, most of them. The few that do have any self-respect won't even look at a GI. Personally I'd be inclined to have the sergeant's CO give him a reprimand and let it go at that. I'm not trying to tell you what to do, Lieutenant, but if it was my case. . . ."

"Captain," the young lieutenant interrupted bluntly, "I'm afraid it isn't your case." The captain shrugged, motioned to the two MP's flanking the dazed sergeant, and led his retinue from the office with drill team precision. The lieutenant looked sadly at Dirkson from behind his desk, and Dirkson had to pretend that he was engrossed in some important paper in order to stay neutral. Dirkson frequently goes to great lengths to keep from becoming involved.

It is quite dark now on the road to Shinabaru. Dirkson sees a light from around the next curve, and remembers that the road passes a small air base officially called Tensan but more often referred to as the gravel pit. The base, set apart from any other military installation, consists almost entirely of a patched-up landing strip used by the Japanese in the last war. For its new owners it has become an auxiliary strip, possibly useful in an emergency; to the greying young pilots who skim their jet wheels uncertainly across its broken surface, it is one of those military abortions that sometimes have to be endured in silence.

Dirkson knows a mechanic who works at the base, a remarkable fellow who, in his spare time, subsidizes his service pay by running tax-free liquor to the thirsty inhabitants of several offshore islands. On an impulse, Dirkson cuts across the meadow separating the enclosed strip from the road. He shows his ID card to the Air Policeman at the gate.

"Ya need a special pass for in here, buddy," the guard says. His tone is unloving. "How the hell do I know who you are?"

"I'm a spy," Dirkson says, noticing with pleasure that the guard is not amused. "Just a joke," he adds, after he has enjoyed the joke. "Billy-Boy Fletcher will vouch for old Dirkson." The guard reluctantly telephones the hangar from his booth, and in a very few minutes the mechanic appears at the gate wearing greasy fatigues and a tired smile.

"Sorry, Dirk, I'm on duty for a while tonight," Billy-Boy says, winking cheerfully at the guard. "Come on in, though, if you don't mind hanging around. I won't be long."

Dirkson follows him in past the frowning guard, and soon finds himself alone on the apron at the edge of the flight line. For a while he amuses himself by inspecting two jets parked under tarpaulins and apparently out of commission. The working-order craft seem to be grouped around one end of the single runway. As Dirkson watches, a sudden flash of light and smoke belches from one of the runway planes. An accompanying low-pitched whine gradually rises in intensity until it booms like thunder in his ears. As it pulls away from the shadows of the hangar, the sleek silver machine is suddenly bathed in floodlights from the control tower.

With no apparent effort except for the protesting roar, the jet races down the runway, passes Dirkson, and silently folds its wheels into its body as it leaves the earth. The white incandescence of its afterburner sears a gently curving line upward into the night sky.

Dirkson is acutely aware of the tenseness inside him. He tries to imagine himself in the pilot's place, to feel what it must be like to be alone with the stars and riding such a potent thunderbolt. With the right combination of quick thinking and perfect reflexes a jet pilot may enjoy a long life, the manual probably says. Of course this particular young warrior, through no fault of his own, really, may never live to see the States again, and his family can cry bitter tears forever over a cheap piece of metal awarded posthumously. Maybe it is better, Dirkson thinks, not having a family to worry about you.

After a while the deafening noise becomes a whisper, and then nothing, and the air strip seems oppressively quiet. Dirkson carefully rolls up his damp shirt sleeves, absently watching the few mechanics on duty shuffling between the hangar and the flight line. He almost decides not to wait for his friend, after all, when he hears the sound of excited voices near one of the darkly outlined jets parked on the apron. Then a piercing yell from that direction shatters the stillness, and almost immediately an Air Policeman waving a huge flashlight races past Dirkson toward the planes, shouting questions no less frightening for being unintelligible.

Quite aware that whatever is happening is none of his business, Dirkson nevertheless follows the AP at a stiff trot. Attracted by the noise, several mechanics and off-duty pilots fall into a run in turn behind Dirkson. The almost total darkness obscures whatever action is taking place up ahead, until a beam of light from the AP's flashlight catches up in its white circle the blurred outlines of half a dozen darting figures.

A second guard carrying an unslung carbine pounds up from behind shouting "Halt!" and then halts himself shortly in front of Dirkson. For a fraction of a second one of the scurrying figures veers into the moving beam of the flashlight, and in one perfectly co-ordinated motion the guard raises the carbine to his shoulder and squeezes the trigger. From fifty feet out in the darkness there comes an agonized, high-pitched cry.

The small crowd stands motionless, listening to the carbine's explosive crack reverberate across the flight line. The two guards, first to move, begin edging cautiously out toward a shapeless mound crumpled on the concrete and impaled by the flashlight's now steady beam.

"What the hell happened?" someone says by Dirkson's ear. No one in the group answers.

A battery of searchlights fixed to the roof of the operations building flash on blindingly, flooding that part of the apron where the two guards stand. Several second elapse before Dirkson realizes that the booming in his ears is the voice of the control tower operator amplified by an immense loudspeaker. The crackling sounds gradually separate and become words: "Flight line security sergeant . . . repeat . . . flight line security sergeant . . . report at once to base ops!"

The sound of a voice barking orders stirs Dirkson and the others into a kind of dazed action. They drift over and form a small knot around the guards, who are staring blankly at the ground. There, sprawled grotesquely on his face, is a native boy about ten years old. The ragged, cut-down army shirt he wears is split open in the back, and is already soggy with the dark blood oozing from the gaping bullet hole.

One of the men whistles softly. "Jesus, it must've broke his back. Look at the funny way he's lying."

"Yeah, he don't look human, hardly."

"Who saw him? I didn't even have time to see him."

"Hell, neither did anybody else."

The guard who fired the shot looks up at the men, the carbine dangling limply from his hand. "Don't any of you guys touch anything," he says, as though someone has to assert some authority. "Just don't touch anything."

"We'll never get the rest of 'em," the other guard says. "They must've got out the same way they got in—right over the barbed wire, or through it."

A mechanic snorts, his black face dripping sweat, "They all a bunch of thieves, no matter how young they is. Hell, man, they'd steal you teeth if you wasn't looking."

"Well, maybe he was lucky at that," one of the pilots says flatly. "I mean, it must have killed him instantly—the poor little bastard never felt a thing."

"A carbine slug goes through you, you feel it," somebody says with finality.

The crash ambulance careens off the runway and screeches to a stop beside the awkwardly grouped men. A white-coated medic hops down beside the body while his partner fishes a stretcher out of the back end. The one on the ground examines the wound quickly and turns the body over. He shakes his head at the other medic. "He's had it."

Dirkson and the others can see the boy's face clearly now for the first time. His round black eyes, still open, stare wildly at the sky. Choking back the bile rising in his throat, Dirkson is compelled to gaze into the terrible reality of the boy's glistening, unseeing eyes.

Together the medics gently lift the small twisted body onto the stretcher. As the other men follow it to the back of the ambulance, Dirkson notices an object on the ground laying close to where the boy fell. He stoops to pick it up, and sees that it is a crudely carved model of a jet airplane, unmistakably the same kind of plane that rose from the runway so beautifully only moments ago.

Dirkson turns the piece of wood over and over in his hands, staring at it, remembering. He remembers that a long time ago he whittled airplanes like this one, working from pictures before he ever saw a real plane. The boy, too, probably came sneaking onto the base for a chance to see the real thing, and was killed for his trouble. As the ambulance pulls away, Dirkson slips the little plane into his pocket and walks quickly toward the main gate. He passes the gate-house without looking at the guard and turns hurriedly back onto the road, back toward Shinabaru.

When he can no longer see the lights of the air base he slows his pace, beginning to feel slightly foolish. He can think of no very good reason why he took the boy's plane. Certainly he will never be able to find anyone to give it to as the last of the boy's personal effects, but then neither would the air force. In all probability the boy will never even be identified—children and dogs run as loose on the island as the breezes. The air force will quietly turn the body over to island officials, the Communists will stage protest rallies in the largest villages, and the boy's relatives, if any, will never know what happened to him. And so he will be buried, and will return to the fertile, steaming earth which spawned him and on which he lived all of his ten years.

The road ends abruptly at Shinabaru in a cluster of thatched-roof huts, and from there a winding dirt path passes an open schoolyard and continues to the center of the village. Dirkson is surprised he has come so far so quickly. Slightly out of breath from descending a sharp hill, he reaches the huts and pauses in their shadows to wipe his forehead. A sudden gust of wind brushing against his dripping face is refreshing and somehow like a good omen. Rested now, he begins picking his way slowly down the path to the schoolyard. As he nears the enclosure the moon slips out of the shadows, causing the simple outlines of the deserted school building to stand out sharply in the yellow-grey light. Breathing heavily and feeling as though someone may be watching him, he pushes inward on the gate.

The violent creaking of rusty hinges startles him. He stands perfectly still, listening, but there is no sound except that issuing eerily from the heart of the village. He enters the open yard and walks toward the building.

At a spot protected from the wind by two large rocks, Dirkson kneels and with his bare hands scrapes out a small hole in the stubborn dirt. Gently, he removes the pitiful wooden lump of a plane from his pocket. He stretches out full length on the ground beside the hole, turning the plane over and over in his hand and watching the moonlight reflect dully from its rough surfaces.

This may have been his school, Dirkson thinks, some teacher

here may have tried to tell him about good citizenship and about
how important it was for all of them to get along well with the
foreigners who now occupied their land. Or maybe he never went to
school, and had been forced to learn about the foreigners the hard
way—begging whatever he could, and stealing what he couldn't
beg. Dirkson looks again at the plane in his hand and wishes the boy
were here now. "It isn't beautiful," he says aloud, surprised and
pleased at the sound of his own voice. "But it's all you had. I'm
sorry, not so much for you but for us. Anyway, we'll give your plane
a decent burial, here in the earth that once belonged to you but
could never belong to me. I'm not a religious man, you understand,
but . . ." and Dirkson, now absorbed by the idea of the ceremony's
importance, wonders if it would be proper to say a few words over
the grave.

As he thinks about this, Dirkson sees or feels a shadow move just
beyond the reach of his peripheral vision. He flips himself on his
back and jerks upright, to find himself staring into the questioning
eyes of a very small, half-naked native boy who is chewing on a
persimmon.

Dirkson snaps his head around the yard, searching the shadows.
It wouldn't have been the first time a serviceman was rolled by a
bunch of kids no bigger than this one. "You scared me, butch," he
says to the child. "Mustn't do that, you know. What if I'd been
packing a .45?"

The boy makes sucking sounds on the persimmon and continues
to stare at Dirkson.

"I'm sorry, I didn't mean that. What's your name? Don't you
understand English at all?"

The child's eyes are as bright as were those of the dead boy. He is
about half the dead boy's age.

"You don't, do you?" Dirkson says. "Understand English, I
mean. But then why should you—this is your country, not mine.
I'm all mixed up, butch. Christ, I'm mixed up!"

Unable to think of anything more to say, or any reason for trying,
Dirkson stands up and brushes the dirt from his pants. His eyes fall
on the hole he dug for the plane. "Listen, butch, I just happen to
have a present for you. It's a very lucky thing you came along when
you did."

He bends over and opens one of the boy's pudgy hands, places the airplane in it, and closes the sticky fingers around it. The boy clutches the plane to his chest and blinks a question at his benefactor. Dirkson nods to him, then turns away and hurriedly leaves the schoolyard. He does not even look back when the gate squeaks shut behind him.

It is ten-thirty. The serpentine road from Shinabaru stretches ahead of him as far as he can see in the dim light. An hour, more or less, will be time enough to reach the barracks. Where the road inclines sharply to the left, Dirkson stops and glances back toward the faint lights of Shinabaru below him. There was once someone he could have told about all this, he remembers—someone who wouldn't have thought him sick, or a fool. Is it possible she could still listen, patiently, undemandingly? It is suddenly very important to Dirkson, this question of whether or not he can ever make her understand at least a part of the things he has felt and seen in this alien environment, so far from the world they knew together.

It is possible, he decides finally; anyway, it is worth trying. He turns away from the village, smiling as he wonders if the sergeant will ask him where he's been. The crisp, staccato sound of the coral beneath his feet is more pleasant, going back.

# *Hugh*

I am standing on the terrace of the Alumnae House, listening to a classmate from Pem East whom I remember chiefly for her gentle wit and acne—which has cleared up completely after twenty-five years—and the egg stains on her pale blue woolen bathrobe.

Suddenly I notice a familiar face from the Class of '47. (They're the ones with owl-shaped name tags; ours are round with "25th" in large Gothic print.) It is a fairly long face, with a nose that is too large for the close-set eyes above it and skin that has been leathered by the sun. From the simple dress the woman's wearing—lime green linen—and gold bracelets on her wrists, I can tell she's rich and social—the Miss Porter's type that always slightly frightened me.

As she leans her shingled gray head back to laugh, she shows a set of teeth which bite into my memory so deeply that I wince with pain. The same kind of pain I felt this morning when I walked through Pembroke Arch and passed the bicycle rack I fell backward over once when Hugh Patterson—the only man I've ever loved in the reckless, headlong way that Cathy loved Heathcliff—was kissing me goodnight.

I fell, sad to say, not from the force of his passion, but from clumsiness. Absent-mindedness. Not noticing the thing was there.

A chaste peck on the cheek was all Hugh Patterson ever offered me in Pembroke Arch, though around us other couples writhed like tangled worms beside the bicycles or beneath the limestone owls that stared down from a shield with the motto: *Veritatem Dilexi:* "I chose Truth."

A rather sad choice I have always thought. And I use the word "sad" the way my mother, a former member of the Sweet Briar May Court, uses it: "She's a nice girl, really. It's a shame that she's so sad." Because it was her firm belief, halfway passed along to me, that Bryn Mawr girls chose truth because they didn't have a better option.

"But I didn't take the job," my classmate's saying now. "Because I need some time, you see. I've just been through the grueling, if useless, ordeal of the Ph.D. Raised three children and lost one. I'm forty-six years old and I have this premonition—if I can give myself a little time this summer, I just may be about to grow up!"

We all laugh at that remark. Me included, though I'm still staring at the teeth of that woman from the Class of '47, moving the unique shape of them across the jigsaw puzzle of my past. Suddenly, they fall right into place. She's Hugh Patterson's cousin. Or, more accurately, the rich girl from the Main Line (was it Bailey, Banks, or Biddle?) who married his cousin. Generally, Hugh's family was as hard up as mine was. But he did have this one cousin who was married to a rich girl with a farm out in Paoli. It had fieldstone fences, I remember, and a long, thin swimming pool, and best of all, a pond where Hugh would take me ice skating at night.

A wave of undiluted longing for Hugh Patterson washes over me. I see him kneeling in pine needles, lacing up my ice skates, his tight blond curls so close to my knee that I can easily reach out and run my fingers through them. But I know, of course, I mustn't. The basis of my strategy—my Five Year Plan to win him—is to hold back all this feeling, since he measures out his love for me in demitasse spoons.

So I have to be content to anticipate the moment, not very far away now, when he'll knot the laces, pull me to my feet and slip his arm around my waist where it will burn through my wool sweaters, as we wobble down the bank in silence. Then step onto the moonlit, pine-fringed pond of ice.

Helen is her name.

My eyes are still OK for reading at a distance, so I work them like two plumber's snakes around the bodies that block me from the woman's name tag. Before I have a chance to read it, a tanned arm reaches across it.

Twenty-two years I have waited to find out what has happened to Hugh Patterson. Here, at last, may be a woman who can tell me. My patience at this moment is inexhaustible. Eventually, that arm will move away.

In the meantime I will stand here, pretending that I'm listening to my classmate's chatter, for this time I am determined to make contact with Hugh.

At my tenth reunion I passed up a chance to see him. Back then one of my classmates—long since divorced and moved with her four children to California—lived down the street from him in a section of Philadelphia called Fairmount that was just then beginning to be restored. She told me they were having a neighborhood street fair the Sunday afternoon of our tenth reunion weekend and that Hugh was going to be the auctioneer. What I ought to do, she said, was stop off at the street fair on my way back to the airport. That way I was bound to see him.

I played with the idea all weekend long, imagining Hugh's face when I stood up at the auction, rehearsing what I'd say when we ducked into a restaurant afterwards to have a drink together. I'd heard rumors that he'd taken up with a Swarthmore girl five years older than he was; that at one point he was actually living with her, unusual in those days, for Hugh particularly, who cared so much about appearances and had been agonizingly celibate with me.

The arm has moved away now, but the woman in the green dress has turned her body slightly. I still can't see the name tag.

In my fantasies, over tenth reunion weekend, I discounted the rumors. Or rather, I decided that if that older woman did exist, she would be out of town. It was only fair that Hugh and I should have one final talk during which I could finally justify my actions to him.

Actions that most certainly did *not* deserve the box he'd sent by parcel post the week after my engagement was announced. When the mailman brought it to the door, I assumed it was a wedding present. I ran back to the dining room, got the carving knife and cut the package open right there in the hall. Out spilled the mementos from the five years Hugh and I had known each other. Theater programs from ballets and plays that we had seen together. The expensive leather belt—with his initials on the buckle—I'd given him one Christmas. Even the five-pound rock we brought home from a hike in the Poconos because we both admired its striated colors. He was going to use it as a doorstop in the house he had just bought in Fairmount to restore.

I was stunned by this evidence of bitterness from a man who almost never showed emotion. And embarrassed, deeply, for Hugh and for myself. I put the things back in the box, before anybody in my family could see them, lugged it out to the garbage can, then went up to my room and wept. If Hugh had shown that much feeling two months earlier, none of this would be happening, I thought. I'd be engaged to him instead. Then suddenly my head popped up from the tearsoaked pillow. Hey, wait a minute. Where were all my letters?

The crafty bastard. He was still saving my letters—on the slim chance that I might fulfill my rapidly diminishing potential and become a famous poet after all. Then he could step forward and reveal to the world that he was the one I had lavished my first fine careless rapture on. Or maybe he was hoping he could sell the letters. God dammit, I thought, it's almost worth the effort of becoming famous to find out what Hugh will do with all my letters.

Even in this final gesture, Hugh could not bring himself to go all the way. And that fact took the sting out of the gesture. Made it easier for me to tell Sam about it when he took me out that night. Actually, I'd found that I could tell Sam anything, which was one reason that I felt relaxed, if not particularly happy, about the fact that I was going to marry him.

But I would not have told Sam if I had stopped off to see Hugh on the way back from my tenth reunion. And it would have been the first time I had deliberately held something back from him. In the end I didn't go; I took the limousine straight to the airport.

It was probably too soon for me to see Hugh anyway. I was still getting postcards signed "As ever, Hugh" which drove Sam up the wall. He had always understood how strong my love for Hugh was, even if Hugh didn't. And I guess I was afraid of Sam's reaction. Maybe even more afraid of my own. For there was always that small chance that if I heard Hugh's voice again, it would catch me like a fish hook in the heart. And there I'd be—in the same old situation—using every ounce of wit and energy to keep the hook from tearing any further, following so fast, to keep the line of pain that tied me to him slack, that I appeared to be moving on my own.

If the hook sank deep enough, it might mean that I would have to leave Sam. And probably, my children, too. And I truly loved my children, though by that time I knew that I would never love Sam the way that I'd loved Hugh.

What I felt for Sam was much more basic. Sam could never be called handsome, except, perhaps, when his brown eyes are burning with a new idea, or amusement at the human situation. He has a dime-size bald spot on the back of his black head which has spread over the years to the size of a golf ball—an emblem of his own mortality I find particularly poignant since he can't see it himself. What I felt for Sam was too day-in-and-out—quotidian would be the word—to work up to the Olympian intensity of my love for Hugh.

If I had seen Hugh then, I might have had to leave, not only Sam, but my children, too. For how could Hugh put up with my runny-nosed, poorly disciplined, frequently nauseated children? I remembered all too well the night he explained to me why he'd decided to switch from general surgery to ophthalmology:

"Because I'm sick of all those people vomiting," he said. "And—if you want to know the truth—I'm also sick of blood."

I figured he was overworked, half kidding when he said that, since it was the middle of his intern year and he was averaging less than four hours of sleep a night. But he was serious. The very next week he took the necessary steps to change his field to ophthalmology.

The eye—he explained, another night when we were necking in his mother's car—the eye seemed to be detached from the rest of the body. Aesthetically interesting. Elegantly fashioned. More appealing, surely, as a lifetime's work, than bursting bowels or spurting arteries.

By the time that tenth reunion came around my youngest child was nine months old; my oldest, barely six. I was absolutely mired in blood and vomit. And I figured that if Hugh swept me off my feet and back into his life again, he might very well refuse to take my children. Even though my oldest daughter and my youngest son are blond.

I remember how he used to say, as if it were a joke, "I can't help it, Tompkins." He sometimes called me Tompkins, as my roommate, Harriet, and the hockey coach did; it made me feel that I was still a long-legged, sexless schoolgirl. "God knows I've tried, but I just can't help it, Tompkins. As a rule, I like blondes best." And there was absolutely no way—short of wigs or bleach—that I could ever be a blonde, though I did point out that I had been a blonde as a child and the chances were my children would be, too.

The only time Hugh came to visit me—in New York, two years before my parents moved back to Virginia—I made him look through a book of photographs of my sister and myself as children. "See there, I'm the smallest one. The *blonde* one. Sitting on the swing." I even engineered an evening at my sister's apartment, ostensibly so that Hugh could meet her husband, a neurology resident at Bellevue, but actually to show him that my niece was blonde, although both of her parents had hair that was darker than mine.

It was pitiful, the way I dragged him down to Peter Cooper Village, changing from the E train to the BMT and then a crosstown bus, to impress on him the fact that I was probably carrying a recessive gene that could give him what he wanted. Beautiful blonde daughters.

By the time we got there, my niece was asleep. So I marched Hugh back into her bedroom and woke the poor child up, and she stood there at the crib rail in her feet pajamas, rubbing sleep from her blue eyes and shaking that bright golden head that was meant to serve as proof that I could be the mother of blonde daughters.

And do you know what Hugh said when he saw her? "I think she has inherited the tendency toward strabismus. That means slightly crossed eyes which can produce a condition called amblyopia—the loss of sight in one eye. You should tell your sister to have her eyes examined. Right away."

Two of my own children have inherited the tendency toward strabismus. The youngest one, Sammy, had to have an eye muscle clipped when he was barely four years old. I remember how he stood there by that hospital bed that was taller than he was, his short, plump toes sticking out from his seersucker pajamas, while Sam and I listened to the casters of the stretcher coming down the hall to take him off to Surgery.

His cornflower blue eyes looked up through the lenses of his horn-rimmed glasses, as he said: "Dr. Cary's gonna move my eye. Right, Daddy? Right, Momma?" Then softly, to himself, "He's gonna move my eye. But just a little bit."

When the orderly came in, he took Sammy's glasses off and set them on the night table against the water pitcher. Then he hooked his thumbs under Sammy's armpits, swung him up onto the stretcher, and rolled him from the room.

For the next two hours, while Sam tried to read a book and I, a newspaper, those tiny horn-rimmed glasses, propped against that water pitcher, stared at me, reproaching me for my genetic flaw, for my stupidity in not taking Sammy to the eye doctor sooner, for all the unnamed failures that mothers carry around with them like birdshot in the heart.

My children have that awful power that Hugh once had of absorbing me completely. And in the process wrecking all my plans.

Back when I was in high school—and my freshman year in college—those plans were all I had. And as long as that was so, anything I put my mind to I could do. But then one February afternoon my sophomore year, I looked up from a snowball fight outside of Pembroke West and saw Hugh Patterson's profile. And a voice inside me said with quiet certainty, "That's the man I want to marry."

It was a sign of things to come that Hugh did not notice me as he stopped one of my friends to ask where Bitsy Smith, a girl he'd met in Europe, lived.

His eyes, I noticed, were a pale, transparent blue, and as he talked, he held them open wide, as if surprised and slightly shocked by what they saw; yet through them came no clues to what he might be feeling. His nose was short and straight with a sudden childish up-tilt at the end, which had the same effect on me as the snubbed nose of a puppy. It made me want to hug him. But what really tore my heart that afternoon and claimed the next five years of my life, was the sight of his sharp-peaked, perfectly formed lips which, when he wasn't speaking, he kept pressed together, as if holding back some sorrow that he could not talk about.

I loved Hugh instantly, and decided I was probably the only person in the world who could draw that sorrow from him. Suddenly I was possessed with a joyful sense of mission. My only problem now was how could I get close enough to him to do the job?

Luckily, Bitsy Smith—the girl he'd come to see—was already engaged to a law student at Penn. So later that same afternoon I dropped by Bitsy's suite and joined the crowd that was having tea and cocoa by her fire. I'd hoped to find Hugh there, but by that time he had left. So I took Bitsy aside and asked if she would fix me up with him sometime.

I "set my cap" for Hugh, as my grandmother would put it. She was much more optimistic about my chances for success with men than Mother, who thought I was too smart for my own good. Nana's theory was that everything depends on strategy. "Any woman but a hunchback can get the man she wants," she said, and I believed her, deeply grateful that although I'd never be a beauty, with my long face and flat chest, I did not have a hunchback. Moreover, I had damn good-looking legs.

There would be times, of course, during the next five years when I questioned Nana's wisdom. The more schemes I devised to show Hugh why he ought to marry me, the more reasons he found why he should not. It was only after I gave up that he came around to almost asking me.

And by that time I'd met Sam. He had slipped into my life the summer I was living with my parents between two teaching jobs. I started going out with him on weekdays—when I couldn't see Hugh—because I liked to be around him. He was so affirmative and interested in everything around him—politics and history, and people. I couldn't help but notice the contrast between Hugh's mincing progress and Sam's reckless careening toward commitment, his eagerness to offer me everything he was and would be, accepting in return anything I had to offer, including the possibility that I might never love him.

It nearly broke my heart to watch Hugh work around to the conclusion that I was probably the best that he could get. I could almost hear him thinking: "Her hair may be brown and her genes ambylopic, but she is well educated, sensitive to the arts, and surprisingly effective socially," as he proceeded, step by cautious step, to the point that he could tell me he was "looking for engagement rings" though he still could not come right out and say who the ring was for. Me, obviously. Wasn't I the only girl he was dating?

When he started all that talk about engagement rings, I could easily have asked him: "Who is the ring for?" But by that time, I was trapped in my own strategy of indirection. Fearful, too, that if I chose the wrong words—honest, blunt, direct words—he would vanish.

As he had vanished once—for my entire senior year—after he had forced me to stand up to him in public.

It happened at a dinner dance that Hugh's class, the junior class, at the medical school was giving for the seniors. One of Hugh's classmates took out a cigar and asked me if I'd like to try it. I debated for a second, then decided to say no. But before I could speak, Hugh said, "Don't smoke that cigar."

Then he announced in the silence that had settled on the table, "I swear to you, Tompkins, if you so much as take a puff from that cigar, I'll never take you out again in my whole life."

The words knocked the breath out of my lungs; I felt as if I'd come down from a high jump and landed on my arm. All I could do at first was gasp to get the air back. By the time I was breathing normally again, I knew I had to smoke the damn cigar. Or give in to Hugh completely. Either way I'd lose him. So I might as well lose him with my pride intact.

I did not answer him. Instead I reached across the heavy-duty tablecloth—by now ringed with stains from our drinks and smudged with ashes from our cigarettes—and plucked the cigar from Hugh's classmate's fingers, brought it over to my mouth and took two puffs from it. Then I passed it back to him—all in total silence, since everybody there, with the possible exception of Hugh, himself, knew how much those two puffs cost.

For the rest of the evening Hugh was exceedingly polite. And when the dance was over, he drove me home in silence, walked me to the door of Pembroke East, and bowed out of my life for a whole year.

The following September I looked for him at the Freshman mixer, which the medical school students usually came to. Finally, one of his friends asked me to dance and told me Hugh had gone to Edinburgh for the year on a research fellowship. It was March before Hugh wrote me. And July before I saw him, at which time neither one of us mentioned that cigar.

It had earned me, by the way, a modest fame at the medical school which provided me with dates to pass the time my senior year. But I had no interest in them. If I couldn't have Hugh, I really did not want another man. Instead, I threw myself into my work, and to the horror of my mother—my grandmother had died before her strategy had worked—graduated first among the English majors, had a poem accepted by a major literary magazine, and won a fellowship to study medieval drama at Cambridge.

Ironically, it was these accomplishments, added to the fact that I had survived without him, that drew Hugh back to me, I think. I delayed sailing to Europe, so that I could see him for another month. And did not apply for a renewal of my Fulbright, but came right back across the ocean to a mediocre job, teaching English and Latin at a private girls' school, just to be in Philadelphia where he was.

And it almost worked. In fact there was a time—twelve blissful hours—when I thought that I had finally won him.

It happened on a Saturday in mid-December, the day before I was to take the train back to Virginia to spend the week of Christmas with my parents. Hugh had the whole day off, so he borrowed his mother's car and drove out to the house in Ardmore I was sharing with two girls who taught at Shipley with me.

He arrived in faded jeans and a ski parka, with a cleaner's bag over his arm. "Guess what?" he said. "We've got free tickets to a dinner dance tonight at the Radnor Hunt Club. I've got my tuxedo. Have you got an evening dress?"

"I've got a bridesmaid's dress," I said. The fact was I had several; that was the year so many of my friends were getting married. I was planning to cook dinner for Hugh there, at the house, since both of my housemates were going to be out. Yet I could tell he really wanted to go to that dance, even though there would be no one there we knew. Still, it was a free dinner. Better yet, a chance to dance with Hugh all evening long.

Hugh was a magnificent dancer. His tall, bony body always seemed to know what it was doing on the dance floor; and it managed to communicate that knowledge to mine. Whenever we assumed the ballroom dance position, with one arm at the other's waist, the other stretched out almost straight, I marveled at the way our long bodies fit together. And as we started dancing we would press our bodies closer till the rhythm of the music merged them into one.

My most recent bridesmaid's dress, smartly tailored in peach-colored organdy, was surprisingly becoming. Hugh had never seen it. The more I thought about that dress and the prospect of going to a dance with him that night, the more I warmed to the idea.

We spent the afternoon working on separate projects in my third-floor attic bedroom. For my birthday Hugh had given me a pine tavern table to use as a writing table. One Sunday afternoon we had driven all the way to the town of York, to a warehouse for antiques, to pick it out. And he had promised to refinish it for me on his afternoons off. We kept the tavern table and his electric sander in my bedroom, so that he could close the door whenever he was sanding and keep the dust from spreading through the house.

Every surface of my bedroom—the floor, the window sills, the jar-tops on my bureau—were coated with a saffron-colored dust, and my clothes and blankets smelled of ground-up varnish. But I loved to have Hugh there, doing his work at one end of the room, while I sat in the middle, at a rickety card table, doing mine.

On this particular day I was planning the assignments for my tenth grade English class. And Hugh was lying on the floor, with his long legs folded up, like a grasshopper's, working on the under-side of the tavern table. It was almost as communal as being married.

Except there was one difference. One enormous difference—in our tortured attitude toward my bed. The presence of that bed—tucked under the eaves at the far end of the room—made us both exquisitely uneasy. And we took great care to avoid even a glance in that direction.

In this respect, I felt a little less than honest. I had had far more experience with beds and sex than Hugh suspected, even though I was, like most of my friends, still technically a virgin. But Hugh blithely assumed that since I was four years younger, I must be four years more innocent than he.

It did not occur to me—concentrating all my thoughts on my strategy to win him—that my experience might be something Hugh could use, something Hugh might need. I was, in fact, reluctant to reveal it. In retrospect, it's hard to reconstruct my elaborately fabricated attitude toward sex then. But I do remember this much. When I read the end of the best seller, *Marjorie Morningstar,* where the fiancé threatens to call the wedding off because he's learned that the heroine is not a virgin, I did not get the point—that this attitude reflected on his character, not hers. I thought he had a perfect right to drop her.

Besides, that afternoon I experienced a pleasure that can come when one has to refrain from sex which surpassed any pleasure I had yet received from yielding to it.

We were on our honor not to misbehave in my bedroom. For me, it was as if I were back in my dormitory room with an unfinished exam book on my desk and a textbook on the shelf with the answers in it. The very proximity of the opportunity made it impossible to consider yielding to it. This was a moral test; if I cracked open the textbook, or fell onto the bed with Hugh, I would forfeit my ability to like myself.

Or so I thought, when Hugh dragged his bentwood chair up to the card table by mine—pulling the round wooden seat through the trim crotch of his jeans and sitting so close to me that his denim-covered thigh rested against mine. A liquid warmth slid through my body, as if I had just swallowed a mouthful of strong brandy. And I felt suddenly limp with longing for him.

"What are you giving them to read?" he asked as he bent over my papers. Hugh liked to read even more, perhaps, than I did, since he read purely for pleasure, while I read for my living now. As he hunched over the table, hugging his bony elbows, his posture struck me as inordinately boyish.

"Aren't you skimping on my hero, Henry James?" he asked. "Just those two short stories? Why don't you give them *Portrait of a Lady?*"

"It's too long," I said. "If you want to know the truth, I've never finished it, myself."

"Oh, you've got to, Tompkins! It's a *wonderful* book. Practically equal to a trip to England, First Class, with the perfect guide. And visually, it beats the Barnes Collection. It's probably my favorite book." He paused. "How can I marry you if you won't even read my favorite book?"

I never knew how to respond when Hugh began to joke about the subject I considered so important. I didn't answer him.

"At least I'm glad to see you're giving a whole week to Emily Dickinson."

"But I can't decide which poems. Have you got any suggestions?"

"Will you really let me choose them?" he asked, delighted as a child would be. It was this hint of innocence, a core of innocence, that made me love Hugh most, I think.

He picked up my small Modern Library edition of the poems, propped it open on his knees at the Index of First Lines and began to check the poems he liked.

Later, after I had finished dressing for the dance and was waiting through that block of time before a date when a girl is too carefully coiffed and powdered to do anything useful, I had a chance to look over his choices. I was shocked to discover that every single one of them dealt with death.

As we were driving to the dance, I asked him: "Do you realize that those poems you checked are all about death?"

"That's not so!" he said. "I know I checked 'The Soul Selects Her Own Society.' And that's a love poem, don't you think?"

" 'I've known her from an ample nation/Choose one;/Then close the valves of her attention/Like stone?' Don't those lines suggest a cemetery vault to you?"

"A bank vault," he said.

"A *stone* bank vault? And what about 'I Heard a Fly Buzz When I Died' . . . 'Because I Could Not Stop for Death' . . . ?"

"OK, OK. You win," he said. "Obviously I have a ghoulish streak in me. Now that you have forced me to the truth. . . ." He turned from the steering wheel to leer at me in the moonlight that was sifting through the windshield, "I'll tell you my dark secret. The fact is I'm a *vampire,* cleverly disguised as a would-be doctor."

On the way back from the dance, though, he brought the subject up again. At that point in the evening, those poems were the last thing on my mind. I was still basking in my unexpected success at the Radnor Hunt Club dance, where several Main Line bachelors who used to take out friends of mine from Pembroke East kept cutting in on me to find out what had happened to the girls they used to date. Each time one of them did, and Hugh came back to me, our long bodies would lock, and the pleasure we derived as they dipped across the dance floor seemed to have been intensified, rather than diminished, by the brief, involuntary separation. For once we did not even feel the need to talk.

I was still suspended in that totally relaxed and satisfied silence which we'd managed to carry from the dance into the car, when Hugh said, "I've been thinking about what you said on the way over. I guess the reason that I checked those particular poems is that death—my father's death—is the most important thing that's happened to me yet."

Then in a steady voice, he started telling me what it had been like the day his father shot himself while he was cleaning some old guns. It happened two days after Hugh's seventh birthday.

"He had given me a litter of puppies for my birthday. Beagles. And was going to help me raise them and train for the hunt. I was down at the barn, playing with the puppies, when I heard the gun go off."

There was silence for a second, but this time it was a silence that I felt unqualified to deal with. I had never experienced a sorrow even roughly comparable to this one.

When he spoke again, his voice was flatter and more guarded: "And to this day the smell of puppies—that sweet oniony smell of a puppy's breath—brings back all the bloody horror of that afternoon. It's positively Proustian, don't you agree?"

For once, I refused to follow his quickstep into intellectuality, as I would have followed the pressure of his hand on the small of my back, or his leg against my leg on the dance floor. I did not want this moment to degenerate so quickly into literary talk.

"I don't know," I said, "I've never had anything that awful happen to me. Did you train those puppies?"

"No," he said, "We sold them three months later when we sold the farm."

"But you still like dogs," I said. "It didn't turn you against dogs. You practically raised that last litter of beagles at your cousin's."

"That's true," he said. "And after I get married, I think I'd like to have a farm, myself."

"It was an accident, right?"

"Oh my God, yes," he said. "I can't believe he would have willed us into everything that happened after that."

We pulled up to a stoplight. "And now, Herr Doctor Tompkins, we have reached Lancaster Pike. Would you like to get a hamburger before I take you home?"

With that, we dropped the subject. But later when we pulled into the driveway behind my housemate's car, I abandoned my strategy for once and acted on an impulse. I slid over in the seat, slipped my arms around his waist, under his tuxedo coat, and hugged him.

He responded with a long, hard kiss. And when we broke from it, to breathe, I thought I heard him whisper, "I love you." But a truck was groaning up the hill below, and I wasn't sure.

"What did you say?" I asked.

He did not repeat it. Instead, he kissed me lightly on the tip of my nose, then harder on my ear, then on my lips again, until I began to feel the same warmth sliding through my body I had felt that afternoon. Only this time we weren't in my bedroom, bound by honor. We were in a parked car.

All the calculations that my roommate, Harriet, and I had worked out, sitting on the window sill of our living room at college, our feet firmly planted on the balcony outside, our cigarette ends glowing several inches from our fingers—all those rules about how far a girl could go and still not run the risk of being thought a slut, seemed suddenly self-serving. Artificial. Trivial. As Hugh's passion rose to meet mine and we fell back on the seat, I would have given anything to him.

If he had wanted it.

But in the middle of our lovemaking, he drew back and sat up straight behind the steering wheel, his white tuxedo shirt gleaming in the moonlight.

"It's all right, Hugh," I said.

"But it may not be all right tomorrow morning," he said evenly. "If we've waited this long, we can wait a little longer."

Then he took me in his arms again, cupped one hand under my breast, and drew my hand into his lap. And held it there, hard, as he kissed me one last time.

"Now let's get out of here," he said, as he opened the car door.

Delirious with joy, I stumbled up the driveway, hand in hand with Hugh, and burst into the kitchen where my housemates and their dates were gathered round the TV set, hissing at some film clips of Senator McCarthy.

At that moment I believed that Hugh and I were engaged.

But when I woke up the next morning I was not so sure. Had I imagined that he said "I love you"?

Before I took the train home for Christmas vacation, I stopped off at the hospital and had lunch with Hugh in the cafeteria, hoping he would do or say something to confirm my sense of a commitment.

But he behaved as if the night before had never happened. He had been working nonstop since six o'clock that morning and was preoccupied with the problems he was having with a patient.

For Christmas, though, he sent me an extravagant present. A gold pin from Tiffany's, shaped like a tiny beagle. And he asked me to go skiing with him over New Year's weekend. But it turned out there was no snow. So we canceled the ski trip, and he worked New Year's weekend, covering for a friend whose wife had gone into labor prematurely.

The next thing I knew, the vacation was over, and I was working harder than I'd ever worked before. In addition to my full-time job at Shipley, I had signed up for two courses in graduate school. Three months of high-school teaching had made me realize that I would rather teach in college, and for that I was going to need some more degrees.

Hugh, poor thing, was even more overworked than I was. Since he was on call almost all the time, he would often get less than two hours of uninterrupted sleep at night. And when we managed to meet briefly at the hospital, the movies, or even at my house (where I sometimes had to leave him working on that tavern table while I rushed off to an evening seminar), we sat and stared at one another across a pool of mutual exhaustion.

I began to wonder if that night of the dance had ever happened.

"You were always so *sure*," he said that final weekend in New York, at Harriet's wedding. At that point Harriet and Hugh were the only people who knew that I'd decided to accept Sam's proposal. And Harriet threw her bouquet at me with so much force that I had to catch it, though I would have given anything not to have seen the expression on Hugh's face as the bouquet fell into my hands.

"You were always so *sure*," he said again, when we were back in Harriet's apartment, standing in her tiny kitchen because another bridesmaid and her fiancé—whom she would marry in a year and divorce in seven—were filling up the living room with a ferocious fight.

Beside two small gas burners and a chipped porcelain sink, we acted out our final scene, my face buried in Hugh's bony shoulder, my tears soaking through his shirt while he held me, lightly, and watched the large electric clock on the wall.

The fact that I had been so sure was apparently the thing that had held him back. And now that I'd decided to marry someone else, he could suddenly afford to show his feeling for me. And I, in turn, had nothing to lose by showing mine.

"You can't imagine what it's like," he said, "to have to argue for your *life*. Suppose I choose the wrong words? Then I lose it. Everything I've planned. It all means nothing now. You must know that, Tompkins. Surely you have noticed that when we're in a room with other people, you're the only one I see. The only one I want to talk to."

But I could not turn back now. If I did, Hugh might retreat again. And even if he didn't, if he went ahead and married me, I knew now how much another man could love me, what it was like to be able to help myself, greedily, to all the love I wanted, anytime I needed it. And knowing that, I did not think that I could live now on the meager rations Hugh would offer me.

At the time, though, I was choking on the sudden flood of feeling for Hugh, and now *from* Hugh, and could not explain a thing to him. So he thought I might recover from my impulse to marry Sam. Why else did he call on a Sunday morning, two weeks later, and announce that he was driving to Virginia to have a talk with me?

"Oh, Hugh. No," I said. "This is the day that I'm announcing my engagement."

"In that case," he said evenly. "There's no point in my coming. Is there?"

And those were the last words I heard him speak.

Across the terrace, now, I see the woman turning her green linen torso, so that, finally, her owl-shaped name tag flashes into view: HELEN BAILEY PATTERSON, 1947.

Before I have a chance to think, I am striding straight across the terrace. Standing by the woman. Stretching out my arm to shake her hand.

I am appalled at my own gall. I never knew this woman, really. When Hugh took me to her farm, we would chat politely, for not one minute longer than was necessary, because we understood, even if the men did not, that we inhabited entirely different worlds. So there is no reason now—except the one huge reason, Hugh—for me to resurrect this accidental, obsolete acquaintance. Yet I will not die without talking to Hugh, once.

So I say, "Hello, Helen. How *are* you?" in a swooping social voice I have never heard before. "I'm Margaret Tompkins Baker." Her flecked green eyes are glazed with lack of recognition. So I press on stupidly: "*Margie* Tompkins. Class of '57. I knew you way back in the fifties when your cousin Hugh and I used to come out to your farm."

"Oh, yes. Yes indeed!" she says, and I detect a flicker behind the dull green gaze. "I know exactly who you are. Where are you living now?"

"In Virginia," I say. Then I notice a plump woman with an owl-shaped name tag bearing down on us with two full tea cups rattling and sloshing in their saucers. I get right to the point. "How is Hugh? Do you ever see him?"

"All the time," she says, "when he comes out to the farm. And he's fine. In fact, I'd say Hugh's thriving. He's assistant head of ophthalmology at Jefferson Hospital now. Did you know that? And into art projects, of course, all over Philadelphia. Restoration, too, in the Fairmount section, mainly. He's restored five houses over there. By now, it may be six."

"Is he married?"

"Hugh? Married?"

She pauses long enough to break the rhythm of her talk, to open a small hole where a person more adept than I am at Main Line understatement might be able to deposit a meaning. But what would that meaning be?

"I don't think Hugh is *interested* in getting married. He's much too involved in other things. You really ought to call him while you're here."

"Do you have his phone number? I think it's unlisted." (Think. Hell, I *know* it is unlisted. At my twentieth reunion I finally worked up the nerve to call him, slipped away from a class meeting and closed myself into a booth. But when I opened up the phone book to the page with Pattersons, Hugh's name was not there.)

"Yes, I have it. Somewhere." Helen's freckled hand dives into her box-shaped pocketbook and retrieves a small red leather book. She thumbs through pale blue tissue-paper pages. "Do you want the one at work? Or home?"

"The one at home," I say. As Helen starts to read the numbers, I pencil them lightly on the cover of my class reunion booklet. Very, very lightly. The first sign of my possibly adulterous intentions. I need to be able to erase the numbers, later.

"Here, Bailey. *Take* this." A tea cup suddenly appears between us. But I have what I want now. "Thank you very much," I say and whirl away before Helen Bailey Patterson is obliged to introduce me to her friend.

The next thing I know I'm marching with an electric sense of purpose off the terrace, out of Wyndham, back through Pembroke Arch, and straight across the campus toward the single room in Denbigh they've assigned me for the weekend. Miracle of miracles, it has a telephone.

I am exhilarated now, because I have a secret. After twenty-two years of shared thoughts and sheets—even toothbrushes, if pressed—I've discovered how liberating one secret can be. This must be the reason that married people find affairs so tempting. What we need is not the sex so much as the affirmation that each of us is still a separate being.

I remember when our youngest son, Sammy, started nursery school, I found an unfamiliar-looking matchbox truck in an ashtray and asked Will, the oldest, who was then about five, "Whose truck is this?"

"Sammy's. He brought it home from school."

"But where did Sammy get it?"

"I don't know," Will said solemnly. "I don't know Sammy's life."

His statement pierced my mind. Until that moment, I had known the origin of practically every toy Sammy touched and every word he uttered. Now, all of a sudden, he had a life outside our life, a constant source of secrets.

Now suddenly, at forty-six, I have a secret, too. I decide that I am game for whatever it may bring me. One secret breeds another, the way a little lie does, and may lead into a tangled situation. But at least it will be a different situation.

There was a time, five or six summers ago, when Sam considered having an affair with a young economist he was working with in

New York City. She was single, bored, and liberated, and made him an offer with no strings attached. But he got drunk first and asked me would I mind. *Open Marriage* was on the best-seller list then. Everyone was reading it, trading it between the beach chairs, and I had expressed fairly liberal opinions on the subject. But the night that Sam got drunk and asked me did I mean it, I found out I most certainly did *not*.

I tried to analyze my unbecomingly conservative reaction. What I minded most was the thought of an ongoing deception. Being made a fool of. Having Sam call me up from dinner with his mistress in a fancy New York restaurant, while I was stuck at home, eating fish sticks with the children. And having him pretend that he was sorry that his business was taking him out of town so much. He's a good sport, Sam. If he was considering having an affair himself, he figured it was only fair to talk to me about it, so that I could have one, too. Would I do the same for him? I hope so.

When I get to Denbigh, I walk straight up the steps into my room, deliberately avoiding contact with my classmates who are draped over the chairs and sofas in the showcase, smoking, gossiping, and reminiscing. But I do not try to make the call until I've had a bath and have almost finished dressing. My ride to our class dinner is leaving at six-thirty. Sam's quartz travel clock, on the scratched, fake-maple desktop, says almost six o'clock.

I will call Hugh now, I think. And I plop down on the metal cot to use the telephone. A private telephone. Imagine. In my day, all we had to link us with the world of men was one pay phone and a bellmaid at the Pembroke switchboard who would buzz a student's room if she had an incoming call.

Our old phone system was tedious and maddening, but oh my God, it was exciting. When my wall buzzer came to life, my legs would react long before my mind did, carrying me halfway down the corridor before I started wondering: Who can that be calling? Oh dear God, please let it be Hugh. And if it was Hugh's voice, that thin, reeded, carefully articulated voice vibrating in my ear, I would collapse with pleasure, sliding down the rough, nubbed plaster wall to sit spreadeagled on the floor, surrendering to the ecstasy of talking to him, not caring that somebody down the hall was probably listening to our conversation, responding to the challenge of imagining the unheard half of it.

This private telephone, on the table here beside me, makes it seem too easy. Obscenely easy. To communicate with Hugh, all I have to do is pick up this receiver. Nobody will be listening, because I've taken the precaution of closing the door. I pick up the receiver, and dial the numbers lightly penciled on the cover of my class reunion booklet, as if they were no different from any other numbers.

I hear a click. Will Hugh be home at six o'clock? On a Friday night? Then a distant ringing.

Suddenly he's with me. I know it is his voice that says "Hello?"

"Hugh! This is Margie. Margie Tompkins Baker. . . ." I meant to speak more slowly, but the words are sputtering. "I'm up here for my twenty-fifth reunion. So I thought I'd call you up and. . . ."

He does not let me stumble any further. "Good heavens. It *is* you. My God. I can't *believe* it. I was just thinking about you. You'll never guess where I was two weeks ago. In Virginia. In Williamsburg, no less. Giving a speech to the Southern Ophthalmologist's Association. In Williamsburg! Can you believe it? The very place I'd planned to give you an engagement ring. We were going to go to Williamsburg the weekend after Harriet's wedding. Do you remember that?"

"Yes, I remember."

"And I kept thinking about you the whole time I was there. So much so, I almost called you up."

His words are so unguarded, plunging all the way back into our old relationship. So why do I feel parried? By the timbre of his voice? The faint hint of laughter vibrating behind it. I never could tell for certain, and I cannot tell now, whether Hugh's laughter is ironic.

And why does he assume the role of the one who was rejected? Actually it's my role, and he's stealing it from me. Is this what I have called him up to tell him? Clearly, he doesn't want to hear it. Any more than he wants to deal with me, the real, breathing me; I might destroy his artfully restored recollections. Hugh always did have a knack for making real things artificial. Once when I was taking a psychology course I gave him a Rorschach test for practice; and he kept saying, "That's a *picture* of a cat. That's a *picture* of a horse." Most people looking at the inkblots will say simply, "That's a cat," or "That's a horse." But Hugh insisted even then on distancing.

What I have failed to recognize all these years is that Hugh prefers to keep it all out there—just beyond his reach—clean and cerebral while the rest of us slosh through the juices—semen, blood, and vomit. He has a mind too fine to mire in an ordinary physical commitment.

This knowledge settles like a ball of dough at the bottom of my stomach, as I chatter on. Answering his questions. Downplaying my children. My four wonderful children. For where are his? Those beautiful blonde daughters I was secretly afraid I could not give him? They may never now exist outside of Hugh's mind, where they roam forever fair and free of acne.

And I am sad that this is so.

He is chatting, happily, telling me about the party he is going to give tomorrow, a buffet dinner for forty people.

"Are you doing it all by yourself?" I ask.

"Yes," he says, "with the help of a few friends. Tonight they're coming over to tear up the lettuce for the salad. Tomorrow they will worry with the meat." It has something to do with a fine-arts center opening, at which Hugh says, "We're having carriage rides, no less."

I have absolutely no desire to come to his dinner party. Or to ride beside him in a carriage. And he has clearly no desire to ask me to.

The fact is, Hugh and I will never meet again, though we are pretending that we will. To be polite, he asks me for my married name. Can he really have forgotten it? Obligingly I give him Sam's full name, and our telephone number, and urge him to get in touch with us the next time he is down our way.

I say good-bye to Hugh then. And wait until I hear the click of his receiver, imagining the scene at his latest Fairmount town house.

His tightly curled blond hair is mixed with gray. Otherwise he is as handsome as he was the night we parted in that tiny New York kitchen. He's been sitting in a wing chair talking on the telephone, but he gets up from it now, and walks over to a bookcase and pulls out a volume of stories by his favorite author, Henry James.

He settles back into the wing chair, opening the book at "The Lesson of the Master," or, better yet, "The Jolly Corner." Then, as he starts to read, his long fingers reach for the stem of the wineglass beside him, not because he wants to drink from it, but just to reassure himself that it is there.

# Where Men Go to Cry

*He had the kind of beauty which*
*defends itself from any caress.*
                    Virginia Woolf, *The Waves*

It was the fatigue that introduced them. On the night Linnea took him home, Paul arranged his drawing board in his customary spot near the back wall. He preferred to let the models stride in, pose, and choose his profiles for him. This time, Linnea set up beside him, just to his right. The model was a young woman, a lean girl that Paul thought he recognized from the local bookstore. He was not surprised when she stepped onto the dais—naked and slim—facing away from him, her long spine curving toward Linnea. Linnea, of course, said nothing. She merely began to sketch—even while the instructor completed his opening remarks—her small hand circling swiftly above the paper before it bore down.

Paul had managed to fling only a few light lines onto his page before Linnea slumped, badly. He had been taking his time with the form of the model's buttocks because he wanted to be sure of what he saw there. When Linnea slumped, her round chin sagging onto the ribbed collar of her sweater, he took his time with that image also. He didn't want to get involved. But when Linnea—her eyes trained on the drawing before her—reached for her cheek with a wavering, unguided hand, he leaned politely toward her.

"Are you all right?" he asked, looking past her at the red-haired woman at the next table, not wanting to be rude.

Linnea nodded rather firmly, her eyes closed, her hand still grasping for her face as if it were after something sinking in water.

"I am fine, thank you. Just weak." He noted that her voice was strung hard, without accent. "Are *you* all right?"

Paul was immediately embarrassed. Linnea was looking right at him, directly into his chest, her unsteadiness apparently cleared away by the force of her words. He noticed, in his discomfort, that though she was not a thin woman, her black sweater engulfed her in a way that made her appear breastless, almost mannish.

"I suppose," he said.

"Good," she answered. "You can help me carry my things. I need to get home."

He was glad, at least, that she allowed him the one thing he took pride in—his efficiency. He placed her charcoal in its box, strapped her shadowy sketch into her firm portfolio, all while she sat on a stool cooly mesmerized by the model's still, white flesh. When he had gathered Linnea's belongings with his, they left the studio one after another, Paul opening the door to the hallway and nodding to the instructor while Linnea slipped out. He was relieved that the other students took little notice of their departure, the soft rasp of charcoal and expressive breathing remaining constant as he turned to leave. Life drawing for him, after all, was a brief hobby, something to do while he waited to leave the country. And Linnea, well, she was obviously talented enough to serve her own whims. Everyone in the class, including the instructor, had to know that. It was Paul's only hope, as he shut the paint-spattered door behind them, that his fellow students didn't also know that he had worked hard to manage this exit; that he, at all costs, had not wanted to leave the light of the studio as if he were just churning flotsam in the wake of this woman Linnea.

The bay breeze was fresh but cool, and Paul felt the skin of his legs crawl as he followed Linnea down the few brick steps that led to the street. Rain was a possibility. The stretches of horizon that he could see between the waterfront warehouses were mottled with the fringe of a cloud bank. After he helped Linnea, he told himself, he would have to hurry home before the car was bathed in a heavy, salt-bearing wind.

"I live on Spring Street, exactly fourteen hundred steps away," she said as they reached the herringbone sidewalk. "I hope you don't mind."

"Not at all," he said, surprised that there was no shiver in her voice. "Not if you will count."

Silence. The shuffle of her flat, cotton slippers on the brick. Paul blushed under his pressed shirt collar. He had wanted to be funny, not biting, not the final word. But this woman had her ideas, and she was weak, perhaps actually ill. He nodded to himself, recognizing the duties of good manners and kindness, and began to follow her whispering steps into the night, hoping at each moment to catch up and move up beside her.

The neighborhood they climbed into was old, only barely rubbed by the distant sounds of the expressway. The houses were hillside remnants, the square-built homes of merchants who had sailed in and out of Portland a hundred years before. Paul's mother had often driven him into that very part of town because, she said, one should develop a clear eye for design. He had always liked his tours. Even now, as they passed a grand clapboard façade, he thought he could smell fresh-cut flowers—the sort his mother adored—though he had to struggle for clarity. The vapors of paint and turpentine rose strongly from Linnea.

"It's my parent's house, this gray one," she said, leading him onto a small varnished porch. "They stay up north now, though. Permanently."

"Nice," he said, examining a carefully restored portico. "Historic."

"Yes." She sounded mildly exasperated, irritable. "You'll have to take my things in, you know. My studio's upstairs."

Once inside, Linnea gamely negotiated the narrow spiral staircase that led from the foyer to the open second floor. Paul could tell that it was a struggle because, even from behind, the deep round intake of her breath was audible. He also noticed what he hadn't seen before—the drag and lean of a slight limp, a crookedness now quite visible in her step.

The studio was still dark when he reached the top of the staircase. Moving toward a black shape that he took to be a table, Paul shifted Linnea's portfolio from under his arm and prepared to lay it down. From somewhere to his left he could hear the suck of breathing.

"No, not there," she told him. "Here. With me."

"Is it clear?" he asked. "The path, I mean. I don't want to ruin anything."

"Just follow my voice," she said.

She turned on a lamp when he was perhaps two steps away, his free hand outstretched, his lips tight with concentration. For a long moment the vaguely lit studio wavered huge in Paul's eyes: four rooms stripped of everything usual except their wallpaper; mantels and windowsill lined with brushes and erasers; doorless closets stacked with canvases. In one corner there was a green easy chair, a coffee-maker, an uneven stack of magazines, and Boston newspapers. A squat radio was on a nearby table. The back wall was covered with sketches of twirling, shifting bodies. Easel after easel, frame upon frame, the rooms gave themselves to the craft at hand.

Paul found himself trying not to stare.

"Yes, it's damn large," Linnea said, her fingers still on the lamp that he could now see was polished brass. "I'm spoiled. My parents, as I said, have moved."

"It's a tremendous opportunity," he said, leaning her portfolio against the bannister, afraid to step away from the staircase until she did.

"I'd say so."

She did not invite him to sit down, to relax, or even help her move some of her larger paintings. Instead, she seemed intent only on looking at him. Without attempting to be polite, she fixed her eyes on him and watched, her fingers kneading the hem of her sweater as she shifted her chin. Paul glanced back at her for the shortest space of time, feeling imposed upon, but the depth of her pupils was too much. Eventually, he found himself staring patiently into the cup of his clasped hands, wondering why she was testing him.

"Shitty light in here, Paul. Would you hit the switches by the mantel over there? All of them."

He took his time. He wanted to be careful. Then, with two movements of his thumb, the room they were standing in, the southeastern one, was fully lit, unshadowed. Paul immediately understood that he was in the naked objectivity of a gallery.

"I thought so," Linnea said from behind him where she was still guarded by the lamp.

"What? What did I do?"

"Brown hair. Brown eyes. Fine buttocks. It's been hard to tell up to now, but I was right. About 185 centimeters. A small Praxiteles Hermes."

Paul smiled, wanting to be ironic. "I measure up?"

"You are a beautiful specimen," she said, rubbing her eyes with hands that now looked plump enough to be nearly flaccid. "That much is clear. If I weren't so tired, I might ask you to take your shirt off although I know, already, what your back has to look like. They must have tried to get you to model down there."

Paul ran his fingers through his hair. "Yes," he said. "They tried."

"But you said no, didn't you." Linnea stepped toward him, her palms out flat, surveying the air before her. "You told them no because I know you, Paul," she said, looking squarely at him, "and I know that you wouldn't show your balls to anyone."

It took a moment. Then Paul felt his stomach tighten beneath his ribs. "I'd better go," he said carefully. "I hope you're not ill."

"Don't be a jerk," she said. "I'm not insulting you. I'm only telling the truth. The studio went after you because they have wonderful taste down there and they couldn't resist. You didn't go for it." She stopped with her fingers in a grip which punched out at the level of his waist. "Because you're so private. That much is easy to tell."

"I had my reasons."

"As you always do, I'm sure. Come here, then, and I'll show you something. Get this friendship started. So that you'll stop looking like some whore has asked you to drop your pants."

Paul followed her into the next room, a tiny solarium that contained only one easel and a chair. The canvas on the easel was covered with a dark blue cloth. He stopped just inside the doorway, letting Linnea fill the room with her weight. As he arranged a series of deep breaths, one after another, he realized that he was sweating.

"Just so you'll know that I'm not after your ass," she said, lifting the cloth from the top of the easel, "let me show you what I've already got. It's not perfect, but it is determined. And, thank God, it is not skittishly private."

Paul expected nudity. What he saw instead was motion, concentration, vigor—all clothed in the garish design of sport. A baseball player, a well-muscled man twisting his way through the batter's box wearing a uniform that seemed as pure and personal as skin.

"Who is he?" Paul was caught off guard. A sports hero? An idol? He had imagined something a little more obscure. More artistic, maybe.

"An infielder, an outfielder. It can't matter to you," she said, looking unabashedly at her own work. "I am thirty-five years old, I am dying. This man is my purity. I could break it down for you, but I won't." She turned toward him and took him in by parts—his head and shoulders, his torso, his crotch. "I can't show you what you can't know," she said.

"You are a very fine artist," he said.

Linnea laughed. "I will trust your judgment, of course."

Paul watched her walk to a bank of small windows that overlooked the edge of the bay. The badly-installed track lighting cut across her face and broke harshly over her hair which he could see was quite dull at the roots. Despite the fact that this woman was obviously baiting him, her face began to etch itself in his mind. Thin, straggling eyebrows. A complexion the uneven color and texture of winter sand. She was, he knew now, quite ugly. But as the narrowness of her shoulders trembled into the ill breadth of her hips, Paul felt his manners give way to interest, to what he might have initially and unkindly called pity. Faced with the wrenching grimace of a nameless ballplayer, what would it be like to touch this woman, he wondered. What would it feel like to feel Linnea?

\*       \*       \*

He came to see her the next day, bringing flowers and two newspapers. "I wasn't sure you'd be able to get out," he said as she answered the door. "I don't have your phone number."

"You are too polite, Paul," she said, taking the bouquet of freesia and laying it in a chair before she frowned at him. "I should have expected as much. There is some coffee ready upstairs."

He followed her to the studio after he put the flowers in a vase he found in the kitchen. Linnea had left them behind. It was clear that she was intent on being gruff or at least blunt with him. The edge that had just shown itself the night before was now clean and unhidden. But he would endure it. She had, after all, issued a challenge of some sort. And God knows, he had few other distractions. How could it hurt, he asked himself. What could it bother?

In the unbroken daylight of the studio, Linnea looked close to wretched. Her straight, home-cut hair was drawn against its will into a thin and uneven ponytail. The brightly patterned housecoat that was snapped tight around her throat did nothing but accentuate the pallor of her face and the disconcerting weakness of her small chin. Looking at her crumpled in her easy chair, Paul realized that it was only the eyes, the still-burning eyes, that held her face together.

"I'm not good today," she said, rubbing her broad, blotched forehead. "I have nothing to say."

"Boston won last night." Paul cleared his throat with his hand over his mouth. He'd worked hard, scanning the morning papers, for that fact. "That's really my only message. I was just wondering. . . ."

"The score was 4–2. Lee gave up six hits. Rice homered. Hobson, thank God, picked up an RBI. The team is now five games out with a current batting average of, let me think, .262."

"I'm sorry."

"For what? For bothering me? Forget it. You can always try to be nice to me," she said, looking at him with two fists curled in her lap. "I just may not like it. As I said, I am dying."

"I'm. . . ."

"Don't you dare apologize for that either." She was shouting now, her voice rising with a heave of her well-covered chest. Somewhere in his head, Paul heard the thud of her own hands against her body. "Just tell me what you want, you fucking beautiful thing. Do you want to be painted? Is that it?"

Paul turned and began to walk, his shoulders slightly hunched. She was exploding, her mouth twisting, her cheeks shaking with sobs. He had not meant to cause that or see it or even ever hear about it. He had just wanted to be nice, to do something that involved a little good spirit before he left to begin his fieldwork.

Did she have the right to ask him those things? He supposed so. From her perspective he must appear to be the worst. An opportunist, a vulture, a camera's eye.

Behind him Linnea blew her nose, signaling to him, he thought, her intention to continue their what? . . . their conversation? Threading his way through the clutter of the studio, Paul decided he would wait for her in the solarium. In there, at least, everything but the light was sparse and controlled.

"Okay," she said from the doorway, her voice softened by swallowed tears. "Why are you here? If you don't want to have that fine butt painted?"

Paul watched the ferry to Nova Scotia glide through Casco Bay. Its motion, even as it edged past the abandoned oil docks, was remarkably predictable. "To be honest, I'm leaving the country in just over a month to finish school, graduate school. I can't answer your question really. I'm at loose ends."

He heard Linnea move behind him, smelled the deep, free smells of her body. It occurred to him that she might be arranging herself for him. "Sit down," she said, somehow having the words warm the back of his neck. "In the chair. I've got some coffee for the two of us."

It was Linnea who suggested that they take things one at a time. "I don't see my old friends anymore, not even the artists. I'm very conscious of having driven them away." She sat on the stained wooden floor of the solarium, a coffee cup balanced on her knee. "But you're untested. We can try to work something out."

"I'll be leaving in five weeks or so. I don't think I'm dangerous." He wanted to stretch out in the chair, but its straight back only allowed for one posture—upright, face forward. "I will not be an imposition though. Only if you need something."

"I need someone to watch me, that's all. My work is changing very quickly. I'd like a measure for that." She nodded toward the covered easel. "Where are you going, anyway?"

"Upper Volta. In Africa."

She laughed, her small teeth spreading above her tongue. For a second, the shape of her face changed completely. "I should have known, I should have known," she said.

"Why?"

"Because there's no hint of it anywhere. Your person is discreet."

"It's true." He smiled back. "I don't own a single dashiki."

"You know what I mean though, Paul," she said, lowering her voice. "You are hiding. You try to tell almost nothing."

So he told her that he was preparing to finish his Ph.D. That he would be a half day's drive from Ouagadougou studying a small village of Bobo tribesmen for a year, maybe two. Afterwards, there would be the dissertation, long months in the library at Berkeley, the degree, a teaching job somewhere in the East. He told her he knew that his plans were thin, vastly general, but if he'd learned one thing from his professors, he said, it was this: you had to be patient. Even in the hot, dry sub-Saharan winds, you had to be patient.

"I'm packed and ready, I guess," he concluded. "As ready as I'll ever be."

Linnea shook her head. "There is a lot you're not admitting to Paul. I can see it. It's all marked out there in your hands. And your jawline." She pointed at him. "You're older, better forged, than you make out to be. Come on. What about the friends, the parents, the bits and pieces of old lovers?"

He did not like her sudden animation. He had hoped that she, at least, would take only what her eye would give her. Shifting his weight in the chair, he watched her push her awkward hips against the door jamb so that she could face him, her eyes resting uneasily beneath the edge of her stringy bangs. "There isn't much to tell, really," he said. "My parents and my brother live an hour away. I've spent the last three years of my life in classrooms. Before that I traveled a little."

Paul sighed somewhere deep in his throat. He was sinking; he could feel it. A brief passage from Tchaikovsky's 6th slipped into his mind and echoed. Her passage, someone else's march. God, even the most veiled references to his past were capable of pulling him back and down. He told himself that he should know that by now.

"No, no," Linnea said. "I want you to try that again. Or better yet, let me try it." Paul could see that her right hand was uncommonly alive as it stroked the worn grain of the floorboards before her. Her fingertips slid as if driven by static. "I am tired of wasting time," she said. "I see things, things that you just barely feel."

Paul put his hands in his pockets. She was pushing him again.

"I don't care about Berkeley," she said. "You've left a woman somewhere. You've perhaps had men or wanted men—you're lovely enough for that—but recently it's been this woman. She's blond, probably in school, and very tall, taller than I am. But her face is not important. It's what you carry with you in the dark that wants to kill you. This woman—she's plaintive, she loves you, she has a softness to her skin that you want, above everything, to forget. You've scared yourself because you've noticed that her small, even breasts have nipples the color of your lips and you're fascinated. Her shoulders are the width of your hips, her wet hair smells faintly like your mother's, her voice has a tone that you've never been able to freeze or break apart. You've noticed all this. You hate it. It's eating you alive."

"You flatter yourself," Paul said, forcing himself to look out to sea.

"I'm not finished yet," Linnea said, both hands working the floor. "The foremost fact is that you've left her. Cleared out. Neat and tidy. Now you're burying her—in sub-Saharan sand, I'd guess. And you know why?"

Paul felt his shell of polite interest shift a bit. Strangely, there was no note of pride in Linnea's declaration. He thought back. No, she'd never done more than narrate. He wondered. Was she baiting him again?

"You do know," she continued. "So do I. You did it because you were afraid you couldn't feel anything. Not that right thing, anyway. You made love to her a hundred times maybe—probably to symphonies, sounds that you chose—but something, something you expected didn't happen."

Paul laughed over the small catch in his throat. "You tell quite a story."

"I'm not wrong about this, Paul. You carry yourself like a ramrod, imperturbable or something. But it's all a defense. Something's broken."

"Her name is Susan," he said. "She is not blond."

"She loves you though, doesn't she?" Linnea was flickering behind her bangs again.

"She's younger."

"I don't mean to pry. I just don't have time. And I have to, have to read the faces I've got."

"Don't worry," Paul said, standing and looking out over the water again. "You only got it half right. It's been worked out."

"You don't see her. Or anybody."

Linnea's voice, he thought, was very cold music. Her age, he supposed.

"I'm going to Africa."

If he had had his way, everything would have ended there at noon in a sunlit pool of understanding. But it did not. Now Linnea could not let him go. He was sure he recognized the signs: a woman temporarily bound by silence, temporarily romanced by tenderness. He heard her push herself up the cream-colored wall with her feet. When she was standing, he realized he was afraid she would move toward him to offer more coffee, to trap him.

"I should be on my way," he said.

The intake of her breath was audible, but it was not followed by admonishment or anger or the scurry of embarrassment. Instead, the piercing clarity of her words dove through him and left him hollow. "I only want to know," she said, "what it's like to be beautiful. Look at me, Paul. You'll know why."

He couldn't gather himself soon enough to help her to the chair. She limped there by herself—broken, red, and furious at her weakness. There were tears in her narrowed eyes and a crippled fury in her shoulders which seemed to shiver into a control of its own. Paul couldn't quite say that she was crying, but she was, it was obvious to him, in some sort of deep, unmet pain.

"Why else do you think I'm so foolish?" she asked. "Look at him, look at *him*," she said throwing her voice at the covered canvas of the baseball player. "I've painted him over and over again. I've met him, talked to him, leaned on the edge of my ballpark seat when he's on the field. And what is he? A ballplayer. A man. An exquisitely proportioned machine of bone and muscle." Paul felt the arc of the painting's hidden motion cut through cloth and air. Its finely rendered twist made its way into Linnea's voice. "And for some goddamned reason I'm cursed with him. I want to know him, I want to know that lovely capturing urge before it's over." She stopped then, her hair loose from her ponytail, dangling about her face and neck like a worn fringe. Paul did not move. He found himself seeing, acquiring, overcome with the setting composition of a picture. One of Linnea's hands fell into her lap like a claw. The other dropped flat, its flutter deadened. An open palm, an offering, a half prayer.

*     *     *

Over the course of the month before he left for Africa, Linnea explained her illness to Paul. She was careful in her divulgence, always speaking to him as if she were teaching him something, impressing him with cold, factual details that he ought to remember. When the sclerosis in her left hand worsened, she opened her books of Renaissance reproductions and showed him—as only she could—the changes in her flesh and structure.

"It's here and here, now," she would say, pressing the gloss of a daVinci and then his own waiting hand with a finger. "It will only get worse, but not steadily. Every day is different. And I know enough not to grieve over surprises."

She was resolutely cheerful even though they both knew it was a game. She would return from her occasional visits to the clinic, smiling stiffly, her sketch pad covered with crosshatched drawings of Paul's face, Paul's arms. On her worst days, when she could barely speak and her face hung like lifeless parchment, she would share their rare laughter by tapping her knuckles or a loosely-swung elbow on her thigh. It was important, she said, for her to keep moving. She had things to accomplish.

But Paul did not have the same driven, finite ambitions. Even before Linnea told him in her most cutting manner that he was drifting, he knew it. The nights of anxious dreams that had ranged his mind in the spring—singing to him in pidgin French, pinning him in blinding, unbroken sunlight—gave way to tiny fragmented visions and sleeplessness. Except in early morning, when he was still in bed and the ocean was the only boundary he could imagine, it was difficult to conjure up Africa. He could hardly believe he was going. The only reality he felt sure of was an awkward consciousness of his body. What he carried from day to day were his tendons, his graceful bones, whatever Linnea seemed to have left with him the day before. And being faced with his own nakedness—in the shower, beneath the looseness of his summer clothing—shocked him, froze him up. It took Linnea to help him stay in motion.

"I would like to finish one series before you leave, " she told him. It was one of her good days. She was wearing a sleeveless red blouse with a daisy dangling in a buttonhole. "More of the baseball stuff. I thought I could do it with your help."

Paul looked at her swaying next to an easel, honest and childlike, her hair pushed back by a blue stretch band. "Baseball? Now?" Her preoccupations still surprised him.

She laughed. "Of course. Their motion is the hardest to follow, Paul. Hardest to reduce. Whatever those men do, they do fast. And alone."

But why not dancers, he wanted to ask. Or just models? Still he didn't question her; he couldn't. He was afraid of what would happen if Linnea ever really thought her fragility was foolish.

"I don't know if I can help," he said. "I don't have many skills like that."

"Just hold a pallet for me." Linnea stomped her foot, perhaps as a joke. "Hold things for me. You always expect so many demands."

It was then that they began to touch each other, tenderly and without secret. Linnea kept it in the air, calling him handsome to his face, pretending to pinch at his skin in rushes of energy. But Paul knew it to be something different, something that he considered too daring and ragged for the both of them. Though he did nothing to change it. Their fingers locked and unlocked as he passed paint and brushes, and he took this home with him to his small, spartan bedroom where it began to curl into his sleep. Time is my arbiter, he thought when he was most anxious. Time will separate us and somehow, as it always does, remake the pain.

Paul then imagined a satisfactory separation into being. He composed what he considered to be a workable plan while he ate his breakfast of toast and poached egg during the habitual time he gave to himself before he visited Linnea. He would spend a few days with his parents; Susan would come into his life for a weekend, a last passage of native joy. Linnea would be his first and most private farewell, but he would have done with it. Dinner, a small well-chosen gift and perhaps, well, a brief engulfing physical contact that would swallow him until he actually left for Paris en route to Dakar and Ouagadougou. He would allow for that possibility and prepare, immediately, to move beyond it. As he drank his morning coffee, looking from his apartment toward the wharves, he was pleased with his own frank thoughts. He could think of being with Linnea—sleeping with her—and it didn't paralyze him. He would, after all, see her in a few months. Nothing would be begun or finished with his departure. As she had told him, her disease was a slow, mysterious, inaccurate one. She could and would, she hoped, live for years.

But Linnea cut him off, beat him to the final mark. When he arrived one morning with a can of linseed oil, some milk and fresh fruit, she answered the door hurriedly, with a sheen of sweat above her lip. "I'm on the phone to Boston," she said. "They want me there tomorrow to start on Hobson, lovely Hobson, and Rice." She went into the kitchen, back to the phone. Vaguely, Paul realized that she was hardly dressed. Her thick, pale legs were bare; her dressing gown was open past her breasts. As she spoke, loudly and surely into the phone, Paul sat at the foot of the polished staircase, the bag of oil and groceries pressed close to his ribs.

"The front office has seen some of my work," she said, coming back into the foyer with her robe pulled tight around her swollen figure. "They want some paintings, at least two. I can hardly turn them down."

"They will be wonderful," he said. "I'm sure."

"The best I can do. Given the time."

"Do you think you will get it this time, this energy or beauty that you want?" He set the groceries on the floor, hoping their rattle would half cover the wry thickness of his question.

Linnea stopped, her mouth an unconscious dent, before she walked past him toward her bedroom. "This reminds me of the time I left Claude," she said. "In New York or Paris, I can't remember. It was over before the door shut."

"You're leaving tomorrow?"

"For quite awhile, I'm afraid. I'm sorry," she said, turning the corner to her room. Paul could barely hear her. "I didn't plan it this way."

But she had planned it. He knew that. Linnea was so desperate about her time—her dwindling time, she called it—that she had not dropped a single moment into the well of open possibility since he had met her. Boston and her ballplayer must have been in the works for weeks; the unsteadiness of her illness allowed for no less. Paul was momentarily furious. How dare she refuse to face him before he left the continent and the only risk he had taken since he had put Susan back from his body and his mind. She knew it was a risk, his being with her and squeezing himself under the lens of her peculiarly magnified world. She knew he trusted her. And she had turned away.

"Life is often like that," he said, raising his voice so that it might follow her into the closet. "It turns swiftly. Susan and I lost each other that way."

"Martín," she shouted back. "Martín . . . I told you about him . . . he is the one I clung to. I was young. And he was so handsome."

When she emerged some minutes later, Paul was pacing, circling the area near her old stereo. A Bach recording was on the turntable, but he had not yet placed the needle in its groove. He was wondering if he should go upstairs or just leave. After all, he and Linnea had never listened to music together.

"A good idea," she said, pausing several feet away from him. "I'll get some wine. We should probably celebrate."

He watched her enter the kitchen. A woman who was, he realized, a sack of shuffled desires and disappointments. He did not miss the fact that she was dressed just as she had been the night he met her. Dark pants, the black misshapen sweater, her hair free and clean around her face. Linnea did not err. Though the female in her might seem buried in her determination, she did not make mistakes.

Then it would just be over. She could not blame him. He had come and gone from her life like a bout of bad weather. Or a sickness. Yes, that was it. Illness bred illness, and he had been like a functional fever. Linnea, working from her stubborn heart, had conquered him in order to cure herself.

He had been used. Pressing a button and taking in the swift ascension of Bach's fugue, Paul allowed himself to think of Susan, to look somewhere in himself for the symptoms of time-killing desire. The scent of her light skin was like . . . was like. . . .

But again, Linnea could not let him go. At least he perceived her distant graciousness that way. "I think we should toast ourselves upstairs," she said, moving quietly past him. "When the music is over, of course."

He found her slouched in her green armchair, an uncorked bottle of chardonnay by her feet. He thought he could smell the wine: a new, heavy perfume. Linnea seemed distracted, the white moon of her chin resting on her knuckles. But she stood when Paul cleared the top of the staircase. "Cheers," she said. "I think we should forgive each other."

"For what?" he asked, impatiently surveying the studio. "Our lack of manners?"

"No, our wish to get out. Leave." She dropped back into her chair, gracelessly. "You know what I mean."

"No, I don't. I wanted to do this without . . . I wanted to do it right."

"You want to do everything right."

Paul looked over her worktables, her scattered sketches and pallets. It was all there—shape, blending, a variety of flesh tones. "I wanted to give you something," he said.

"What?" she said, a fresh edge in her voice. "You never made love to me. You never even told me what it was like with Susan. I don't see that you've given me anything that's worth a fuck."

"That's all you wanted, then." He spoke through his set teeth, anger moving to trembling in his knees.

"No, I think that's all you wanted. An ugly woman, some adoration. A pitiful piece of leave-taking ass." Linnea rocked herself with rage, though her chair was anchored and ungiving. The wine bottle rattled at her heels.

"You're bitter," he said.

"No, you are," she shouted, hammering the air with a whole arm. "You god damn fucking are."

Paul left her, the broken tattoo of her pounding feet following him down the stairs and through the bare foyer. She wasn't helpless, he told himself. She never had been. A woman like that would eat him alive.

*     *     *

He only made it to Ouagadougou about once a month. The American attaché and his wife were always encouraging him to visit, to give himself time to adjust to the broad, unbroken patterns of the village. But Paul was hard on himself; he insisted on making it all work, allowing himself time off only when he needed supplies— batteries, film, new cassettes. He wasn't worried about burnout. Where could he go, where would he want to go if he failed?

At the end of the rainy season, he gave himself a brief vacation, a trip east to the sacred crocodile lake at Sabou. On his way back, he stopped in Ouagadougou for a complete French meal at the attaché's expense and a mail check.

In his fan-cooled hotel room, Paul opened a bulky packet from his mother. Inside, he found a heavy cotton shirt, two English novels, and an envelope of newspaper clippings. His mother also included a lengthy letter spiced with dry, crisp wit and pertinent news from home. She answered his various questions and praised him for his frequent and detailed corrrespondence. It remains so fascinating, even on the page, she wrote. Your tales from Africa have you sounding so strong and well.

Paul read her letter twice before he folded it beneath the fly-leaf of one of the novels. He wondered if he would ever tell her how bad it was.

The envelope of clippings contained two surprises. The first was a brief letter from Susan saying that she might or might not fly into Dakar for a Christmas visit. The stationery was cool and very smooth in his hand. Reading her rounded handwriting, Paul felt his heart beat with the thud of the Belgian-made window fan. He needed her to visit. Weeks ago he had realized, rather crudely, what it meant to need a woman. The warm native malt, the exquisitely barren landscape, the bound and shifting sun were never enough. The scents and sighs of the Bobo women were only cruel flavoring. He was not quite in love with Susan, but he had told her that. She hadn't seemed to mind. I'm trying, her letter said, to work something out.

The last surprise was a trio of postcards addressed to him in care of his parents. They all bore Portland postmarks. Their messages were brief. *I'm sorry. I'm sorry. Thank you.* Paul flipped them over, spreading them out on the poorly-dyed bedspread. daVinci. Michelangelo. daVinci.

Linnea. She had done it to him. Caught him in the middle. He tried to remember if he had thought of her since the flight from Paris to Dakar when he dreamed that he slept with her, dreamed that he made love to her as her skin moved like dough. In that turbulent sleep, she had pulled him into her as if his thrusts, his flesh, his desires were never-ending. She had read his face with her fingers while they moved together. No, no, he convinced himself that he had not thought of her. But she had gotten to him in any case. *I'm sorry.* She must be dying. *Thank you.*

He would call her. The cards were, according to their dates, more than three weeks old. But where would she be? The hospital? With her parents? Under the care of a twenty-four-hour nurse

who, Linnea used to say, would surely be cursedly color blind? Paul
left the hotel with his wallet, following the vague directions of the
drowsy concierge. The Intertel booth was only a few blocks away.

What would he say to her? Paul remembered the way she had
named the sunlight as it changed through the arc of a day, moving
from the broad sea gray of early morning to the hot, unforgiving
shafts of noon. Notice the difference when you're away, Paul, she
had said. The dawn will be so different when you're in Africa. The
dusk will be so harsh.

He stopped on a broken street corner, already sweating. A young
native boy tried desperately to sell him a newspaper, then some
fruit. What would he say to her? A woman who couldn't speak, who
might be paralyzed or even—he looked at the sky—dead. Here I
am, Linnea. Not so far away. Here I am. In a country where even
the mighty Mossi emperor still rules cross-legged in the dust.

# A Part

Old Isabel Lanier, the actress (remembered for her Viola and Portia) backed her Audi out of her friend Esther's drive. She paused. For a moment something stopped her from driving home to her own retirement cottage, identical to Esther's except for the roof over the front door. The thing that stopped her was her host and hostess, still standing outdoors after bidding her good-bye, slowly moving about their yard. Esther had spied some neighbor and was strolling toward the boundary fence. John was picking up random branches. They looked, in the dusk of early spring, ineffably beautiful to Isabel, so that she did not want to move.

Yet it was the end of a very long day. After her morning's regular ballet exercises, there had been necessary shopping in the shopping center—dishtowels—and the kind they carried nowadays were horrid, made of Turkish toweling; after lunch a tiring session with the dentist. Lying stretched back, with no place to spit, if there had been anything left in her mouth to spit after the thorough vacuum cleaning given it by the dentist's assistant (*was* she a nurse?) made Isabel unhappier than anything little Dr. Bellows, looking about 18, could do to her. How she did miss her own old Dr. Ross in New York, exuding confidence and reassurance, with, at her elbow, a nice basin to spit into. They said growing old was not for sissies, but the world kept finding new and disagreeable things to make it harder.

Going to tea at Esther Green's had been just what she needed after that. She loved Esther. As she went to sleep at night, she loved to visualize her new friend in her own little cottage here, with her aging, handsome husband, John; she making cookies for her grandson. Isabel had no grandson, but if she had, she swore to herself that at this point she was ready to make cookies for him. There was nothing tragic or distressed about Esther. Her mind was happy and serene. A teacher in an independent school all her life, she diverted herself now by writing reminiscences for her college magazine and doing research for the local historical society. She was sensible and occupied, like an elderly Barbara Pym character. She lived appropriately. Just thinking about her made Isabel happy.

For her own part, Esther seemed enchanted with Isabel's reminiscences of life in the theater in the twenties and thirties—the good days. Her closest friends, she had entranced Esther by telling her, had been Blanche Yurka, Rollo Peters, and Jane Cowl.

For tea today they had some of the grandson's cookies and also croissants Esther had made. It seemed a marvel to Isabel. Croissants! The table looked charming with two silver pheasants stalking in opposite directions, lace place mats revealing the polished dark mahogany. Isabel sat sideways in her chair, still slim and elegant. After a while, John Green, who took a cup with them, began to descant upon the glories of the Washington Redskins. About then Isabel began to feel she must go home; the accumulated fatigue of the day began to descend, inch by inch. By the time she had got her coat and gloves on, she could hardly wait to go.

Yet now, sitting in the car she had backed partway out of the drive, she experienced a sudden shift of feeling. They looked so beautiful, she felt smitten by fortune just to be in their vicinity. Dusk adorned them, in their classic old age, and they seemed filled with a mysterious life—they *were* life.

Why not get out of the car, now, and rejoin them? Something beatific might result. Isabel thought of the times, in her 80 years, when she had seized a high and ridden far away on it. Beatific things *had* resulted—sometimes. And now, since the reality of the future lay in dying, why not live life as hard as you could while you still had it to live? To drive away, now, felt more like the road to death.

Isabel turned off the car. She got out and walked, almost timidly, toward her friends, as if she were approaching deity.

"Oh, Esther! I just thought—"

In the shock when her sensibility met Esther's good sense head on, Isabel's high collapsed under her as if she had been standing on a soap bubble. Now she was just terribly tired. She had seen something beautiful, for which she longed, but this was not it.

Under the weight of exhaustion, heavy and black, she did not have the strength to continue pursuing an apotheosis. "I—I—" she stammered, like an old child, "I think I left my gloves."

Esther, ever a good friend, said gently. "Honey, you've got them on."

"Why, so I have."

"We all do it, sweetie."

"We certainly do," Isabel replied, smiling brilliantly.

Although she was not a religious woman, it occurred to her, as she drove away in the Audi, that, even though you were old, you still had to live life as if it were going to go on forever—take rest, eat food.

She drove home as fast as she dared, looking forward to cooking her supper—oh, but such a cooking! To stand in front of her stove, the way Esther would. She could visualize each turn of the wrist. Every biting of the lower lip, the dashing the strand of hair away with the back of her hand. She could, as escape from fatigue, *be* Esther—that was what her longing had been about—hadn't it?

She felt a moment's doubt, as she always did feel before going on stage. Yet, she reminded herself, even if it was not the real thing— not life—it would be, as they said, a reasonable facsimile thereof. And it *was* life.

# Sweet Armageddon

Quiet winter thunder during the blowing night caused Amos to turn his head on the pillow and lift his thin aching body to stare toward the nailed window. Skeletal branches of a leafless redbud jerked as if suffering. His breathing slowed, though Martha sighed beside him, hers a gentle wheeze. Fingers of her right hand drifted across the sheet in search of him.

*. . . a great earthquake . . . the moon became as blood. . . .*

The thunder was a CSX coal drag passing through Richmond's freight yard on a journey to Newport News and the bay. The coal would be dumped into a ship's hold, blackness showering down, and if a man lay under it, could he know a deeper darkness? Yes. At the end would come the perfection of everything, even of blackness itself.

He lowered himself to the bed so as not to disturb Martha. He no longer minded his body's pain. Pain was honest and spoke the truth. When an arm, a shoulder, a spinal disc hurt, the message signaled a malfunctioning of parts. Pain, too, would be perfected. Was not that the message given mankind these last days?

*. . . thrust in thy sickle and reap . . . for the time is come . . . the harvest of the earth is ripe. . . .*

Signs were incessant, their velocity increasing like a whirlwind. Everywhere his eyes fell on destruction. INFANT BABY FOUND IN DUMPSTER. He'd wakened during the chilled night and pictured a newborn child among egg shells, rinds, and moist coffee

grounds. Images of wickedness no longer sickened him. They confirmed.

        . . . *I will turn thee back and put hooks in thy jaws* . . . .

He listened to sounds from the street: a pickup starting, dogs
barking, shoes slapping cracked pavement. In this neighborhood
somebody was always running, flight in their feet, rapacity in their
stride. Wind gusted, causing a limb of the redbud to scrape the
gutter. Noise easily penetrated the flimsy siding of the tiny house.

Despite the constant scouring of limb against gutter, he slipped
back into a dusky sleep for 30 minutes, brought fully awake by
squealing tires and the gunning of an engine in front of the house, a
residence never new for him and Martha, lived in dozens of times
before they rented it from a dark man who came late Friday nights
to collect his money. Floors were covered with buckled linoleum,
windows needed caulking, and the water heater leaked. About was
the faint smell of gas. Down at the corner the neighborhood became
black. Numberless raucous children spun frantically or climbed
misshapen apple trees to throw hard, shriveled fruit at one another.

He and Martha had never owned a house, not in 42 years of
marriage. They possessed only a few sticks of furniture. All their
lives together they had been sojourners. How many decrepit resi-
dences filled with cast-off sofas, chairs whose legs were not substantial, dishes stained yellow, knives never sharp? If they wanted
to discard an item, the hullabaloo among the congregations.

        *How long, O Lord? How long?*

He dressed slowly, careful of his balance, or lack of it, steadying
himself on the antique chest of drawers from Martha's family as he
pulled at his long johns and heavy trousers. He wore also a plaid
shirt, a sweater, and a wool cap. He'd once been tall, had run the
distances at Davidson, and established a North Carolina collegiate
record for the mile which remained on the books nearly a decade.
Age, the relentless wear of the ministry, had honed him down.

        . . . *even to hoar hairs will I carry you.* . . .

For a time a black-and-white photograph of him hung in the gym
passageway, framed behind glass, and during years he returned to
homecomings, he walked past that picture, not eyeing it openly,
glancing sidelong shyly. The October afternoon he passed and it
was gone, he broke stride and felt breathless, as if he'd been robbed
of his body.

*. . . God will not hear vanity. . . .*

He walked softly down through the cold house to the kitchen, so small and dismal in spite of paintings—flaming mums, pink roses, blue iris—Martha had put up, none new, most done years before she gave herself entirely to him, her life, her dreams, in the old way of women to men. He clenched his eyes as if he stood in a storm at thoughts of what he'd given her in return.

Her hair had once been thickly dark, and she'd been gladdened by all sights before her violet eyes, a child at a feast till he took her into the mountains where they lived in little more than a shack, the wind a skinning knife, howling like the damned, their water frozen, she in a mink coat as she chipped ice from their sink and tried not to weep. He held her shivering body against his own, trying to keep her from knowing winter.

*. . . they seemed unto him but a few days, for the love he had to her. . . .*

He stopped before this scarred sink, blackened where dripping had worn away enamel. The faucets he'd fixed countless times ate washers. He bent to look out the window at the narrow back yard and the unpainted plank fence. His patching hadn't prevented children from using his yard as a short cut to an alley which in turn led to a street and middle-school playground. They left a trail which ruined his meager grass. Children climbed over, dogs dug under despite brickbats and rocks he'd stomped into holes. A mongrel turned on him snarling, backing Amos into his own house.

*. . . then shall be great tribulation . . . one stone not left upon another. . . .*

He peered at the sky. For an instant a growing redness thrilled him, a celestial conflagration, yet even as his knees gave, he saw it was only the sun's first scarlet rays striking breaking clouds. He pictured the cataclysm, the rolling thunder and terrifying lightning streaking down black corridors of earth, the dazzling rapture in the heavens.

He heated a pan of water for his tea. He did not drink coffee or other stronger stimulants. His freshman year in college he'd become tipsy when an upperclassman fed him grapefruit juice spiked with tasteless vodka. Amos climbed an ancient sycamore beside the river and alarmed others, who called for him to come down from the white branches. Like a tightrope walker, he made his way along a limb, not realizing what he'd drunk, believing his feeling the joy of life on a languid June day, the goodness of God's world. He spread his arms and dived into the fast tawny water. They thought him dead, broken and drowned, but he was merely knocked windless, his face and chest lacerated. They cheered him that afternoon, girls too, and he received a bid to a good fraternity, which he declined not only from lack of funds but also the suspicion he was already promised.

> *. . . wine . . . at the last it biteth like a serpent and stingeth like an adder. . . .*

So many doors had been open to him, hallways of marble and power. A recruiter offered a position with the trust department of the largest bank in Virginia; yet Amos made his irrevocable choice, which came not on a mountaintop or even a scene of beauty and peace, but along a busy Richmond street when he while wrestling with decision looked upward among shadows of tomb-like buildings to a simple cross touched by resplendent sunlight atop the belfry of a colonial church as out of place in the business district as milk among oil. That cross sparkled in his eyes, seemed to detach itself and float down like a shimmering blossom and settle burning on his forehead, a divine kiss. At the same time over the din of traffic, under it, from within, from everywhere, he heard a still small voice say, "Take my hand and walk with me."

> *. . . choose you this day whom you will serve. . . .*

His water was ready, the boiling sounding hollow in the nearly empty pan. He sat at a small table he himself had built. He was no handyman, no person with a gift for tools, but he'd been forced through necessity to adapt his fingers to hammer and saw. He could repair leaks, mend furniture, and had wired the extra telephone to the bedroom upstairs.

As if his thinking caused it, those phones rang now. He hurried to the one at the foot of the steps so Martha would not be disturbed.

"Shiner," the voice said. "Blind my eyes!"

Laughter before the connection broke. Neighborhood children who made fun of his baldness, the sunlight reflecting from it. They would never believe he'd had fine hair once, auburn locks which fell across his brow when he preached. He hardly remembered losing it, as if he'd wakened one winter morning, gazed into the mirror, and seen for the first time the deterioration wrought by service and age.

*. . . Thou shalt come to thy grave in a full age, like as a shock of
corn cometh in his season. . . .*

A rumbling, a vibration which reached his feet through the floor.
He stood from the table, rushed to the front door, and opened it.
Sounds of traffic, always, night or day. Wet discolored leaves lay flat
against broken pavement. A flight of pigeons flew over so close he
heard the wash of their wings. Then sonic boom, the plane unseen,
perhaps an aircraft to be used by God for the last closing of His
angry hand. The plane flew on.

He knelt for the newspaper on the stoop. During the summer
glossy blue lizards had crept from crumbled mortar to sun themselves and made him think of Brazil and his years among Indians at
the jungle's edge—quiet, dark-eyed people whose aroused savagery
was like the wrath of terrible children. Now he lived in the American jungle proclaimed by the *Times-Dispatch* he held: MAN
KNIFES TWO DAUGHTERS, WIFE, NEIGHBOR.

He stopped reading and would allow his subscription to lapse.
Did he not know what appeared in the papers and periodicals before
they lay at his door?

*. . . nation shall rise against nation . . . earthquakes . . .
famine . . . pestilences . . . fearful sights. . . .*

Fearful sights: LONG VIOLATED CHILDREN CLAIM
THEY LOVE THEIR FATHER. God's omnipotent hand was lifted
against the world's culminating evil.

*. . . she shall be burned with fire; for strong is the Lord God who
judgeth her. . . .*

As he returned to the kitchen, he heard Martha rise from their
bed and scuff her way to the house's single bathroom. He listened to
her cough and the gurgling of the old plumbing. She washed herself. He knew every sound of her. Long ago they reached the point
when nothing was hidden. Dissected each was before the other's
eye, but tenderly.

*. . . better a dinner of herbs where love is. . . .*

She came down the steps, a brittle woman now, her skin old
linen, her arms crossed against cold, her posture pulled forward by
the arms. She'd wrapped herself in a mended lilac housecoat. She
wore her white wool socks pulled high on her shrinking calves and
the rose-colored slippers he'd bought for her last birthday. Her hair,
now sparsely white and carefully brushed, had been what first

attracted him as he walked behind her from a Grace Street market—long, bouncy, alive with a sunlit vibrancy.

"I'll do your tea," he said, again haunted by her face, time's leaching of it. Her smile was automatic, her brave banner. She could've come from some great misfortune, a ghastly hurt or death, and her eyes darted at him as if surprised he was in the house.

    . . . *bring down my gray hairs with sorrow to the grave. . . .*

"Will you be going to the post office?" she asked, her voice a slight tremolo. With a ladylike sweep of hands, she sat at the table and prayed. Her bluish fingers curved to her cup. He felt he could've reached to her hair and plucked it from her head like cotton. I never wanted this to happen to you, he thought. I meant to bring you treasure.

Yes, he said, he would go to the post office, but first he fixed her a slice of toast, buttered it, and spread it with orange marmalade. He didn't realize the hot water had again failed till he rinsed his cup at the sink. She'd washed herself in cold and not complained.

He crossed to the utility closet at the rear of the kitchen where the heater was enclosed, pipes rusty and corroded around the joints. As he sniffed, he adjusted the burner, yet no matter how he fooled with the controls, the yellow flame burned feebly and as if about to expire. He'd telephoned the gas company and been told it was not their responsibility since the heater was inside the house. That meant asking a plumber to come, and the last insolent bloodsucker had charged $25.00 just for walking in the door.

On his knees he shut off the gas, cleaned the burner nozzle with a snip of stove wire, and again lit the flame. He looked for Martha and found her in the parlor dusting—parlor too grand a word for the shadowy room hardly large enough to hold the love seat, the black upright piano, and two chairs. He'd taped the rosebud wallpaper at the top to keep it from peeling farther. A dampness prevailed even in summer.

At times she played the piano, leaning to the hymnal open upon it, her delicate fingers arched to the keys as if touching flesh. From walls hung more of her flower paintings and sunny landscapes as well as the enlargement of him and her young and shining on a Brazil beach with Mary standing between them—Mary, four years old, a bright grinning little girl who held a seashell toward the camera while beyond lay the ocean, not blue, but a shimmering undisturbed green, like a pasture, solid enough to walk across.

*. . . the flocks of my pasture are men. . . .*

"Let me," he said, drawing the dust rag, a piece of old flannel nightgown, from her hand. She'd been running it over the coffee table which held the theological pamphlets, his Bible, and the one book he'd authored, *The Ever Perfect God*, published not by any notable press but a private Memphis house with the last money Martha had held onto from her inheritance. The volume received one review, that in a conservative Presbyterian journal, and sold less than 200 copies over a decade. Cardboard boxes containing the remainder of the limited printing were stored in the cramped, dirt-dauber infested attic.

"I'm stronger today," she told him, not wishing to give up the cloth.

"Better to rest."

What was wrong with her? Nothing specific, no ailment the doctor could positively identify and say do this, do that. She had simply broken down physically, her body called on too long to bear weight and function. At times a hand would not obey or a leg wobble. In lifting her cup, she might bump her chin. She stumbled when no obstruction existed to tangle her feet.

He accompanied her up to their bed, the room displaying pots of flowers on a bench before the window. All windows were nailed against thieves. She kept plants growing no matter where they traveled over the earth. The view was to the east and brown frame houses nearly identical to the one they lived in, dwellings built for employees at the Philip Morris stemmery from which the coarse odor of tobacco seeped through the neighborhood.

A middle-age man who worked for the city lived directly across the street, and Amos had seen him beat his wife—on a Saturday night, a silent, flat drama during which the woman simply hunched against a wall and held fingers curved over her face. She was passive, sullen, and never raised her eyes. Her flaxen hair flung about with the blows.

*. . . woman is the glory of man. . . .*

Martha turned on her side toward the flowers. He went back downstairs, buttoned up his overcoat, and reset his cap. When he left the house, he relocked the door behind, though anyone half determined could easily force entrance.

Break-ins around the neighborhood were almost as common as the arrogant quarreling starlings, and during late summer he'd wakened with the certainty somebody stood outside touching the house. He switched on the bedside lamp, hoping to scare off whoever was there, but pretended to Martha he wished only to rearrange the coverlet.

> *. . . I come as a thief. . . .*

Wind gusted, punching him, gathering street grit to throw against his face, stirring trash of the gutters. A bristling cur barked at him, the stiffly moving dog member of a gang which dug in his yard. He walked wide to pass, careful to keep his gaze from meeting the animal's bulging lustrous eyes, a contact, he'd read, which often prompted attack.

He needed gloves. He turned up his coat collar and again adjusted the cap loose on his head. Was he actually shrinking? He felt smaller, lighter, as if his bones were twigs and his skin paperish fabric over them. If he knocked against an object, he might tear.

He glanced at the sky, a silverish blue, cumulous clouds bunching, steeds of the heavens.

> *. . . behold a pale horse . . . his name that sat on him was Death. . . .*

Two blacks ran down the sidewalk toward him, causing fear to squeeze up through his chest to his throat. As they flew past, he whirled. They sped across a lot where a house had burned to cinders. At the rear they leaped through a fence gap. No one gave chase. His heart beat wildly.

At the corner he walked toward Belvedere and his post office. He allowed no mail delivery to the house. Too much was stolen on the block, including a check that had required months to straighten out with the Board of Missions. For an entire week he and Martha lived mostly on breakfast food, peanut butter, and A&P pancake mix.

Sirens startled him, and he winced as fire engines swept by, red lights flaring and reflecting from the trucks' yellow sheen. Their power pushed against him like a flow of water, and he reached both hands to his cap to hold it in place. The roar cause his ears to ache. Great tires beat the pavement, and the tromboning exhausts left behind an oily blue pall.

*. . . power was given unto him to scorch men with fire. . . .*

Again he walked, on the fringe of commerce now, a beauty parlor, a music store displaying a trumpet in its dusty window, a doughnut shop, a launderette where women slouched smoking and waiting in plastic orange chairs, used furniture sold on the sidewalk, motorcycles, some disemboweled. Across a wall an obscene word had been sprayed with red paint.

Then the gauntlet, the youths loitering, both black and white, a few older, yet not men either, people in society's limbo, only dangerous. They leaned against storefronts and power poles, hands in jackets, their eyes weighing passersby. Amos believed they sensed when he carried money, that those feral eyes invaded his pockets and it was only a matter of time and opportunity till he was seized and shaken to be emptied.

"Give us the word, Shiner," one said, though Amos saw no lips move. The laughter contained no mirth, and he willed himself not to hurry or show his fright. Blood pounded his ears.

*. . . in the last days scoffers, walking after their own lusts. . . .*

The post office was a substation where clerks worked behind caged windows. Tarnished combination boxes were no longer used, their glass insets shattered. A trash bin overflowed. The spray painter had been here too, the same filthy word written this time over a spotless young sailor proclaiming GO WITH THE BEST.

Amos stood in line. Ahead were two black women, one holding a baby which peered over its mother's shoulder at him, the ebony eyes unblinking and seemingly worldly. The other woman bought a money order and stamped envelope, acts which required shifts of a shopping bag and pocketbook. Suddenly the baby started crying, still staring at Amos, and the mother faced him as if he'd done something to cause it.

When Amos reached the window, the clerk recognized him and turned to ranks of wooden alphabetized pigeonholes. Apprehension gripped Amos when he failed to see the grayish envelope sent by Ministerial Retirement, but then it appeared, lodged between unsolicited catalogues. He kept all catalogues, not that he ordered from them, but it pleased Martha to leaf through the pages.

A fourth piece of mail was a letter from the development office at Davidson. He no longer sent money, yet the college continued to carry him on its roll. Once he'd welcomed the magazine, eager to learn what classmates were doing. Now it was as if the time he knew those men had been in another century. At least the hurt was gone, his sense of failure caused by turning page after page listing accomplishments and awards. The year his book came out, Davidson mentioned it—not with a review of recommendation, but merely a sentence in the alumni notes.

    *. . . envy is the rottenness of the bones. . . .*

He began the second leg of his journey, the walk from the post office to the bank. He fitted the check into the breast pocket of his shirt and pulled his sweater down tight against it. As he crossed the street with the light, a city bus rolled by so close he felt its diesel exhaust blow against his legs. Passengers stared at him from the superiority of elevation. The rear of the bus displayed a poster of a beautiful black girl wearing a skimpy pink bathing suit and drinking a diet cola.

He passed the tattoo parlor, relieved that this time of morning no gangs loitered at the entrance, and averted his eyes from the coiled green dragon with its yellow fiery mouth and split red tongue. There were carmine hearts, serpents, and a voluptuous Asiatic woman who grew from petals of a blue tulip. The whore, he thought, of Babylon.

Then a series of empty stores, one with headless unclothed manikins in the window. He heard a moan, perhaps human, or the wind, and thought of hideous perversions taking place in darkness. He was glad to see in the distance a city policeman mounted on a plodding sorrel.

    *. . . Behold a red horse. . . .*

He pressed his inner arm against the check, so little for what he'd given the church. It, his social security, and the pittance from the Board of Missions were all he had in this world. For a time he held services in the abandoned bakery, preaching the word to men whose drink- and life-ravaged faces were glazed with doom and despair.

He passed an alley, careful to curve out from it in case anyone lay in wait, and saw two grown men fighting—hitting each other with quiet deadliness, both bloody, clothes torn, their bodies bunched in violence. He hurried past.

    *. . . every man's sword shall be against his brother. . . .*

Even this paltry check had to be cashed at a bank. For that he needed to cross Broad Street, like a border where one stepped into a more prosperous country. White buildings rose in the sunshine, concrete gleamed, and tinted glass shone as if lavender insect eyes. A fountain splashed above a scalloped pond before the temple of money.

. . . *I will rain upon him an overflowing rain.* . . .

Swift doors hissed open before him, and he walked among potted shrubs, blond furniture, and sculptured birds on pedestals. Vultures, he thought. He signed the back of the check before a teller's eyes, a young woman painted and doll-like who always asked whether he had an account, though certain he did not. She'd seen him a hundred times, yet required identification which she studied before accepting the check and subtracting the bank's five-dollar fee. He and Martha could eat an entire day on that fee.

Cash in hand, he feared the return to the house. He thought of himself as an unarmed ship making its way among mines and submarines. His routine was to travel extra blocks to avoid the route used to come to the bank. Often he wove a path through a Safeway store to throw off anyone who might be following.

He had another trick. He sat in a chair near the bank's entrance and when nobody watched bent quickly to shape the dollar bills around his skinny ankle. He jerked his white cotton sock up over it. Elastic bound the money tight. A surprised woman customer glanced down at him. He pretended to be retying his shoelaces.

The large man walked laughing from the manager's office beside the radiant vault. He wore a gray overcoat and matching homburg. Despite his size, he moved easily, and his skin shone under the gilded lighting. His dark trousers were creased, his black shoes polished. He pulled on yellow pigskin gloves as he talked back over his shoulder to the manager, who followed with an air of subservience. The large man's green eyes swept past Amos and leaped back.

"Speed, is it you?" he asked.

"Whale?" Amos replied, and they held out their arms to each other and hugged. Whale buffeted him, pounded his back, danced him while the branch manager, tellers, and customers watched and smiled.

"Look at him, will you!" Whale cried, holding Amos at arms' length and turning him for all to see. Whale's complexion was rosy, his teeth outsized. Swept-back silverish hair had been precisely barbered, the flesh of his jowls shaved to a gloss. He smelled of cologne. Those heavy jowls quivered with happiness.

"Thinking about you just this morning, telling Pam how you and I stole the class bell and hid it in the cemetery!" Whale said, still manhandling Amos. "Listen, you're eating breakfast with me."

Denying Whale was like standing up to a force of nature. He was all encompassing arms and pressing body. Amos explained he had to get back to Martha, and Whale offered to pick her up too. Amos didn't want him to see the shabby little house, the decaying neighborhood, his diminished wife.

"She can't," he said. "She's under the care of a doctor."

A bent truth, and he hated lying. All his life in the big things he'd told the truth, but he would protect Martha from being shocked and humiliated by having Whale appear at the door while she had no time to prepare herself, mask her frailty, induce color into her cheeks, lift from the closet some last sheer garment.

"We'll take her flowers," Whale said, and Amos dissuaded him from that too. The easiest thing was to go to breakfast and escape as soon as possible. The manager invited Amos into the paneled office and handed him a modish phone. His fingers shaky, Amos touched the lighted buttons while Whale and the manager stood in the doorway talking of new accounts. The manager, a fair young man, wore a charcoal suit with vest.

The phone rang seven times before Martha answered, and Amos almost panicked. He pictured her lying on the floor of the cold house, her robe loose, her feet bare. He thought of her violated and bloody. Then her voice—well-bred, friendly, despite the tremolo expressing no alarm.

"Why I'm fine," she said. "I was playing the piano. Whale? You mean Thomas Ferguson? How nice. You were such friends. Don't you worry about me. I'm warm. He used to ask me out. Always breaking things. Tell him I send my love."

"If you smell gas—"

"Amos, I'm not helpless."

Then Whale had the phone from his hand, talking to Martha, his voice loud and hearty, speaking so everybody in the bank could hear, calling her beautiful, telling her she'd always been his favorite girl, promising that his Pam would get them together for dinner. Though dinner was never likely—Amos had learned to come up with excuses—he knew how pleased and flattered Martha must be. He imagined her lifting fingers to her hair in the immemorial primping gesture of women.

He received the phone back but was hardly able to hang up before Whale had hold of him again, crowding him out through the lobby and glass doors. They crossed to the lot at the side of the bank where a bluish black limousine was parked in a reserved space. The upholstery was tan leather, and the dash controls had the stainless steel complexity of a laboratory. It is, Amos thought, the kind of car I've ridden in only at funerals. The smiling manager opened the door for Whale and waved as they backed away.

> . . . *all the chariots of Egypt, and captains over every one of them.* . . .

"I no longer need to work," Whale told Amos. "They kicked me upstairs, use me mostly on consulting stuff. But I love it."

He drove aggressively, pushing the car's nose into the street so boldly the other traffic had to swerve, honk, make room. Whale grinned and winked as he sped them downtown.

"Where you carrying us?" Amos asked.

"Going to fatten you up, buddy. Now give me a playback on your life these past years."

Amos wouldn't even attempt to explain he'd been to the mountains, runty towns, the muddied Amazon, to Philistines everywhere, that he'd been mocked and rejected and was not only waiting for the end but praying for it. Each morning he opened his eyes hoping the dawn the last the heavens were denied to the faithful. Whale couldn't understand. Amos might as well be speaking a dead language. He said he'd merely been occupied with duties of the ministry till his retirement of the last 18 months.

"I noticed you limping," Whale said.

"The gnawings of arthritis."

"Thought maybe a witch doctor got you. You were down in the jungle, weren't you? Poisoned spear or arrow. Makes a better story."

They'd roomed together at Davidson, both athletes, Whale center on the football team, yet they were never alike. Whale worshiped in chapel with no more change of spirit than when snapping his wet towel through the locker room or lying beside a girl in the grass. Amos loved him, however, and helped him graduate, while Whale in his turn wished to share every delight he came upon with Amos.

They moved along stately Monument Avenue now, before the granite mansions artfully restored under the gaze of Confederate heroes on horses forever prancing. Stylish people walked between painted black jockeys and wrought-iron lamps and gates. Brass nameplates on elegant porches glinted. Cars parked at the curbs had the European flair.

*. . . riches profit not in the days of wrath. . . .*

"You took Martha away, you know that," Whale said. "Why she picked a brain like you instead of a warm lovable human being like me, I can't figure. And you dragged her to the jungle."

Whale drove too fast and waved at a policeman beyond Lee's statue. Amos had taken Martha down there and remembered the pain in her violet eyes when she first saw children with open sores. She'd kept the clinic running even as funds were withdrawn, till in her weakness and despair at the death of their daughter Mary she'd also fallen prey to meningitis and lain burning with fever on a straw mattress for 20 days. He would lift her mosquito neting and sponge her parchment-like face, and during the 20th day she raised fingers to his wrist, making no words with her trembling lips but a sound like the rasping of sandpaper.

*. . . beauty is vain but a woman that feareth the Lord shall be praised. . . .*

"Me, I've tied the knot again," Whale said, slowing at a light, yet impatient, the signal a personal affront for changing against him. They stopped beside a church built of hewn stone in the Gothic manner, a soaring structure whose arched stained-glass windows portrayed the feeding of the multitude, Christ's walking on water, and the dolorous procession of the cross. It was a society church, the sort of pulpit Amos had never been offered. His largest congregation was less than 200 souls, and in the end he lost even that because of the stand he'd taken.

"What happened to your first wife?" he asked.

"Becky left me for a Winston-Salem horse breeder. Parting was friendly, unlike Tess who was looking for a fancy man—which God knows I'm not—and tried to empty my pockets."

"Tess?" Amos asked, turning to him. "You've been married three times?"

"I believe in family," Whale said and laughed as he punched at Amos with gloved knuckles.

Whale apparently traded in women like his cars for newer sleeker models. During Amos' life it never occurred to him his helpmate could be other than Martha. She was more than anything he believed he would ever possess or deserve. When in Cumberland Gap the pretty redheaded organist entered his study and bared her breasts for him, he'd bowed his head and covered his eyes, causing her to pull furiously at her blouse and leave the church not to come back.

> . . . *thy wife shall be as a fruitful vine by the side of thine house.* . . .

Whale swerved at one of the grander brownstones. Before the entrance was a green canopy with white initials in English script. Amos glimpsed an empty terrace, balconies, and a uniformed door-man. The place was a private men's club.

"I'm not dressed for this!" Amos protested.

"Saturday mornings make no difference," Whale said. "Men come anyway they want. I've been in Bermudas."

He parked in a fenced lot, waved their way past the guard, and they entered the club by a side entrance which led to a plush foyer and elevator. They went up from street level to the first floor with its wine carpets and gilt portraits of Lee, Jackson, and Stuart. Wooden columns and wainscoting reflected an amber light. They hung their coats on numbered brass-capped pegs.

Amos, aware of his seediness, felt a surge of inferiority. He seemed insubstantial and as if he'd cast no shadow in these opulent rooms hung with hunting tapestries and glittering teardrop chandeliers. Whale, laying an arm around Amos's shoulder, forced him along.

They passed through double doors into a vaulted chamber where three long rows of banquet tables had been set and men were already eating, drinking, calling to one another. Whale had been correct about dress. Some were indeed properly turned out while others wore jeans, boots, and a few who'd been playing squash or paddle tennis had on sweat suits. The room was too warm, logs burning in a stone fireplace large enough to enclose a small car. Above the fireplace another portrait, this one of a stern periwigged George Washington. Whale hauled Amos around to make introductions.

"This character got me through college," Whale said. "I'd flunked everything except women without him."

Big men, beefy, important, who shook hands strongly, and Amos felt the emanations of power from their florid fingers. Casual dress or not, there were fine watches, diamonds, and the tables were covered with heavy linen, silver, and delicate crystal. Shiny black waiters in white jackets carried trays steaming with meat, eggs, pastries, and pewter pots of jams, coffee, cream.

The world's victors, Amos thought, and stiffened his back. He held their eyes. They possessed the sureness and strength of those dedicated to money. He sat and ate at the urgings of Whale, who heaped his plate, but the hotly spiced abundance was dust in his mouth. He felt small, old, and angry he'd devoted his life to God's work for so little while these men reveled in vulgar abundance.

Immediately he was shamed at himself and silently asked forgiveness. Their time would come. It was written:

> . . . *the merchants of the earth shall weep and mourn . . . for no man buyeth their merchandise any longer . . . the gold and silver, the precious stones . . . purple and silk . . . ivory . . . chariots . . . and souls of men. . . .*

"He was better than the rest of us," Whale said, talking loud enough to be heard down the table. "He made us feel we'd spit on the floor. One hell of a guy."

Let him talk, Amos thought, not attempting to explain his life now, for it would be inconceivable to Whale and those gathered here to feast that before the church court he'd charged his denomination was becoming too liberal and worldly. He argued men of the cloth no longer believed fully in the sacred inviolability of Scripture, that pastors stood in the pulpit who denied the Virgin birth and the very deity of Jesus Himself, calling Him merely a window on the nature of God. Christ a window! What blasphemy!

So he'd written his book, *The Ever Perfect God*, the volume he'd spent the last of Martha's inheritance on, and named names, called lords of the church Pharisees whose interests were their own ambitions and not the spread of the pure and holy Word.

*. . . they shall lay hands on you and persecute you. . . .*

He wasn't banished. The church no longer did that, believing itself too civilized. He was given a softly worded warning by the Committee on Ministers, yet afterwards had slight chance of finding a congregation. The story spread he was a belligerent fundamentalist and trouble maker. He would've accepted even a country pulpit, but no delegation arrived to hear him preach or question his theology. In a sick, facile society which had forgotten its roots, he carried spiritual contagion.

Finally it had been left to him to nail up a sign Martha painted over the doorway of the closed neighborhood bakery. Daily he preached to those off the street who sat in second-hand chairs and sang from tattered hymnals while Martha played a piano the keys of which stuck. The lost, the drunks, the derelicts, men and women who hoped for a little warmth, coffee, a kind word. Yet he taught them. Truth isn't partial, he said. The absolute cannot be modified.

The pitiful collection of battered coins and grimy dollars wasn't enough for him and Martha to live on. He worked part time as an orderly in a nursing home while she clerked in a florist shop, arriving home nights so weary she dropped onto the sofa and sighed as if giving up the ghost. It was a question of their persevering and keeping the faith till he reached the age to qualify for his pensions, including the Board of Missions one he'd had to battle for.

"What are you if not denominational?" an obese attorney down the table asked, a speared link of sausage dripping egg yolk held before his yearning lips.

"I'm a believer in God's sovereignty and the sole efficacy of Christ's blood," Amos answered, chin raised as if challenged.

"Well, okay," the attorney said and looked mystified as he fed the sopped meat into his mouth.

Amos wanted out, to be away from this pagan table, this heated temple of excess, to go back to his loving wife and his Bible. He stood and made excuses. Men raised their glasses to him. Whale, his mouth flashing food gobs, rose to go to the door with him. Others called farewell.

"I mean we got to get together," Whale said, helping Amos on with his coat. "I intend to plant a big wet kiss on Martha. Give me your phone number."

Whale drew a silver pencil and a small notebook with a leather cover from the jacket of his banker's suit, the leather having his initials embossed on it in gold. Amos gave a number, one digit of which was incorrect. Still Whale might be able to track them down. Refusals would then have to be constructed.

The doorman saluted Amos as he moved quickly out the great front entrance flanked by stone horses. Under the blowing canopy, Whale again hugged him, laying his cheek alongside Amos', and for an instant Amos fought tears. He felt if he didn't hurry away, he might weep. What kind of tears would they be? For the loss of the world and the dear ones left behind.

"Let me drive you," Whale called after him.

"I've business to attend to," Amos said and walked rapidly in the direction of downtown, but as soon as he reached the corner, he doubled back to the rear of the club where a clanging fan exhausted odors of the indulgent repast inside.

> *. . . and the great men, and the rich men, and the chief captains, and all the mighty men . . . hid themselves in the dens of the rocks of the mountains and said, Fall on us and hide us from the face of him that sitteth on the throne. . . .*

Worried about Martha he waited for a city bus that seemed would never arrive. He sat near the driver and door so he could be off fast, yet still had four blocks to cover. He half ran, his breath came in gasps, and the stitch in his side caused him to bend. Keep her well, he prayed. Keep her well.

At the house he fitted the trembling key to the lock. He thought he smelled gas, but Martha was all right. She had put on her wool dress, dark sweater, and cotton stockings. She sat at the kitchen table dealing out a hand of solitaire, using cards she'd carried all these years, white fleurs-de-lis on a royal blue background, perhaps from a sorority or bridge club, a deck from another life.

> *O thou whom my soul loveth. . . .*

Her fingers were so fragile, made for the holding of roses and fine porcelain. He checked the gas heater. The pilot flame burned feebly. He laid out his money on the table, and they made small piles of bills, each dollar allotted to its purpose. He answered questions about Whale and pretended to have enjoyed the breakfast.

During the afternoon they napped side by side, prayed, and he read to her, not another volume from the free library, but his own book, the passage they both loved:

22222222222

22222222

222

"Whom the Lord loveth, he chaseneth." How the words shock till one understands that what appears to be misfortune is merely correction arising from the loving concern of a father preparing his child for a feast at his gorgeous table. The pagan is lost. The Father will not waste Himself but allow them to have what they wish in this world because at the end they will be wisped away like smoke in a whirlwind; but when at last God collects His loving family, He will minister unto them through the golden corridors of a joyous eternity.

Amos believed it with all his being.

For supper he served them lettuce, apple sauce, a portion of chicken, and a glass of low-fat milk. By night they had prayed and were again in bed. They lay singing the old hymns to one another as fingers touched.

Dogs barked. A plane flew over. Amos thought he heard a shout, perhaps a scream, but his ears were no longer trustworthy, and the sound might have been wind on the skeletal branch scraping the gutter. A police car raced up the street, its siren shrilling, the flashing red lights penetrating darkness of the bedroom's cold ceiling.

During the night, half sleeping, half dreaming, he became confused, and his eyes fluttered and brightened with visions of the dazzling rapture, the gathering of the faithful into the aureate Heavens as the world and those abandoned upon it passed away with great noise, terrible fire, the blood and cries of the dying.

*. . . Blessed is he that watchest. . . .*

He woke fully, not knowing the time, but at the nailed window he saw a crimson glow and simultaneously felt a tremor through the earth. Was that a trumpet he heard? Stretching upward, his heart drumming, he pushed one hand to Martha and lifted the other toward the rattling panes as if offering her and himself skyward on his own agitated palm.

# *Journalism*

She had a patron, and in that way advanced in the business exactly like any man. After an apprenticeship in North Carolina, she went to New York for a newsmagazine and then to Africa and the Middle East for a wire service. She remained very fond of her patron, an old-fashioned editor who'd refused to obey tradition and assign her to women's news. He understood from the beginning that she had not gone into journalism to describe women's clubs or marriages or charity balls. She was attractive and serious and somewhat shy, and the editor was not certain that she belonged in journalism at all. He thought, mistakenly, that she was fragile. But he trained her well in North Carolina and then recommended her to the newsmagazine.

She had wanted to be an historian and in the beginning entered journalism only to learn how things worked: impatient with theory, she was eager to learn the ethics of the street. To her surprise, she liked the milieu, its confusion and haste and chagrin and the instant obsolescence of yesterday's dispatch. After North Carolina and New York, she knew she would have to go abroad because she wanted to cover politics and war, and she wanted to see at firsthand the countries she knew only from books. In Africa and the Middle East, there were countless opportunities to witness politics and war, disorder and suffering, and no opportunity was ever missed. In time she became senior correspondent for the region, always traveling and often in danger. Her seriousness deepened, but her experi-

ences did not make her either gallant or cynical as they often did her
male colleagues. She did not care for cynicism as an attitude and
had no need for the protection it gave. She was determined to stay
afraid and grinning.

She was a professional and intended to dominate the environment and in the privacy of her own heart was exhilarated by her
success. She loved her work, and although she collected numerous
offers from newspapers and television networks, she remained with
the wire service; a matter of loyalty. Her years as a war correspondent gave her a hard sense of reality and of her place in reality's
scheme. She need not have worried about fear. In the year 1972, a
women's group gave her an award for a series of articles describing
the destruction of a village in a west African country. The citation
took particular note of the effect of her pieces and concluded that
through her courage and compassion she had advanced the cause of
women in journalism. She was unaware of the nature of the citation
until it was read to her at the banquet. She said then that she would
be happy to accept the award on behalf of the dead and dying and
the homeless. Then she turned to the president of the women's
group and agreed that she had been fortunate to witness the particular war that had resulted in the destruction of the village. In
order that she might win the valuable award and the honorarium
that went with it, and be worthy of the citation; surely a small price
for those thousands of dead and homeless to pay. Thank God they'd
been present, willing, and accessible and available for interviews.
She tactfully corrected the president's pronunciation of the name of
the village. She said she hoped that before too long there'd be
another war for perhaps another woman to write about, in order
that the cause of women in journalism be advanced yet another
notch. Thank you, thank you. God bless. The audience of women
received these comments in shocked silence. She'd been so unfair,
so savage and perverse. . . .

"You didn't have to do that, Paige," the president said later.

"Yes, I did," Paige replied.

"You took it and twisted it—"

"Not as hard as I could have," Paige said.

The truth was, she did not believe that journalism advanced the
cause of anything, except her own understanding. It was for that
reason that the women's award outraged her. Better that they give

an award to male journalists, war correspondents, whose writing advanced the cause of men. She hated the idea of being a spokesman or spokeswoman or, God forbid, spokesperson of or for anything beyond herself, and agreed with Auden that no poem had ever saved a single Jew from the ovens; journalism's record was a little better, but not much. She understood that she had certain responsibilities as a result of the work that she did, so she had no objection to appearing at fund-raising rallies for refugees or other displaced persons. If her presence could guarantee a few extra dollars for a good cause, she felt obliged to comply. She'd speak, if called upon, or simply lend her name to a list of sponsors. They were always the same sponsors. She disliked the commotion that attended the rallies, but she believed that it was criminal to stand aside on grounds of temperament or of professional neutrality. In this world there were no neutral professions. Journalism was the least neutral of any of them.

Paige spent most of her professional life abroad in the company of men. She travelled with them in the war zones because soldiers did not react well to women reporters working alone; they became imposters, self-conscious bullies or thin-lipped stoics or Don Juans unless other men were present to keep them honest. She believed she could not discover the truth about men at war unless she saw them with their own kind, at a distance; when she was alone with them, she was the living proof of the Heisenberg Principle.

In the various zones, the journalists behaved like a large and unruly family, and after the first few assignments she was accepted as one of them. She shared her notes with them and "covered" for them, as they did for her. It was obvious from the outset that she was no den mother or casual mistress either, yet being with so many men so far from home was unsettling to her. The love affairs that she had always involved men far removed from both journalism and the war. It was essential for her to keep the two parts of herself separate. The older correspondents beguiled her with their European manners and old-fashioned pride. Like journalists everywhere, they believed they could easily have been something else: soldiers, diplomats, ministers of the interior, novelists, innkeepers. They used their profession like a suit of armor. She thought of them sometimes as crazed medieval warriors, clanking around the battlefield in cuirass and basinet, invulnerable to the calamities they witnessed. They were not heartless men, far from it, but they saw themselves as recorders and nothing more and had contempt for younger colleagues who sought personal and professional involvement. She found herself personally closer to the older men, though of course intellectually she ran with the others (up to a point). She passionately desired change, by which she meant an end to the killing; she believed herself temperamentally a revolutionary, though she could never kill in the service of an idea. She knew that her affection for the older men was a contradiction, but because she was on the far side of thirty-five-years-old herself she had sympathy for anyone in early middle age who had spent his best years in combat zones. And the men had a certain gaiety.

Some of them were in flight from women and some from bourgeois respectability, and some were merely footloose adventurers. Journalism was a safe haven. They were men who understood and appreciated drama and mystery and who prided themselves on being dry. They did not like it when she praised their work. Yet late at night, when drinking, the emotions would come tumbling out in a torrent. It took only the smallest crack in the armor, a chance word or gesture (if it were late enough), and she would find herself listening to muddled tales of ruined love and opportunities lost; of loosened grips and lives gone to seed. The first time she listened to one of these stories she began to giggle, believing that she was listening to a *story*, a joke. Then she realized that the speaker was relating events he believed to be true, a part of his own personal history, lachrymose and melodramatic. These episodes were by turns hilarious and heartbreaking and without exception ironic in tone. They seemed to be able to deal with the facts of their lives only through irony: heroic gestures, commonplace ends. Most of the men were excellent storytellers with a sure grasp of idiom and a phenomenal memory for dialogue, their own and others. The stories had been distilled by memory and were now more vivid than the originals.

The conversations were not one-way. She'd collected numerous amusing stories of her own, and while she was less operatic than the men, she was no less forceful. She found them sympathetic and intelligent listeners. Of course the longer she stayed the more the stories, hers and theirs, tended to overlap.

But the men frightened her. She was physically afraid of them, sensing nascent violence. She knew that literally the last thing any of them would do was harm her; indeed, they protected her as they protected each other. She was afraid of an accident. She was afraid they would fall on her. She tried to avoid them in large groups, although that was difficult; they all travelled in a pack. When they were drinking, they had a tendency to surround her and pepper her with stories; at those times she felt under siege. Typically, she would be seated, and they would gather around her, looming over her chair. She was not a small woman, but she was delicate; and the men always seemed robust. A recurring nightmare had her surrounded by large men, who as if on signal commenced to fall like giant trees, crushing the life out of her. It would happen by accident, one of them would stumble and fall and they would all go down like heavy dominoes; there would be no escape for her, she would be smothered where she sat. She would not be discovered until later, like one of the wounded always left behind in any retreat.

She took care to avoid them when they were drinking heavily. Once in Cairo, one of them fell down a flight of stairs, an everywhichway slow motion fall, flailing arms and drunken thuds down a dozen steps. Athough there was a good deal of laughter and no one was hurt, she could not expel from her mind's eye the image of herself crushed beneath the huge body. In her mind's eye, Paige saw herself walking up the stairs and the man tumbling down toward her, the man out of control. She waited patiently for him, there was no route of escape in the narrow passage; there was no sanctuary at all.

She told an abbreviated version of this story one night to one of the younger men, who at first laughed in appreciation (assuming that he was hearing a joke). Then he turned serious, nodding with sympathy and understanding.

"It's sexual of course," he said at last.

She looked at him earnestly, her features softening; she was careful to arrange the expression on her face.

"You've been here too long, your time's up," the young man said.

"Is that right?"

He said, "Sure."

She looked at him again, and a wave of compassion for the older men swept over her. How could she have been so foolish? She said, "It is not sex. It is fear. Do you understand fear?" He stared back at her, startled by her intensity. Her expression was benign, but her voice was cold. "That is when you are afraid physically. If you like, I will describe the difference between sex and violence, ecstasy and fear. Would you like me to do that for you?" She bent toward him, her taut face resembling a snake about to strike. But the young man was already rising, excusing himself, thinking that it was a tragedy when editors sent neurotic women to combat zones.

After that, she kept her fear mostly to herself. But there were moments when she was unable to do this. These were moments of terrible incongruity, when her world seemed to turn upside down. One night she and a friend, the wife of one of the correspondents, returned late to the hotel after dinner. It had been a pleasant dinner, they had not talked of the war at all. The others were in the lobby, sitting, when the two of them walked in, cheerful after a stroll through the darkened streets. All of the men stood up as they approached, their faces polite and composed; the wife nudged Paige, smiling, a silent comment on the good manners of these men. But Paige knew better. She knew right away that something was wrong. There was one moment of awful silence, and then one of them turned to the wife and said they'd just got word that her husband had been hurt. Paige moved to put her arm around the girl, but the men quickly gathered round, the largest of them reaching for her, cradling her almost. Then Paige caught a glance from one of them, and she knew that "hurt" meant "dead." After a moment, they all sat down again, and when the wife had stopped crying they told her what they knew. They told the story as they might write a dispatch. Each fact was given a source and its own special value. Conjecture was labelled as such. They all spoke in very low tones and assured the wife that everything possible was being done. Her husband was very popular, and they felt the loss as keenly as she did.

There was nothing more to be done. The embassy had been notified. Each man had rung up his best source in the government and appealed, as a personal favor, for verification; for any verified fact at all. Incredibly, the wife then reached out and touched each man—as if the men were talismans. They waited in the lobby until dawn, when the deputy ambassador called with a complete account. They had found the body, and it was being returned to the capital. For the rest of that day and the next, they remained at the wife's side. But Paige never forgot the moment when they entered the lobby, the men slowly rising, Paige knowing that something was greatly wrong.

She'd been abroad for seven years. She decided that the eighth year would be her last. She believed she belonged now in America. The eighth year was a horror, it opened with a letter from her mother; she and her father were separating after forty years of marriage. It was a terse letter, no details supplied. A month later a friend in North Carolina sent her an obituary notice; her old editor, long retired now, had died of a heart attack. Some weeks after that a close friend, a young American foreign service officer, was killed in Indochina. She was thirty-seven now and understood that there would be years like this one. She decided that the best way to get through it was to concentrate on her work, and to do that she needed a holiday. She arranged for a month's leave in Cyprus, intending to do nothing but lie on the beach and read. However, after a week, she found herself living in O'Ryan's apartment. He was one of the resident British journalists, a friend of a friend, the largest and most reckless of all of them, though he did not wear what she had come to regard as the usual badges of instability. He had not been wounded in action, was not divorced, and did not drink heavily. However, he had a high tolerance for pain and a jaunty attitude toward his work. He seldom drank because he wanted his senses keen for journalism.

They knew each other by reputation but had never met. He'd worked the Far East and had only recently arrived in the Mediterranean. During her holiday, the ceasefire on the island collapsed, and she cabled her office that as long as she was there she might as well cover for them. She and the Englishman began to cover the war together.

You see, he said to her one night. We make an ideal team. I do the military, you do the civilian.

Oh yes, she said. It's perfect.

I describe the search, you describe the destroy. We are the yin and yang of journalism.

Yes, wonderful, she said.

I can see us sharing the Pulitzer Prize or whatever it is they give you Ameddicuns.

Smashing, she said. Just what I've always wanted. But don't forget Stockholm.

I'd quite forgotten, he said. I do *beg* your pardon. Now look here. I've found this new village. You've never seen so many wounded people. Wounded and dead everywhere. They're preparing a new attack tomorrow, I've been assured of that on highly reliable author-ity. It'll be an especially heavy barrage. We can go to it. I've hired a car and driver, we can double-team the battle. How would that be?

Oh *lovely,* she said.

I knew you'd like it.

I can't wait.

Car's hired for six in the morning. We get there by nine, watch the shooting 'til noon; we can be back to file in the afternoon. Rest of the bastards will be climbing out of the rack, or finishing their lunch drinks—

Will you be *armed?*

Bloody right I'll be armed. You too.

Well then, why don't we stage our own firefight?

No managing of the news, he said. We take the dead where we can find them.

How wonderful for us.

Now go to sleep, he said. We've got to be keen for tomorrow.

Is that really true, why you don't drink? To keep your senses sharp?

Certainly.

For journalism? You want them sharp?

Of course. Otherwise there's no point, is there?

I suppose not, she said.

I can already hear the sound of incoming.

Yes, I expected that you might.

And you, the cries of the wounded.

Go to hell, she said.

Yes, I can hear them in your head. The screaming. Inside your lovely head are all the casualties trying to escape. To escape their prison. That head of yours, it's Lubyanka or Flanders Field, depending on your point of view.

Go to bed!

I'm in bed.

Go to sleep!

Not before a goodnight kiss, he said.

No kiss, she replied. By no means no kiss. I'm afraid I might catch whatever it is you've got.

No, he said. You're immune. But you can give me a goodnight kiss anyway. A kiss from Paige, angel of mercy, journalism's nanny. You ought to show me the same consideration you show the damned casualties!

Screw you, she said, grinning in spite of herself.

That's what I've been waiting for! he roared, shaking with laughter and burying his face in her neck.

He was in many ways the worst of all of them. But he made her laugh. His nickname in the Far East had been Wretched Excess; at times she thought of him as a character out of Camus or Beckett. She believed he was the most thoroughly rootless man she had ever met, anywhere. He couldn't even be bothered to follow up on a story. Wretch was a man without a memory; each day was absolutely new, no dawn like any other; no one moment had any connection to any other moment. History was discontinuous, except of course for women; women marked the various stages of his life. In that way they were a convenience. The one thing to be said for Wretch was that he did not frighten her, despite the obvious and alarming fact that he was the most violent man she knew. He was the one man she had good reason to fear but did not.

She believed it was his sense of limitless possibility that enchanted her; he had a morning cheerfulness, a kind of rampant gaiety, that drew her to him. She thought he led an utterly seamless existence, his life and his work were one, each reinforcing the other. She'd begun her career with a search, and she knew she'd abandoned that search some time back. There wasn't any single detail of war with which she wasn't familiar. But her hard-won knowledge had gained her nothing. She had it all firsthand, and all she knew for certain was fear. Perhaps that was all there was to know. She had hoped that the details would lead her to some larger understanding—of herself or of humanity in general. She had hoped her experience would lead her to a General Historical Theory, something beyond cliché. For a very brief period, she thought she would find the answer in Wretch. Every morning they drove to a burning village, a village no different from the one the day before; similar casualties, identical acrid odor; "the stench of cordite." How many times had she written that? His enthusiasm never diminished; he charged from the car in the direction of rifle fire like a child chasing a pot at the end of the rainbow.

She asked him one day what he hoped to find.

He'd looked at her, puzzled. What was there to find? It was not a question of searching and finding or of hoping either. It was just describing what was there. *They* searched, you didn't. It was interesting describing the search—

Interesting?

Of course, he'd said.

You never lose interest in it?

No, he said. Certainly not. It's what I do. What I've always done.

Why not? she persisted. Why don't you lose interest?

He'd shaken his head, exasperated. Stupid female questions.

Sincerely, she said. I want to know. And I want to know another thing. I want to know what you think you're doing. I mean, you write about it—O.K. But then what? Do you see yourself improving matters? Or is it just personal?

*Christ,* he muttered.

No, really, she said. I want to know.

It's very simple, he said. Too simple for you. You don't grasp that I'm not like you. You like things complicated. That's the big thing with you. The more complicated the better. The more complicated the more depressing. You thrive on it! He was sneering now and his voice was rough. Anything *natural,* he said, you're not up for it—

Oh *really,* she'd replied, stung. That wasn't fair, she was just trying to understand. She said, If you had any imagination—

He turned on her then, furious; she thought for a moment that he was going to hit her. But he rose from the bed, pale and shaking with anger, moving deliberately to the clothes closet. He began to remove her things, dropping each garment on the floor; then he pitched her suitcase on top of the clothes. He said, Go cry on someone else's shoulder. Take your bloody theories to someone else's bed. She wanted to reach out to him, but didn't, and in a moment he was gone, leaving the door ajar.

The next day she left Cyprus and returned to her base in Africa. She was glad to be home, all the old crowd was there and they welcomed her with open arms. The first night at dinner they asked her if it were true, they'd heard rumors, she and Wretched Excess O'Ryan. . . .

It's over, she said.

There was a general sigh of relief; they were glad to hear it.

Strange to say, he drifted out of her life as easily as he had drifted into it. In retrospect, the entire episode seemed fantastic. She realized now how deeply she had hurt him with the remark about imagination, though she did not completely understand why. The thought of it stirred her to melancholy; but she was angry, too. What was there about him? Opposites attract, she concluded finally; live by the sword, die by it, etcetera.

In Africa a week, she found herself fatigued. She was seldom tired and thought that a good night's sleep was all she needed. That night, tumbling into bed, she knew that she would dream; she found herself looking forward to sleep, and to the dreams that sleep would bring. She thought she would try to transport herself to another time and place, assume a new persona altogether; falling asleep, she remembered that her birthday was next week. Thirty-eight years old; six months to go in Africa. Suddenly, just then, she decided that she would leave right away. She would cable the office the next morning and leave as quickly as she could arrange passage. She hugged her pillow and fell asleep, though she did not dream.

She woke on her birthday, understanding nothing. She was surrounded by white. White walls, a white net over her; she was clad in white, in a bed with white sheets. Her arms were chalk white, there was a white plastic band around her wrist. Then, slowly coming to, she understood she was in a hospital. She was frightened, what was she doing there? Still wondering, she dozed, then wakened, then dozed again. A nurse looked in, smiled, and left. She dozed. The nurse returned and moved to her bed when Paige's eyes fluttered. Seeing her eyes open, the nurse smiled broadly; pink teeth in a lean black face.

She would be all right now, the nurse explained in French. They had been worried, Madame was in a coma for almost a week. But she had responded to treatment. The nurse gave her a complicated name, apparently the name of the disease; a tropical disorder of some kind. Paige knew after a moment that this was not the nurse but the doctor. She was suddenly overwhelmingly grateful that the doctor was a woman. She began to cry, they were tears of relief. The doctor smiled distantly.

There were a number of men, colleagues apparently, who wished to see Madame, but perhaps not just yet.

No, she said.

Perhaps in two days or three.

Three days. Paige said.

The doctor smiled. Three days, then.

When will I be free to leave?

A week, ten days.

Paige smiled. Ten days, make it ten days.

The doctor shrugged. The beds were in demand.

I can pay, Paige said.

In that case, Madame, the bed is yours.


Three nights later they all came, the regulars. They brought with them bottles of liquor and mixer and a Scotch cooler of ice. They'd had hors d'oeuvres prepared at the hotel and passed these around. They brought a fistful of cables with them, messages from friends everywhere. It was a regular party, they joked and laughed for some time. They looked at her like jewellers examining a gem and told her she seemed quite fit for someone who'd been in a coma seventy-two hours before. And they were indelicate, as always.

You almost bought the farm, one of them said.

. . . the fellow in the bright nightgown.

She looked up, puzzled. What was that?

A joke of W. C. Fields's. That was what he called death, "the fellow in the bright nightgown."

Why? she asked.

I don't know, he said, I don't know why.

They all laughed again. The party was getting rowdy, and one of the nurses came in to disapprove. They waved her away. Paige was tired, but she did not tell them to go. She couldn't, these were her oldest, dearest friends.

It grew noisy. One of them bumped her bed and moved away, laughing. They were telling an old story now, hard for her to follow; it was a story about Wretch. She was getting sleepy, she was more tired than she realized. The drugs clouded her mind, she felt she was living in slow motion. Her bones ached. The nurse came in again and was told to leave. There was an argument, more laughter. Than a pause, and she saw they were all looking at her, knowing now that they'd overstayed their welcome. She was ill, she needed rest. They gathered around her bed, leaning down one by one to kiss her on the cheek, staring into her sad blue eyes. One of them touched her hair. She smelled the fumes of the whiskey and the smoke from their cigarettes. She moved her face on the pillow, they each kissed her in turn and mumbled their pleasure that she was all right, and that her illness was nothing permanent. Her eyes had been half-closed, she was looking sideways at the door. Then she glanced up, their faces were above her, expressions blank, like masked surgeons in an operating theater. They loomed, large and misshapen. She looked away and they slipped out of her vision and she felt them all, every man, as a potential fallen; leaning over her, seductive, not anchored, teetering, not fastened to anything. If she was not careful they would smother her, one more random killing. She looked back, trembling. She was terrified now, beginning to go to pieces, fighting it, knowing it was only a matter of seconds. Then one of them moved, and when she flung up her hands to protect herself he kissed her fingers and danced away.

# The Lost Glove

## I. BEGINNINGS

A. *Three possible ways to begin.*

Dear Jeanne,                                    Sept. 6, 1953

When I left you on Thursday I was bursting with pride. I never thought I'd see the day that my daughter would be going to a college like Wellesley. A real atmosphere for learning—a peacefulness and serenity. How lovely the campus is—and the girls, the one I met seemed very high caliber. Have you gotten to know anyone yet? What about Ann Nichols? I got a big kick out of her. Is she always so friendly and outgoing? (Or is she just a loud mouth?)

On the way home I went over in my mind the clothes we unpacked. It seemed to me, Dolly, you had everything you needed and that you and I did a pretty good job in getting your stuff together. Not an excessive amount—but just right. If you find that you need something, let me know and I'll see what I can do.

The biggest surprise was when I got home. Of course Daddy wanted to hear all about it—what your room was like (I didn't tell him how much we spent on that blue scatter rug!)—and what the girls were like—but the surprise was . . . a large bouquet of bright yellow chrysanthemums on the lowboy chest in the foyer with a note that said, "Welcome Home from a Job Well Done." Isn't that a lovely gesture!

Of course, Dolly, you are the "job well done." I can't take all the credit. Daddy and Almighty God helped! But enough such nonsense. I was proud of you on Thursday—your wholesomeness, your calm, and your sense of responsibility. I pray that your first year of college is everything you hope it will be. I'm sure that there is much to be gained there and that you will learn a lot.

I must close and go and visit Grandma.

All my love,
Mother

B.

Jeanne rode her bicycle from the library to the dormitory on dark evenings, gulping cold air. At the dorm, girls in plaid shorts and woolen knee socks played bridge for hours at a time, smoking cigarettes. The air smelled stale.

She wore green slacks and spent time in the library, rooted in a carrel in the stacks of the basement mezzanine, behind the dusty volumes of old philosophical journals. She was reading about the Fabian Society, Sidney and Beatrice Webb, and "The greatest happiness of the greatest number." She was reading Stendhal in French. Her renderings of paramecia and amoebae were growing lovelier; she bought colored ink. But something was wrong, some growing pain that made it hard to breathe deeply. Cold air, a draft? What was it? And for the first time in her life, 18 years, she knew she longed for Rita, her mother.

C.

Dear Folks,                                          Feb. 6, 1954

Needless to say, there is little time to write a long letter. A biology quiz and a French test tomorrow. A long term paper for English is due in three weeks. The weather is freezing and my boots aren't really that warm. Would it be O.K. if I bought some new ones? My coat is warm enough if I wear my crew sweater under it.

I met with my class advisor, Mrs. Reynolds, the other day. She wanted apparently, just to talk. She said she had spoken to Mr. Lazarus, my English teacher, and that he thought very highly of me. I told her that I disliked French and about my other courses—she was very warm and called me Jeannie—and asked about my family (YOU!) and my summer plans.

The big English paper is getting me down, but I have finally decided on the subject: Thomas Mann and his ideas about the connection of art and illness. Have you ever read anything by him? He wrote *The Magic Mountain* and *Death in Venice* which is a novella (a very short novel).

By the way, Mom, I just found out there is a guest room on the first floor of the dorm where visitors can stay for only $3 a night. I would really like you to come up. You seem so curious. We could spend a few days together and you could go to classes with me and eat your meals in the dorm. There probably would be a concert or lecture we could go to together. Please consider it seriously. I checked it out with the house-mother and she says "Fine!"—So when will you arrive?

Now stay well and get some rest—(sound familiar?)

Love and Kisses,
Jeanne

## II. CHARACTERS

A. JEANNE. *Jeanne describes herself.*
1. A Salinger fan. I read *Catcher in the Rye* a couple of times, but I don't believe that in real life a boy of Holden Caufield's age can be such a big deal personality. My mother buys me a book of T. S. Eliot for my birthday at my request. Want to read Virginia Woolf, especially *To the Lighthouse.*

2. I become friends with an intelligent, loudmouthed girl from the Bronx—who walks like a bear and is as shaggy as a yak. Her name is Dodo.

3. I discover that if I listen to the Brandenburg Concerto #5 while watching the leaves of the maple tree outside my window flutter in the breeze—that the leaves will actually dance beautifully and in perfect time to the music. Ann Nichols says, "Oh, you're nuts, Jeannie!" She speaks with a Maine accent and is second generation Wellesley. Dodo believes me but isn't impressed. "What's the big deal about leaves dancing to Bach!" she says. "The question is 'Will they dance to Arnold Schönberg?'" "Who's he?" I ask.

4. Flexibility is one of my strong points. Teachers have always commented on my cheerful adaptability. In art class I am able to integrate a spilled splotch of ink into my design. My gym teacher calls me "Jeannie Limber Legs." My American History teacher commends me for my "balanced perspective," my ability to see all sides of an argument.

5. My father is quiet, formal. As he drives along the West Side Highway he keeps a record in the back of his mind of which ships are in port and which ones have sailed. He knows how long each ship has been away. He doesn't know what subjects I'm taking in school. On Valentine's Day he sends me a corsage of pink tea roses. For my birthday he carefully chooses a greeting card that conveys his deepest feelings. His business is on Seventh Avenue: girls' coats.

6. Alan, a boy who was two years ahead of me in high school, comes to visit me from Williams College. Gray eyes, and nice lips and teeth and beautiful hands. A physics major, spends hours explaining how the internal combustion engine works. Then we neck. I like boys, am very horny, but a virgin. Suddenly he gets really passionate and wild. Something happens. He excuses himself and goes to the bathroom. I blush, ashamed of my bungling awkwardness. Afterwards he isn't friendly. He never writes or calls.

7. I take a job cleaning the dorm living room and sweeping the hall steps and must get up at 6 a.m. I empty ashtrays, dust, straighten out chairs and tables. Don't mind the dirty work. Like being the only one awake. Night gives way to day with the exact swiftness as at the Hayden Planetarium, but w/o music. I watch out of the window.

8. I start reading Thomas Mann and decide to write my English term paper on "The Changing Attitudes of Thomas Mann as shown through his Changing Concepts of Disease and Death." This is Mr. Lazarus', my English teacher's, comment when he returns the paper about Thomas Mann:

> B+    Extremely difficult subject—you do amazingly well with it.
> The first page or so are in need of re-working: after that
> your presentation is less obtrusive and Mann's attitudes

come through. Your organization is fine. Curiously, main trouble appears to be in the construction of single sentences—often you write with a Germanic structure.

9. Mr. Lazarus, slightly smashed from drinking beers at the local bar, where he was watching the McCarthy hearings on TV, asks me whether I have any plans for the future. I tell him I've thought about becoming a teacher or a lawyer or a journalist. How can I tell him that I alternate between wanting to be a horserider and trainer on an enormous ranch in New Mexico (leather chaps, embossed boots—and I wrangle a wild herd of horses by myself from a distant pasture back to the corral at full gallop) and a scholar or brilliant humanitarian like Albert Schweitzer or Jane Addams? I find that I can't talk freely about myself to Mr. Lazarus.

10. In my college room with its blue plaid Bates bedspread, I think of my mother and of home—the smell of pot roast cooking and the taste of potatoes seeped in rich gravy—and her sorting out the laundry on Sunday nights: the sheets and towels, light-colored clothes, dark clothes. So much handling of clothes (sprinkling, folding, ironing), of objects, dishes, food. Women are always touching things: folding, smoothing, paring, dicing. My father watches the ships enter and leave the piers, thinks about missions fulfilled, continents connected—while lightly holding the lacquered steering wheel of his car. He listens to World News on the radio during dinner. My mother holds an onion in one hand and a small knife with a brown wood handle in the other. She peels and slices. Tears run down her face.

11. Often times she seems preoccupied. I'm not sure why. Of course she worries: about right and wrong and about us (my father, my sister and her husband, about me). For example, when I was late sending my father a card for his birthday, she wrote, "I beseech the Almighty in Heaven to tell me where I have failed as a mother." She was serious. Her reaction, as far as I'm concerned, was a little extreme. I don't think she had failed just because a birthday card to my father was a couple of days late.

B. RITA. *Jeanne describes her mother.*

1. Rita has violet-blue eyes and dark brows. She walks with sharp, determined steps like a sandpiper at the water's edge. She dashes here-there, sometimes across the street quickly, sometimes carelessly. Seems to be mumbling and frowning; about what? Perhaps about news or how statesmanship is going downhill. About Eisenhower who may have been a great general during The War but is a lousy president.

2. Rita's frowning: Is it "what the world is coming to," or is it that she never feels she looks as chic and smartly dressed as Aunt Selma, who wears peacock blue silk Shantung dresses on Sunday afternoons when the family gathers in Grandma's dim living room?

Sometimes Rita's worried face makes me mad. How to make her happy? Once when I was about 12 (and she was well into her 40's) she asked me what I would think of her and Dad's adopting a baby. I was at the kitchen table watching her cut string beans and tried to imagine what it would be like to have a baby brother or sister. Guarding my place as youngest, I said I didn't think it was such a hot idea. She laughed and said no more about it. Perhaps I should have been enthusiastic. Perhaps she needed another child.

3. When she and I are edgy with each other, I expect her to reach out and brush the hair off my forehead or criticize my appearance. More often than not, she doesn't, and it's just a feeling I get.

4. On a trip to New Hampshire, the family passes a pony farm with a riding rink. I dare my mother to go on a pony. She does. The pony, with a mouthful of saliva and half-chewed apple, smears the runny mess on Rita's coat sleeve. That doesn't stop her. My father, seeing his wife sitting so straight on the pony, calls her "Stonewall Jackson." Something erect and brave about Rita.

5. She tries to please. Pleasing parents even when she is herself a parent, an adult, a wife. So many people to do right by: aging parents, aunts, uncles, cousins, her husband, her

children; even her oldest daughter's in-laws; even nieces and nephews, old friends, and so on, and so on.

Once a long time ago she hired a "Home Efficiency Counselor" to come to the house and assist her in working out a daily schedule, or routine, that would help her feel she was getting more accomplished. When the counselor, a neat slim woman with a chignon that looked like a chocolate donut, left the house there was an index card with a weekly timetable on it left on the kitchen counter; for a while it was tacked up on the cupboard door.

6. I don't understand where she derived her sense that there was more to education than getting information or status. She had gone to old-fashioned public schools and a commercial high school; however, without financial support from my father or approval from anyone else in the family, she squeezed tuition out of her household allowance (scrimping on her clothes—buying basic black and changing accessories) and sent me to a small progressive school—à la John Dewey. She adored that little progressive school with its trips to the Fulton Fish Market and a lighthouse in the bay—and its sanctioned tumult, its affection, its freedom. When I was older and begging to go to public schools like other kids, she explained, "I wanted you to feel like an individual."

7. Recently she wrote that she was at a loss to figure out what to do with her time. She was trying a short course in Emergency First Aid and Nursing. Her letter read, "I had to pretend I was the patient. (The others in the class had to make the bed with me in it.) Of course I wore my underwear underneath my nightgown. I was burning up."

8. A letter from Rita:

Dear Dolly,                                    Feb. 11, 1954

I was so flattered that you invited me up to college. Are you sure that my presence won't interfere with you—your classes, studies, etc.? I would love to witness the "inside story." I think I can take the train up there a week from Wednesday. Daddy says I should go and not give it a second thought but I hate leaving him alone. Of course he can have dinner with Aunt Selma and Uncle Max.

Poor Uncle Bert got held up in his store—about ten minutes after Aunt Helen and Ricky walked out to shop at the A & P. When they came back he had been stripped of the beautiful new Benrus watch Helen had given him for their anniversary, his wallet, his papers, some money. Everything happens to them.

Dad says I definitely should take the train and go up to see you. He says he'll manage. He's such a generous, good-hearted guy. He doesn't stand in my way. I've even been thinking of taking driving lessons.

Oh yes, Jeanne—I took *The Magic Mountain* out of the library and started it. Very interesting. I want to read your paper on Thomas Mann—I hope I can understand it. Dolly, it certainly sounds like a big topic. I admire you for taking on such a large subject, but hope you didn't bite off more than you can chew.

See you soon.

Love and Kisses,
Mommy

P.S. Your comment was well received. It is rather biased of me and uncalled for. Perhaps you are right. I stand corrected.

### III. PLOT

Jeanne becomes aware during the winter months of an amorphous sense of loss. It dawns on her that she is missing her mother. She invites Rita up to college to visit with her for a few days.

A. *Rita arrives.* She does not own slacks but wears a maroon and wool dress and a black coat with velvet trim, black kid gloves, and a light blue gauzy wool scarf instead of a hat, and galoshes, rather dainty ones like a Russian Princess, that are molded for high heels.

Rita has a flair for joining things, enjoying the atmosphere; her eyes sparkle, she smiles a lot; now there is an easy air between J. and R. They avoid inflammatory topics like religion and sex.

B. *Classes.* Rita goes to Jeanne's English class, where Mr. Lazarus is discussing Dickens' use of imagery in *Our Mutual Friend.* After class, Rita tells Mr. Lazarus how impressed she is with the high caliber work he gives the class. In turn he tells Rita how well Jeanne is doing. Jeanne, somewhat embarrassed, stands about six feet away from these adults . . . but she is not as embarrassed as she would once have been; her mother's and teacher's brief words have resonance for her, tie different parts of her life together.

The same feeling occurs on the way home from Intro. to Music. They are walking up a steep hill; it is night; not a clear, high-ceilinged black night—but rather a deep violet one that hangs close overhead. A light snow is falling. The class had been listening to *The Marriage of Figaro*. A strong wind is blowing directly at them as they walk back to the dorm after class, and Rita bows her head to it, but speaks. "What a thrill Grandma would have gotten if she knew you were studying opera. She used to insist on Grandpa's taking her to the Metropolitan even when they had no money. I still remember when Grandma and I went to hear Puccini's *Tosca*. We had seats in the top tier." Rita's eyes are tearing. She blows her nose. Her eyes always tear in the cold, but this time Jeanne is unsure whether it is the cold or deep feeling; not sure if it is sadness or joy.

C. *Dialogue at the Local Rathskellar.*
  —How was your weekend at Cornell? Did Frank act like a gentleman? (R. knows better than to ask this, but does anyway, coyly, tentatively.)
  —What is that supposed to mean, Mother?
  —I've heard about what goes on at college weekends and fraternity house parties.
  —What have you heard?
  —That there's a lot of drinking and sex. Lights-out and carrying-on. I hope you didn't do anything you're ashamed of, young lady.
  —I try to do what feels right to me, Mother.
  —What does that mean exactly?
  —It means what it means, J. says, smiling reassuringly; then she changes the subject.

D. *Railroad Station.* Jeanne is wearing one of those red slicker raincoats fashionable at that time, with her heavy crew sweater underneath. She has urged her mother to stay for at least one more day: there are still other classes to attend—European history, modern dance, and a biology lab, but Rita is worrying about her husband and also says, "Jeanne, there wasn't one other parent on the whole campus. Not one."

J. What difference does that make! Why can't you stay just one
more day?

R. I'd like to stay, I love it here, but I want to be home in time to
make Dad dinner. Dolly, these couple of days have been
among the happiest in my life.

J. So stay then! Change your plans! Dad will understand, he
won't mind.

R. Dolly, I'd like to stay. In fact, I'd like to go to college with you,
but I can't. That's impossible.

*Here Rita draws the line.*

Once the train pulls into the station and her mother boards it,
Jeanne must leave immediately, for she finds that she can't watch
the train with her mother on it pull out of the station. She cannot
bear the objectivization of that distancing. Moreover, the idea of
seeing the bare railroad tracks, where the train had stood, frightens
her, seems violent to her. "Why am I living with strangers?" She is
surprised by the intensity of her feelings. She takes a cab directly
back to the dorm and goes to her room and closes the door. For a
short time she avoids her friends.

*Later J. is aware of something unfinished, some omission. There was
something she didn't say to her mother—or was it a question she forgot to
ask?*

E. *Several Days Later.* Her mother writes: "When the train was
pulling out of the station I looked for you and didn't see you. What
happened? Was something wrong? Where did you disappear to? By
the way Jeannie, you didn't happen to find one of my black leather
gloves? I must have dropped it onto the track as I got on the train.
Look for it anyway in your room or in the guest room at the dorm."
Jeanne shudders. The glove probably fell onto the track. She pictures her mother searching for the glove, then walking out into
New York City wearing only one glove, one hand naked. Five years
of trying to escape this connection end in a rush of pain: seeing her
mother with her bare palm extended like a hungry beggar.

Jeanne answers the letter: "This may sound really stupid and you
may not believe it but I left the station and couldn't watch the train
leave with you in it because I didn't want you to leave."

F. *Two Weeks Later.* Sixteen days exactly from her mother's visit, Jeanne calls home collect. It's 6:05 P.M. Her dad answers, sounds puzzled and doesn't accept the charges. "Tell her to call in fifteen minutes," he says to the operator. Jeanne puts the call through again in fifteen minutes. Still her father refuses to accept the call. Again she waits fifteen minutes and then calls. It's 7 o'clock now. Her father answers, accepts the charges, sounds nervous and tells her that Mommy isn't home yet. "The supper table is all set but she hasn't even called. That's not like Rita," he says to Jeanne and adds, "I'll call you as soon as she comes home."

Jeanne walks up and down the corridor but is unable to put in words what seems to be happening, so she doesn't tell Dodo anything. In twenty minutes the phone in the dormitory rings. It's neither her father nor her mother. It's her aunt, who can barely speak. She mumbles, "Come home quick. Something terrible has happened to your mother."

Jeanne goes up to her room and packs her charcoal flannel suit. In her drawer she finds a black wool jersey blouse with a Peter Pan collar. The housemother drives her to the airport. Dodo goes along to help Jeanne. They drive to the airport in the dark, in silence. The weather is still cold but now in March it is also damp. Jeanne is grateful that the housemother is quiet. The housemother knows Rita from when she stayed in the guest room in the dorm just two weeks ago, and likes her very much. Dodo is also silent—but shaking, partly because she has never flown before and is petrified. The plane is small and the trip takes forty-five minutes. Jeanne thinks about nothing. A cab takes them through the city to home.

No one tells Jeanne directly but she can see from her father's and sister's faces that what she had already guessed from her aunt's mumbled phone call in the dorm is correct. Only when she goes into the kitchen, which Rita had repapered the year before, and sees the small table carefully set for two, with a few jonquils in the center and green plaid napkins folded in triangles on the plates, does she begin to believe it. She notices the chairs that Rita had recently reupholstered in dark red vinyl according to instructions in her prized book, *Handyman's Guide to Small Home Repairs.* In her own room, on her dresser top is a small envelope with two tickets for a Martha Graham concert during spring vacation, undoubtedly a surprise for her from Rita. Should she go?

## IV. ENDINGS

A. My aunt told me that the coat my mother wore when she was run over was folded in a paper bag in the bottom of the foyer closet. She suggested that I have it cleaned and put away for the following winter. It was in perfectly good condition. Before I returned to college I took out the coat; it was black with velvet trim. It had a small drop of blood on the collar. I tried it on; it fit. My mother and I were exactly the same size. I noticed that there was another blood stain on the cuff. The stain was shaped like the state of Texas and was the size of a half-dollar. My mother must have raised her hand to her head where the wound was. I took the coat off and rubbed my finger over the blood stain. I shivered. Without the coat around me, I felt cold.

B. Lying stomach-down on my bed, my head hanging over the side, I stared at the blue shag rug. I thought of the ocean: not blue, but rather a steely gray ocean, rough and swirling. An ocean of broken glass. I was in a small rowboat. Something like the scene towards the end of *To the Lighthouse* by Virginia Woolf except that I was alone, without my father or sister. The boat was rocking and tossing, rising and falling in the swells; the water was rough; the oars yanked out of my hands. I braced my arms against the sides of the boat. The shore was now out of sight. Mainly, I was alone, alone.

*"Where are you now?" turns into "Mother, who were you?" The omission: not having asked the right questions, enough questions. The story—maybe more Rita's than Jeanne's. Need more about Rita.*

# Secrets of Sweet Baby Jesus

"It's only for the weekend," Bucky said.

"I just don't know," Willy McCullough told her. "I never really saw myself as a father figure. Teaching is one thing, being responsible for them is another."

"Willy, what are you talking about?"

"I thought I was talking about me, about how I'm probably not the guy to keep track of two energetic teenage kids for that long."

"What you are talking about, Willy, is total bullshit. Nobody has to be a father figure if it's just two days, is Point A. And the fact that if Mississippi had come back from Beaumont the way she was supposed to, then I wouldn't be in this jam in the first place, is Point B. It's just a matter of seeing that they eat, the poor things."

They were sitting on chaise lounges beside the pool at Bucky's condo. No, not a pool for the condo complex. After Bucky got her enormous divorce settlement, she thought that it was time to move out of the sprawling house near the U. of Texas in Hyde Park, a home of stately red brick and white pillars that seemed like it was ready for the Tara look-alike contest. All Bucky's divorcée girl-friends were moving into condos, and seeing Bucky's two teen-age kids were away at schools then, she decided that such a life style would be right for her too. But when Bucky found her supposed "unit," it was this spot, one of the two genuinely luxury-class models studding the ends of the complex with its tastefully gray-stained wood siding and yellow canvas awnings, for which Bucky

had yellow canvas cushions on these chaises made to match. The
setup had a full four bedrooms, enough fenced-in grounds back
there (more of that tasteful gray on the planks) for Bucky to employ
a full-time Mexican yardman, and, yes, the private pool. In spring
now, the grass greened, the wisteria spilled its purple. It was truly
the best time of year in Austin, Willy told himself.

Closing in on forty, Bucky had on a white string bikini. She was
tanned, and if you saw her stretched out with one knee cocked up
like this, a copy of the new American edition of *Elle* there on the
terra cotta tiles beside her, you would have knocked ten off that.
She wore oversized sunglasses. She had her honey-streaked hair
pulled back from her forehead, a single looping elastic at the back
for a girlish colt's tail.

Willy closed his eyes. He liked that, well, holiness, to the fra-
grance of her milky French tanning cream in the warm day, as
somehow cut by the chlorine sharpness of the shimmering pool
water itself. Birds chirped.

"If it weren't for this problem with Mississippi, Willy," Bucky
said, softening her approach.

Rich Texans like Bucky were probably the last people in this
confused universe of ours, Willy thought, who could believe in
things as passé as black maids named after Southern states, without
a qualm.

"Willy, are you listening?"

"Of course I'm listening, and of course I'll do it."

And of course he must be as nuts as a trapped coyote to agree to it.

"You're so sweet, Willy McCullough, you are."

On the other hand, Willy did love that drawl of hers. It was
Galveston syrupy and as exotic as Parisian French for somebody like
Willy, who had grown up to the twanging of cotton farmers out in
the flatter-than-flatness of West Texas, near Odessa.

*       *       *

Bucky believed in Things Eastern, Willy knew. And, with money
like hers (old enough, apparently, not to be affected all that much by
the current Texas oil bust), such belief seemed to be her option.
Actually, the money was her ex-husband's, Jack Mobley's. He was
directly descended from that pack of Tennessee settlers who were
bravely waiting to defend their own mission in San Marcos while

the Alamo was being swallowed in orange flames down in San Antonio. Bucky liked to think, even pride herself on the fact, that vicious Santa Anna and his horde of barbaric regulars were nothing to compare to the lawyers she had sicked on Jack after he fooled around with just one 22-year-old too many. Bucky had had her fill, and handsome Jack, in the Texas House and in line for something maybe as big as Washington some day, didn't want any more bad publicity than necessary over the split. He folded fast. He handed Bucky a deal that in the end she herself said she couldn't believe.

Bucky had been raised in Galveston, from a somewhat old and somewhat moneyed family herself. For her Things Eastern began when she went away to college, at one of those places in the velvety green hills of Virginia. She said she picked the particular school because it allowed you to board your horses at the campus stables, which could make for a comfortable afternoon of riding after classes in jodhpurs and a peaked black equestrian cap; that was the way Willy liked to picture her. But after her coming-out ball in Galveston, and after she married Jack, Things Eastern took on a purer dimension—New England. For six years the family had spent summers on Martha's Vineyard in Massachusetts, and Willy had seen glossy snapshots of them all sunburned up there. There were pictures of the white clapboard house with black shutters they rented. Bucky explained that it had once belonged to a bona fide Bay State whaling captain, pointing out the little turret and widow's walk on top. There were pictures of Jack and his pals on the deck of a sailboat during the famed Edgartown Races. Bucky pointed out (proudly) that she was pretty sure that the little stretch of blue, bordered by lime green on either side, was the span that Teddy Kennedy Australian-crawled back from Chappaquiddick that fateful night. Willy was amazed at how short the distance was, nothing at all for somebody with only elementary YMCA credentials, and anybody who said that old square-jawed Teddy was just fanning some Hyannis Port breeze when he claimed he did it, had surely never actually seen the lay of the place.

And then, when Bucky's two kids were old enough, Things Eastern became prep schools up there. Lane, the older, went to Concord Academy for a while. It didn't really take. Lane railed against the whole scene of prepdom right from the start there in

Henry D.'s home town. And if Concord Academy worked out just
fine for toothy, wild-haired Caroline Kennedy (a note Becky added;
why were well-off Texans so taken by the Kennedy thing, now that
Willy thought of it) it threw up some hurdles for Lane. In short, she
went instant punk to show how much she detested the school. Or as
punk as she could get, understandably, at a place like Concord
Academy, which meant black everything in clothes, death-mask-
white makeup as often as possible, and four pierce marks on her left
earlobe for affixing assorted dangling paraphernalia. Bucky got concerned. She brought Lane back to Austin, and she enrolled her in a
local Episcopal day school. Then all the rebellion effervesced. Out
were the ragged black jeans and the black leather jacket heavy with
chrome chain of a thickness seemingly strong enough for a tractor
pull, and in were tartan-plaid skirts and blouses with genuine Peter
Pan collars. And Jesus. Lane joined an evangelical Christian group
that met as an after-school activity, and this now seemed to worry
Bucky as much as the previous bondage get-ups. "What I can't
stand is the way she goes on with this Jesus, just the word, saying it
over and over again no matter what you're talking about, sounding
like some goddamn cracker dirt farmer." Willy didn't want to remind Bucky, surely, that not only were his own people such farmers
who did try to churn patches of cinnamon-brown dirt into something vaguely suitable for a fleshly green cotton crop, but "Jesus"
was a common word indeed in their rickety frame house, right down
to its being embroidered in the carpet-thick wall hangings of Biblical scenes (always lots of lambs in them) that his grandmother
worked on endlessly.

   Bucky's son, Cameron, was at St. George's School in Newport,
Rhode Island. He was a year younger than Lane, a sophomore now.
Cameron had his father's black hair and strong, handsome features,
though maybe the pale-green eyes, Bucky's eyes, betrayed a certain
softness. Apparently, Cameron took to St. George's immediately. He
played lacrosse and rowed for the crew, and Bucky said that his
literature teacher, genuinely Oxford-educated, had gotten Cameron quite interested in British poetry. "I think he'll be a poet
someday," Bucky said, proud and entirely serious about it. He was
home from the school for spring break right now. And from what
Willy had seen of him, all shy politeness. Willy didn't consider that

the kid would be any problem in the course of the weekend that he, Willy, would be staying at Bucky's condo to keep an eye on them. Willy could ask him more questions about lacrosse and crew. They were sports that Willy, once a decent 440 man on scholarship at the state teachers' college in Abilene, knew little about, and such questions had made for good conversation starters so far, a little awkward, but overall smooth enough. But Lane. Willy had no idea how he would deal with her, and most exchanges between them so far in Willy's month or so of dating Bucky had boiled down to Lane trying to engage him in her ongoing heated debate on issues like whether the current AIDS problem wasn't Jesus' way of trying to tell the world something.

Maybe Willy simply didn't relish the whole idea of it. First, even if Bucky had to see her own mother in Galveston that weekend, and even if Bucky didn't want to drag the two kids through the ordeal of having to put in time with the old woman who was pretty tough to deal with now that she had slipped into that perpetual blue smoke of sad Alzheimer's disease, Willy didn't like to see himself being a glorified baby-sitter. It seemed to emphasize the situation of his being so nakedly unemployed now, having a while back quit his job as a junior high history teacher and assistant track coach to go into a partnership on a ridiculous attempt at a Cajun cuisine restaurant. Naturally, that went flat quickly enough, and Willy, who knew nothing about the food business, later thought that at least he might have had a chance if it had been a restaurant that stuck to West Texas home style or even fiery Tex-Mex, rather than that trendy blackened redfish on dirty rice, the okra-laden oyster gumbo and the rest, all of which he knew less than nothing about. Secondly, being asked to oversee the kids indicated something in his relationship with Bucky, that when she proposed that he fill in for the maid Mississippi, who was still up in Beaumont with a family illness problem herself, Bucky brought out the fact that, after all, Willy had been using Bucky's new red Dodge convertible for the last week, so he sort of owed her.

But who was Willy trying to kid? In a way his real uneasiness had nothing to do with this weekend. In a way it had everything to do with the fact that Willy had done more than watch that restaurant business go under after his partner hurriedly bailed out. Willy got

so scared that he lied on both tax and bank refinancing forms to try
to save it all, and there was a good possibility that now Willy would
land in prison.

Honestly.

*          *          *

Willy was wearing a sort of white jumpsuit. He was in a sort of
lounge, a room of orange fiberglass scoop chairs (those pressed-out
things), functional masonite-topped tables, and a white linoleum
floor.

In the lounge were a lot of other men in white jumpsuits. Some
were Anglo, but more were black and Hispanic. Yet the jumpsuits
gave everybody a veritable uniformity, even if, Willy noticed, they
all seemed to be wearing different kinds of shoes. And they were all
in groups at those tables or clusters of those chairs, except for
Willy, who sat in a corner by himself. Willy was worried that they
didn't understand him, and it seemed that he couldn't even explain
who he was, what he thought, because of a severe case of laryngitis.
Willy was worried that they suspected that he was an informer, and
he felt so alone. And then it seemed that Willy had one of those
little writing pads kids used, a flat board with a milky plastic sheet
that had a waxy coating behind it, so when you bore down on the
plastic via the leadless red wooden stylus provided, you could etch
out something. Willy wanted to write, to tell them he was simply
Willy McCullough—and *certainly* not a snitch. But it seemed that
each time he went to put down words to that effect on the plastic, a
light breeze would lift up the sheet and the writing would disappear. He tried again, and the breeze lifted it again. It blew gently
through a half-opened window, and when Willy looked over that
way with a gesture that signaled he was going to get up and close it,
a lot of the faces of the dark men looked right at him. The mean eyes
of one thick-necked specimen said without words that he better not
fucking attempt to shut that window.

Willy tried writing again, and again the breeze lifted the sheet in
a slow crackle, like satin ripping. Or maybe it was more than that.
Maybe Willy wanted to tell something more than just his name and
that he wasn't an informer to these men. Maybe Willy was trying to
write down before him a message to *himself* as to just who the hell he
was, what he was all about. But now, when he merely touched the
stylus to the plastic, the breeze lifted it again.

Willy told his lawyer about these dreams he had been suffering lately. Dreams about prison in general, maybe Huntsville specifically. The lawyer was a bearded man who wore eight-hundred-dollar python boots with his cheap suits. He told Willy flatly, "Don't get into that, pal. That ain't gonna help one goddamn bit, that dreaming shit."

Honestly.

*       *       *

By that Saturday afternoon, Willy had to admit to himself that he was doing all right.

Lane read her Bible in the kitchen most of the day, which was fine with Willy. And Willy and Cameron headed out to Zilker Park for some elementary lacrosse.

"Indian ball is its real name," Cameron said.

"I know," Willy said. "Or, I remember you were telling me that before."

"It's the national sport of Canada." Cameron spoke so politely.

"Come on, what about ice hockey?"

"I know. It's easy to get somebody on that, isn't it. But a guy at St. George's showed me in a *World Almanac of Facts*. At first I didn't believe it."

"I guess it's at least some concession to the Indians," Willy said. "More than we made here. Rip off their land, but at least give them a national sport."

"You're right." Cameron smiled. What a gentleman.

Cameron wore chinos, tastefully scuffed boatshoes that had maybe seen some time there on the Newport, R.I., docks where the sleek twelve-meters once made their home, and a light-blue oxford-cloth button-down shirt, the sleeves rolled to the elbow. He had on teardrop Ray-Ban sunglasses.

Half the city seemed to be out there this weekend enjoying games, the other half sunbathing there or flying kites snapping like happily untethered neckties up in the blue. The park was huge, an ongoing spread of greenness right to a distant brace of leafy old live oaks, behind which rose the pastel high rises of the city's skyline that featured all that whacky, somehow fun too, postmodernism put up in the last few years.

Willy, once such a track man, had played only one game in which you used any implement you held in your hands, and that was plebeian baseball. He had never attempted tennis or golf, let alone the strangeness of lacrosse or ice hockey. But he liked the way that the whole trick now to moving with this lacrosse stick was to make sure that the ball was always gently swaying in the worn rawhide net on the stick, its handle taped with comfortable white adhesive. Cameron said the move was dubbed "cradling it," and that made sense, as it did feel strongly akin to rocking to keep an ever-so-tiny baby content in there so it wouldn't bounce out as you jogged. And before long Willy had the hang of simple tosses to the patient Cameron, and not long after that they had found a stretch of open, daisy-speckled grass for themselves, and they spread a good 30 or so yards apart. They let go with mile-high pop-ups. Willy liked that too. The ball seemed to hang aloft forever, almost not moving at all, like a beeping satellite, while he slowly circled and circled—till he detected the very crest and the inevitable drop, which happened with all the sudden velocity that Galileo himself discovered letting go with that red McIntosh from the Tower of Pisa. Willy savored the final gentle thud, the way that he was getting the hang too of recoiling a bit when it hit, using that elastic give to keep it spongily socked smack in the sweet spot and not out again in an instantaneous ricochet.

"Nice!" Cameron called from across the way.

"Sure is!" Willy shouted back.

"You're a natural!"

And Willy wondered. He wondered if he hadn't maybe missed the message of America. Wasn't this the whole idea? Not end up an even 40, a bachelor and busted to boot. But to have locked up something earlier, to have established a family, surely, and every week to find yourself in a city park on a day that was right out of a Chamber of Commerce promotional film, relaxing with, in a way, a son.

Riding back in the Dodge convertible, Willy felt nicely tired. He thought about a good shower, thought too that maybe they shouldn't have let the strange Lane stay at the condo by herself. Even if she had said that she had no desire to go to any park, Willy should have pressed her some and at least gotten her out of the house. But she did have her Jesus. Cameron scanned on the car's radio and found some jazz on an FM station.

"You like jazz?" Willy asked him.

"Yeah, I really do, I guess," Cameron said, from behind those dark Ray-Bans.

So they talked some about music. Willy remembered the names of some of the be-boppers, like Charlie Parker and Dizzy Gillespie of that upturned custom horn that could have been trying to poke out its easily whispering riffs to heaven itself. How gentlemanly Cameron was about this too. And as with the lacrosse, Cameron realized that Willy had no expertise, but he seemed to listen to everything Willy said with good nature and give-and-take. The guy was what every parent wanted their kid to be—a considerate adult.

At the condo, Willy started making plans for dinner. He had proven a hit with brunch, preparing about the only brunch in his slim repertoire. Huevos rancheros. Which basically meant fried eggs, fresh chopped onions added to basic tomatoey Pace brand picante sauce, Old El Paso refried beans, and his coup, corn tortillas. He drove clear over to the Mexican neighborhood in East Austin to buy the fresh tortillas and then warmed them up between moist aqua-and-white-checked dishtowels in the oven; the towel method was the only way to ensure the things kept vaguely supple and didn't turn fiberglass-hard in the course of the heating. But now, Willy wasn't encountering such smooth waters, and though Cameron appeared to like Willy's suggestion that they grill up some chicken, Lane, in her challenging way, would hear nothing of it.

"Chicken's full of bacteria. Each one of them is just a pimply bag of salmonella. I saw it on 'Sixty Minutes.' They had these guys out at some chicken processing plant in Missouri who blew the old whistle, claimed that if truth be known 50 percent of the stuff isn't fit for humanoid consumption."

In the end, even easy-going Cameron had to admit that the harangue hadn't exactly left him in the mood for poultry either. So they all somewhat agreed on Wendy's hamburgers, a common denominator. Both Willy and Cameron were obviously enjoying the square-cut things with genuinely golden fries and genuinely extra-thick vanilla shakes. A shake was something Willy hadn't had since who knows when, yet it reminded him of relaxed nights as a teenager with his pals in his dusty West Texas town at the Dairy Queen, one of those standard places featuring red-and-white trim and

yellow fluorescent bug lights along the sloping roof, a spot that was
as much of an institution in the Lone Star state as the armadillo or
Bob Wills himself. Lane was having her problems with the burger.

"Thick and juicy is what they advertise," she said. "Which is
another way of saying thick and greasy. Look." She had the corner of
her burger in its seeded roll remaining, and she held it atop the
white styrofoam carton. She tugged out a couple of lettuce shreds,
then she let it all drip, drip, drip that supposed juice. She even
squeezed it some, as if it were a kitchen sponge, saturated.

"Seeing is believing, huh?"

Eventually, what Willy feared would happen did happen. Cameron was on the phone for a while at the condo with a friend of his,
and when he hung up and asked if he could use the Dodge convertible to drive over to the pal's house, Willy consented. Bucky had
given Willy no directive on the use of the car by either of the kids,
but who was he to deny Cameron? After all, Willy himself had
indeed been freeloading on using the new red thing with its rolled
leather upholstery for a week. So why shouldn't the kid have access
to it when it belonged to his own mother? But, again, that brought
about Willy's worst apprehensions, because for the evening he and
Lane would be left solo. This could turn out to be a few hours as
long as one of those interminable European wars of succession that
Willy slogged through in the classroom for ninth-grade World History in the old days.

Lane once punk. Now Lane close to a Jesus freak. Maybe it was
her edge that led to these extremes. It certainly didn't grow out of
any reaction to or rebellion against what had been doled out to her
in that looming category called "looks," of ultra-importance to a
teenage girl. Lane may have been slightly pudgy, simply because a
good deal of her time spent hanging around the condo with her
pebble-grained Bible, the size of an overnight suitcase, was also
devoted to big-league snacking. A lot of the diet Pepsi that Becky
insisted on rather than the regular cola, along with a lot of Chip-
Ahoys or, her current favorite, the new cheeze-filled cone of a corn
chip called Corn-Quistos; the product was apparently being test-
marketed only in Texas, the way that Dallas-based Frito-Lay stuck
to their home territory for trying out all new fare. Yet Lane's dose of
extra weight was to be expected in a kid her age, and, in essence, if

she hadn't opted for scrubbing her face free of nonexistent make-up till it was almost beet-raw and wearing those outfits of pleated skirts and pressed sleeveless cotton blouses (intended to be All-American, but looking austere as any post Vatican II nun's attire) she would have been another true Texas beauty. All of it from Bucky: the strong cheekbones, the even white teeth, the long, slim legs that even this temporary pudginess couldn't alter.

Willy sat with her in the condo's airy living room. It was an expanse with walls painted gray, 15-foot cathedral ceilings, tasteful bone-white broadloom in the center of the waxed kiln-tile floor, and just enough gray, German-designed furniture. Two of the bold modern paintings, all abstract angles, on the far wall were so valuable they were actually insured with Lloyds of London. When Bucky first told Willy that, he thought it was a joke; yet she assured him that as her ex-husband Jack had told her long ago: "When it comes to art, honey, I don't know much about it, except you don't piss around with Dallas or Houston for insurance. You got to call Lloyds, go that extra mile." She was adept at putting on Jack's wheeler-dealer voice.

"Christian TV?" Willy asked Lane now.

"What are we supposed to watch, MTV? It's all soft porn, anyway."

"You could have a point there," Willy acknowledged. Besides, she held the remote for cable channel selection.

"Preachers?" Willy asked.

"Not on Saturday. It's family entertainment now."

Willy thought about suggesting the Cable News as a compromise or even trying one of the regular networks. They always liked to run those television movies about the life of Jesus or sometimes even remakes of *Spartacus* around Eastertime. But he didn't want to provoke any argument. As it turned out, family entertainment meant old black-and-white reruns. Willy did fine with "The Donna Reed Show," which in the early sixties ran on the one network station that could be barely picked up in this West Texas town. He had more problems with "Leave It to Beaver," which should have been the more known, but wasn't hooked up to his town via that solitary network station. So it failed to qualify as even a nostalgia trip for him, as he watched the supposed intrigue about whether or not brother Wally would invite the freckled, overcute "Beav" to a party Mom and Dad had agreed to let Wally have in their evenly lit living room.

It finally, mercifully, finished, and Lane flicked off the set just as the hoppy theme song started to sound and the white credits rolled up the screen.

"About an hour of television is right, wouldn't you say," Lane said.

"I guess," What else could Willy say?

"Families should spend less time with television, more with just talk."

And though Willy wasn't part of the family, he should have spotted this coming. There was no way he was going to dodge that AIDS debate. Lane had just been waiting to confront him, the proverbial cornered squirrel—or maybe skunk. Willy watched as she first staked out her territory by heading to the kitchen and returning with a bag of Corn-Quistos (on the side it announced in huge letters, "The One-Pounder") and a Dr. Pepper. It was the original stuff distilled from sugary syrup as thick as 10–50 motor oil, to be sure. She had that afternoon bought a six-pack of it rather than of the Diet Pepsi, now that Bucky and her orders were gone for the weekend. Lane set the chow on the glass-topped coffee table, tucked her legs under her skirt, and prepared for a good session of it.

"It seems to me that there are two questions," she said, taking a sip. Her true blonde hair was done in a big braid, tossing as she spoke. "First, just the simple matter of sex education in the schools, whether all this talk of safe sex is just something to promote sex in the end. Second, the bigger question I always think of. Is Jesus trying to tell the world something, maybe America more than anybody else, with all this stuff about AIDS. Scripture says, John X:24, that He will watch them in their wicked ways, and then He will talk to them with a sign."

"Talk to who?" Willy asked. "The Central Africans? The Haitians who are supposedly living in the poorest country in the Western Hemisphere? Jesus' own poor who suffer if ever there was a poor who suffer. He's trying to tell them something? Because those are the places where the incidence is so high it was already of epidemic proportions before we ever heard of it here. So why isn't it them, not America, He's trying to tell something to?"

"Because." She paused. She scooped out more of those squiggly corn cones, popped them in her mouth. She reached for another long belt of Dr. Pepper, maybe to give her the power that she needed to fuel her for what she saw as the long and yummy argument on the way. "Because. . . ." And without even listening, Willy knew that he had made the big mistake, bitten for her bait. An hour later, Lane continued to do most of the talking, and Willy would have gladly settled for the Beav (slighted and eventually deciding to buy some rubber ice cubes for the otherwise harmless punch bowl at brother Wally's party, to get even with Wally for not inviting him to hang out with the older guys) rather than this talk, or what soon became an ongoing bombardment, aimed point-blank at Willy, of more chapter and verse.

Nine-fifteen; nine-thirty; nine-forty-five; ten; ten-fifteen; ten-twenty . . . and by five-of-eleven Lane herself admitted she was growing tired of the blab, and Willy suddenly felt that without his noticing it he had made it over the hump of his duties for the weekend. And now that he had let Lane vent what she had to, Willy admitted he had done a good job, told himself what he had told himself earlier out at the park with Cameron playing lacrosse catch, those white dots of the high flies still playing slow on the forever blue of the screen of his own drifting imagination at the moment, softly announcing to him that he too was close to sleep, and. . . .

And then the call from the police station downtown. Cameron was being held at that new yellowbrick mausoleum right on Fifth Street, and he was physically OK. But just about everything else was wrecked.

"Between you and me," the cop admitted to Willy, for whom he must have felt bad, "the kid is a real Captain Destructo if I ever saw one." The cop's name was Sergeant Kells.

Willy tried to picture the details the cop recounted. The way Willy understood it, Cameron and his pal, high on something, had headed out into the already charged Austin Saturday night, downtown with a mission. Or at least Cameron had a mission. It seemed that his pal, Kirk, wanted to abandon ship when he realized that Cameron was really going through with it, and Kirk bounded out of the convertible at a red light at Guadalupe and 24th. Cameron slowly continued on. Past the university, and past the pink stone dome of the statehouse, and past the starry slabs of those new high rises downtown, right to the parking lot of Basil's, the poshest club in town. Luckily, the valet for the valet parking was loafing inside, so there wasn't any personal injury. Cameron managed to repeatedly floor the accelerator of the Dodge and repeatedly slam it into a half dozen shimmering specimens of sky-high-priced German sheet metal (two Mercedes and four BMW's, according to Sergeant Kells' count) even some Italian fare (yes, there was the inevitable red Ferrari).

"You know what he told me?" Sergeant Kells asked.

"What's that?"

"It was just work he had to do."

Willy agreed to come down there fast, and he hung up, rattled. He gave Lane a brief summary, as he jumpingly waited for a taxi. Her first response was that it was definitely "X," a tablet of so-called Ecstasy, that Cameron's blood corpuscles were thumpingly supercharged on; she said that it was true, he did the stuff all the time. Her second response was that Cameron did not, in fact, have a driver's license. Willy had been conned into letting him use the Dodge, though she didn't want to say anything at the time; she was just hoping for him to go out and return safely, that it would all blow over.

But it was stranger than that. Suddenly, there was no edge to what Lane said, and this was a Lane Willy hadn't seen before. She had softened, seemed so sadly *concerned* that Cameron had that problem with "X," seemed so sadly *concerned* that Cameron didn't possess a laminated document from the Texas Department of Public Safety attesting that he was legally allowed to operate a vehicle. She was crying softly, scared.

"He's a good kid, Willy. Except all this divorce stuff has hurt him a lot more than me. He wants a family, and these drugs and this hating of rich people, something like this wrecking their expensive cars, is maybe not his fault, because—"

The driver of the Yellow Cab leaned on the horn again. Willy didn't have time right then to take this in, with the driver already pulling away. Willy shouted that he was coming and jogged to catch him, thinking that Lane had surprised him so, the poor kid, and thinking too that those mirroring Ray-Bans on Cameron that afternoon were probably a clue—Willy should have known that behind the mirrors that bounced back only your own image when you looked, the kid was slightly crazed.

\*       \*       \*

The next afternoon the trio of them were moving along a two-lane road through freshly planted farmland so flat that it could have been drawn with a draftsman's rule. On bicycles.

Bicycles of very differing qualities. Lane had her Raleigh twelve-speed, silver metallic and new enough that the spokes shimmered in the sunlight like rolling rainbows you weren't quite sure of. And in front of her was Cameron on what at first appeared to be a two-wheeler small enough for a clown, seeing he was an even six-feet tall. But he said before that he didn't mind a bit; he had had the thing with its yellow vinyl banana seat when he was about ten, and he was surprised as anybody else when Willy found it in the condo's garage. And in front of Cameron, leading this parade of sorts, was Willy himself atop a true crate, a repainted, wide-tired blue thing made by a gone American company called Columbia and probably weighing as much as some luxury sedans; it was all he could dig up in his door-to-door quest to find a third bike back at the condo complex.

Willy had known around two that weird afternoon that they had to get out. To do something. And he got the idea of a bike ride, remembering how Lane herself had gone on her Raleigh that morning for services at that Pentacostal church she had joined on her own. Otherwise, the day would simply degenerate to more ongoing naps. On Lane's part, seeing she had waited up for Willy and Cameron to return from the police station the night before then rose so early for church. And on Cameron and Willy's parts, seeing they didn't leave the station till close to four, and even if they didn't get up early, that ordeal had taken its toll. Was that station ever a mess. Actually, with Willy simply signing a few documents, the cops were almost ready to release the "juvenile" to his custody—without Willy having to resort to a phone call to his sleazy lawyer of those python boots. And all that Sergeant Kells wanted was to be certain that "the kid has come down" from whatever he was on. Though while they waited in the front lobby of the place that was as busy as a Greyhound terminal on a three-day holiday weekend, it seemed that Sergeant Kells forgot about them entirely, before they did receive—a full two hours later—his "permission" to leave.

The bike ride developed its own inevitable problems.

Willy had thought he had done right in suggesting they head east of town. There Texas turned to farmland flatness all the way to the green-and-aqua coast; on the west side of Austin, it started off with some Hollywood-style hills, which soon gave way to the High Plains, then, much further on, real mountains out toward El Paso. Willy said that he knew for a fact that due east was a great catfish farm and restaurant (man-made "tanks," the local vernacular for ponds, where hundreds and hundreds of massive sacks of Purina catfish chow were lugged to feed the critters to fatness); that would give them a destination, a goal. And nobody had eaten much of anything since those maligned burgers of the evening before, except for Lane and her Corn-Quistos con Dr. Pepper. But on the way, first the slim, gum-walled tire of Lane's Raleigh blew. Probably a goathead burr popped it. Which meant, to protect the aluminum rim, they all walked a full mile to the intersection of this farm-to-market road and another one, where at a Texaco station in the true middle of nowhere the attendant finally dug up a patch kit. Then the Sunday National Guard convoy. The phalanx of olive-colored vehicles, their turned-on headlights looking like watered down scotch drinks in the daytime bright, chugged along in the throbbing heat, slow as a jam, giving Willy a lot of time to dwell on the phone call from Bucky that morning and how he told her everything was just fine. The lie had seemed sound then, but now it also seemed worse and worse, in the course of the three of them on this goofy collection of bikes actually becoming blanketed with soot from the trucks. Willy could grind it like pumice between his molars. Add to that the situation that the whole operation seemed to have slowed even more, while the drivers took their time in checking out Lane in her white tennis shorts and white tank-top shirt. Her chubbiness must have seemed nothing more than tanned Playmate-of-the-Month plenitude to this crew.

"I'm sorry," Willy said. They had stopped, the truck convoy having finally passed, and, as before, the road empty. Lime-green spring sproutings, a white barn with a white farmhouse, and some huge shading liveoaks out there.

"Big deal, some trucks," Cameron said.

"They did wreck this shirt," Lane said. Loose strands of that golden hair stuck glued to her sweaty forehead. She tugged out on the cotton lisle to examine the polka-dotting of black. "But you don't have to worry, Willy."

"No, really," Cameron said, "you're the last one who should worry about anything."

"He's right, you know," Lane said.

Gentlemanly Cameron, then whacked-out Cameron. Aggressive Lane, then softly crying Lane, who seemed to understand so much about the world and its sadness when Willy rushed out the door the night before. One-eighty turns from both of them in the last twenty-four hours. And now all of that gone. They were just kids now, willing and grateful to follow Willy wherever he led them. Despite Willy watching that confidence in him sink some when they discovered that the catfish place had apparently shut down months before, the farm itself foreclosed on, as attested to by an auction sign.

"Closed?" Cameron said, staring vacantly at the placard.

"This shirt is really ruined," Lane said; she looked down at it more.

But then there was a Seven-Eleven miraculously waiting at the intersection of two more farm-to-market roads further on. They stopped. And then they found a field of fresh alfalfa beyond a gully of roadside wildflowers—red Indian paintbrush, yellow false daisy, and those so-blue Texas bluebonnets, all benevolently planted like this by the highway department—and then they were picnicking on soft drinks and sandwiches they made of cold cuts, loaded with mustard, on Mrs. Baird's white bread; they agreed it had to be the best meal they ever tasted. The smell of the grass's sugary chlorophyll, the softening of the light on the trio of them beside the bicycles that shed surreally long shadows. Stretched out, they ate.

In a half hour, they would be caught in a cloudburst on the long, long way back, exhausted and soaked. But right now there was just the alfalfa, the technicolor of the wildflowers, the fluttering of a wave of delicate white butterflies that they gawked at in dreamy silence.

And suddenly it hit Willy. He maybe didn't notice himself talking out loud.

"I haven't thought of it in two days. I haven't thought about the fact that this time next year I could be in prison. You know, I don't know when I last went through two full days *without* thinking about it."

The other two didn't seem to listen. Cameron was back in his own private universe. Lane was saying something about the fragile butterflies being special, "like little secrets of Sweet Baby Jesus," though Willy wasn't sure if that was exactly what it was.

Ah, spring in Austin, Willy assured himself.

# Children of Esau

In the stateroom Steve shared with Bob Layton aboard the U.S.S. *Independence*, there was a small electric fan. Damn fan went back and forth, back and forth, and now Steve remembers it—how funny, how important, how dumb and stupid it was—as he sits opposite his old man in the living room of the Bethesda, Maryland, house he grew up in. Thanksgiving. Dad thumbs *Time*, his wheelchair by the picture window overlooking the back yard. From the kitchen come the good steamy smells of roasting turkey, of cornbread dressing. From there with the clatter of pans also come the slow, indistinct lift and fall of Mother's and Milly's voices. Steve wonders (in a broken bottle way) about other Thanksgivings—the times before the old man was busted up with a stroke and before brother Greg was zonked out in a nuthouse over in Baltimore (expensive, of course, only the best for Greg!) and before Steve got hitched to Daffy and they had a kid named Harry Jr. (after Dad, after the old man), she and the kid now upstairs and Daff trying to keep him occupied until dinner is ready. Those Thanksgivings back then, before the damn knots of complication. . . . Down in Williamsburg, Virginia, Steve once got himself lost in the garden maze at the Governor's Mansion. Started to blubber, yelled for help. Greg's voice answered out of the boxwood smell and hot white sky: "Where are you, Steve? Just tell us where you are!" Happy idiotic fan went back and forth, back and forth, back and forth. Twisted wire face on it looked like a gap-mouthed grin sometimes, and at

others like the blade-guard it was. Nice to come in from a shower
and lie down on the bunk naked and let the fan dry and cool you off
while you tried to slide your head out of the last mission—the blue-
green ocean of jungle, the village like an island in the sky reflecting
paddies, the roiling lines of black napalm smoke rising from the
targets they had just hit. Their stateroom was hot, anyway; as
junior officers he and Layton had the lousiest place to bunk—where
the air conditioning ducts ran too close to the steam and hot water
lines. Some nights it was so hot they went up to the squadron ready
room to sleep. There the air conditioning had the temp down
around fifty-five degrees. Wild dreams of snapping dogs (St. Ber-
nards) and snakes and a bitchy woman who kept lifting her long
black skirt to show her naked private parts to him. In another
dream he was in his bedroom at home, upstairs in this house, and
there was a big black snake on his bed and Mother was knocking
urgently on the door. The snake raised his head, smiled, and began
to talk like Franchot Tone.

In the ready room there was a lot of kidding around. A bull of a
guy named Sullivan gave a very bad porno calendar to a prissy
lieutenant commander who was rotating back to the States. The
guy was expecting a formal-type gift, something like a squadron
mug. Standing up there in front of everybody—big green and
brown Nam map behind him, spotlights glaring off his bald pink
head—he unrolled the calendar to a big color picture of a guy and a
broad going at it. He got a stupid grin on his face, shuffled his feet,
couldn't think what to say. Couldn't shift out of the formal-type
remarks he had all set in his head—the little speech about how
much it had meant to him to serve in the squadron and how there
was no finer group of men anywhere. After at least a minute of
suspense the guy said: "Thank you all very much. This means a lot
to me." Laughter. The place exploded. There was never anything
like it. Guys were on the floor. Some started honest-to-god crying. It
was at least five minutes before the ready room started to settle
down. Later heard that the lieutenant commander had, when he
got back to San Diego, found out that his wife had been doing a
number with a college kid. Beat the hell out of her. Broke bones.
Put her in sick bay. Left aching knots of complication in Steve's
belly, a brassy taste even now. For God's sake, why? Everybody had
laughed at the poor jerk. Along in here Steve and Layton decided

(silently) to keep the little fan running at all times. To never turn it off. Knowing even then it was dumb, acting like kids, but goddamn doing it anyway.

Over at Blair High School and out at College Park, Steve had avoided all the broads and talk about broads and the cold snarls that could be. Stayed clear of home, too—*this house* that always felt like the old lady's, like a puzzle he didn't want to bother with. Away from Greg's heavy raps to the old lady about A-pluses on his papers and Honor Society and being first string on the varsity basketball team. Away from the old lady's sweet whining at Dad on Friday nights when Dad got home from a week of traveling so tired he could hardly hold his head up over his dinner plate. Hunted. Pumped gas. Hung around out at the Rockville airport. Took flying lessons. But even when he soloed, when his head and nerves were full of all that and the emptiness of the sky and the steady drone of the engine, he hadn't been able to get outside the goddamn icy knots of complication. Not then, not with the stupid little fan on the Indy. . . . And not now damnit damnit damnit.

The senior guys in the squadron talked all the time about their wives and their forty-two thousand dollar houses ("Today I could get an easy fifty-five nine-fifty for it") and their kids in Little League and their kids with 94 averages in the academic course at Miramar High School. Like idiot TV families. They had wallets stuffed full of pictures they wanted to haul out and show you. Wife slim-looking, not bad. The kids in a staggered smiling row in front of a California ranch house. Regular issue pictures. Except for the house, the picture could have been of Steve's family (not his, really, but his old man's; not his yet, anyway). And the pictures would have been just as much a lie. Behind the old lady's smile she was scared of her own shadow, her eyes glazed over most of the time like she was going to cry. Greg—though mister good guy to everybody, was, behind that, like an autumn fly buzzing and zinging around, afraid to land anywhere. And Milly, Milly who always looked peppy and pretty, even in Christmas morning pictures—she's been doing her act so long, her Milly act, that she's forgotten (if she ever knew) where she's at. Dad's no-nonsense voice when he talked by phone to somebody at the office. Otherwise the old man was asleep in front of the TV or in his pajamas in the kitchen eating crackers and milk before going to bed. Dad was mostly gone, even when he was there.

But since getting wiped out by the stroke, he's had a different look to him—like down inside of him he has a huge belly laugh which is boiling, thickly churning, but he can't quite get it out. "Hey old man! What the hell is so funny?" He would look up from *Time,* his eyes warm with that secret joke of his. And that look and his silence would be his answer. Answer the same as the reason for the goddamn question! Steve's belly is wrung like the old lady used to wring out her dish towels. In the window behind Dad, the bare tree limbs jump in the November wind. Smells from the kitchen. The furnace running in the basement.

None of them believes Steve has a thought in his head. Dumb old Steve with his airplanes and *Sporting News* and *Playboy.* Hated *Siddhartha* and *The Invisible Man* which Milly and Greg went nuts over in high school. Knew before he made himself read them that he would hate them. Dumb happy-go-lucky Steve who aboard ship never said a serious word to those fakes (fools, too) who spouted off all the time about their wives and families and houses. Kidded them to keep them off his back, out of his way. Wanted none of that TV show garbage. Had gone into the Navy to get away from it. On the day he was commissioned at Kingsville, Texas, he married Daff in the Naval Air Station chapel. While he was aboard the *Independence,* she stayed with her folks in Clover, Mississippi. While out there, he sometimes forgot he was married—seemed more like a washy dream. Caught himself thinking home was this house in Bethesda, and not the big old country house in Mississippi where Daff was, and pregnant with their kid. Aboard ship he had a picture of her. Was taken by her old man in the wisteria arbor out behind their Mississippi house. She looked dreamy, sweet. Wisteria thick and blooming all around her. A few bees. All this he liked, though the old lady and old man and Greg and Milly would never for a minute believe he liked anything for being sweet. But he did, he did. Marrying Daff, that whole confusing nice mess, had to do with being then a NAVCAD at Pensacola, with the dusty wire-insulation smell of the trainer cockpits, and the blazing sun on the concrete of the flight line, on the aircraft, and with the sweat of PT and the sop of his uniform to his back when they marched in that terrific heat. Worse than Washington, D.C., worse than that. These and the smell of disinfectant as he swilled out the barracks toilets, and the drone and drone and drone of hours in the classroom where the navigation problems or details of engine design would slide in and out of focus, in and out of mind, as he struggled to stay awake and wanted to go to sleep.

Marrying Daff had to do with all that, with the fact that the guy who bunked next to him was Daff's brother William (not Bill) and with the cool oil and vinegar smell of the front hall at the Burnam's house, the deep shade of the woods which were thicker and greener than any he had ever walked through—doing this with her, Daff, who was content not to talk all the time, to let silences fill with the sounds of katydids, jays, crows, and the chatter of leaves, like their footprints in the sandbars along the creeks filling quickly with water as they hurried to firmer ground. These and the sweet urge he had when he was with her to run around on all fours barking like a dog, and to crawl under the porch into the dry dust there and sleep with the hounds, and—this later, when she was in her room, and he in his, the house dark around them—the urge to go out into the night woods behind the house to kill whatever it was lurking there. It was all this that became marrying Daff. And it was all this that made him hate the picture of her just because it was a picture (in a leather frame that kept tipping over, falling flat), and it got into Steve's head so much that when he thought of Daff he thought mainly of the picture of her in the wisteria arbor. All the crazy, wild insanity of the times with her, both before and after they got married, had begun to fade, dim behind that single stupid image snapped one afternoon out of a wisteria arbor. Christ.

One day (April 10th) Steve's bunkmate, Layton, picked up some bomb blast—didn't haul his A-7 up fast enough from a run that was too low for heavy ordnance anyway. Sloppy flying. Caught his own bomb blast, and the shrapnel began to tear the hell out of his turbine blades. Steve wasn't flying Layton's wing, but when the report crackled over the radio he and his wingman swung to the south to intersect Layton's course back to the ship. After managing to climb to about nine hundred feet, Layton started slowly to lose airspeed, altitude. Too low to punch out. Steve heard him report it, then saw Layton's A-7 down low, skimming the jungle. Layton said the aircraft felt like it was shaking itself to pieces. Over the radio Steve could hear the rattling behind Layton's pretty steady voice. Layton's wingman, a guy named Kraus, was down there with him, flying above and a little behind. When they crossed the coast

everybody knew Layton wasn't going to make it back to the ship.
Losing too much airspeed, altitude. The A-7 would take him into
the Gulf before that. The sea was fairly calm. A rescue helicopter
was already on the way from the carrier. For about five or six
minutes everybody held course, and there was a little chatter on the
radio. The ship reported a rendezvous with the helicopter in about
six minutes. Layton decided to drop into the sea while he still had a
little control. Said she was getting unresponsive, mushy. Steve
remembered the little fan in their stateroom—how it was going
back and forth, back and forth, regular as a heart beat. And remembers remembering. One night in Subic Bay he and Layton had
raised hell. Like he was in a lousy war movie, Layton took the O
Club singer back to his hotel room. Layton was from Wyoming, and
his old man was a preacher. Layton had been a tight end on the
University of Wyoming football team. Layton loved to play golf.
After Layton settled the A-7 into the sea, Steve and his wingman
and Kraus would fly a cap until the helicopter showed up. Back at
the ship they would all have a little brandy. Layton took the aircraft
down very slowly. His wingman talked him through the ditching
checklist. Nose high, good approach. Steve told him the helicopter
was in sight. Quiet on the radio. Just as he settled into the sea,
Layton mumbled something nobody understood. A terrific splash,
spray—no skim at all! Steve cut power, turned tightly, dropped the
port wing. Kraus was yelling, "You dumb shit!" The helicopter
wanted to know what had happened. Steve said, "O Christ." Layton's A-7 lay upside down, belly skyward in the churned-up sea
where it had gone in, evidently caught the big air intake, and been
violently flipped over on its back. If he had survived the impact (a
bad if, a bad if) and wasn't unconscious, Layton was now upside
down in a cockpit filling with sea water, and trying to clear all his
wet harness. Steve and the others held tight turns hoping to see a
bright raft or life-jacket bob up beside the plane. Nothing nothing
nothing. Just as the helicopter arrived, the A-7's nose reared up; the
sea had flooded in and now pulled the aircraft down tail first. The
canopy flashed in the sun. Then Steve saw the plane go beneath the
sea, leaving only a creamy white froth and big gasp-like bubbles of
air.

   In these churning memories he has drifted down to the basement
of the Bethesda house, and now he stands by the old Ping-Pong

table, bouncing the ball and hearing Milly overhead in the living room now, laughing and talking with Dad. The old lady stepping around briskly in the kitchen. And, distant, up on the second floor, a faint faint voice (Daff's). Very far away. Steve puts the Ping-Pong ball under a racket on the table. He steps over to the door which leads to the furnace room. He remembers the strange fascination this little room has always had for him. Used to hide in here. Goes in, shuts the door. The warm cement-dust smell. The oil. Does not flick the light switch. Opens the front panel of the furnace. The forced air fan is running, shoving the warm air up through the ducts. Steve flips off the firebox door, just as he did (in spite of threats of punishment) when he was a kid. For a few minutes he lets the flames inside play through the dark of the furnace room, be alive on his clothes and arms, warm his skin. The cold churn of recollections ceases for a while. Then feeling self-conscious he closes the firebox, the furnace, and goes upstairs to see if any of the games are on TV yet. His belly still feels tight—a long wait for Thanksgiving dinner.

Steve packed up Layton's gear. Rolled his mattress. When the squadron exec officer and a yeoman showed up to do the job (it was their duty), Steve ran them off. After Layton's gear had been stowed for shipment to Wyoming, Steve sat down at the desk and wrote a dumb letter to Layton's old man and old lady. The fan had not stopped swinging back and forth. When Steve came back from mailing the letter, he noticed the wisteria arbor picture of Daff. Without Layton's stuff on the desk, the picture jumped out at him. He picked it up, took it out on the catwalk, and pitched it into the night, the sea. Stood there a while. Slept that night on deck, under the belly of an aircraft. Just after dawn the next morning they were back at the same cluster of villages they had worked over the day before. Nothing but charred sticks and burned trees, but the AO on the ground said there was a network of tunnels and he wanted another strike. After again dumping all their ordnance on the village (no damage to aircraft this time) it looked just as burned and charred as it had looked when they started. More bomb craters was all. Eleven pilots were lost by the squadron, most of those in the Panhandle and when they did Hanoi-Haiphong. The senior guys in the squadron (the old maids) sat around with long faces deliberating on the politico-strategic implications of the raids into the North. All had done a tour at the War College, or some place like that, and thought they knew what they were talking about. But didn't; it was all hot air. Steve played Ping-Pong and poker. Went out on deck to see what kind of a night it was. Dropped down to the crew berthing compartments to find J. T. Smith, a black guy in ordnance who loaded aircraft. Was also from Washington, D.C., and liked to talk the Redskins and smoke Steve's Hong Kong Cuban cigars. (Once sent a box of these to the old man; his four sentence thank-you letter was the first letter from him Steve had ever received. Carried it in his flight suit for a couple of weeks.) When the mission was into the North, especially Hanoi-Haiphong, the old maids had a good many mechanical problems. Got scrubbed, or aborted back to the ship. At night in the wardroom mess the guy would do a big number about punk luck and lousy maintenance people. Silence. The click of utensils on heavy Navy china. Everybody afraid to meet anyone else's eyes. On those missions a bile taste in the back of Steve's throat. The rippling shiver when the Sams were reported. The urge to pee. The flopping lump in his belly when he wasn't precisely sure where he was unloading ordnance. Briefing and debriefing officers talking hard about military-industrial targets; words, goddamnit, didn't put the ordnance where it should be. Busy as hell, busy as hell with aircraft maintenance, TAC reports, all the mickey-mouse squadron duties. Busy, and in the cockpit letting himself think of nothing except the aircraft, his mission— *nothing else*—until the hook caught the cables and he climbed out, back on deck. Sappy tired then. But couldn't avoid the goddamn magazine pictures of bombed out hospitals, of dead kids being rocked in their old ladies' laps, of the villages, towns, torched and destroyed and made into black blots. Saw these from the cool unreal of the sky, too. Saw these with his own eyes. A province chief, his wife and kids, were just as dead after they'd had their throats laid open by the VC—the tendons white, the arc of the knife a bloody smile—as the families which were crushed or burned to death by the bombings. Maybe he'd swallowed U.S. propaganda about the VC. Maybe he'd swallowed VC propaganda about the U.S. Maybe none of the nightmare was true; maybe it was all twice as bad as he thought. Maybe . . . goddamn, goddamn word. Knots that made his fingers ache and his belly churn. Like now, like now.

Steve has come up from the basement, wandered into the den,

flipped on the TV. A college football game is on. He watches the play flow back and forth over the regularly spaced lines of the field, not exactly paying attention or not paying attention. Just there. Feels like he's forgotten something but can't remember what it is. The Venetian blinds are closed against the light outside. A Hollywood style war. Everything in a blur so that nothing seems real. Believed Layton had disappeared, not that he was dead, was dead. VC were killed and NVA and civilians—Steve knowing in his brain he had done it, taken it to them, but not *believing* that he had. Circuit never quite closed. Frayed insulation, sparks all over the place, but no completed connection between what he did in the closed cockpit (that familiar world which smelled vaguely of him) and what he saw on the ground or in the magazines in the wardroom. Seeing this now and remembering the way the old man spread a newspaper over the mouth of the fireplace, and the newspaper, the print, the pictures caught fire, burned out from the center until Dad had to drop it all.

Once caught a regular NVA battalion in a clump of jungle up near the DMZ. Hit them with heavy stuff and napalm until the bastards started to break and run across open ground. Chewed them up then with 20 mm while the jarheads on the ground did the same with small arms. Got excited as hell. Steve and his wingman (Huppleman, the new guy he bunked with) turned tight as hell at minimum airspeeds so they could work more passes over the field and drop more of the bastards into the dust. Dust an iron-red color—the same color as Maryland's clay. Felt lucky going back to the ship. Felt like it was a good day. The Marine CO sent a written commendation to the skipper. The skipper gave them a box of cigars. There was a Ping-Pong tournament, and Steve finished second behind a lanky kid from Cincinnati who had a real killer-type smash shot. Huppleman had the habit of taking showers in the middle of the night. Tossed and turned in his bunk for a couple of hours trying to get to sleep. Then he would get up, take a shower. One night Steve went into the head to check on him. See if he was okay. Huppleman was in the shower, but inside the splashing water sound there was the noise of him crying, blubbering like a baby. Without being seen Steve beat it out of the head. Never said anything to Huppleman.

For three weeks they had been operating continuously—not even a day off for bad weather—when one of the signalmen from the comm center rapped at the hatch to Steve's stateroom. It was 0430; he was up and dressing for an early hop. Huppleman had already left for chow. Steve saw, in the red-lighted passageway, the signalman's grin. The guy handed Steve a message: LTJG STEVEN L. PRICE 077283 VA-147 040868:1245 YOUR SON HAROLD JR. BORN THIS AM SEVEN POUNDS ELEVEN OUNCES BOTH DO-ING WELL COUNTY HOSPITAL CONGRATS JJ BURNHAM RR1 CLOVER MISS. The signalman remained in the passageway, grinning. Steve broke out one of the cheap cigars he had bought for the occasion and gave it to the guy, who then hustled off. Steve stuck the message in his pocket. He felt only sleepy. Daff and Mississippi and a baby seemed more something from a dream he was trying to remember in bits and snatches. Not something real. As he ate chow, sat through the briefing, did a close air support mission, Steve waited for the news to sink in. It never did. Back aboard ship he passed out the cigars anyway. It was the third time a guy in the squadron had become a father. Thinking of himself as a father was as dreamy and unreal as thinking there was a real kid somewhere who was his son. Short circuits. Feel even now this way—that the kid Daff has upstairs isn't really his, of his flesh and blood. One of the teams (Arkansas? Nebraska?) has scored a touchdown on a bomb-like pass. The TV shows the crowd jumping up and down, the football players jumping up and down. Everybody looks happy as hell. When Steve was born his old man was driving between Wash-ington and Richmond on old US 1; that road was a death trap. A path, a strip of red clay along the top of a dike, shooting by as he flies over—this sight in his mind. Something churning in his chest as he remembers that morning a few weeks after the telegram. Torching a VC village. Coming down in shallow dives, laying in the napalm and rockets, climbing back for another run. Just Steve and one of the old maids, Lt. Comdr. Jarvis. Steve had finished a drop and was pulling out to the right when he picked up some scurrying movement on the ground. Wiggling along one of the rice dikes. Radioed Jarvis that the VC were bugging out, using tunnels, and surfacing along the dike northwest of the village. Jarvis acknowledged. Diverted his run from the village to the dike and laid two rockets real close to what must've been the mouth of the tunnel. Red dirt in the explosion. Steve was coming around and down again. VC running like hell along the dike. Put the 20 mm on them (no more rockets). Saw one guy in black fold up like a rag doll. A little further down the dike—a running clump of them. Kept the 20 mm going. Saw them drop as the rounds caught up with them. Excited as hell by this time. Jarvis laid the rest of his rockets into what was left of the village and told the ground AO their ordnance was expended and they were returning to the ship. Steve told Jarvis he was going down for one more pass to see if anything moved. Looked pretty still. Dead VC where the rockets had hit. The long guy Steve had caught on the dike. Then he saw her—an old lady in plain sight on the dike. On her haunches. Around her the dead ones from Steve's last pass. On the old lady's lap a bundle of rags. As he approached she lifted her face and her fist—shook it at him as he passed overhead. Bright sunlight. Steve laughed: she had a hell of a lot of guts. Pulling up and starting his climb up to Jarvis, Steve realized—and again feels the rip of it on the couch in the den with the idiot TV football game on—that the thing in her lap had been a kid. A dead kid he must have got with his 20 mm. Also realized—this with the terrific jaw-locking sourness of then—that none of the dead had any weapons. *That he had not seen a single weapon.* Steve gets up, snaps off the TV. He remembers the time he was hunting down in Tidewater, Maryland, and fell into a shallow brick-walled well—the mossy smell, the cold slime up to his knees, the reverberations and echoes of his voice calling to the guy he was hunting with. The silence when the echoes died away. The debriefing officer said the VC did this kind of thing to undercut pilot morale. That the VC drove those civilians out of the tunnels just so the striking planes would waste them and then discover they were civilians. "Cuts our combat effectiveness. They know we don't like to kill women, kids. A damn low trick. Makes you sick to your stomach." Steve played basketball for three hours on the hangar deck with some enlisted guys. He heaved everything he had eaten all day into the urinal trough.

He almost stopped writing letters home to Daff. Greg, poor dumb Greg used to beg the old man to write a postcard home while he was out traveling; the old man would laugh, promise, and then Greg would spend the week clawing in the mail for a picture postcard which never came. Steve never begged the old man for anything. He wanted to ask, but didn't. In there, in the dining room, on a rainy Saturday night when nobody in the family was going out, nobody had anything to do, Steve told Dad that he (Dad) wouldn't know what was going on in the family because he was never home. Dad came straight out of his chair and across the table—it seemed so—and decked Steve, knocked him over backwards in his chair. Milly and Mother began to laugh, high and shrieky. The pain in his chest (where Dad hit him), and the pain in the back of his head (where the wall hit him) stung-ached pleasantly. Felt as if he had just awakened from years and years of sleep. Steve picked himself up, cocked his fists to take on the old man. Greg grabbed him from behind, pinned his arms, yelled, "Don't do it! Don't do anything dumb!" Never had he hated Greg so much, wanted to kill him so much. He struggled but couldn't free his arms. Greg laughed. Steve stormed out into the autumn night and ran and ran and ran through the streets of the neighborhood until his lungs ached. Spent the rest of the night in the furnace room. Sunday evenings the old man left for his business trips. The family had to drive him out to National Airport, but Steve didn't like to go. Didn't like the way he felt when the plane's red and green lights slid away, dropped into the night. Didn't like the way they all trooped silently back to the cold car. Hid or pretended he didn't hear when they called him to go to the airport. Didn't go with the others. Once after Greg and Milly and Mother had returned from the airport, Greg started in on Steve—how he was a rotten son and didn't give a damn about Dad and hurt Dad everytime he didn't go to the airport. Stepping out into the yard (it was dark, cold) Steve and Greg had the worst and bloodiest fight they ever had. It was Sunday evening. Milly finally discovered them and got Mother to break it up. Always after this there was a cool distance between Steve and Greg—too polite with each other. "How's it going?" "Not bad. You?" The churning in Steve's belly is bad as he passes through the kitchen and goes out to the driveway basketball set-up. He shoots baskets—long jump shots that mainly miss. The ball is too soft, needs air. He wonders if Greg can play basketball at the asylum. Greg was always better, ten times smoother and quicker than Steve. Steve begins to play harder, to dribble, to get a little sweat going. His belly eases a little.

A few days after the incident with the old lady and dead kid, the doc took Steve off flight status. Couldn't keep a damn thing on his stomach. Could be ulcers, nerves, both. Steve told the doc it wouldn't do any good for his nerves if he lay around while the squadron was flying. The doc arranged an R & R for him to Hong Kong. With a couple of other zoomies, Steve took the mail plane over to Subic, in the Philippines, and then caught a hop back to Hong Kong. Steve shacked up with a sweet bar girl he met in the Tiger Garden in Kowloon. Named Soo-loo, or something like that. She had a little two-room apartment that looked down on King Street. Had a cute kid, a baby named Lin who was a Eurasian. When Steve asked about the kid's old man, Soo-loo giggled. She showed Steve the sights—the cable car up the mountain behind Hong Kong, the junks and sampans over at Aberdeen. They had lunch in a floating restaurant. Spent a morning on the beach at Halfmoon Bay with the kid. Soo-loo looked skinny, ribby in a bathing suit. Did a couple of night clubs one night, but mostly stayed in the apartment, talking and laughing at the pidgin English they conversed in, playing with the kid. And eating—Steve ate and ate and ate. Steaks, fat hamburgers, mounds of Chinese stuff she fixed. Picked up some lost weight. Mornings Soo-loo spread a pink quilt in the sunlight on the floor in the front room, and put the baby on it to play. Reflected pink light touched everything, Lin, Soo-loo, even him. Steve loved to watch the kid, play with him. The last day Soo-loo helped him pick out some wool blankets for Harry Jr. and an alligator purse for Daff. She never carries it, uses it. Steve put $200 in the sugar can, and was sorry as hell to leave. Back on the *Independence*, the doc grinned when he weighed and checked Steve over. Huppleman had kept the electric fan running. Steve was put back on flight status. Went straight into a long series of runs into the North. Was okay, perfectly all right for the rest of the tour.

Feeling calmer now, and a little winded from the basketball, Steve is back in the kitchen. Mother is carving the turkey, laying back the richly brown skin, the thick white pieces steaming, smelling so good he can taste it. Dad used to carve the turkey, but no more, no more. Mother is saying she's sorry Greg couldn't be with them, but the hospital (she always calls it that, never asylum, never nuthouse) and the doctors had been adamant, and anyway they would all see him later this afternoon during visiting hours. Without pause she asks Steve to call Dad and Daff and Harold Jr. He walks through the dining room—Milly stands alone and sad-seeming at the picture window, looking out into the leafless limbs of the backyard. What's with her? In the living room Dad is still reading.

He now has a book on his lap. His left arm has fallen off the armrest and dangles loosely by the spoked wheels of the wheelchair. Hasn't realized it yet. Now from upstairs a sharp knocking and kathunking and scuttering noise. Blocks: Harold Jr. has kicked over, destroyed in frustration, whatever it was he was building with the blocks Mother had found for him in the attic. Steve's blocks? Greg's? Both? Daff is shushing him now, telling him to behave and not disturb his Granddaddy. In Steve's belly something starts to tremble, then pump fiercely. What the hell is this? Feeling about to choke, holding it down. Not let it out cause he might not be able to stop if he did. Prickly sweat. Dad hasn't looked up. Holding the back of the Queen Anne chair. Kicking over the blocks, hearing them fall, scutter on the bare floor. Snapping thoughts of loony Greg, of opening the firebox on the furnace. The clear urge—with the goddamn guilt of it—to start throwing chairs and lamps, to break up Mother's living room that drowns Dad like a bee in a jar of honey. Jams his fists down into his pockets.

"Dad," he says, his voice sounding peculiar, almost damn weepy. "Dad?"

Dad looks up from his book and realizes with a flick of embarrassment that his arm is hanging limp. He reaches over with his other hand, and replaces the arm on the wheelchair armrest. Paralyzed at fifty, but his eyes again bright with that supersize joke he has down inside of him.

"Dad?" Prickles up Steve's spine, out over his shoulders—like a child's sick nightmare. This voice, his voice, sounds like it is asking a question, almost pleading, not calling Dad for Thanksgiving dinner. For god's sake, what question!? Jesus Christ!

"We're ready to eat," Steve says to the floor. "Dinner's ready."

"Smells good," Dad says, slurring.

Steve feels at the edge of sick as he goes into the front hall. Looking into the dining room—Milly is gone—he sees the golden turkey, the steam rising from the bowls of peas and dressing and gravy. The bile taste is in his mouth.

He looks up the tight closed stairway. He hears the quiet song of Daff's voice talking to the child. He calls to them, trying to sound good-natured, but with some trembling and thickness still in his voice: "You all come and eat. Thanksgiving dinner is ready."

More sweeps of warm prickles up his spine.

Daff answers cheerfully, and for an instant he despises her for being that way. He hears her soft voice speak to the child, and the two of them start to come down the upstairs hall from the sewing room. Dad wheels into view. Mother comes in from the kitchen, her bright brave smile already in place. Milly follows, chattering to fill up the silences.

Steve goes into the dining room, the sick feeling trembling his belly, the taste of bile at the back of his throat—fear: goddamn taste of fear. Of what? Of what? Of nothing, he thinks, and therefore as pure as you can get. He hopes to hell he can eat some Thanksgiving dinner; he hopes to hell he won't have to make up a reason why he can't eat it. Daff and the child, talking about turkey-lurkey, are coming down the stairs.

# The Janeites

$M$r. Owen is reading *Emma*, his favorite book. He has, in fact, been reviewing it for several days so that the details will be fresh in his mind for this afternoon's meeting. He has laid the book open on the kitchen table, and when he runs across a passage he thinks his wife would like, he reads it aloud.

"'Human nature is so well disposed toward those who are in interesting situations,'" he says, "'that a young person, who either marries or dies, is sure to be kindly spoken of.' You remember this now, don't you, Alma? Mr. Elton is going to marry Augusta Hawkins, and she'll become Mrs. Elton. I know you'll remember her— the odious Mrs. Elton?"

Alma looks at him for a moment, sets her mouth in a tiny O, then looks away.

"She's the one like Mrs. Salesby," Mr. Owen says. "Remember Mrs. Salesby?"

Mrs. Salesby was a neighbor of theirs years ago, whom Alma one day had decided was Mrs. Elton in the flesh. A vulgar woman, contemptuous of everyone except her family, she possessed a wealthy sister, whom no one ever saw but about whom she talked constantly. "The people she has working for her," she would say. "Why, I really *don't* think she knows how many there *are*, exactly: oh, not that they're numberless, of course. You shouldn't think *that*" (with a laugh) "but there are some—in the *nether* regions, so to speak—whom she has never seen. 'They also serve who only stand' as *Shake*speare said." And Alma's eyes would widen with amusement as she listened, standing there on the front steps of the house and pulling her sweater tightly around her, and in the evenings—after their daughters were asleep and they had finished the dishes and done whatever reading they had—she would sometimes imitate Mrs. Salesby: "But my *dear,* so much *mon*ey, and all in*her*ited, of *course.* Her husband's never earned a *pen*ny of it, not *he!*" The odious Mrs. Salesby.

Mr. Owen looks at his wife: her eyes appear dilated, and there is no clear separation between the blue and the white. Her eyes are the colors of the Dutch tiles lined up on the shelf behind her head, and her white hair—chopped short and in straight bangs—makes her look like a little Dutch girl grown suddenly old.

Mrs. Armstrong, who has been putting dishes in the cabinet, comes and stands at the table and holds out three pills: one round and white, one white with a red band, one orange (shaped, Dr. Sandys observed, like a tiny football). Mr. Owen takes the white pill and holds it to Alma's mouth, which opens instantly in a way which reminds him of the games they played when their daughters were children. (*Here comes the airplane,* he or Alma would say. *Zoom, zoom! Where is the airport? Where is the hangar?* And Randall, or Eleanor, would open her mouth and receive the Cream of Wheat, or the single green bean stuck to the prongs of a tiny fork.) He places the pill on Alma's tongue and holds the glass of water to her lips, and before she drinks, her eyes almost focus on him, but then her face goes blank again and she swallows. He gives her the red and white pill and, as Mrs. Armstrong turns away, puts the orange one in his shirt pocket. When he touches his wife, she seems to understand who he is.

"Good girl," Mrs. Armstrong says when she turns back to them. ("So well named," Mr. Owen told Alma when they hired Mrs. Armstrong and Alma could still appreciate some of what he said. "I imagine her in front of mirrors, grimace and groan, admiring her own biceps.") Now she is a necessary third in their household and no longer anyone to laugh at.

"'The charming Augusta Hawkins,'" he continues, "'in addition to all the usual advantages of perfect beauty and merit, was in possession of an independent fortune, of so many thousands as would always be called ten.' 'The *usual* advantages,' " he repeats. "A wonderful touch. I've never noticed it before."

Later that morning, Mr. Owen sits at the desk in the living room, writing a letter to Randall and Eleanor. He writes the same message to both, copying each paragraph, as he finishes it, from one sheet of stationery to another. "I think your mother still enjoys the reading at breakfast: I'm not so sure about Mrs. Armstrong. I thought she would leave us over Proust, such clearing of throat and heaving of shoulders. I *do* skip passages until I find something your mother might enjoy. Perhaps that disturbs Mrs. Armstrong's natural sense of continuity, or perhaps it's just impatience. She is truly wonderful for us, though. She cooks, cleans, even handles your mother's medicine to make certain I don't forget. Dr. Sandys insisted on that when she came to us. She hoards it up and parcels it out like candy."

He wants to avoid writing about their mother's condition. He wants Randall and Eleanor to feel cheered by everything he has to say, as if he were telling them an interesting story.

"We are thriving," he writes. "Your mother and I have lived together for forty years with very little to vex or disturb us." He knows Eleanor will hear the echo from *Emma*—Randall will merely think the words sound old-fashioned—but he doesn't write it just to give his younger daughter the pleasure of recognition. He always tries to think of his life that way. He and Alma *have* had no serious problems—minor illnesses, both theirs and their daughters, financial problems in the early 1950s when he decided to return to college—but nothing until now has been more than temporarily perturbing. "I can still manage," he writes. "I have a firm grip on everything. I manage to keep myself occupied."

He hesitates to mention the Society. To his daughters and their husbands—Randall in California, Eleanor north and east of there near Helena, Montana—the Society seems like very little. "I wish you hadn't given up golf," Randall said recently. "There are people in Richmond who golf, I know." Her voice over the phone is always strident, as if she can't accept the 3000 miles between her father and herself and wants the fervor of her words to pull him closer. And even Eleanor, witty like her mother and yet mild and preoccupied, wrote in a letter recently that she was happy he enjoyed the

Society but didn't he think he should get away more? "Once every other month," she said, and he could feel her attention wandering even on the blue note paper. "Only six times a year. That's hardly enough to say it's anything."

He can't think how to tell them that the Society is all he wants now, how to confide in them at all, to tell them how the diminishing of everything seems right to him. Whenever he thinks of his daughters, in fact, he is reminded how distant, how unreal, *their* lives are to *him*, how much more vivid the two of them are in photographs, Randall behind a huge bouquet of roses at the Academy graduation, Eleanor posed over the piano keyboard in the den of the house they sold fifteen years ago.

He looks at the two pieces of stationery on the desk top. He has written less than half a page, but he can think of nothing more to say. He decides that he will have more to tell them in the evening, and he folds both sheets of paper and slips them into one of the pigeon holes at the back of the desk.

After lunch, when he is sure Alma is safely in bed, he leaves the apartment and walks the three blocks to the bus stop. The last block lies beyond the area he is familiar with, but he has the bus schedule in his pocket and knows exactly when he can board and where he will get off, so he is not anxious. Once he gets to the Club, he will again be on familiar ground. He thinks of himself as moving from island to island, the bus like a benign ship over which he has to exercise no control.

At the stop a large unpleasant-looking woman is already sitting on the bench. Mr. Owen prepares to speak to her, but she glances at him and then shuts her eyes. She is wearing a black straw hat and a purple dress with a slip strap white against her arm, and she is apparently living out an interior scene of some consequence to herself, even of some violence, for she occasionally bites her lip and sits forward as if she wants to say something. Once she speaks— "And I'd just like him to *try!*"—but catches herself before saying more, then turns her massive back to Mr. Owen.

When the bus pulls to the curb, he isn't surprised that the woman shoves ahead, grabs both metal bars, and then heaves herself up the steps as if no one else is waiting to board. He tries to think of the name of the woman in *Persuasion* whose substantial size (he can almost quote the description) makes her comic even when she is weeping for her scapegrace son, but the name will not come to him.

There are two black boys on the bus, young men really. One is wearing a cap, and the other is wearing a felt hat with the front brim turned up. They are sitting on the back seat with their radio, a large silver and grey box with two round speakers like saucers, between them. The volume is so high that the bus seems to have room for nothing besides the sound. Mr. Owen can tell by the stiff set of the driver's back that *he* will not do anything about the noise. The other people on the bus—the fat woman, two younger women, a man who looks disreputable despite his coat and tie (an unsuccessful salesman, Mr. Owen guesses)—cluster near the front. Everyone seems determined to pretend the music isn't there.

Seated, Mr. Owen unfolds the notice of today's meeting: it is printed on heavy cream paper with Anna Lefroy's drawing of Chawton Cottage at the top. "At October's meeting," he reads, "we'll enjoy something different, a general discussion of *Emma*. Come prepared to speak about any of the characters. We want a lively discussion." The notice says that Professor Mary Sturm from the University will read a paper. He has never heard of Professor Mary Sturm, but he has hopes despite her name. Her paper is entitled "A Defense of Mrs. Elton." Mr. Owen enjoys irony, and he looks forward to Professor Sturm's brand.

He himself has thought of some interesting things to say about Mrs. Elton. She has long been a favorite villainess of his. When he tries to imagine her now, he sees Mrs. Salesby again, and he remembers when Alma first saw the resemblance: "I think she must have read the book," Alma said. "I think she models herself after Mrs. Elton on purpose. She has some devious purpose in mind we can't begin to *guess* at." Mr. Owen decides the other members of the Society would like to hear about Mrs. Salesby.

As the bus gets closer to the University, several more people get on, but no one gets off. Outside, through the windows, the houses grow larger and statelier, and he sees people walking, singly or in twos or threes, along the sidewalks, in a way they never do around his apartment building. Because of the loud music in the bus, he imagines the people outside walking in silence, or whispering to one another. The bus passes the Museum, and he begins to look for the

Civil War monuments which tell him he is near the University. After that, he will be at the Club. He thinks of how quiet it will be there.

When the two boys exit, suddenly and jerkily, disturbing the old men and the pigeons in the tiny park which stretches out from the bus door, the bus seems empty and hollow. The boys were not so bad, he decides—silly and thoughtless, but not bad. He watches them, shoving at each other and laughing, until the bus moves forward and leaves them behind.

As he expected, the Club meeting room is quiet. He takes a seat on the second row. Only a few members are here before him, and he recognizes them all. The only other man is Mr. Asquith, whose wife leads him into and out of every meeting like a sad, obedient dog. Mr. Owen has never heard him speak—though *Mrs.* Asquith is quite vocal—but there is always in his face a look of resigned disagreement with everything anyone says. Mr. Owen nods to Mrs. Beatty, tightly done up today in brown wool with what looks like a cameo at her throat, and to Mrs. McAteer, who wiggles her fingers beside her cheek in response. He remembers that the fat woman in *Persuasion* is Mrs. Musgrove.

At the front of the paneled room are a long table and a lectern, from the top of which an empty microphone holder hooks meaninglessly into the air. Mrs. Arnold, the day's moderator, comes in a side door with a thin woman in red, obviously Professor Mary Sturm, and the two of them stand talking at the table while Mrs. Arnold eyes the flexible microphone neck with disapproval and Professor Sturm glances down at the notebook she has placed on the table top.

As he looks at Professor Sturm, his enthusiasm for the discussion wanes. She is a tall woman with a protruding chin. Her dress looks too big for her, and her black hair is already falling from the loose twist on the back of her head. She looks like someone who wouldn't enjoy reading Jane Austen, let alone talking about her.

Most of the other people who begin to fill up the room are familiar to him, the sort of people who relish the novels they're here to discuss. He wonders what Alma would say about Professor Sturm: *We should really give her a chance, don't you think? Still. . . .* For the first few months of his membership he brought Alma to the meetings and she was able to understand some of what was said. There followed several months when, although Alma stayed home, he took notes to share with her in the evening. Now he doesn't do that.

Mrs. Arnold introduces Professor Sturm. "A wonderful opportunity," she says, "to hear a true scholar share with us her interesting—and I think you will find 'provocative'—ideas about Miss Austen." Mrs. Arnold clears her throat, as if she wants to say more, then pulls the offending neck of the microphone stand down and forward. "I know you'll listen eagerly to what she has to say." Mr. Owen is reminded of a teacher telling her children to be polite.

When she begins to speak, Professor Sturm pitches her voice so low that Mr. Owen has to lean forward and cup his hand behind his ear to make out the words. She is so clearly uncomfortable that Mr. Owen begins to feel sorry for her. He tries to catch her eye so that he can nod reassuringly, but she fixes her gaze on the paper she is reading.

As she reads, though, she grows calmer. After some introductory comments—how critics have responded to *Emma*—she begins summarizing the plot, and Mr. Owen sits back. The material is so familiar to him that he needn't pay close attention; he enjoys the sensation of being reminded of what he already knows, and he begins to feel grateful to the speaker and sorry for his first reaction to her. Then, however, without any warning, she begins speaking nonsense: "And it is this Mrs. Elton who has been universally despised by Austen's critics. But is there really any difference in the final analysis between Mrs. Elton and any other character in the novel? Is she really worse than the heroine, in fact? If she violates the norms of the society depicted in the novel, isn't it possible that the norms, indeed the society, are corrupt and her violence against them—despite her own lack of self-knowledge—is justified."

Mr. Owen thinks he has misunderstood, for no one else looks disturbed. Mrs. Arnold has her eyes fixed on something in the back of the room which she seems to find mildly hypnotic. To the left of him Mrs. Beatty plays absentmindedly with her cameo; to his right Mrs. McAteer is looking at her hands folded in her lap.

Professor Sturm talks about each character in the novel. Everyone, according to her, is caught in a vile world whose standards of order and taste corrupt and dehumanize. The things she says seem so wrong to Mr. Owen that he tries not to listen: he tries to think of something else instead. But her voice, which has grown louder, is as insistent as the music on the bus.

"And so Mrs. Elton only *seems* vulgar to a reader who identifies him/herself with a landed gentry—and perhaps to that part of Austen attached through rudimentary longing to such a world. But Mrs. Elton's vulgarity is, in fact, the energetic challenge to the complacency which lulls, which in fact deadens, the other characters. She is Austen's clearer self attacking a world Austen herself could no longer embrace: a world smug and decadent, ripe for change or death, no longer attached to any reality outside the minds of snobs." Mr. Owen feels as if the woman has walked directly up to him and spat in his face.

When she sits down, there is applause, but when Mrs. Arnold asks for questions, no one responds. "No questions?" she says. "I can't believe it." She turns to Professor Sturm. "They're usually very talkative," she says, as if she were discussing a classroom of children. "You've given us a lot to think about." Professor Sturm smiles in a way which shows she agrees.

Because someone has to reply, Mr. Owen stands up. "I have a question," he says, but he cannot think yet exactly what it is. Everyone watches him, and Mr. Asquith, still the only other man in the room, smiles—surprisingly—as if something pleasant has happened.

"I don't see how you can believe any of that," Mr. Owen thinks at last to say. "We knew someone just like Mrs. Elton, and she was rude and loud-mouthed. A braggart, that's what she really was. She always had to tell us how much better she was than anyone else, when all along we knew we were—I know it sounds wrong to say this—better than she. I can't describe her manners." He pauses, and everyone in the room looks at him. He knows they expect a question, but he cannot attach his indignation to any idea. His mind will not connect anything. "I just wish my wife could be here to show you how vulgar she was and how. . . . The point is she was just like Mrs. Elton and it *matters* that she not be. . . ." But what should she not be? Accepted? Defended? He hasn't said what he wants to say. It is something else that matters, something entirely different.

"I'm not sure what your question is," Professor Sturm says, "but I *am* sure that vulgarity isn't as bad as it's cracked up to be." She pauses for the laughter her remark calls forth, and Mr. Owen realizes everyone is grateful to her for relieving the embarrassment he has caused. "I'm also sure a life spent merely avoiding vulgarity isn't good enough. I think Austen would agree with me."

When he fails to sit down, Mrs. Arnold tells him that she has asked for questions and if he has one, she's certain Professor Sturm will be happy to respond. She adds that Professor Sturm has to leave in a few minutes and then the Society members will have a general discussion. "Perhaps," she says, "you could save your own comments for then."

"You don't know, do you?" he says. He is speaking to Professor Sturm. "You don't know how anything you say touches something else, do you? In what other people care about? That's my question." Professor Sturm's face has grown blank, as if he has committed a blunder she chooses to ignore, and, when he looks all around him, the faces of the people he knows grow blank also. Their expressions erased, they hold their heads still in the neutral air, waiting.

The bus ride home is uneventful, and he thinks, not about the Society meeting, but about something else, like a page from a novel:

"There's nothing we can do," Dr. Sandys told him. "I could send you somewhere, to a neurosurgeon or the University hospital, but there's nothing anyone can do. She'll get worse, more and more confused. There's just nothing. Look," he said. He held a book open and showed Mr. Owen a picture. "It's what happens in the brain. Here, the synapses allow connections: little electrical impulses jump back and forth and carry signals. Here they can't do that. You can see why."

To Mr. Owen both pictures looked like nothing which could be important to him or Alma. They were black and white and they depicted what looked like coral or fungus, nothing that either he or Alma could care about. He could not imagine the picture having anything to do with Alma's brain. He could not understand how the shredded fungus in the picture could mean anything.

"Here," Dr. Sandys continued. "I'm giving her three prescriptions and some samples. First, a tranquilizer, very mild. This second one is mostly phenobarbitol, to prevent seizures. And this is amitriptyline. It's an anti-depressant. Make certain she only has one each day: they're very powerful!" He held his palm open so that

Mr. Owen could look at the oddly shaped pill. "Doesn't it remind you of a little orange football?"

Mr. Owen drove Alma into the city. There was a drugstore which had been there when they were children and which had been restored to look the way it had then. They sat in wirebacked chairs at a small marble topped table and ate ice cream. The smell of the drugstore was disinfectant and alcohol, like the doctor's office.

"I'm sorry," Alma said. "I feel as if I'm moving in and out of the sunlight. It's hard sometimes to remember what things are and what I should do with them."

She held up her spoon. "Fork," she said. And they both laughed as if she had never in her life said anything more clever.

"She had a restless afternoon," Mrs. Armstrong says. "I think she knew you were gone." She puts Alma to bed at 8:00 and then goes to her own room, and Mr. Owen can hear the sound of her television set through the wall.

When he thinks it is safe, he opens the drawer of the sideboard. Under the linen tablecloths, which they no longer use, is a small mahogany box, divided into two sections, for two decks of cards. Only one side, however, contains cards: in the other are several orange pills—he counts twenty-two. He has averaged keeping one out of every three Mrs. Armstrong has given him, and he has been building the collection for two months, ever since he decided what to do. He drops in the twenty-third pill: in less than two more months, before Christmas, he will have forty, twenty for Alma and twenty for himself.

He is tired but wants to finish his letter before he goes to bed.

"I had an interesting day," he writes. "I rode the bus to the Society meeting: that always makes me feel like someone on a boat being taken somewhere nice. There was a woman—a large woman, all wrapped up in purple like Lent—who reminded me of Mrs. Musgrove in *Persuasion:* I suppose I had Jane Austen on my mind. There were two boys on the bus who were more active than the rest of us could live up to. They reminded me of you girls as children, full of noise and mischief. At the meeting a woman from the University said some outrageous things, but I think I set her straight (not as well as your mother would have done, of course). I told her about Mrs. Salesby—do you remember our old neighbor?—and I explained how she was like the characters Jane Austen clearly despises. I think the University woman saw my point, though maybe *she* was too much like Mrs. Salesby herself. Both *very* vulgar women."

He hears the footsteps before Alma appears at the entrance to the living room. He watches her as she goes to the mirror and looks at herself. Then he gets up and walks to her side. The two of them in the mirror, with the single lamp burning, look very old, older than they are. Alma's face is puzzled, and she starts making little whimpering noises as she stares at her reflection.

He takes her arm and, when she tries to pull away from him, grasps her by the elbow and begins to guide her around the room. In a few minutes, he knows, she will grow calm and he can take her back to her bed.

He imagines they are strolling along a sidewalk, passing other couples. The sun is shining, but there is a cool breeze. Something significant has happened which they do not yet understand, and the two of them are enjoying a well-deserved rest. They lean towards each other and whisper. Their conversation probes the meaning of whatever it is they have experienced, and through their talk they begin to see the pattern in what has occurred. When they tire of walking, they will go into one of the stately houses set back from the street on green lawns. He imagines that the rooms will be white with high ceilings: he cannot imagine any furniture, or any sound. The rooms will be very quiet, empty like the pages at the ends of all the books they have ever read. He realizes that he yearns for the emptiness.

As Alma's restlessness subsides, she begins touching everything they pass—the roll-top desk, the back of the wing chair, the arms of the sofa. Then, as he leads her out of the room, she opens and closes her hand along the smooth wall, as if there might be something there to clutch.

# A Mechanic's Life

How's your martini?" she asked.

He nodded and brought the glass to his lips. The pale, near colorless liquid mirrored the hill across from the terrace. He drank the view. He could almost taste the spruce trees, the pond, the road down to the village as the whole prospect passed across his palate like a savory.

His wife had shrugged and sipped some wine and leaned forward to hug herself as if to give him more time in his reverie, but then, with a shift of feet, she returned to their conversation. "You have so much machinery already." Her voice was almost casual. "How did you know he wanted to sell it?"

"Little Bink called me. His father had asked him to call me. It's in first-class condition, you can be sure of that. After all it was Bink Card's own brush cutter, and he only used it to keep down the fence lines. And he serviced it himself. I really need it to keep down the brush from around these spruce trees." He gestured toward the hillside. "The slope is too steep for the tractor."

"How much was it?" she asked, lighting a cigarette, one of the unfiltered kind that she continued to smoke, though he had stopped all tobacco use years before.

"Only five hundred dollars," he replied, thinking how easy her questions were to answer. That hillside, for the first time since they had lived here, would now really look right. He would be able to control the undergrowth. "The same machine with attachments costs three or four times that brand new," he continued as he took a handful of peanuts. "Also, now that he's in the hospital, old Bink needs the money. There are a lot of things I'll be able to do with it. I really do need it."

His wife had turned her gaze upon the hillside. There was a search in her expression, an old bemused search of familiar ground, as if she might come across something she had never seen there but, at the same time, did not expect to find. Since they moved to this old farm ten years before, she had returned to the city almost once a week. He used to think she was having an affair, even half-enjoyed the idea, for it made her more glamorous to him, more interesting, so it was with a strange disappointment that he discovered the hairdresser appointments and theatre matinees were alibis laid down to cover long and pointless walks through the city's streets rather than some passionate assignation.

"Well, that's fine," she said, letting the cigarette smoke drift from her lips. "Of course you do need it."

He remembered her saying this when he bought the cultivator, his first piece of genuine equipment. He did not count the lawn-mower, though it had been his first machinery purchase, because the lawnmower was the sort of cosmetic appliance that could be found on any suburban lawn and not at all in the same category with the cultivator nor the powered snow thrower and certainly not the high-wheeled tractor that occupied most of the space in the small barn. But the cultivator was still his favorite; it could turn and modify the soil. Its Saracen blades sliced through the earth's helm to transform an old feed lot into a sultan's paradise. He had always planted gardens that were too abundant.

When he would appear at the back door with baskets of green beans and squash, eggplant, and Brussels sprouts or onions, his wife would say, "What am I supposed to do with all these?" The tomatoes seemed to depress her even more. She would let them grow soft in their casual pyramids on the back-room bench until they had been compressed and juiced by their own weight. She had tried to can some, to freeze some of the other vegetables, but, in the end, he stopped looking for easier recipes for her to try and reduced the variety and number of vegetables to be planted, though the area of the garden remained the same, the blades of the powerful cultivator churning and chopping the same plot of ground he had originally fenced off.

"I haven't seen Little Bink in a long time," she said with a final drag on her cigarette. She only smoked it halfway down, a habit originally meant to appease his criticism.

"He'll be taking over the machine shop now. He's done most of the heavy work for his father the last couple of years anyway." In fact, the younger Card had not called him about the brush cutter, as he had told her, but it had been the other way around. He had called Little Bink when he heard the old man had become seriously ill, had been hospitalized. He mentioned the young man's name to confuse her opposition to his new purchase.

Little Bink had been an inventive kid in high school, using his father's tools, and particularly the welding equipment, to fashion weird and wonderful constructions from the scrap and parts of machinery that littered the Card place. They could easily pass for modern sculpture. His wife had taken an interest in Little Bink, tried to get special attention for him at the local school, even spoke to a friend of hers at the Art Students League, but it came to nothing when the boy dropped out of school and into the oily darkness of his father's machine shop. Some weeks later, after some special apprenticeship, he showed up at a church supper with his left hand completely bandaged; he had crushed his fingers in a power press. The old man had lost several fingers, walked with a stoop, and bore numerous scars on his body as though the machinery he repaired had become impatient, had turned and nipped him as he worked over it.

The boy even looked different, something in his eyes when they met him, a note of suppressed laughter, as if he had played some outrageous joke upon them but they would never know its nature. It was about then that his wife began going to the city.

"It's so wonderfully peaceful here," he said to her. He fished for the olive at the bottom of his cocktail glass. "You don't know what it means to me to get back here and just soak up this silence, savor this—this peace."

"Yes, it is peaceful," she said and stood up. "Bring in the glasses will you. It's time we have something to eat."

*       *       *

The next morning he backed the old pickup truck out of the barn. It was a rolling testament to Bink Card's ingenuity; he had welded its rusts together and kept it going long after it should have been junked, and, as the man settled into the lumpy seat behind the wheel, he was overcome with an appreciation for Card's skill and craftmanship. It was to signal this feeling, as well as to wave to his wife if she were looking out the window, that he raised his hand in a cavalier salute and tapped the horn button as he passed down their driveway.

"Bink Card is the last of an American breed," he would tell weekend guests. Some excuse would be found, perhaps a broken axe handle, to take these friends down to the country garage so they could observe a native genius in action. Sometimes on the long plane trips that were a part of his life, he would find himself talking about Bink Card to the stranger in the next seat, about how he could fix anything, put anything right while at the same time delivering a salty commentary on the times, local personalities, or women. "Bink Card said," became a familiar prefix for the pithy remarks he had heard at the man's garage. He would repeat them to his wife, claiming some of them to be folklore, almost. But she would never laugh.

"You know very well," she would say, "that if anyone else said things like that, you would call them a bigot. He's nothing more than a mean-spirited, dirty old man." She was still angry about losing the contest for Little Bink.

Even now, as he rounded the curve in the road, he half expected to see the familiar figure standing in the open doorway of the ramshackle garage, the black metal mask tipped up on his head and a cigarette smoking in one hand, like the acetyline torch he held in the other needed help. But it was Little Bink who waited for him there now.

He turned the pickup off the highway and onto the dirt road that always looked to him like the path of a beaten but glorious army. Broken machinery lay in the weeds on both sides, parts of combines and threshers, tractors and cutters—all left behind under a camouflage of rust. The farm wagon Little Bink was spraying with paint had been salvaged from this junk, had been put together from this junk by Bink Card, and had been, no doubt, his last piece of work before he had been taken to the hospital. Two-inch oak planks had been bolted to the chasis of a three-ton truck, and the tongue assembly and front axle of a manure spreader had been fixed to the front. The whole rig was being painted a brilliant yellow, the wheels were already an unearthly green, and the two colors set up a vibration in the morning light that hurt the man's eyes. The boy continued to operate the spray gun, the unhurried motion of his arm conducting an even coat of paint to wood and metal, and the glistening pigment accumulated on the rusted bolt heads, the joints, and hardened seams of manure until the whole assembly resembled a bizarre confection. Little Bink had not turned to greet him nor did he pause when the truck stopped nor did he acknowledge the older man as he got out of the ancient pickup. It was as if there were some point on the wagon frame where the different films of paint would be joined and that everything, everyone would have to wait until he methodically reached that point which was known only to him. The man leaned against the fender of his truck to wait his turn, even enjoying the idea that he had a turn in the younger man's schedule. He studied the manufacture of the wagon and could see the new enamel-covered faults and corrosion that should have been restored before they were painted over and wondered if Bink Card had had only time enough to teach his son a few of his skills, those with the paint sprayer and the acetylene torch.

Abruptly, Little Bink stopped the spray gun and walked to the barn, holding the coils of hose to one side. The compressor was shut off. It was suddenly very quiet. A herd of black-and-white cows moved slowly across a distant field like pieces of torn paper adrift on a dark pond. The young man reappeared in the wide doorway. He stood there, blinking like his father as if he had just come up for air, or for light, and even held a cigarette the same way, fingers together and chest high in the elegant pose of a woodchuck by its hole.

"Nice looking wagon," the man said. Little Bink sucked on his cigarette and smiled, suggesting there had been no point telling him something he already knew. "How's your dad?"

"Coming along," he answered. His voice was higher than his father's, nor did he resemble him much. His hair and complexion were very light, so light that his face looked bald, without eyebrows or hairline. "His kidneys aren't so good." It sounded like he talked of a worn part, the flaw in a transmission.

"Well, if there's anything we can do," the man stopped because Little Bink had smiled again, that same sidewise smile he seemed to reserve for them when they met. "So here she is," the man turned and quickly crossed the yard to the brush cutter. "Here she is," he repeated and tentatively touched one of the hand grips.

The brush cutter looked like something Bink Card might have thrown together on a Sunday afternoon, using a week's spare parts, but this was the way it was supposed to look. This was the way it looked in every catalog, the way it appeared in every showroom, and that was the beauty of it, the man reminded himself, because the original design had been so perfect that no changes had ever been made. There were no frivolous fenders over the two substantial wheels, no tinny cowling around its engine; nothing had been put on the machine that was not directly geared to its function of heavy duty work. The mechanical construction was frankly exposed and was the embodiment of raw power. He grasped the two shafts by which it was steered. It was so perfectly balanced on its two wheels that he could raise its seven hundred pounds with only the slightest pressure, could see-saw the whole rig on the axle's fulcrum, so that the horizontal cutting bar lifted like the jaw of a hammerhead shark against the soft gray belly of morning.

"Boy, she's a real man-killer, isn't she?" the man said exultantly. . It was a description of the machine he had heard others make.

"She'll get the work done, no question," Little Bink said. "But you got to let the machine do it. Don't try to push it or wrestle with her. That paragon gear onto it drives her at its own speed, no more, no less. You can't rush her or turn her by force. She's in A-one shape too. Pap used it only to keep down the fence lines."

"Yes, you told me that," the man replied. "But I guess she'll cut through almost anything."

"Well, I've seen her go through a stand of inch-and-a-half maples like they was straw."

"Inch-and-a-half, think of that," the new owner said. He knelt and pulled out the dip stick to check the oil level.

"Sumac, of course," the boy continued, "why, hell, she'll take on three inches without a whimper."

"Sumac, three inches," the man repeated. He inspected the cables that went from the battery to the ground and to another part; the starter probably. "And the beauty of it," he said, "is that it's all right out here in the open; easy to get at, easy to fix—if there's a need to. Well, here." He stood up and took a folded check from his pocket and handed it to Little Bink. The amount was for a hundred dollars more than he had told his wife.

The boy carefully inspected the check, as though it was the first sort of paper he had even seen. "Is it all right?" the man asked, after a bit. Little Bink nodded and smiled, then tucked the check into the top pocket of his coveralls. They pulled a couple of heavy boards out of the weeds and placed them against the edge of the pick-up's bed. Little Bink stretched out a toe in the graceful attitude of a dancer, the man thought, and touched the starter button fixed near the drive-chain. The engine coughed and started instantly.

The boy adjusted the throttle on one of the steering shafts and let the machine idle while he returned to the barn to retrieve loose tools. He replaced them on the proper racks inside. The noise of the engine, only partially muffled, carved out a wondrous space around the new owner to put him in a joyous isolation from the day and from all men. He could not yet believe that he owned this machine. He tried to imagine the glistening parts working smoothly within the roar; tried to picture them, tried—within the limits of his ex-pertise—to name them.

The two men made no effort to talk above the engine's noise, and Little Bink signaled and then demonstrated that the new owner should run the cutter up the planks and onto the truck bed. The man tried to align the wheels with the planks and received his first lesson in the machine's huge inertia. It seemed like trying to adjust the Sphinx.

Impatiently, Little Bink reached across him and pulled a gear level and the cutter responded immediately, going into reverse and backing the older man up and into the barn and almost over a large anvil before he could locate the neutral position and stop it. Care-fully, he moved the lever into forward gear, and the machine began to roll. He steered it with only a slight pressure on the hand grips. The wheels bumped over the ends of the planks and, with no hesitation, pulled the whole mass up the ramped boards and onto the truck. He found neutral, rather deftly he thought, and Little Bink lay a screwdriver across the sparkplug and the cylinder head to short the ignition. With several mournful gasps, like it was only warming up to its full power and was sorry to quit, the engine quit.

As he drove home, he looked at the brush cutter through the rear-view mirror. There had been an imperial quality about its power, slow but relentless. His ambition for it had already multiplied itself; to merely trim a little brush from around young conifers would be a puny utilization of its power. He could foresee empires of clover where barbaric growth now rioted.

He was sorry his wife was not home, her car was gone, but he backed the truck into a bank to run the cutter off since Little Bink had been reluctant to loan him the two planks. He had hoped she would be there to hear the smooth power of its engine. With the malicious raw teeth thrust out in front, the brush cutter slowly wheeled toward the barn, and he walked behind it, hands resting on the grips to steer it, like an invalid recovering from paralysis. At the barn, he maneuvered and parked it beside the tractor and between the cultivator and the lawnmower, just behind the roller and the snow blower. Its bare, utilitarian manufacture shamed their superficial designs; it was as if an honest, simple working man had been set down in a drawing room full of dilettantes. He took a screwdriver and shut down the engine the way he had seen Little Bink do, sorry for its silence, for he was eager to try it out, but he had to prepare for a business trip in the morning.

I I

By the time he returned from his trip, Bink Card had died and been buried. His wife gave him the details as they had drinks on the terrace his first night home; it had been a small funeral and Little Bink was to continue the machine shop.

"I'm glad I went to see him," he said. "The veterans hospital is near the airport, so I went by for a few minutes before my plane left."

"That was good of you," she said and lit a cigarette. She seemed more nervous than usual and drank a martini with him.

"They had him hooked up to a dialysis machine, but I guess there had been too much damage. He didn't say much."

In fact, Bink Card had not talked to him at all, had even turned his head away and left him with the companionship of the machine at bedside. It hardly made any noise, only a low hum, and that surprised him as if the mechanic should be associated only with noisy machinery. Card's skin had become the color of old-fashioned laundry soap; perhaps all the fumes he had inhaled in his machine shop, all the smoke of his cigarettes had surfaced, had been sucked to the surface by the tubes that connected him to this humming box. Maybe that explained his silence; maybe the machine had also filtered Bink Card's talk, those folksy monologues rinsed of their meanness and bigotry so that there had been nothing left for him to say.

After about ten minutes, a nurse came into the room, and he had stood up. She regarded them curiously to establish their relationship, and he had almost started to explain it, he told his wife, but then only nodded and started to go. He had leaned over the sick man and said, "Bink, I promise to take good care of your brush cutter." He didn't tell his wife this part, nor that the three fingers left on Card's right hand had lifted from the counterpane and turned in the air. It was an ambiguous gesture.

"Listen," his wife was saying. "I'm going to the city tomorrow."

"Tomorrow?" he replied. "But I just got home."

"That's right," she answered as if it explained something. She had let her legs sprawl and then closed them together to trap a fold of skirt around her hands. "Though I don't feel I belong there anymore. All the taxis seem to be full and I can't find the corner where the empty ones pass. But there's a Monet show at the Met and lots of other things."

He smiled and looked away from her, toward the hillside. They had had a dry spell and the underbrush around the conifers would cut very cleanly, but he had hoped she would be there to witness his first day with the cutter—to hear it. He had an agenda. In the morning, he'd trim around the evergreens, just to get the feel of the new equipment. Then, in the afternoon, he'd turn it loose in a lower lot where brambles and sumac competed. So, he would be alone, but as he ate breakfast the next morning, the idea of doing it alone appealed to him; there was a purity about it.

When he pulled open the barn door, he found the brush cutter just where he had left it, though it seemed ready to chase the other equipment, to snap at the lawnmower's plump tires. He reviewed the check list for starting (he had owned an official manual for the machine for some time) and then pressed his toe against the starter button. The engine turned over, coughed, and almost caught. He toed the button again. It almost started. He readjusted the throttle, checked the choke's position, and pressed the button. Blue smoke puffed from the exhaust. He held his foot against the starter button, contrary to the warning in the manual, and the crankshaft turned and turned and turned, but there was no ignition. Yes, there was gas; he checked the tank.

It was probably in the ignition, he thought, probably some part of the ignition like the coil or the condenser. Maybe it was the spark-plug. With a wrench, he quickly removed the plug and was gladdened to see its gap fouled by a gooey deposit of oil. He wiped it off and, whistling as he worked, cleaned the metal with a piece of emery paper until it gleamed like new. He checked and adjusted the plug's gap, he had all the tools for this right at hand, replaced it, and hooked back the wire. He touched the starter button. It almost kicked over, but he could tell that the battery was now getting weak.

It would probably be a good idea to let the battery rest while he checked out the coil and condenser. Moreover, the engine might have flooded. Again, the functional simplicity of the machine impressed him as he began to take it apart. Even if he had not owned a manual, even if he had not almost memorized the manual, he could have done exactly what he was doing now. As he removed each part, he laid it on the floor in a workmanlike manner. Every nut and bolt was easily accessible.

The coil and condenser were neatly tucked beneath the metal platform that held the battery. Four bolts held this shelf to the chassis. The pure logic of the arrangement thrilled him. He tried to visualize the genius who had designed the cutter, his name must be somewhere, for this invention could not have been the product of any anonymous corporate effort. When he withdrew the four bolts, he discovered them to be longer than he had supposed, apparently they were seated far in the engine block. One by one, he set them down on the floor with the other parts. However, the battery platform did not fall off, did not even budge, but remained fixed over the coil and condenser. It remained as solidly a part of the chassis like it were a piece of it, like it had been welded to it. In fact, it had been welded to it.

With a rag, he wiped the metal clean and saw the neat scar left by Bink Card's skillful application of the acetyline torch. No doubt the threads on those long bolts had become worn and some extra bonding had been needed at this point. But the beauty of a machine like this, he told himself, was that there was more than one way to get at a problem. He took the manual to the open doorway where the light was better and studied it. His stomach rebuked him for the quick breakfast, and he noted the sun was higher than he expected. Then he found the right page. The diagram illustrated another way of reaching the coil and condenser; by coming from behind and through the space where the starter motor and the timing gear were located. They would be easy to remove.

In fact, he didn't even have to change the socket wrench because all the fittings had been standardized. As he twirled off these bolts, he reflected on the modification Bink Card had made on the machine, to appreciate the idea of the man's practical wisdom joined to the original conception, almost a synthesis. The driving chain and the rotor slipped off. It was all going much faster than he thought it would.

Three bolts had held the starter motor, and a couple of screws fastened a small black box that contained something that looked like fuses. The garage floor was beginning to resemble one of the illustrations in the manual, everything neatly laid out. Now he could put his hand through this space and, with a small screwdriver, undo the condenser fitting; but a piece of steel, shaped like a keystone, had been welded partially over the opening so he could not insert the screwdriver in such a way to get a good purchase on the screwhead. He could plainly see the screwhead. It gleamed on the other end of the narrow channel like a pearl in an inner sanctum. He deduced that Bink or maybe Little Bink had welded this brace at the axle for extra strength.

On his knees, he was clearly at a point of decision. He could reassemble the machine and, by then, the battery would have probably recharged itself and the carburetor cleared. It would probably start with one touch on the button. But what if it didn't start? Then he would have to tear it down all over to the point he had just reached and that would be a waste of time. The morning was already gone. He heard a car motor down at the house. He got up and went to the corner of the barn, though he would have been surprised if it had been his wife. It was only the dry cleaning man, delivering some clothes, who waved to him as he got into his truck and he waved back. He watched the truck turn and pass down the driveway and out of sight. Some birds sang behind him that sounded like robins or they might have been sparrows.

The left side of the brush cutter was even simpler than the right; that is, there were fewer parts to remove. Only three cotter pins held the clutch assembly and its control rod together. He left the carburetor intact, having read enough to know that this was a specialty in itself, and chose to remove the left wheel. With the wheel off, he would have a clear shot at the coil and condenser from this other side.

As he levered the machine onto a piece of cement block, he was again impressed by its substance and mass and by the great power within it, a power he knew to be there but momentarily at rest. If he could only get to it, he knew he could fix it. The heavy duty tire spun free of the ground, turning easily, well-lubricated and per-fectly balanced. The wheel's ball bearings kissed like the tumblers of a combination lock falling into place. The plastic cap pulled off easily and then the large pin that it protected. Several washers slipped off, and he could see the wedge-shaped key snugged in the channel of wheel and axle. He put both hands on the wheel, braced his feet against the chassis and pulled. It didn't move. After several more efforts he took to whacking it from behind with a crowbar. Nothing could move it. It was fixed on the axle as if permanently attached. Yet, when he spun the wheel, it turned as if set into perpetual motion. It was curious, he thought, that anything could move so effortlessly, so easily in one direction, and still not slip an inch in another.

He stood up to stretch and walked into the small yard before the barn, pulling and massaging the muscles of his back. Far above him, a tiny jet plane was silently scoring the afternoon sky, appearing to divide the day into halves that would break apart along the white scratch it left behind. There was a whiff of pine on the breeze, and he looked over at the hillside. Actually, there wasn't that much brush to worry about yet.

He began to whistle again as he put the machine back together. Even though he had not been able to repair it, even though he had not been able to get inside its steel case and reach the problem, he was gratified that he was able to return every nut and bolt to its proper place on the outside. Everything snapped back, he now worked with the precise familiarity of a professional; every part disappeared off the floor and found its right location on the machine like one of those trick photography sequences. Finally, the brush cutter was put together and looked like nothing had ever happened to it. No one would know, he thought, that he had practically torn it apart. Well, Little Bink could probably tell, and he would have to call the boy and ask him to come and see what was wrong with it. Just before he left the barn, he touched the starter button. The engine did not start, but it still turned over, just as before, so he had not made it worse and there was some kind of victory in that.

His wife had returned from the city very late so he did not see her until morning, and then he found her in the backroom, preparing to load the washing machine. She did not answer his *good morning*, but held up the pants he had worn yesterday, then dropped them into the tub. "Those *were* your good jeans," she said sorrowfully, but she was not angry. "You should wear old clothes when you work around your machinery."

"Well, it was the brush cutter," he replied. "I hadn't intended to work on it, but it wouldn't start and I tried to fix it and one bolt led to another and. . . ." She nodded and smiled and looked away from him, into the tub that slowly filled with water. He was eased by her manner. "It's probably just a little thing wrong with it. It ran great yesterday. You should have heard it. But it's something I can't fix, so I called Little Bink to come up."

"That's good," she nodded again.

Just as she spoke a flat bed truck came up the driveway and continued on to the barn. There was a large motor generator mounted on the back and several cylinders of compressed gas. It was a familiar rig on local roads, as Bink Card had used it on his rounds to repair broken-down farm equipment.

"How was the city?" he asked her. "Did you meet some friends? I couldn't wait up."

"It's still there," she shrugged. "I had to do a lot of little things that took a lot of time." She closed the top of the washer and reached into her shirt pocket for a cigarette. She faced him.

"What?" he asked.

"What?"

"You were about to say something, I thought."

She waved smoke toward the ceiling. "You can help me with the house. I'm way behind and have to get caught up."

"Sure," he replied, though he wanted to be at the barn, wanted to be there when Little Bink got the cutter going. He could picture the

young man studying the machine, reviewing a list of possible problems coupled with their solutions, but it would be wiser to stay here
and help his wife. She usually hated housework and let the different chores pile up until they would press a bitterness on her
usual good nature, but this morning she turned to the different
tasks with a joyous bustle. They dusted and vacuumed, washed the
woodwork, did mirrors and the windows inside, beat the rugs,
polished the bathrooms, waxed the floors; husband and wife paired
up. Sometimes, as they worked, they would hear the clang of metal
on metal, the blows of a hammer and clatter of tools. The generator
had started up, and its whine cut through the morning calm.

"Sounds like he's using the torch," he said to his wife. "I guess
it's not a simple problem after all."

She nodded and smiled and handed him a dustpan; she had the
broom. They had come, at last, to the guest room. He wondered if
there were to be weekend guests; perhaps someone she had met in
the city and had invited up and was waiting to tell him when they
took a coffee break. They had even changed the linen on the bed in
the guest room, and she had displayed the same sedulous attention
to mundane details, such as the precise corner folds of the top
sheet, that always seemed to key her preparations for someone's
arrival.

She aligned several journals on the bedside table. "There," she
said. "That's done." The bed was between them. It was a double
bed but looked larger because of the design of its counterpane. She
looked around; her cigarettes were in the kitchen.

"I'll buy the coffee," he said.

"Good." As they walked back through the neat and expectant
rooms, he noted the sounds from the barn were fewer but more
emphatic. There was an exactness to the hammer blows; their
number selected carefully, their delivery timed. He heated up the
coffee she had made earlier and brought cups to the table. She had
already sat down, already held a smoking cigarette.

They sipped their coffee, and he was about to speak and then saw
she was also going to say something and then a geyser of noise
erupted in the barn, an engine roar that permeated the air, an
explosion of sound that caught all the particles of light in its
billowing racket.

"Listen," she almost shouted.

"I know, I know," he cried. He was laughing and clapped his hands. "Do you hear that? Listen to that. He's got it started!" He reached across to squeeze her hand. She brushed some bread crumbs together and then swept them off the table. They fell to the floor.

"No. Listen. That's not it. Listen." She shook her head. The engine noise had moderated, become more tuned. "Listen to me. I've taken an apartment in the city. I guess, I'm leaving you."

He had heard what she said, heard the way she said it; the slight hesitation in her voice that had been poised for him to turn her in whatever direction he cared to take. But he was also listening to the powerful sound of the engine and a tempo that rhymed his own heavy pulse as all the nameless parts worked smoothly.

# On the Shore
# of Chad Creek

Melvin Combs, his wife she died. Turned her head to the wall, her arms crossed. She was 81 year old.

Melvin he was 83.

The 2 of them live alone up there. You walk a footbridge across Chad Creek, and climb a footpath about 18 rod up there to the house. You cain't see the house from the road, but you can see it oncet you get across Chad Creek.

Melvin sit down and stare at his old woman for a long time. Her name was Maude. Everybody know them 2 for a long time, Melvin and Maude Combs.

Melvin sat there and sighed. He know in his heart it got to happen. She been waking up ever night since the middle of winter, saying, I am cold, I cain't seem to git warm.

Now it was spring time, and they was a dozen blackbirds out in back of the house, 3 or 4 of them on the roof of the shed. The trees was flowering. Maude loved to see the trees flower in the spring, but now she had turned to the wall with her arms crossed over her breast and died.

Melvin was alone. He sat there in his rocking chair without rocking none at all, and stared at the dead woman's back. He could see from the slope of the covers that her 2 feet was curled around behind, like she was only a little baby sleeping.

Outside, the birds was chirping and a fresh breeze was pushing against the window near her head. But she didn't feel nothing, and neither did Melvin, because the window was closed and the door was closed.

Melvin went over and open the door. When he did, he heard a car driving somewhere down on the road, but he couldn't see the car. You couldn't see the house from the road, and you couldn't see the road from the house. But you could hear the cars go past, and the trucks go past.

Melvin went out on the front porch and looked down the steep and crooked path, past the pine trees that grew on this slope but hardly anywhere else in the valley. Melvin stared down at the edge of the foot bridge, and he said to hisself, I am going to have to carry the body down there. Ain't nobody coming up here to git the body. Hit will be for me to carry the body down and across the foot bridge.

When he talked, he rub his wrinkled old hand on the porch banister, which he put up fifty year ago, and sanded down smooth and fine.

She ain't all that heavy, he said. Hit won't be nothing at all to carry the body down there and across the bridge.

He went back inside the house and said to his wife, I am going to have me a little sip. Then he recited, Early in the morning or late at night, a sip of corn will go just right.

She didn't like him to speak that poem. Melvin didn't drink very much, but he sure like to take his sip. He take a sip most any time he feel like it, but he didn't get cross-eye drunk like a lot of men do.

Now he walk into the little kitchen and stared out through the checkered muslin curtains she had bought only 5 or 10 year ago. The sun was out for a minute, and then it turn dark from the April clouds a drifting by overhead in the sky.

Melvin sighed and pulled out a jug from underneath the sink. Then he poured a couple fingers in a jelly glass and sat down in a chair. Then he change his mind and got up and open the back door, so's he could hear the blackbirds that was busy out in back. The breeze come in through the door and made the little flowery dish towel on the rack by the counter flap around.

Hit's a right nice spring breeze, Melvin said.

He took hisself a little sip of the corn whiskey and smack his lips. Sweet tit, he said.

After a bit, he lean around the corner and look at the dead body, but it was still right there in the same place, the feet curled around like a baby's and the head half buried in the pillow.

She was a good wife, Melvin said out loud.

Then he sat and sip some more of the corn whiskey, and after a little bit, he got up out of his chair and walk outside onto the old splintered wood porch and down the cement block they use for a step and onto the bare ground. The grass was a growing high for April.

He walk out a little, took 2 or 3 steps in the sun and then a cloud pass overhead and he was walking 2 or 3 steps in cool dark shade. Then it was sunny again, and the blackbirds was flying here and there.

Melvin stood still and he sip the last of his whiskey. Then he turn around and look at the little house where he and Maude had lived for 50 years and more.

Maybe I better go down and get me some hep, Melvin said out loud. Maybe I better stop me a car and get some body to come up here and hep me with the body.

He stood and took a long breath and studied the back of the house. Then he said, No, she didn't like no body coming up here, unless they was invited. Unless she knowed they was a coming.

He walk back to the back door, step up on the cement block and stood on the tiny porch again.

Hit won't be no trouble, he said.

He went inside the house and put on his hat. Then he went over to the bed and look at the body.

I am strong, he said, and hit won't be no trouble for me to carry that body down to the foot bridge.

But it was heavier than he thought. He wrap it in a blanket and pick it up and was surprised to find out it was already getting to be a little bit stiff. No telling what time she had died in the night.

But he got her through the front door, and part way down the path. It was steep, but Melvin he knowed ever step, ever little turn, down through the dark pine trees.

He got the body halfway down, so's he could see parts of the road, and his feet slip out from under him, and both of them went just a sprawling. The body bounced a couple times and half rolled out of the blanket, and Melvin he skin his elbow and jarred his shoulder so's he could hardly move for a minute.

He decided he need some hep, so he wrapped the body up comfortable and went back up to the house. Then he went into the kitchen and poured hisself another 2 fingers of whiskey. He sat there in the chair. He could feel the numb feeling in his shoulder and he was a wondering if he should go down to the road for hep.

No, he said, I will do hit myself.

So after he finish the whiskey, he was feeling better. When he walk down the path, he said out loud, Ain't many 83 year old men can carry a dead body down a mountain path.

Maude was laying right there where he had dropped her, and he got downhill from her on the path, and then he pick her up pretty good and start walking once again. His old legs was a shaking, though, and it look pretty bad for about 50 or 60 feet, but then he made it to the foot bridge, and by God went all the ways across that foot bridge, without stopping once, and the foot bridge kind of jump and wiggle the way it does, but Melvin, he knowed it like the wobble in his own 2 knees and didn't stumble or fall down once.

When he got to the other side, he tried to set the body down gentle, but dropped it, and again it roll about half way out of the blanket. Poor Maude's face was pale and dead, and her arms was still crossed on her breast, the way she'd died. Her jaw was fixed open, and her eyes showed a little crack, like she was a taking a peek at him now and then to see how he was making out.

Melvin he sat there and breathed hard and tried to catch his breath, which took a pretty long time in coming back.

Then he got up and got the body in his car, which was parked there. He didn't drive it much, and ever now and then the battery was run down, but Melvin he always park it right there on the hill with the brake on, so's all he had to do if the battery was run down was let go the brake and the old car started a rolling down the hill, and before long, he just let out the clutch and the engine catch and start a running as smooth as ever.

This is what he done this time, too. Maude's body was laying half on the floor and half on the back seat, with its arms still crossed, like it was cold and was trying to keep warm.

Melvin drove all the way to town that way, a couple times moving over after cars had come up fast behind and honk for a while, because they want to pass.

When he got to town, he went to the undertaker who also had

new and used furniture for sale in front of his store. The undertaker was Wilkie Thomas.

Melvin said, Wilkie, hit's Maude. She is outside there in the car.

What's the matter with her? Wilkie ask him.

She is dead, Melvin said.

Wilkie just raise up his eyebrows and stared long and hard at
Melvin. You mean, your wife has died and you done brought her all
this way by your *self?*

Who you think would bring her? Melvin said.

Then Wilkie said, Melvin, you been drinking?

Never mind about my drinking, Melvin said. Are you going to
come out and get my dead wife's body or not?

Wilkie just raise his eyebrows once more, and stuck a toothpick
in his mouth and said, Come on, then. Let's go take us a look.

When he saw the body lying in the back seat, all wrapped up like
an Indian in a blanket, and with its arms crossed and its mouth
open, Wilkie said, Well, lookee there!

How much for you to take care of it? Melvin said.

Well, Wilkie said. Well.

I said, how much will it cost to bury her? I ain't got much money,
Wilkie.

Well, Wilkie said. How long she been dead?

She died last night, Melvin said. She told me she felt funny
before she went to sleep. Didn't say she felt bad, just funny.

They say that a lot before they go, Wilkie said. Yes sir, they say
they feel funny, and brother that's *it!* Know what I say when I hear
that?

What? Melvin ask, rubbing his right shoulder with his hand.

I say that's a funny sense of humor, to think it's funny when
you're about ready to die!

Wilkie give a little laugh then, but didn't keep it up when Melvin
didn't join in.

When they went back inside, Wilkie got behind his desk and just
sat there a few minutes, chewing on his toothpick. Finally, he said,
Well, Melvin, I guess we better git started. Are you ready?

That's why I come here, Melvin said.

Wilkie nodded and then he yell out, Hey, Paul!

A voice answered from a room in back.

Come in here, Wilkie said.

A big young fellow wearing dark-rim glasses opened the door and asked Wilkie what he wanted.

Mr. Combs here, Wilkie said, has recently suffered the hardest blow of all. His wife of many years has passed away.

50 years, Melvin said. 52 years, to be exact. We was married 52 years ago. She was going on 30. She was a widow. I had been too busy a whoring around and a gaming and a traveling and a carousing and a drinking to settle down before that. I was 31.

While Melvin was talking, Wilkie and Paul was both a watching him, like what he was saying was the most important thing they had ever heard. They was paying so much attention that Melvin finally stopped, because he was not used to having other people listen very close to what he was saying.

When Melvin stop talking, Wilkie he just sat there nodding. He even pulled the toothpick out of his mouth and dropped it on the floor. He look like he was studying Melvin's words.

Then he started talking again, explaining to Paul what had happened. Paul, he said, this here's Mr. Combs, in case you haven't had the pleasure of meeting him yet. Mr. Melvin Combs and his wife, Rachel. . . .

Her name's Maude, Melvin said.

. . . which is what I meant to say, but I suffered a little slip of the tongue, momentarily; his dear wife, Maude, of 52 years went to a better realm in her sleep last night.

Died with her arms crossed, Melvin said.

Died with her arms crossed, Wilkie said, nodding.

You want me to go pick her up in the hearse? Paul said.

That won't be necessary, Wilkie said. Mr. Combs his self has brought his dear departed wife to us, saving us the trouble.

And gas, Melvin said.

And gas, Wilkie said.

Where is she? Paul asked.

Out in Mr. Combs' automobile, Wilkie said, passing his hand slowly through the air in the direction of the door.

I'll go out and get it, Paul said, and he walk out the door.

Smart fellow, Wilkie said. He goes away to college, and works for me part time.

Then Wilkie started a smacking his lips and shaking his head back and forth. Melvin, he said, do you have a death certificate?

No, Melvin said. You are the first person that seen her. Except for me.

Wilkie sighed and slapped both of his hands on the top of his desk. Well, he said, there are forms that have to be filled out and things that have to be done. I'll call Doc Wilson and see if he can come over and make out the death certificate. Meanwhile, you better fill out this form here.

Wilkie pulled a sheet of paper out of the desk drawer and shoved it toward Melvin. But Melvin he was just standing there a shaking his head no.

What's the matter, Wilkie said. You can write, cain't you?

Yes, I can write, Melvin said, but I cain't lift my arm. I done hurt my shoulder.

Hmmm, Wilkie said. If I lift your hand up onto the paper, do you think you can sign your name?

I can try, Melvin said.

It worked. Melvin he signed his name, and Wilkie filled out the form, explaining what was on it.

When they had finished with it, Wilkie said, Melvin, would you like to take a couple aspirin for that there sore shoulder of yours?

No, Melvin said, hit's all right.

Must not be all right, or you could write with it, Wilkie said.

No, Melvin said, the writing is over and done with, so I don't need my shoulder no more.

Maybe you broke something, Wilkie said.

No, Melvin said, it don't feel like anything is broke.

Wilkie took his watch out and look at it. I thought so, he said.

What did you think? Melvin asked.

I thought it was getting close to lunch time, Wilkie said. Would you like something to eat?

Melvin thought a second, and said, Yes, I could maybe eat a little something.

So could I, Wilkie said.

Then Paul he come back in, and Wilkie said, She was stiff, wasn't she?

Paul took a quick look at Melvin and then nodded, and said, Yes, she was getting pretty far along that way.

I thought so, Wilkie said. You get so's you can tell by just a looking.

I put her in the back room, Paul said.

You done right, Wilkie said. And wait here a minute, because we are going to have a little bite to eat.

Good idea, Paul said. I'm hungry.

Wilkie reached over and picked up the telephone. He dialed it, and said, Hazel, this is Wilkie. How about cooking six hamburgers with everything for us. I'll send Paul over in a couple minutes. Also a bag of potato chips. Also a six pack of ice cold Rolling Rock beer, and a can of 7 Up for Paul.

When he hung up, he looked at Melvin and said, Paul here don't drink, do you, Paul?

No sir, Paul said.

How much you weigh, Paul? Wilkie asked.

Oh about 230, Paul said.

If you drank beer, you would probably weigh more than that, Wilkie said.

Two hundred thirty is enough, Paul said.

Melvin said, I knowed her long before that. Long before she was married, even.

What? Wilkie said.

We was in school together, Melvin said. Just little shavers. I pushed her in the creek one time.

He's speaking of his wife, Wilkie explained to Paul in a low voice.

I figured, Paul said.

Then we growed up and went our own separate ways, Melvin said. Maude was married to a man named Chambers. He was killed in a mine accident about sixty years ago. And then I come back and there she was, a waiting for me.

Things certainly do work out funny, Wilkie said. Yes sir, they work out funny. You put that in a story book, and no body in the whole blessed world would believe it.

Chad Creek, Melvin said.

What? Paul said.

That's the creek he pushed his future wife in, Wilkie said. When she was a little girl. Then he said, Paul, you better go git on over and pick up our lunch, because it will be ready before long.

Yes sir, Paul said, and he went on out the door.

Where we been a living all these years, Melvin said. Right on Chad Creek.

Things certainly work out funny, Wilkie said.

When Paul come back with the hamburgers and things, all 3 of them sat down and started eating, right there in the office. Paul sat in a chair near the door, and read a book while he was eating.

He is studying his lessons, Wilkie said to Melvin.

Melvin drank 2 Rolling Rock beers, and Wilkie drank 4.

Paul went into the back room and went to work.

Doc Wilson came a little after 1 and pronounced Maude Combs dead.

Who crossed her arms? he asked.

She died that way, Melvin said.

Wilkie nodded and said, She told Melvin she felt funny before she died.

Doc Wilson just stood there and kind of looked at the 2 men, and then left.

Is that all there is to hit? Melvin asked after a little bit.

For right now, Wilkie said. Except for the funeral arrangements. However, you can come back later today and take care of them if you just want a simple service.

Melvin he didn't say any thing for a minute, and then he said, Hit just don't seem like enough, some how.

Oh it's enough, all right, Wilkie said.

But hit don't *seem* like it, Melvin said.

But it is, Wilkie said. Then he said, Melvin, did you carry the deceased's body all the way down that footpath and across the foot bridge?

Melvin nodded. Hit wasn't much, he said. Only thing was, I fell down like a blame fool and hurt my shoulder.

Can you move your arm now? Wilkie asked.

Melvin he move his arm a little bit and said, Looks like maybe I can.

You think you can get back to your place all right?

Why sure I can, Melvin said.

Well, just so's you can manage, Wilkie said.

A few minutes later, Melvin said good-by, and went out to his car. He got in and drove back to the foot bridge.

He parked the car right on the rim and set the hand brake hard. He also put it in reverse gear. Then he got out of the car and walked across the foot bridge and went up the hill to the house. Then he turn around and look back at the road, but you couldn't see the road from his house. Only the pine trees a standing there thick and dark on the hillside.

Melvin stood there for a few minutes and listen to a car go past. Then he was sleepy, so he went inside the house and laid himself down on the bed, next to where she had died with her arms crossed.

For a while he didn't think of nothing very much, and then he remember that he hadn't even told them that he could remember when she had worn pigtails. This was even before he had pushed her into Chad Creek.

Seventy-five years ago.

His shoulder still hurt, but he knew he would go to sleep before long. He had always been a powerful sleeper.

He thought of her head sunk in the pillow, her legs curled up and her feet tucked back, her eyes not quite closed, so's she looked like she might be taking a peek at him, seeing how he was bearing up under it.

Stiff as a side of beef.

The whiskey and the beer was working on him, though. And he was drowsy.

He thought of her pigtails, and how he had pulled them until she give out with a yell that was so loud, ever body heard. The teacher had punished him then. Made him stand in the corner by his self.

It had all started way back then. Maybe even before.

WILLIAM MEREDITH

# The Dolly Varden

*An Incident in the Aleutian Campaign*

A gust riffled the surface of the brook. When it cleared, the big trout he had seen downstream lay there almost at his feet. Captain Hideo Yoshida, a small, springy man wearing a parka, stood on the bank in hip-boots. The little Aleutian brook was so narrow here there was no need to wade. Watching the fish, he knelt and took a jar from the wicker creel which already held four trout. The first salmon egg burst as he put it on the hook, leaving only a rag of pink tissue. The oil ran over his fingers. He took another egg and threaded it more gingerly, like a little bead, over the barb. He breathed through his teeth as though to cover up the noise his stiff rubber clothing made when he moved.

Downstream he could hear the rancher Dawn, who kept sheep on the island, and the corporal splashing and shouting back and forth as they fished with nets and spears. Yoshida was glad to be rid of them and wouldn't concern himself further about how they fished. There was plenty of stream. Down where they were it widened, as it meandered, to one huge trout pool that dropped over the black beach into the Bering Sea. Behind him, in the direction he was working, there seemed to be several miles of brook before it lost itself in the grass-tufts. The green treeless mountains that fed the stream were cut off by a low ceiling of cloud as grey and lifeless as rice-paper.

When the salmon egg was set on the hook Yoshida rose and swung the line lightly over the water to lay it on the surface a few yards upstream of the big trout. What a beauty he was, as he lay there under the opposite brow, dark and submarine, switching his tail to turn a little from time to time, holding steady in the current with imperceptible motions of the fins under his gills. This was the species they called Dolly Varden. Its colors had reminded some literate fisherman of the bright clothes one of Dickens' heroines wore.

As the red bead sank and moved downstream in the clear water, a school of little trout, two and three inches long, materialized ravenously around it like iron-filings drawn to a magnet. One of them broke open the red sac of the salmon egg and the taste of oil made the others bolder. Then when the lure was only a few feet from the big fish, one of the fry hooked himself and set up a panicky splashing that frightened the rest away as invisibly as they had appeared. With a little curse, Yoshida jerked the minnow from the stream and over his shoulder onto the grass. But the prize had not been frightened. It lay motionless above the billowing water-weeds.

Yoshida tore the hook roughly from the minnow's mouth and holding the fish in his left hand cut it in half with his hunting knife. Next he cut a strip of the tough pink flesh and carefully sheathed the point and barb of the hook. He took a salmon egg and crushed it, letting the oil run down the bait.

This time he lowered the lure nearer to the fish. The oil made a rainbow on the surface, and for a second it seemed that the whole leader and hook might float, from the surface tension of the oil. But then the fry started at it again, the first one tugging it under. The meat was too tough for the little cannibals to tear, and Yoshida had cut the bait too large for them to swallow. Downstream and deeper it moved until as it neared the dark brow where the fish lay it appeared only a white spot. Yoshida was doubtful that he would rise to this bait. It looked clumsy and raw when the little fish left it. Besides, the brook would be full of fresh eggs at this season.

The hook came nearer the fish and Yoshida raised it slowly so it would pass above him. As it passed over, the trout rose. The man watching saw the white shape engulfed by the dark. Delaying a fraction of a second, he jerked the rod sharply and hooked the trout.

To keep his line taut, he rose and stepped back from the bank. He played the fish without exaggerated ritual. He let it take only a few feet of line and then bent the rod against it. The trout rose to the surface and danced for an instant on the air, showing its silver belly in the spray. Then the fisherman settled his footing on the springy turf and with one motion drew rod and line and fish up and onto the grass. Before the fish had tossed once, Yoshida had pounced on it and with the handle of his knife struck it sharply between the eyes until it lay still. With the fish on the ground in front of him, he rocked back on his heels to a squatting position. His hands felt up under his parka for a cigarette. He smiled to notice they were trembling.

This was his first day away from his battalion in four months, the first morning he hadn't had to prepare himself—it wasn't his report he prepared every morning, it was himself—for the daily conference with Major Smedley. The major counted on him for what he called the Jap point of view in assessing the day's dispatches. Yoshida had learned to read the dispatches first and to isolate a minor detail of the enemy's movements for comment. It had taken him several weeks to believe that this was what the major wanted, and during those first weeks the major had taken a dislike to him. This holiday was not the major's idea but part of a scheme of the new general's to prevent fatigue.

He was still smoking when Corporal Doherty and the rancher came across the loop of land described by the brook just below. In his big, knotty hand Dawn carried a gunnysack partly filled with fish. He too wore hip-boots and he had a cartridge belt around his jeans and a .45 in a holster. Doherty, a fresh-faced boy of twenty, carried two dip-nets and a home-made spear over his shoulder.

"Well, how did the complete angler make out?" Dawn shouted from some distance away. Yoshida was irritated less by the mockery of the question than by the assumption that the afternoon's sport was finished. The rancher saw his last catch. "Say, that's a pretty fair Dolly. They're not as good eating as the Rainbows, but they're all right. I'll bet you didn't catch him with your flies or salmon eggs."

"No, I tried what you said, baiting with a piece of trout. The fry took too many eggs, and nothing would touch my flies."

"Well, the boy and me got a bigger one than that, I think. We found a deep place down there a way. We must have pulled out ten the first dip."

"Yeah, Captain, you ought to try it down there. There's thousands of them, big as this, I saw one." The corporal held his hands apart.

"Where's the rod?" Yoshida asked.

The big face showed dismay. "Gosh, I must have left it where I set it down by the pool, sir." He was already turned away, the nets and spear on the grass where he'd dropped them. "I'll be right back, sir," he called as he ran off across the tundra.

The rancher sat down next to Yoshida, dropping the sack of fish with an odd thud between them. He was a big man, as big as the major and as noisy.

"I'm afraid you're undoing my efforts to make a fisherman out of that boy, Mr. Dawn," Yoshida said. "Some day, you know, he's going to want to fish a stream where the trout don't want to be netted or where the law is better enforced. Did you do much fishing before you came up here?"

The rancher seemed to acknowledge no criticism. "Oh, I fished some in Colorado, in the mountains. Here I just fish to eat, and I've found netting's the best way."

Yoshida looked over Dawn's head to where Doherty was returning over the flat grass. He held a light bamboo rod in front of him. "That's where it was, by the big pool," he said. "I couldn't get those eggs to stay on, sir, and when they did the little fish always got there first."

"That's what I found, too," the captain said. "I was baiting with trout just now when I landed this fellow."

"He's a beauty, sir. Bigger than any we got."

Yoshida was breaking down his rod and the boy followed his example. When they stood up, the rancher picked up Yoshida's eagled cap and extended it to him with a smile. Yoshida could find nothing but politeness in the act.

They had come out on horseback. Now they walked toward the base of the hills where they had found some scrub big enough to tie the horses. Halfway across the little delta, they flushed a ptarmigan. It seemed to materialize from the grass under Yoshida's feet. It still had its white winter plumage. As it drummed away up the misty tundra it seemed like a ghost bird. The report of Dawn's pistol near his ear was like a blow. The bird was out of range, almost out of sight.

"They're harder than a partridge to drop," Dawn said, putting the automatic back in its holster. "Same family. They're better eating in the fall than now, though."

They came to where the horses were tied. The three men mounted and went up the low hill and over it. The cloud was only a hundred feet above them, quick and irregular, scudding with the air. The wind was cold. Dawn rode in front. He buttoned the top button of his flannel shirt. Doherty rode behind Yoshida. He was a farm boy and easy in his saddle. Yoshida was not at ease on a horse, but these were slow, fat animals. Since the war, Dawn had explained, he had no men and the only exercise the horses got was what he and an occasional Army officer from the base gave them.

When they came over the hill they saw the Army base on the edge of the bay below them. It scarred the green April landscape with mud roads, camouflaged buildings, spidery communication wires. Yoshida's eyes involuntarily found the communications building and then the window of Major Smedley's office at the near end of the quonset. "I hope the rest will do you good, Yoshida," he had said. "We all get a little tense with the inactivity here. I know I do. Remember, it takes ten men like us to put one soldier out where he can kill a Jap."

The sheen of the bay was broken with the forms of ships. The sky over them held the unnatural brightness of sunset after an overcast day. They didn't follow the jeep tracks that ran down to the camp but turned up along the ridge where the ranch buildings stood. The rising trail took them through the ragged underskirts and into the base of the cloud. Somehow they had changed places and Yoshida could see the corporal but not Dawn.

"This is why I thought we ought to start back," the rancher's voice said from close beside him. He had let Doherty pass him and was riding beside the captain. "The horses can find their way in most weather, though. I got lost on my trapping lines last winter in the snow, and Fencer here brought me all the way back from Chamchak Bay on the other side of the island, as near as I could figure. I never put a hand to the reins once I knew I was lost. The wind was blowing thirty-forty miles an hour."

Cloud was all around them now, fixing the radius of visibility as evenly as beneath a street-light.

"Fog don't bother them either," the voice went on, "except sometimes they see things, sheep for instance, that shy them. I remember one time I came on some Japanese fishermen cooking on the beach, in a fog like this." But the narrative ended as abruptly as it had begun.

From the rolling elevation of horseback Yoshida could see only the rumps of the two horses and the milky outlines of the riders. There was the drone of an airplane from the direction of the bay. He had a momentary insight of what an airman's vertigo must be. The corporal had the same thought. Turning half around in his saddle, he said, "It's a good thing horses don't spin in. I haven't any idea which is up or down any more."

"They're better than airplanes that way," Dawn's voice came. "You just set them on automatic pilot and they'll make the landing for you."

The remark surprised Yoshida. But then the first time he had met the rancher he had been surprised by a similar display of unexpected knowledge. Soon after Yoshida had come to the island he had heard some officers speak of the ranch, and one clear winter morning he had climbed the hill on foot. Entering the three-sided yard of the ranchhouse, he had found Dawn shoveling a path through the light snow that had fallen in the night. Although Yoshida wore no insignia on his heavy parka, Dawn had evidently heard he was on the island because he said in tolerable Japanese, "Good morning, Captain." But he had seemed not to understand the greeting Yoshida returned, and later Yoshida had not found occasion to ask how much Japanese he knew or how he had come by it. Like this remark about aircraft, it was probably the result of a quick intelligence rather than a trained one.

It was the rancher's horse that saw the fence first and led the others along it to the gate. They passed Yoshida's jeep, beaded with fog, and continued across the paddock. A paddock and barnyard seemed almost exotic here.

Mrs. Dawn called out from the doorway of the house. "Hello," she said, a dark figure silhouetted by the electric light. "You must be wet through if it was like this down below." Then she saw it was only her husband who wasn't wearing waterproof clothing. "Why can't you dress sensibly, like the others, John?"

They unsaddled the horses and the two older men left Doherty to rub them down with a gunny-sack and went into the house. Mrs. Dawn had stayed in the open door and shook hands with Yoshida.

She might have been a few years older than her husband. She moved with a quick energy. To Yoshida her thin body suggested a Japanese girl's except that her legs were long, making her as tall as he was.

"You and the boy won't be starting back in that jeep tonight if I have anything to say about it," she said as the men pulled off their wet clothes—Yoshida his outer garments only, Dawn his flannel shirt and undershirt, revealing a white, bony torso. "I don't know what you two do down there, I don't know what any of you soldiers do here where there isn't anybody to fight, though there's enough of you, heaven knows. But I'm sure they can wait till tomorrow for you to do it."

Yoshida knew that Major Smedley would expect him to be at the ten o'clock conference the next morning, briefed on the communications that had come in overnight. "What do you make of this, Captain?" he liked to ask, passing Yoshida a perfectly self-explanatory report of a reconnaisance patrol. "Why do you figure they'd leave planes on the strip at Holtz Bay but none at Attu?" Then Yoshida was expected to play his rôle of Oriental psychologist. The object was to find an explanation—any explanation—that the.intelligence officer would accept but had not thought of for himself. Sometimes Yoshida would hand the dispatch back to the big man and say, "I have no idea, really, sir," and then Smedley would study him for a long moment and say, "I see." Yoshida supposed that at such times the major was wondering how far he could be trusted.

He decided suddenly he would take his twenty-four hour pass literally and present himself next morning without having read the day's traffic. "If you're sure you have room for us," he said to his hostess, "I'd like very much to stay. I don't think either the corporal or I could be described as indispensable to the war."

"I hope we can make you quite comfortable," Mrs. Dawn said and he realized that like any housewife she resented the implication that her hospitality had bounds.

"Gee, this'll be the first time I've slept in anything but a G.I. sack in over a year, I bet." Doherty had come in and was washing at the sink.

"Or under a lady's roof." Yoshida turned his hand toward her in an odd, not ungraceful gesture.

"Oh, you'll sleep in army beds just the same." She laughed. "That's all we have."

"The captain's an intelligence officer," Dawn said. He came from the bedroom, pulling a sweater on over a clean undershirt. "And Doherty here's your aide, is that right?"

"You promote me," Yoshida said, smiling. "Only general officers have aides, I think. No, he's called my orderly on battalion records, except nobody has orderlies to speak of in wartime. He works with me in the office down there, and we . . . well, we do intelligence work, as you say." It sounded self-important and mysterious, but he couldn't think of any other way to say it. "I read reports and brief the base personnel on enemy weapons and tactics, especially what's happening in this theater. Sometimes we actually see captured material, and occasionally prisoners are brought here to interview before they take them back east."

Dawn was spilling the bag of fish onto the counter by the sink.

"Here, let me clean them, Mr. Dawn," Doherty said. "At least I can do that."

Dawn gave him the hunting knife and stood behind him for a minute, watching. "Leave the head and tail on those little ones," he said, "just gut them."

Yoshida went to the coat-rack by the door and took a pint of whiskey out of his parka. Putting it on the table, he looked to the woman. "May we all have a little drink before dinner?" he said.

Mrs. Dawn exchanged a look with her husband. "Why, fine," she said. "I'll just get some ice and things. I don't take anything myself, but you men can do what you like while I'm cooking."

"I wouldn't care for any, either, sir," Doherty said, turning around at his chore.

When he and Dawn had their drinks, Yoshida asked about the electricity that ran up to the ranch.

"We didn't ask for it, of course," Dawn said. "We have a generator of our own. But they thought it would be good to have communication with the ranch, and they ran electricity up on the same poles with the telephone. Then Colonel Graydon lent us the refrigerator and the water-pump."

"And is that a Signal Corps radio?" Yoshida asked. He had seen an elaborate short-wave set in the bedroom when Dawn had switched on the light.

"No," Dawn said. "No, I built that myself a couple of years ago."

"Do you have a transmitter here?"

Dawn didn't answer right away. "I used to," he said. "I gave it to Colonel Graydon. It will be returned to me when the war's over."

"Oh, of course," Yoshida said. It was a delicate subject. "Some of these regulations seem pretty arbitrary when it comes to our own affairs. I've never agreed with what the government has done with the Japanese-Americans on the West Coast, for instance."

"What have they done with them?" Dawn asked.

"They've herded them all into compounds in the Middle West. They're there now, thousands of them. Like prisoners."

But this infringement of liberty must not have struck the big man as comparable to his own case, for he said nothing and held a hand over his glass as Yoshida offered to fill it. Yoshida poured himself a third glass. He sometimes relied on whiskey to put himself at ease.

The room was silent for a moment. The woman came to the table and transferred the drinking things to a tray. Then she picked up the drop-leaf table and moved it easily from where the two men were sitting to the corner of the room where a wall bench was to provide the two extra seats for them at dinner.

"Gee whiz, lady, there's enough men on this island so you don't have to move furniture," Doherty said. There was a pleasant kind of play between him and the woman. She had tied a flowered apron around him and he was frying the first of the trout.

When they were seated, Mrs. Dawn offered Yoshida the platter with a big trout on top which he guessed was his final catch. Crisp and brown, it looked smaller now.

"The big one is yours, Captain," she said. He was surprised that they had cooked his fish along with the rest, without asking him. When he took a bite he had a moment of real irritation. It had been fried in mutton fat instead of butter. It tasted slightly of the strong, unaged meat which Yoshida supposed was their usual fare.

"I saw a picture in Life," Dawn said as he boned one of the fish. "A lot of Japanese cabinet ministers and princes rigged out in top hats and tailcoats and spats, fishing for goldfish in a pond. It was an artificial pond, with a little house on the edge of it and rocks set up in it to walk on. It said underneath that it was the emperor's goldfish pond and the emperor was having a fishing party. What do you suppose they do that for?" Dawn didn't look up from his plate.

It was the kind of question Yoshida was used to. He might have been at a briefing.

He had seen the picture himself. It was one of those occasions of imperial hospitality at which the amusement—carp-fishing, duck-netting or whatever it was—was as stylized as the personal relationships. The peers and statesmen were in Western morning clothes. If they had worn Japanese clothing, Yoshida thought, he could perhaps have told a man like Dawn what the scene meant. But in the ridiculous tailcoats and silk hats, casting elaborate fishing tackle into a contrived tank of tame fish, there seemed no simple way to explain that these were men who knew themselves to be descended from gods and in the presence of a god.

"The easiest explanation is not a very satisfactory one, I'm afraid," he said. "It's an old Japanese custom, in a culture where the customs are stylized. It looks foolish to us because of the clothes—the Japanese are half-Western now, and the two cultures produce some absurd incongruities." This was the way his answers to the major sometimes trailed off. It was always a mistake to oversimplify.

"They make a great thing of saving face, don't they, sir?" Doherty's question seemed a devastating comment on his answer.

"How long have you lived here, I mean in America?" the woman asked.

"As a matter of fact, I've never been to Japan," Yoshida replied. "I only learned to read Japanese when I was in college. My grandparents went to Hawaii as farm-workers. I studied it in college so I could teach." Nobody said anything, so he went on. "I was teaching Oriental art in California when the war started."

He felt quite alone at the table. He was aware that the Dawns, like most of his colleagues in uniform, were finding it hard to believe that a man with his physical characteristics could be an American like themselves.

"Let's all have a drink to settle this very excellent dinner," he said. His voice sounded loud. He got up and brought back the two glasses that had been rinsed and left by the sink and two more he found on the shelf above. Without looking at his hostess he poured an inch of whiskey into each of the little glasses. The bottle was almost empty. He handed the glasses around.

"But tell me, how does it happen that you speak Japanese?" he asked Dawn. There was a flicker of surprise on the woman's face.

"They used to come in here a lot for water, sometimes to buy mutton, before the war," Dawn said. "Fishing boats, small ones mostly, with six or eight men aboard. They poached all this water pretty openly then. Sometimes even the mother ships with canneries on them." He took a sip of whiskey. Yoshida noticed that Mrs. Dawn had drunk some of hers. Only the corporal's was untouched. Yoshida thought irrelevantly that he was a minor.

"When they came ashore there was usually someone who spoke a little English," Dawn went on. "They traded us things for mutton, and for the water and American coffee. Helen got some cups one time, and that knife is a Jap knife. Well, this one boat came in several times the summer before the war. I figure now they were charting the harbor. Anyhow, the captain got to be pretty friendly. His name was Yamasaki. He was a nice guy. He even came up here for a meal once. He was the one taught me to say a few things in Japanese."

While he was talking, his wife went to a cupboard and brought back a white cup and saucer. It had no handle. The glaze was grey white and the only decoration was a blue line-drawing of a sea-bird in the bottom of the cup. It had a kind of elegance, Yoshida thought. He handled it slowly and read the little manufacturer's cypher on the bottom before passing it to Doherty. Then he took up the bone-handled knife that Dawn had indicated and looked at that for a long time. It seemed to him that they were all waiting for something. He swallowed the rest of his drink. He was feeling the whiskey.

"It's odd they didn't send a landing party in here last June during the raids, isn't it?" Yoshida said. "They seem to have put forces ashore to reconnoiter on all the other islands."

"That's what Colonel Graydon told us, when the first troops came," Mrs. Dawn answered. "He asked us a lot of questions about what we'd done, and he said we were very lucky."

"You were indeed," Yoshida said. He had read the transcript of Graydon's interview and had agreed with the colonel that the Dawns were telling the truth. Only at this moment did the story begin to seem too simple. The transmitter. The generator. "You were indeed. The people on Kiska, and the Jones and those Aleuts with them on Attu, they all disappeared. We don't know yet whether they were taken prisoner or killed."

Again it was Mrs. Dawn who answered. She seemed to be talking to herself rather than Yoshida. "There were planes overhead for days, some of them ours I guess, but we couldn't tell in that weather. We kept the guns loaded. John watched the beach all the first day. Naturally there wasn't anything about it on the radio till it was all over."

Doherty was listening very carefully too now.

"When was the last time the Japanese fisherman—Yamasaki, you said?—put in here?" Yoshida turned and put the question to Dawn.

"They were in and out of here all that summer. I think they usually headed home toward the end of September, maybe a little later. I remember one time the Coast Guard told me to watch my trapping lines because they were poaching them too out west of here. That wouldn't be until October, November." He talked slowly, as if he were speaking to a foreigner.

"But this knife," Yoshida said, holding it handle-first in his small palm and placing it before Dawn with the characters on the blade showing, "it says *showa jushichi—enlightened peace sixteenth year.* That means it wasn't made until 1942. It couldn't have been made *before* the fishing season of 1941."

The woman leaned forward into the circle of light drawn by the hanging lamp and studied the little characters. Yoshida held the knife in front of Dawn still, committed by the gesture.

Dawn took the knife at last and looked at the characters from left to right and then at Yoshida. "That's funny it should say that, because we got that knife in the summer of '41." His voice was heavy and patient, as if he were explaining something not to a foreigner but to someone stupid.

While the big man looked at him Yoshida felt his absurd melodrama ebbing away, leaving him without excuses, as naked and wrong as in a nightmare. He smiled. He might have tried to pretend it had been a joke, but the woman straightened up in her chair and said in a low, bitter voice, "You better go now. I don't want you here tonight. I don't want you to come up here again. You're as bad as the rest of them in Japan. I suppose they need men like you. I suppose it takes a Jap to catch a Jap. But I don't want you up here any more." Her voice was flat and weary. "If they still think we're spies, let them send up an American to fetch us."

"That's not right, Helen," her husband said. Yoshida wondered how he had ever come to vent his feelings toward Major Smedley against this straightforward man. "He was only trying to do his job.

Although"—he turned back to Yoshida—"I don't think you'd catch anybody but a rank amateur with a lure like that one. You know, if we were spies, we'd have to be good to be here. We'd have to know that kitchen knives aren't dated, for instance, that that's just some kind of trademark."

"It was stupid of me," Yoshida said. "It was a stupid trick. Go turn the lights on on the jeep," he said to Doherty. The boy looked crestfallen and foolish. He put on his foul-weather gear and went out.

"I apologize to both of you. It was stupid of me," he said again. "I think it was the whiskey. I've been drinking too much since I came here."

He went to the coat-rack and pulled on his parka. On the floor by the door he saw his open creel. The big trout was still there. He had been wrong even about that. They hadn't touched his fish. What the woman had meant was simply that as a guest he was to have the largest one.

When he had fastened his parka he picked up the creel. The big Dolly Varden had begun to lose its color. You could have taken it for an ordinary sea-fish.

Neither of the Dawns had spoken. Yoshida looked at Mrs. Dawn a little more openly than he generally permitted himself to look at an Occidental woman. "I know what it's like to be accused of treason," he said. "It happens to me from time to time. It is not pleasant. I hope you will try to forgive me."

The man would have said something but his wife touched his sleeve and they were still sitting there at the round table when Yoshida closed the door.

# Roses and Limes

Henschel held the last note and gazed at Mattie. It was easy in the joy of the moment to forget everything else. Her long brown hair wisped in a gust of street wind, and she looked away to God-knows-where, but Henschel loved that last harmony, the blend of spirit that kept the crowd on their tiptoes three or four deep on the park sidewalk.

When the song ended, Henschel did his riff on the guitar. Mattie turned her back to the crowd and said, "Let's get the hell out of here."

But the crowd clapped and shouted, and Henschel tipped his blue seaman's cap, letting his unkempt red curls spill out. "Just one more," he said to Mattie. "They love you." He kept smiling and nodding at the crowd.

Mattie had already put her harmonica into her purse.

Henschel shrugged and finally held out his hands, palms up. "Sorry, folks, but we know you've got to keep the economy rolling. And we have to see a man about a dog. We accept spare change and bills in denominations of ten or more."

He lifted his guitar over his head, freeing his body from the strap, and thanked the people who came forward and dropped money into the case on the sidewalk. "We'll be back tomorrow," he said. "If it's not snowing, we'll be back."

When the crowd dispersed, Henschel packed up his guitar.

Mattie split the money on the spot. Then they walked together
along West 4th toward The Avenue of the Americas. It was a sunny
day, but cool, with September settling in.

"Where to now?" Henschel asked.

"I'm going to my brother's," said Mattie. She looked up at the tall
buildings as she always did when she lied. She had the look in her
eyes, wide and innocent, as if she were looking at cathedrals.

"Shit you are," Henschel said.

"Look, do I ask you where you go? To those damned arcades or
wherever. Do I ask you?"

"We could go to Blumenthal's and practice."

Mattie shook her head. "I'm going to my brother's."

At the corner a man in a long, shabby, black overcoat was direct-
ing traffic, yelling and gesticulating at the taxis and Caddies. "Hey,
Ragout!" Henschel shouted. "Long time, no see. You just get back?"

The man waved and grinned with rotten teeth. He whistled for
cars to move.

Mattie had hurried up, and Henschel ran to catch her. "So you're
not taking your medicine," he said. "I don't see why you lie."

"I lie because you ask questions."

"If you ran out, get some more. Isn't the stuff free?"

"I have to go all the way to the Bronx."

"So big deal. It's a subway ride." He hated to think of her being
without. She'd told him once, late one night when she was high,
how it was like darkness closing around her, little by little. Like
dusk, she said, only not pretty. "If you want I'll go with you," he
said.

"No you won't."

"Then I'll pay the taxi." He pulled some dollar bills from his
pocket and held them out to her.

Mattie took the money and kept walking. Down the street Ragout
had held up traffic for no apparent reason, and Mattie took the
opportunity to cut across. Henschel let her go, watching her sadly
until she disappeared behind the plywood barricade of a construction site. She had no brother, he knew, at least not in New York.

Blumenthal did not go out, ever. He lived above a tuxedo rental
store on West 36th, where he sat in his wheelchair all day long.
Because of his illness, he looked older and wearier than thirty. His

hair was nearly gone, and his eyes were sunken. Nothing shocked him anymore. One time the Chinese restaurant next door caught fire and the firemen had called for the tenants of his building to evacuate, but Blumenthal stayed in his room pretending he wasn't home. And when the woman upstairs shot herself in the head and her blood seeped through his pasteboard ceiling, Blumenthal said, "It's just a reminder. That's how I'll go out, under a sheet."

Blumenthal was sitting beside the closed window, newspaper in his lap, beer in hand when Henschel came in. Blumenthal always read the obituaries for entertainment. The kitchen fan from the Chinese restaurant blew smoke directly against Blumenthal's building, and even with the window closed, the aroma of soy and rice and meat permeated the air. "It ain't roses and limes," Blumenthal said. "You ever smell roses and limes, Hen?"

"No," Henschel said.

"You have something to look forward to."

"So how are you?" Henschel asked, "Anyone die?"

Blumenthal folded back the paper. "Are you kidding? This is New York."

"I mean anyone famous."

Blumenthal pretended to read from the long list. "Martin Henschel, age nineteen, address unknown, died today. He had too many dreams."

Henschel smiled, took his guitar from the case, and did a riff.

"How'd it go in the park?" Blumenthal asked. "Did she show?"

Henschel nodded. "It went okay. You eaten yet?"

"Sandwich," Blumenthal said.

"What kind of sandwich?"

"Peanut butter."

"That all?"

Blumenthal put the paper back in his lap. "Anchovies, pheasant under glass, and hearts of artichokes."

"Don't be bitter," Henschel said. "I bought squash and lettuce and chicken."

"Jesus Christ would gag. You expect me to cook all that?"

"Not the lettuce," Henschel said. He played a few chords.

"You must have done all right today."

"Some rich woman gave me a loan," Henschel said. He put down the guitar and went across the room to the tiny kitchenette. "I saw

Ragout. They should send him to the police academy instead of to The Farm."

Blumenthal shrugged. "I still think you should go solo."

"We had a crowd," Henschel said. "I'd rather have thirty-five people each with a buck than one guy with a fifty. Mattie brings the people." He put some lettuce on a plate and some dressing on the side and took the plate to Blumenthal.

"She'll kill you," Blumenthal said.

"No, she won't."

"She's nutso."

"She's dynamite." Henschel said. He looked out at the restaurant fan which was a gray blur in dirty brick. "She's just fragile."

Blumenthal stuck a fork into his salad. "She's tough," he said. "And she's good at picking out a sucker."

Henschel played pool in an arcade for a couple of hours in the afternoon. When he'd lost six dollars, he quit and walked up Greenwich Ave, humming a song that Mattie had taught him.

> *Riding, riding. . . .*
> *How we got here with no past*
> *Disappearing as we came*
> *What's the matter with the story*
> *When there isn't any name?*
> *Riding, riding. . . .*

The light slipped away. People moved from place to place, always by sidewalk or street. Henschel somehow knew places he had never seen, places he wanted to go. He'd take Mattie. He still saw her as she was that first day eight months ago, playing her blues harp with her back against the brick wall of Blumenthal's building. She'd had a thin jacket around her shoulders, a cup on the sidewalk, and when she'd sung to him in that honey voice, he'd sat down beside her just to listen. Afterwards he'd asked her to Brigham's, out of the cold.

"I've got to return the cup," she said. "Will you come with me? It's Blumenthal's."

So he had met Blumenthal, and over the course of days, he heard Blumenthal's story. A couple of times he sang with Mattie in Blumenthal's apartment where it was warm, and the music sounded easy and clean, without frills or foot-stomping. They fit by feeling; even Blumenthal said so.

"What about you and Blumenthal?" Henschel had asked her once.

"Nothing," Mattie said. "He used to be a friend of mine."

So where was he going to take her, Henschel wondered. South. Where did roses grow, or limes? He turned off Greenwich Ave and stopped a little way down at a cart vendor's. "A bag of almonds," Henschel said to Erzio.

"No almond," the man said. "I got pretzel."

Henschel bought a pretzel and warmed his hands. The lights of the stores were on, and above him he could see silhouettes in the windows of offices. Erzio raked the coals in his cart. Henschel bought a sausage.

Along the fringe of the garment district, people thinned out. In the middle of an empty block was a row of huge windows which reflected the blue dusk and the pale orange clouds which looked as cheerful as wash on the line. When the clouds faded to gray, Henschel crossed the street, unlocked the padlock on the door, locked it again from the inside, and climbed the stairs.

The deserted loft was a half-block deep, with eight-foot windows facing the street, and smaller, broken, never-washed windows higher up in the nave. He had bought the key for ten dollars from a man who was heading to Virginia. Henschel shared the space with bats. The bats were his partners, and together they guarded that blank room from which nobody wanted to steal anything. The bats departed in the evening when Henschel arrived, and came back the next morning when he left. They rose through the cracked walls and broken windows, and when the room was deserted, Henschel played. He spun out his songs into the cavernous air, and with music all around him, echoing through that immense room, he felt as much at home as he could ever feel.

He had learned to sleep cautiously in places that were not his. He napped in libraries, sometimes empty classrooms, even in garbage dumpsters. His sleep was always tenuous, ephemeral, transient, and that night, in his culled moments of rest, he dreamed of Mattie. She lay beside him, but she was so thin! He could feel her ribs showing through her smooth skin, could feel the bones of her arms. Her face—those wide eyes and sweet bow mouth—was turned

away from him, but he knew she was awake. He could feel her
restlessness even when she didn't move, could feel her staring into
the darkness. All he wanted was that she would sleep. He loved her,
yes. He wanted to soothe her. But how could he love so much what
she was and still hope for her to be different?

He was wakened by the crack of a tin can hitting the sidewalk
outside his window. Disturbances frightened him—sirens, dull
talking, breaking glass. People stole everything in the city, searched
for food in the most unlikely places. Another can clattered on the
street, and he pulled his thin sleeping bag tightly over his shoulders
and covered his ears with his hands.

He was up before dawn. He rinsed his face with water from his
canteen, then huddled in his blanket and waited for the bats. The
nights lasted longer now, and cold seeped through the walls and
windows. Where had Mattie spent the night? Had she gone to a bar
and gone home with someone? Or to a cafeteria? He thought of the
bats. Usually he could hear them as they sifted in through the
windows and skirmished for places along the rafters. But that
morning the nave was silent. Light oozed through the huge windows, a gray pall without sun, and he felt uneasy.

When it was full light, and the bats had not appeared, he dressed
quickly and took his guitar down the stairs. He unlocked the
padlock and pushed open the door. An empty beer can fell from the
latch. A scrap of paper had been tucked into the top.

> I feel bad. I have done everything wrong.
> Can't get warm. Where are you?
> M.

He bought a newspaper for Blumenthal and walked up to 32nd
Street. Blumenthal would be awake at that hour because the pain in
his legs allowed him only fitful sleep. He got up early to have more
time to blame everyone for everything.

Once in his beer haze and a fit of self-pity, Blumenthal had told
the truth. He had been a reporter once for the *Voice*, a man who'd
known which strings to pull and whom to harass. He had written
up characters like Ragout and Erzio and the psychotic ranters in
front of the library. He liked the races at Yonkers, the late night
cafes in Soho, and his own position of power.

"Then one night, Granger, this friend of mine, and I came out of the Market Diner at two in the morning, I mean shit-faced, Hen, and we decided to go interview Thomas McGuane, the Western writer. McGuane had left his wife back in Montana and was on a rampage with Elizabeth Ashley up at the Plaza. If McGuane wanted to ruin himself with movie stars that was his business. Ours was reportage, and we were going to knock on his fucking door and make him the most notorious kick-ass cowboy in New York." Blumenthal had stopped for a moment then and had pulled the blanket from his mangled legs. "We never made it to the Plaza, Hen. We never saw old Tom McGuane. Instead we got side-tracked by two whores. We were walking up Broadway kissy-facing, and some maniac drove his car through us. He killed Granger and one of the women and crushed my legs. Mattie, she was the other whore. She was unscathed."

Henschel took the stairs to Blumenthal's by twos and opened the door with his key. He threw the newspaper across the room and sat down on the couch.

"She's not here," Blumenthal said.

"How did you know I wanted to find her?"

"I guessed." Blumenthal wheeled around to face him. His expression was ashen, as if he'd been awake all night. "She was here."

"When?"

"I don't know. I don't keep track of time. A few hours ago. It was dark." Blumenthal planed his hand through the air. "She was flying and wanted some more uppers."

Henschel closed his eyes. "She needs the medicine," he said. "She was doing okay."

"The whole world is sick," Blumenthal said. "Nobody's okay."

"Did she say anything? She say where she was going?"

"To her brother's," Blumenthal said. "Shit, she wouldn't give me the time of day. How the fuck should I know where she goes?"

"You used to know," Henschel said quietly. He got up and looked out the window. It was too early for the restaurant to be open, and the fan blades were still. They looked like a gray star in a reddish-black sky. "You tried something," Henschel whispered. "She wanted some money, and you tried something on her."

"No."

"She needed comfort."

"I need comfort, too," Blumenthal said, suddenly angry.

Henschel stared at him. "You? You sit in this God-awful room and feel sorry for yourself."

"Nobody could have helped her," Blumenthal said. "She's crazy, I tell you."

"You *assume.*"

"Fuck you."

"That's right, fuck me," Henschel said. "Somebody *cares,* but so what? Fuck everybody else in the world, because on the bottom you feel pretty safe."

Henschel picked up the dirty plate with two half-eaten pieces of chicken and some leftover squash on it and threw the mess against the wall. Bones and ceramic fragments exploded across the room.

It was still cold when Henschel left Blumenthal's. Papers were blowing along the street, and steam rose from manholes and grates and dissipated on the wind. He ducked a shoulder to the cold blast, turned the corner, and went into Brigham's. Usually he had coffee at the stand-up kiosk because Anita Sosnowski needed the money more than Brigham's, but that morning he wanted warmth. Uppers: was that what Mattie had wanted from him in the middle of the night?

He didn't know much about her, really. He didn't even know how old she was. She'd come from the West, from some small town in a huge land with blue mountains in the distance. That's the way she said it. But he hadn't asked why she'd run away. He knew why: she was lonely, she could not get along with her family or her friends, she wanted more than a landscape. All that sorrow—that was where the music came from.

For a half hour he sat with his coffee. Maybe he'd take her to Homestead, Florida, a place near Miami he'd read about once. They'd hitch, practicing while they waited for rides. They'd play in small towns on the way, a stop in Virginia, the Carolinas. He'd never been anywhere himself except over to Jersey and once to Providence. Why not Homestead? They could get along just as well where it was warm. That was where the bats went. And what was so wrong with dreams?

He finished his coffee and looked around Brigham's. He counted 17 people. An old woman with a bandana around her neck was staring idly out the window at the street. A man of no ascertainable age was pushing together the crumbs on his plate. Another man, younger, unshaved for days, was asleep with his head on the formica tabletop. Some of them Henschel had seen before; he would see them again.

He got up and edged toward the woman by the window. He stared at her until she felt his presence. "Can you sing?" Henschel asked her.

The woman did not look at him.

"Can you sing?" Henschel repeated, raising his voice.

He knew some of the other people were watching him, but no one moved. The woman did not answer.

He turned to another table where a middle-aged man in a filthy suit jacket smiled up at him. He opened his lapel and offered Henschel a drink. Henschel bent down so close to the man's face he could see the gray at the tips of his black whiskers. There was bourbon on the man's breath. "If you hurt her," Henschel whispered, "I'll kill you."

Henschel went to another woman who stared blankly at him as he approached. "Can you sing?" he asked.

The woman got up and hurried away.

"Hey!" he called after her. "Just one note?"

Finally the manager came out from the office behind the cafeteria counter. "All right, pal," he said. "Move along."

Henschel dodged among the tables.

"What's the idea of hassling these people?"

"Can anybody sing?" Henschel yelled out, still backing away, keeping the manager at bay. He circled toward the door. "Anybody? Just one goddamn note?"

Henschel sat in the park on a wire bench and tuned his guitar. Pigeons hobbled across the asphalt sidewalk, picking up stale popcorn. A few old men drank from their brown bags. Henschel cocked his head toward the O-hole, tapped a string with his right hand, and with his left twisted the plastic eye at the end of the neck. When he finished each string, he lifted his head and scanned for Mattie.

Usually she came through the park, her long stride noticeably faster than other people's. She was often late. But if she needed money, she'd be there. Once he thought he saw her rounding the corner—her hair was pulled back and tied behind her head, and she was wearing jeans and an old leather coat—but it wasn't Mattie.

He played a couple of songs, softly mouthing the words to himself, singing so quietly no one else could hear. He leaned his head close to the guitar to hear the chords and the tune to his own new song. He made up the words as he went along.

> *Nothing but the morning*
> *Makes me feel all right*
> *A little bit of evening*
> *Turns into night.*
> *We don't always have roses and limes*
> *To take us away, away, away.*

He thought of the migrating bats gone from the loft, sweeping through the starry sky with unerring accuracy. They navigated by night, miles above the earth and spoke to one another in high-pitched squeaks, knowing without knowing they depended upon one another for survival. Did they know, Henschel wondered, that he was left behind?

Maybe Mattie had gone up to the Bronx. The bad night had scared her into getting what she needed, and convinced her of her lack. It took time to get there and back; it took time at the clinic. He fine-tuned, scoured the park. Still no Mattie.

He played through the lunch hour alone, singing, nodding, trying to smile, but the mood was not there. Inertia was missing. Impulse. He got a small group, but not the crowd they'd had the day before when Mattie was with him. At one o'clock he was done. He played on for a few stragglers until he saw Ragout in the middle of his street with his hand raised.

Cars were honking and drivers shouted at him, but Ragout blocked the traffic. Henschel stood on the bench to look over the cars parked at the curb. And there was Blumenthal, trying to maneuver his wheelchair out of a pothole in the middle of the street. Blumenthal turned and lifted and cursed, then finally he jerked the wheel out, nearly tipping himself over. He continued across the street, and Ragout waved his arms and whistled for the cars to get moving again.

Blumenthal mounted the curb and came down the sidewalk, his face sweaty from exertion. His wisps of long thin hair were damp, his skin pale for having been so long without the light of the sun.

So where would Mattie want to go, Henschel wondered. Tampa, maybe, instead of Homestead. Puerto Rico. Somewhere there were banana trees and grapefruits and tropical flowers. Mattie would sometimes sing right through the lunch hour, not caring how much money they made. She would forget everything else but the words. She would move with the beat and close her eyes, and her clear voice would rise as though she were in a country of clean and vivid air.

Blumenthal's lips moved as he came closer, but it was a nervous gesture without sound. His eyes did not meet Henschel's. His hands moved slowly and tentatively on the wheels, as though he did not want to cover the last distance. But Henschel knew why Blumenthal had come. A newspaper was open on the blanket in his lap.

WILLIAM PEDEN

# *Hurricane*

The cottage where they had spent all those summers when the children were little was falling apart, but a couple of roses were blooming on the bush by the doorsill where he and Old Hetty buried the mason jars the last day of each summer at Gwynns Island. The colonel's house, always so neat and tidy, needed paint, the shingles on the roof were loose, the front door screen was rusting, and the lawn was ankle-deep in yellowing grass. The fig bushes had not survived the hurricane, and Hetty's kitchen garden was a mass of weeds. The chicken coop had gone the way of the fig bushes, but the privy where he had been temporarily imprisoned during the hurricane still leaned crazily beneath the loblolly pines. The captain's bench was gone, too, along with the wooden steps which had led from the gently-sloping lawn to the sandy spit between pines and bay where the children had played through so many golden afternoons. As he had remembered, the hurricane had devoured half of the beach, but the sand near the wrinkling waterline was as firm and clear as ever. He removed his shoes and socks and rolled up the cuffs of his gray flannel trousers. It was low tide but the water was clear and clean-smelling and surprisingly warm for early November, so he took off his jacket, shirt, and t-shirt, and draped them over a tree-stump. Then he turned again to the water and began the long walk up the deserted, curving shore.

That afternoon, before the hurricane began, I had walked along the beach with Dad. There had been no sun that day. Almost always there was a breeze from the bay, but that day the air was heavy and smelt like fish. We sat down on the captain's bench and looked at the water. Usually you could almost see across the bay to Courthouse but that day you couldn't even see beyond the crabpots, and the gulls weren't soaring and swooping, and there were no sandpipers dancing right next to the water. Always that time in the afternoon people were out on the beach or in the water but that day Dad and I were alone. I edged up against him. He looked like an Indian. Your father was raised near Gwynns, Mama would say, and that's why he tans so quickly, and she would wrinkle her nose in exasperation because she had been raised in the mountains and she never tanned no matter how long we stayed on the island, and neither did Ellen, but I did. My skin was like Dad's, everybody said. Ellen favors her Mother, Grandma would say, but Sarah takes after her father. I edged closer to him, and he put his arm around me and looked out at the bay, a cigarette hanging from his lips and the ashes falling onto his gray sweatshirt.

Then he threw the cigarette away and he swung me off the captain's bench and we walked across the grass and down the wooden steps. It was about three o'clock and Mama was still resting and Ellen was doing a jigsaw puzzle on the dining-room table, but the sky was so dark you could hardly see the poles sticking up out of the water where the crabpots were fastened. The water was dark, too, and cold-looking, though it was usually so warm on the beach that Mama had to sit up under the loblollys because she had trouble breathing and the sun made her feel faint and she couldn't walk up the beach to Spook Woods with us the way she used to when we first started coming to Gwynns the year after I was born, driving all the way from South Carolina in the big green Buick that had been owned by The College before Dad bought it.

Dad pulled off his sweatshirt. There were some goose-pimples on his shoulders and his back looked like coffee after he had poured cream in it.

"Are you comin' in, Sarah?"

I started to shake my head no because it was so cold, even my feet felt cold, but I thought Dad wanted me to so I ran into the water but it didn't feel like it usually did so I came out and got Dad's sweat-shirt and wrapped it around my shoulders while Dad waded out beyond the crabpots. He was a good swimmer, almost the best at the university when he was a student, Mama said, and I liked to see the water bubbling up behind him when he swam and his arms would be dipping up and over like the porpoises that sometimes late in the summer we could see out in the bay. They're patrolling the beach, Dad would say. They're keeping their eye on us; they're taking good care of us. I always felt happy when I could see the porpoises.

But today you couldn't see far enough out to know whether the porpoises were patrolling the beach or not. There were only ugly yellow thunderscads where you could usually almost see across the bay to Courthouse, and the sky looked as if it was falling into the water.

Then Dad waved at me and turned and dived, and then I couldn't see him so I began counting. After I got to twenty-five I started getting scared and I ran into the water and called him, and then way, way out beyond the crabpots I could see his head come out of the water, and he turned over on his back and shot a stream of water out of his mouth, like a whale. He turned over again and started swimming towards me, and then he was walking, first just his shoulders and arms coming out of the water, and he waved to me. I waved back and got out of the water and sat down. Then Dad was there beside me.

"Everything O.K.?"

"Yes," I said. "Just fine."

"The water was good," he said. "You should have gone in."

He took my hand and we ran across the beach and up the wooden steps and across the grass. Old Hetty, Colonel's housekeeper, was sitting in front of Colonel's house, shelling crabs. She had a laundry basket full of crabs and she was cracking them and picking the meat and dipping it into a big bowl of water the color of the clouds with small pieces of shell and meat and other things floating around in it, and then she would put the washed crabmeat into a smaller bowl. Speckled pink and red crab shells were scattered all around her bare brown feet and a ragged piece of crabmeat like a Punch and Judy nose was stuck in her gray hair.

"What's with you, Hetty?" Dad asked and sat down on the bench beside her and reached a crab out of the laundry basket and began breaking it with Hetty's hammer.

"Tol'able, thank God." She turned towards me. "How you, Sary?" Her face was as wrinkled as an old apple and her eyes were very blue; she has a good face, that Hetty, Dad always said. She laid down a nutcracker and pointed towards the water and the sky. "Bad weather comin'."

"Do you think so?" Dad asked, looking at me and then at Hetty and then back at me again. "Air's heavy, all right, but it doesn't seem really *bad*."

Hetty grunted. "People leavin'." She waved her hand towards the cluster of cottages far down the beach where the summer people stayed. Hetty didn't like the summer people. Except us, that is.

"Oh?" Dad said.

She pointed at the antenna on top of Colonel's house. "Weather man said a hurracan' was comin'. Said would be worst since 1923."

Everybody on Gwynns always talked about the hurricane-of-1923. Pop Haskins who ran the general store had been a boy then when the whole island got covered with water and four people were drown-ded, the only time since the lynching anyone ever got killed on Gwynns except for when the pirates used to come to the island and the Revolution. I looked beyond the captain's bench where the sky was getting lower and yellower, and I edged down on the seat between Hetty and Dad.

"Yes, we heard that on the radio this morning." Dad had lowered his voice. "What do you think, Hetty? Are *you* leaving?"

She wrinkled her nose and sniffed the air. "Naw, I'm not leavin'."

Dad took his arm from my shoulder. "Honey," he said, "Why don't you go over to the cottage and see if Mama's waked up yet?"

I slid off the seat and walked across the grass. At Colonel's boathouse I squinted into the shadows behind the steps to see if Willy was sleeping in the gray powdery dirt, but the ground was damp and he wasn't there. When I passed the chickencoop I picked up some gravels and threw them at the ugly red chickens and they flapped their wings and ran around in circles squawking. I liked coming to Gwynns for the summers but I didn't like the chickens. They were smelly and always were squawking when I had to go to the privy. I didn't like the privy either. It's really very unsanitary, Mama would say to Dad. I don't know why the Colonel lets Hetty keep those awful chickens. Smelly, awful things. Just *awful*.

Willy was asleep at the door of our cottage. When I stepped over him, he opened one eye, and yawned, and beat his tail against the steps, and went back to sleep.

Ellen didn't look up from the table.

"Hi," I said, but she didn't answer so I looked over her shoulder. The puzzle was a picture of a big red barn and a hay wagon with horses and a boy with a pitchfork. It was almost finished, so I ran into Ellen's and my bedroom and fished around under my pillow until I found the piece of the puzzle I'd hidden there after breakfast so I could be the one to put in the last piece. I stuck it beneath my pigtail and went back and sat down.

"Hi," I said again.

Ellen looked at me as though I'd just finished the last of the Kool-Aid in the icebox, and went back to the puzzle.

"I'm almost finished," she said. "There's just a few pieces left." I saw one piece shaped like a star and I thought I knew where it would fit, so I reached across Ellen's arm to pick it up but she grabbed it away from me and snapped it into place the way she did when she'd hand me the old maid card. "Go 'way," she said.

"Ellen!" Mama's voice sounded a long way off, like it always did when she was waking up. "Ellen, be nice to your sister."

"But she's messing up the puzzle."

"*Sary!*" Mama's voice had *that* sound in it. "Come here," she called, and as I went into her bedroom I turned and stuck my tongue out at Ellen.

Mama was sitting up in bed, and her hair was mussed up, and she looked as though she still needed some sleep. "You know you shouldn't bother Ellen when she's doing the puzzle."

"But, mama," I began, but she shook her head at me.

"Where's your Daddy?" she asked.

"He's pickin' crabs with Hetty," I answered. "And there's goin' to be a hurracan'."

Mama's hand flew to her throat the way it did when she was starting to cough.

"Don't say that, Sarah, don't say that. What makes you say that?"

I pointed towards Colonel's house. "Hetty said so. It was on tee-vee this morning."

"I wish we had a tee-vee," Ellen called from the dining room.

"Hetty said the summer people were leavin'," I added. "They're going to 'vacuate."

Mama's face was white and she jumped up in the bed. "Ellen, will you turn on the radio?"

"There's a piece of the puzzle missing," Ellen screeched. Her voice sounded like my kindergarten teacher's. "Oh, mama, Sarah's done it again," and she rushed into mama's bedroom and grabbed me by the pigtails. "Sarah did it again," she hollered, and yanked out the piece of the puzzle and waved it in the air. Then she rushed back to the dining room and stuck it in the puzzle, and she looked at me like I was one of the dead fish you find on the beach in the mornings after the fishing boats have been out, and I started to cry.

Mama came to the doorway in her wrapper. I always thought she looked better with her clothes on. "Children! Stop that, both of you! That's no way to treat your sister, Ellen." I started to smile, but mama's eyes were angry and scared both. "And, Sarah, you've been told not to do that." She went to the front door. "I want to talk to your father. You two stay here." She went out on the porch and I could hear her calling Dad, and then the screen door slammed.

"You're awful," Ellen said, and I stuck my tongue out at her again, and ran out through the porch to look for Willy, but he wasn't asleep by the door of the cottage.

I woke up in the middle of the night and I could hardly breathe. At first I didn't know where I was. There was such a racket I couldn't think. The rain was beating against the roof and windows. It didn't sound like anything I'd ever heard before, except maybe a train when you're standing along the track and the train goes by very fast. Only thing, it didn't die away and stop. It just kept on roaring and beating against the roof. It had begun earlier, after I'd tried to find Willy and Mama was fixing dinner, and then all the lights went out, and we couldn't listen to the radio any more. Dad lit the Coleman lantern and we'd eaten cold sandwiches and gone to bed early. Do you think we should try to get out and go to Aunt Marg's? I heard Mama whispering to Dad while I was getting undressed. Oh I don't think so, he said, it's too late. I knew he was putting his arm around Mama and kissing her, and I think I heard him say something about the road being too bad to get to the bridge to Courthouse where Aunt Marg and Uncle Edmond lived, and besides, he said, there's nothing to worry about. Then I had fallen off to sleep until the pounding woke me up. My pillow was soggy and the sheets were so damp they stuck to my legs. I had forgotten to put my flashlight under the pillow so I reached out in the dark for

Ellen; when my hand touched her arm she gave a screech and I jumped out of my bed and into hers.

"What *is* it?" I hollered in her ear.

"I guess it's the hurracan'," she said, and we lay there for a while and I was just going to get up and see what Dad would say about it when there was a tearing and a ripping, and it sounded like an airplane had fallen onto the roof. Cold water was coming down on us and the cottage shook and then dark things were poking through the ceiling. Ellen and I jumped out of bed and ran into Dad who was at the doorway with his flashlight, and we all began yelling at once.

"What's happened?" Mama was calling from her bedroom. "Oh, good Lord, I knew we should have gone to Aunt Marg's."

"You all calm down, all of you," Dad yelled. "Are you kids all right?" He ran his hand through my wet hair. "Ellen, you O.K.? You, Sarah?" He stumbled into our bedroom and shined his flashlight up at the ceiling. "You stay in bed, honey," he called to Mama.

Together we pulled our beds out into the main room and Dad closed the door to our bedroom. "How many people you know ever had a tree fall into *their* house?" he asked. "You can tell *that* to our friends in South Carolina."

After Dad went back in with Mama, I pretended to sleep. I got used to the roaring and the pounding, but the air was sticky and smelly. I crept out of bed and stuck my nose against the window but all I could see was dark and splashes of water. Ellen came up beside me and I put my arm around her and she didn't shake it off.

"Hetty says the whole island was covered with water when they had the hurracan'-of-1923," I said. "And four people were drown-ded." I pressed my face as close to the window as I could and tried to see out. "Will we be drown-ded?"

"Pshaw, no." Ellen said. "We won't be drown-ded. I don't think so anyhow."

All through the night the rain kept beating down and the roaring and pounding seemed worse than ever when I woke up. It was so dark and cold that I felt sick, so I crawled into bed with Ellen who was wide awake and looking straight up at the ceiling.

"I think we should go to Aunt Marg's," I yelled into her ear. "I don't like this. Let's ask Dad to take us to Aunt Marg's." Once a week we always used to go to Aunt Marg's, over the new bridge between the Island and Courthouse. Dad and Uncle Edmond would sit in the library and drink whiskey and talk, and Mama and Ellen and I would go upstairs and take hot baths and wash our hair, and then we'd all have dinner in the dining room that was bigger than our whole cottage was. I always liked those afternoons at Aunt Marg's.

"Just how do you think we could get to the bridge?" Ellen yelled. "The road's all covered with water. I heard Dad telling Mama." She lifted her nose in the air and sniffed, the way Willy does when he smells Mama cooking dinner.

I jumped out of bed and ran across the cold wet floor to the window near the sink, and tried to look out.

"Where *is* Willy?" All I could see was rain. It wasn't coming down straight the way it usually does. It was almost flat against the ground, the wind was blowing it so.

"Where's Willy?" I yelled again, and turned from the window and ran smack into Dad and Mama as they were coming out of their bedroom. Dad had on an old sweatsuit and Mama was in her bathrobe. She didn't look very good. "Where's Willy?" I hollered again and grabbed Dad's hand.

"Good Lord," Mama cried. "We've forgotten him!"

I ran to the door to the porch but I couldn't push it open, and Dad had to help me. The cement floor was covered with water. My lifejacket and Willy's bowl were floating in one of the corners, and I ran to it in my bare feet. Ellen came out too and was just opening her mouth to yell something when I saw her face turn white like it had the day she'd swum into a school of stinging nettles and you could hear her hollering all the way to Courthouse. She was pointing towards the bay and I turned just in time to see the captain's bench lift up and turn upside down in a swirl of spray. A fringe of dirty-looking water was creeping up at the edge of the grass where the steps that led down to the beach had been. Good God Almighty, I heard Dad say behind me, and then there was a ripping tearing sound, and one of the green and white metal awnings from Colonel's house went flying past me and I ducked and closed my eyes just as the big tee-vee antenna crumpled up and where it had been fastened to Colonel's roof there was just a big black hole. Mama, Ellen yelled, look, and I heard a big thump above the beating of the wind; it was our car, the second-hand big green Buick, but I didn't see it turn over because Dad grabbed me by the arm and dragged me into the main room and shoved me under the dining-room table, so hard that I bit my tongue and banged my head. Then Ellen tumbled in head over heels, and then Mama, and Dad was outside the table kneeling down and squinting in at us.

"You all just stay there and everything will be O.K." His face had a white look, like Mama's, and I had never heard his voice sound like that before, ever. "Just stay there and be quiet, do you hear?" He patted Mama's shoulder and crawled away from the table. I looked at the backs of his dirty gray tennis shoes and hoped he would come back to the table soon.

"There goes another of Bob's awnings," he called from the window a little later. His voice still had that strange sound that I didn't like.

"The water," Mama called. "What about the water?"

"It's no higher," he yelled back. "It's a real dog, but everything will be O.K. You all just stay there. Everything will be all right."

"What about Willy?" Ellen asked.

"Don't worry about Willy," Dad said. "He'll make it, somehow."

"I wish we had something to do," Ellen said.

"Is it all right, honey?" Mama called. "The water?"

"It's no worse," he yelled back. "I think maybe it's slowing down a little. Not much, but a little."

Mama's breathing sounded like a balloon when you let the air out.

"It wouldn't be so bad if we had something to do," Ellen yelled, and Mama began to smile a little.

"If the water doesn't get any higher we'll . . . we'll go over to the Colonel's house. You can help Hetty make bread. Can't she, honey?" Mama called out to Dad.

"Sure," Dad said. "That would be fine. She can help Hetty make bread."

I knew this was silly, cause Colonel's house is nearer to the bay than our cottage is.

"Colonel's house is closer to the water than ours," I yelled.

"Hush!" was all Mama said.

Ellen was kicking the table with her feet. "I wish we had something to do," she grumbled.

"You all are being very good sports," Dad called from the window. "Oh, oh, there goes the last of the shutters."

I stuck my head out from the table to try to see the last of the shutters. "Go back in there, honey," Dad shouted.

"Is our car still there?"

"Yes, Ellen, the car's still there. It's upside down, but it's still there."

Ellen started to bawl, but Mama shushed her. "How about the water?" she called to Dad. "Is it any better?"

Dad's voice sounded very tired. "No, it isn't any better. But it isn't any worse either. Why don't you all try to rest a little? I'll let you know if it gets any worse."

"How can we rest here?" Ellen yelled. "My legs are getting cramps."

It kept pouring down rain and howling all through the morning. Mama would call to Dad to ask if the water was getting any higher, and he would call back that it wasn't any worse, and then I must have dozed because then Mama was shaking me and we all crawled out from under the table, and Dad was grinning at us. My head still hurt where I'd bumped it but the sick feeling in my stomach wasn't there any more. The electricity was still off and every time I thought of poor Willy out there in the storm somewhere I felt like I might throw up or something awful like that. But Mama fixed some cold sandwiches and they tasted better than I thought they would. Then Dad said to Mama that he thought that if possible he would try to go out to the privy to empty the slop bucket. Oh honey do you think you can make it, Mama asked. I think I can make it, Dad said, I think I can make it if I can wait for a lull in the storm. Don't do it, honey, if you don't think you can make it, Mama said, but it would be real good if you could. So in a little while Dad put on his raincoat and an old beach hat and got the slop bucket out of their bedroom. He sloshed across the porch and started out for the privy. He was up to his ankles in the water and all bent over against the wind and his hat almost blew off, and without thinking he reached for it and almost dropped the slop bucket but somehow he didn't drop it. His hat blew away and he bent into the wind again and fought his way across the lawn and finally to the loblollys where the privy was. He pushed and pushed at the door with one hand and held the slop bucket with the other and then finally he got the door open and he disappeared into the privy.

Mama was smiling. "Your Daddy is a great man," she said, and we both went back to the table. Ellen had tried to start another puzzle but the pieces were too wet, so she had propped up a book and was reading by the light of the Coleman lantern. I looked at my Mickey Mouse watch. It was wet but it was still running. Dad had been gone almost five minutes.

"I wonder when Dad will be back," I said. "Isn't it time Dad was back?"

"Oh, any minute now," Mama yelled. "Go to the porch and watch for him."

I went to the window: my heart seemed to stop.

"Mama! Mama! The privy's fallen over!"

"Oh, good Lord!" Mama's face was white and she started to cough. She ran to the porch, but Ellen and I grabbed her. "Get my raincoat," she was crying. "Get my raincoat! We must go help your father." Ellen let go her arm and Mama ran in to her and Dad's bedroom. "Oh, good Lord. Good Lord. We must help your father." She was running around in circles and her face was white. I was just going to leave her and try to get to the privy without her when Ellen gave a whoop.

"It's O.K.," she called from the window. "Dad got out."

The privy was almost flat against the ground; only the stump of a small pine tree was propping it up. When I got to the window Dad was halfway between the privy and the cottage. He was waving the slop bucket like a flag and when he came closer to the house I could see that he was laughing and I ran through the porch and shoved the screen door open. Dad put down the slop bucket and slapped me on the shoulder and kissed the top of my head. We went inside and Mama and Ellen were hugging him and me, and we were all laughing at once.

"I got in there," Dad was saying, "Lord knows how, but I got in there." He stopped and wiped his eyes and hair with the towel I had brought him. "And all of a sudden there was this gust." He kept rubbing his hair and began to laugh again. He doubled over and laughed so hard I thought he'd never stop. "What a way to go," he said. "All of a sudden there was this gust and I thought we were going to take off like one of Bob's awnings. What a way to go, I kept thinking. What a way to go." He straightened up, and looked at us. "Fortunately, I had just emptied the slop bucket. And I kept thinking about Thurber. Even when I thought the privy was going to take off like one of Bob's awnings. I kept thinking of Thurber. What he could do with a situation like that!"

"It's wonderful," Mama said. "Really wonderful. But stop shouting!"

"Shouting? Who's shouting?" Dad looked around, first at the ceiling, then at the floor, then at the windows. A strange look came over his face. I was almost scared for a minute. Then he gave a yell, like the kind of whooping yahhhhooooooOOOOOOO! he always gave when we crossed over into Virginia when we'd been away a long time, only louder, a lot louder, so loud that it almost hurt my ears.

"Listen," Dad was yelling. "LISTEN, YOU ALL!!!"

All of a sudden it happened. Just like that, it had happened. For the first time since I'd waked up in the middle of the night, we could hear each other without yelling. Just like that it had happened. We could *hear* each other again.

All that night and all the next morning and part of the afternoon it kept on raining, but the roaring and the pounding were over. We tried again to do a puzzle but the pieces were still wet and the electricity was still off. We had damp cereal and cold sandwiches for lunch and then I tried to get interested in a picture book. When I woke up Dad was leaning over my cot. He gave me a kiss, and his breath smelled like the fruitjar of dried peaches that he and Hetty buried beside the rosebush at the end of each summer and then he would open up the next year when we came back to Gwynns.

"It's all over, sleepy-head," he said, and shook my shoulder. "The storm's over."

We all put on our sweatshirts and our raincoats and slopped through the porch where the water was still as high as our ankles, and went outside. The clouds were low and the air was still heavy and there was a yellowish-greenish light over everything, but you knew that the hurricane was over. The rosebush by the front door was flattened out on the wet grass and so were the fig bushes; there were squashed green figs everywhere, floating in little patches and pools of water. I didn't even look at our car because I knew how bad it must have made Dad feel to see it lying on its side like an elephant I'd seen at the zoo. One side of Colonel's roof was mashed in and the tee-vee antenna was all twisted on the ground and the green and

white awnings were all torn off except for one over the front door
that was hanging and sort of swinging. I ran to the boathouse to see
if Willy was there, but there was nothing but mud and water under
the steps. Dad took my hand then, and we squished over to Colonel's, and Dad beat on the door. Hetty came out barefooted and
smiling and with a big towel wrapped around her head.

"Well," Dad said. "Are you all right?" He waved his hand at the
dent in the roof and the awnings and the tee-vee.

Hetty made a sound like a horse. "Nothin' like the hurracan' of
1923," she said, and wrinkled up her nose and laughed, and turned
back to the house. "Colonel be down from Richmond tomorra or
Sadday to see what's happened. Got some cleanin' to do." She
stopped and looked at me. "You come over before supper, Sary; I've
got some crabmeat and fresh bread for yourall's supper."

We walked down to where the captain's bench had been where
we had seen the dirty foaming water creeping up on us. I couldn't
believe it. The steps to the beach were gone and so was most of the
beach. What was left was a mess of dirty yellow globs of foam and
seaweed and dead fish and driftwood and what looked like just
garbage. One of the loblollys was stretched out where I had built my
sandcastles, and its roots were sticking out like a huge dirty mop.
The whole place looked like I'd never seen it, and before I knew it I
felt like I was beginning to cry.

"I'm going back to the cottage," I said. I slopped up through all
the mess, up the little bit of a slope that was all that was left of
where the beach and the steps and the captain's bench had been.
Just then I heard a squeal and from somewhere behind a flattened-
out patch of moss roses out crawled Willy, looking like a drownded
rat. Dad and Ellen and even Mama saw him, but I was there first. I
grabbed him up and he was wagging his tail and coughing and
licking my face like crazy, and we all ran to the cottage and Mama
got a big towel and Dad squeezed it out and we wrapped Willy up
and we were all talking at once.

Dad went to the kitchen sink and poured some whiskey into a
glass and held it up towards the ceiling. "The dove has returned,"
he said to Mama, and took a sip from the glass. "Don't ask me how,
and without an olive branch, but the dove has returned."

"That's right, Noah," Mama said, and they both laughed, so I
laughed, too.

"I wish we had something to do," Ellen said. "I wish I could take a bath."

"It's been a long day," Mama said; "I think you should all rest for a while."

Ellen sniffed and went back to the table and rummaged around with the pieces of the puzzle. I took Willy in my arms and sat down on the cot near the window.

"The road may be open by tomorrow," Dad said. "And we'll all go to Aunt Marg's."

Ellen looked outside and waved her hands.

"How can we go to Aunt Marg's? The car. . . ."

"We'll think about that tomorrow," Dad said, and finished the whiskey in his glass and went back to the sink.

I looked at Willy and he looked at me. Mama went to the icebox and Dad lit the Coleman lamp.

"I expect they'll have the power back on tomorrow," he said.

"I wish there was something we could do," Ellen said.

I started to look at the book that was by my pillow but I could hardly see the pictures. I love you all, I thought, and I closed my eyes, and before I knew it I was asleep.

# Secrets

Oh how I loved her! my father said on the plane back to the States. But he said it was over now, his affair with the girl at the Institute, Clara Springel. How she had wept at my grandmother's book party in London, what a scene she had made.

The boy I was with wanted to know who the redhead was. That's Clara Springel, my father's lover, I said.

My mother wrote to say she had big welcome home plans, had arranged for another doctor to be on call so she could pick us up at Kennedy and we could all go out to eat. My father handed the letter to me. Now isn't that nice of her? he said. She doesn't have to do that. I was planning. . . . I had hoped you and I could just take a quiet ride home in a taxi.

My mother was a pediatrician in New York. She kept toy whistles in her pocket and passed out sugarless gum at the desk.

In the crowd at the buffet table, I stuffed myself with something fried in tempura and watched my grandmother, whose nose was as red as her garden gnome's, hug an older man in the book business around his neck. Impossible to imagine, I actually had to see my English grandmother having a good time. My mother's mother, an Italian Mama from Far Rockaway, never stopped laughing, her fat neck and great bosom, everything jiggling at once. My mother was beginning to take after her, her bosom already hung low, and she wore polyester pants with elasticized waists and flowered tunic tops. The boy I was with, something my English grandma had arranged, loved to hear me talk Long Islandese. He really wanted to get to the States someday, he said. He held a copy of my grandmother's new gardening book, *From Aubergine to Zucchini with Mrs. Slipper,* waiting for her to sign it for his mother as a birthday present. "I say," he said, "I wish I'd met you earlier, Liz. And what a lovely party. That girl's your father's lover? She looks rather unhappy. My father doesn't have a lover."

Yes, Clara Springel. The one hanging onto the arm of the man with the big head of steely curls, my father, whose shoulder looks good to lean on. That's her, turning her face into his shoulder when someone comes up and wants to talk to them. Because he can't introduce her as his wife, he calls her his "friend," and she says the word frightens her, but she understands. "Oh why do you have to be married? It must be something to have two women love you at the same time," she says. My father scoops up a glob of chick-pea paté on a piece of toast and guides her to a tattered pink love seat. The boy I'm with, named Jasper, suggests a look at the Parliament building by night and leads me away from the food to the balcony of the hotel. He puts the book down. I let him kiss me, and then see my father looking for me inside at the party. It's time to take Clara back to her hotel, crying in the taxi.

My father, a geneticist, is somewhat of a celebrity in scientific circles. My grandmother is proud of him, but she still said sternly to me, "There is nothing wrong with being ordinary, Elizabeth."

Clara would say the same thing when I told her I was not cut out for science and doubted I would write books like my grandmother. "I like you just the way you are," she said. We stood in the park at the edge of the duck pond, in the town of Bath, on her break from the Institute, where she sat at a Bunsen burner all day. I'd met her before my father did, feeding the big, sloppy ducks pellets from a paper cone. We met in the George Lillo Park. It was named for a minor 18th-century English playwright in my literature book, with its muddy duck bank and groups of boys who liked to call to Clara and me over the water and push each other into trash cans. Clara's red hair always attracted attention.

Then when I told her whose daughter I was, she was flustered.

Her hand flew up to her identification badge on her breast. "Dr. Slipper's a great man. How lucky you are." I was amused, but then everyone here thought he was wonderful. Clara asked me his first name.

"George," she murmured. "Such a refined name. Does it fit him?"

"Except when he's playing the saxophone," I said.

Every Wednesday morning, my father and I would leave Oxford on the six A.M. bus for his lecture in Bath at the Institute. Out of the dusty, rattling windows at the back of the bus I'd watch dawn break over Oxford's spires. Below us, students huffed up the streets on their bicycles, oblivious to the roar and soot from our tailpipe. My grandmother said the air in Oxford was unbreathable with its exhaust and factory smoke. I thought worse of the damp chill that the ancient stone gave off.

I was always glad for our weekly excursion to Bath, though it meant an encounter with my grandmother in her garden. Since 1954, her eggplants had won first prize at the Bath Fair, and last year the London *Times* had sent a photographer to immortalize her spading around the foxgloves. The first day we met, in late August, she gave me a present of gardening gloves, and together we ripped out the dying annuals. She had the hands of an Irish potato farmer, and for a writer she didn't talk much. I did all the talking and told her about home, our unmown yard, and the wild woods so different from all this English order. At home, we swam in a private cove in Cold Spring Harbor. I did my homework upstairs at my window overlooking squirrels' nests and my dilapidated treehouse. When my father wasn't working in his lab down in the woods, he blew his cheeks out on his saxophone in the basement. "Road Runner" was his showpiece, but I liked better the bluesy improvisations that sounded like a big fish undulating in the current. The Cold Spring Harbor Fish Hatchery was only a mile away from our house. We would leave a block of my mother's frozen spaghetti sauce out to thaw for dinner and walk down to see the bass in their concrete houses. We fed them Purina Fish Chow you could get out of a gumball machine for a dime and watched them flip and dive for the pellets.

My English grandma didn't understand how my mother could live in the city during the week and only come home on weekends. My mother was now five years into building her pediatrics practice. "But she should be home with her family," Grandma said to me in an anger so strong that she tore a five-foot rope of mint out of the ground and went tumbling backwards.

She knew the Springels of Bath. Clara's father was a butcher. They were a little too High Church for my grandmother's blood but still very nice. Clara was their only child, born the year my father left for his freshman year at Oxford. If my grandmother could have predicted that there he would meet Anna Maria Multari from Far Rockaway and run off to America with her, she would have done anything to stop him. She would have welcomed the saxophone in a Blackpool jazz band over the microscope and months of silence from overseas. When he did write, she said, they were the letters of a lonely man, swamped in the chores of maintaining a household while his wife went off to medical school. "Baby doctor!" she said. "Why didn't your mother want to stay home and tend to her own baby?

". . . but your father was marvelous. He didn't complain. He kept your boopy clean and your fingernails cut and in the meantime made a name for himself. A great man, he is. The great minds of England appreciate him."

Clara Springel wasn't everything she could have hoped for for his mate either, but at least she knew Clara's parents, and Clara was an English girl. Clara wasn't brought up having her diaper rash rubbed with olive oil. And Clara's mother, the butcher's wife, could vouch that she was ambitious, yes, but basically a good, ordinary girl who mainly wanted a family of her own.

The fact that my father still had a wife in the States while carrying on an affair with Clara didn't embarrass my grandmother. Her best friend, Mrs. Feeney, had a nephew who was a convicted bigamist. And my grandmother's deep kinship with the natural world also enhanced such freethinking. She had the butcher's wife agreeing with her that the artificial bonds of matrimony would not make the crows or foxes lead more happy lives.

Clara, the butcher's daughter, my father's lover, threw a handful of pellets to the ducks and leaned back next to me on the bench.

"My mother ought to stick with slicing sausage," she said to me. "And my father, he'll like it when your Dr. Slipper leaves for the States again and I marry a nice local boy."

Their lovemaking took place in Oxford, most of it clandestinely in the house we rented on Beaumont Street, after I had gone to bed. But some of it in a punt on the river in broad daylight in the pious presence of the swans. Clara left her flat in Bath to move in with us, but the commute every day to the Institute was too exhausting, and she and my father quarreled. Clara would accuse him of having an easier life than hers because all he had to do was teach one Monday afternoon tutorial at Oxford and present a Wednesday lecture at the Institute. Seeing the newspaper in the bathroom would send her into a rage because he'd had the luxury of sitting there reading. He, in turn, roared about her wet stockings hanging in the shower. He insulted her television shows. When my mother telephoned, Clara was difficult to talk to for days afterward. Although my friendship with her began before she became his lover, I found myself barely able to tolerate her moods. My attitude—I could not seem to help it—was that if she were going to make my father unfaithful, she had better make him happy. I didn't think she had any right to demand that same happiness herself.

After a long winter of rain and quarreling, she moved out. Spring came, and sunlight broke across the pocked stone and shot through stained glass windows. My father's students brought him daffodils. Clara sometimes telephoned before breakfast with a breezy "Good morning" and then an intense interest in what my father had prepared himself to eat and what we had done the evening before. I finally realized who she was, a girl only seven years older than I, hopelessly locked in a situation sordid even in the eyes of my father. By spring, he still would not consider divorcing my mother for her. I certainly did not want that either, and Clara, wisely, never asked my help in the matter.

In the spring, we resumed meeting at the George Lillo Park on Wednesdays during her break from the Institute. When my father couldn't get away to join us, we had a better time because Clara would let herself relax. She never acted silly when he was around, but if it were only me, she would bend over the fence at the ducks and insult them, calling them cows, sluts, ignoramuses. Still, they waddled up to her and let her stroke their sleek heads. When she was sad, she called them her beauties. I told her she'd love the fish hatchery at home. There was nothing more beautiful than a school of big brown bass swimming in perfect synchronization along the slippery walls of their tanks.

In some ways, it would have been fun to have Clara come home with us. She thought my father's saxophone improvisations exquisite and encouraged him to practice on the roof. She would love the cove and the woods. I could show her around New York. When June came, my father's tutorials at Oxford would end, and we would be going home. Thinking there might be something more she could have done, Clara permed her hair and bought a tailored suit to make herself look older. She took French cooking lessons and wore the opal ring my father gave her on her left hand. He still introduced her to his acquaintances as his friend. Or worse, his "daughter's friend," which would make her inconsolable.

London. The dim corridor of her hotel which stood across the Thames from ours. We had moved into London for a week before our plane left for New York. My grandmother's book party. My stomachache from the rancid mayonnaise in the seafood dip. That boy Jasper trailing me on and off buses and leaving messages at the desk. Clara refused to board at our hotel, let alone sleep with my father. It was part of breaking away, she said. I shouldn't have even followed him to London. In the excitement of seeing London for the first time, I dreaded Clara's brave, buttoned-up face every morning when we met for breakfast, either at her hotel or ours. She put up a fuss if my father offered to take her out somewhere alone. In the booth, she insisted on sitting across from us. If my father ordered coffee, she would order tea.

Our last day, we stood at Piccadilly Circus. My father told me as I fed the pigeons some popcorn that if you stood here long enough you always saw someone you knew. Not five minutes later, I saw my third grade teacher from home. And not ten minutes after that, I saw Clara edging her way off a bus with a crisp paper shopping bag. Two teenage boys barged past her, and she lost her balance at the curb. A little crowd milled around her, and someone helped her up. Then I caught sight of her again, bag torn, glumly looking at a menu in a cafe window. If she turned her head but a few degrees, she would see us. My father yanked me up by the arm and pulled me down the steps, through the traffic circle, away. He explained later, as I examined my arm in the taxi, that no matter how pathetic Clara looked, he must now try to think only of my mother. Because he would be going home to love her just the same as before he left.

Our first Saturday back home, the three of us went for a sail at my mother's instigation in my little boat. While we'd been gone in England, she'd sent it to the marina for new tackle and bottom paint so that I might get interested in sailing again. "Take advantage of your last free summer," she said. Once I entered college, I was to get a summer job to help pay. I'd value my studies more that way. She hung her beeper in a plastic bag from the mast, we stowed away a motor in case she should get called, and off we set. She opened a thermos of tomato soup and passed around mugs. She was very pleased at having us home.

Then the wind picked up as we left the lee of the land, and we flew in sleek elegance toward a public beach across the harbor. Elegant until I forgot to head the boat into the wind as we approached, and scraped us along the rocks. She said nothing about the bottom paint, but rolled her pants as I held the boat steady, and slowly lowered herself over the other side. We fastened a line, and my father took the anchor to dig into the sand up the beach. I helped her over the shells and slippery rocks. Summers ago, my mother had worn a bathing suit with a little pleated skirt that my father used to flick up in back to annoy her. Now he seemed to prefer to be alone, thinking no doubt of how Clara would look in a bikini.

Clara sunned herself in my grandmother's eggplant patch that summer and wrote him letters, parts of which he read aloud to me when I walked down to the lab for a visit. As I looked at the pages in his hand, I saw not one crossed-out word. Obviously, she had toiled over her letter on scratch paper and copied the whole thing over to please him with her neatness. I learned she had joined a badminton team and had to have a tooth filled. She wrote like a child and not a very clever one. Her letters came in scented pink envelopes to the post-office box he used in town for his scientific correspondence.

Barnacles attacked the underside of my boat where the paint had been scraped. One hot August morning, I dragged it up onto our beach and cracked at them with a kitchen spatula. Chips of calcium flew, but after an hour I'd made no significant progress, so I heaved her back over and pushed her into the water on her tether. My mother would have stayed at it until the job was finished.

That same August, one of her patients got leukemia, a five-year-old boy named Daniel who was now being kept alive with transfusions. My mother was sleeping at the hospital, most weekends included, so determined she was to be with him when he died. Talking to me one night on the phone, she said she'd never had a patient die before. It was terrible but a great relief in a way. She'd known that eventually she would have to face it with one of them, but which one would it be? When it didn't happen and didn't happen, she began to dwell on any idiosyncrasy and wrote pages of notes after each child she examined. Daniel had been with her since she'd opened her practice, a 9½-pound healthy newborn. She'd given him his first examination in the delivery room and swore now that she remembered his trembling tongue inside that screaming blue mouth, and how her gloves felt on his slippery skin, and that the mother had said to her from the table, "I don't know what I'm going to do with another boy. Please doctor, tell this one he has to be good."

My lack of interest in the boat aggravated her. Here was a five-year-old fighting for his life, who tried to slap a hockey puck down the hospital corridor from his wheelchair. Daniel had become her child for the summer.

On a Sunday when my father and I had risen late and were having newspaper and coffee at the bottom of the stairs, the phone rang. My father grumbled and rose to get it, the sash of his bathrobe trailing into the kitchen.

"Oh hello, Baby," he said. It was my mother. There was a long stretch of silence after which I heard him hang up, but he didn't come back. "What did she want?" I called. I walked into the kitchen and saw him looking into the refrigerator.

"Do we have any eggs?" And then, bump, he shut the door and leaned back against it. "Oh dear. Oh what have I done?" he said.

And then my heart took a leap. She had found out about Clara at last.

My mother had called to say that she had had lunch yesterday with an old friend of *hers* from Oxford, Lavinia Stewart. "She's a widow now, your mother told me. Poor, dear, prying Lavinia."

Lavinia was in Oxford last April for a reunion of her class and stayed over to browse in the bookstores. "And crossing Magdalen Bridge in her widow's weeds, whom do you think she saw in a punt? And whom else do you think she saw in that punt? And what do you think these two people were doing?" my father asked.

But an hour later, a towel around his waist, he was laughing at himself in the mirror. He had called me in to powder his back before he dressed. "Your mother's going to make me sweat it out, but I'll win her over, don't you worry." As my fingers slipped over the moles and gray hairs that grew out of them, I wondered how Clara had overcome such a sight during their lovemaking. He was going into the city to deliver a confession and apology to my mother over lunch. He asked me if I thought he ought to wear some aftershave.

"She can't be won over that easily," I said.

"You make me sound like a buffoon." He ordered me downstairs to the kitchen junk drawer to find a Long Island Railroad schedule. I opened my mouth to say, do it yourself, but I wanted him to go through with this. He needed to give Clara up before things could go back to normal. One evening recently, I had brought his supper to the lab and saw him hastily shove a pink letter under some magazines. He was supposed to be injecting duck eggs with mutant cells. But ducks reminded him of Clara. I told him I was sick of his absurd passion for an assistant lab technician. I didn't care if he now hated the cancers he'd manufactured and loved the duck eggs. The great minds of England who so appreciated him were waiting for the genius to do something.

So now I ran upstairs with a train schedule, with all my will trying to muffle my excitement, when I heard him call, "Elizabeth!" He lay on the bed clawing at his tie. I loosened the knot and tore it off. "I can't breathe!" he said. He grabbed his chest, his nostrils snorting for air. I called an ambulance and then my mother's office. But it was Sunday. I only reached her answering service. She was on her rounds at the hospital. What was the nature of the call? In an emergency, here was a number I could call. I beat his jacket pocket for a pencil. I looked in the nightstand. "I don't have a pencil!" I shouted at the woman. "Look, just tell her to call home right away."

"Am I going to die?" my father asked.

"No. Just keep calm. Try to breathe normally."

"It's beating again."

"Good."

"I'm frightened."

"Don't talk."

"I was thinking of Clara when it happened. Did she ever say anything bad about me? Anything to make you think, even for a moment, that I was disgusting?"

"No. Will you shut up and save your breath?"

"I wouldn't blame her if she had. It was wrong. It was wrong."

The ambulance arrived before my mother called back. We shot to the local hospital, siren and all. Sitting next to his stretcher, I watched the road rip away through the back window. Cars pulled off at odd angles. People coming out of a church heard us and were riveted there on the marble steps. The pristine steeple reminded me of Oxford's sooty spires and gargoyles. I heard Clara's midnight giggling. My father's eyes held on to me. His cheeks felt like stone.

His heart attack turned out to be nothing more than palpitations, something everyone under stress feels now and then. But it took all morning to convince him of that. He ran a treadmill test to prove there was something wrong, as if he thought my mother would go easy on him if she saw him in a hospital bed. But his heart pumped beautifully. The doctor said he had the heart of a 20-year-old-man.

"Get me out of here," my father said, and I rushed off to call a taxi while the doctor removed the wires from his chest.

While we waited outside the hospital, my father paced the walk from the flagpole to the brick wall where I sat. "When we were in the ambulance, I knew you were worried. What were you thinking?" he asked.

"I was in a trance. You know the way you feel in an emergency. I wasn't thinking much about anything other than that I didn't want you to die."

"Were you thinking that I deserved to die, maybe just a little, for my behavior with Clara?" He looked hard at me.

"No," I said. Yes, the old bitterness had flickered in me for a moment in the siren's screaming.

A breeze came up, sending a paper cup clattering across the hospital drive. It blew my hair in front of my eyes and obscured his image. And I pretended for a moment, the way I sometimes did when I watched them together in Oxford, that I wasn't connected to him, not connected and therefore not responsible for an opinion.

Sometimes when I would first look into a tank at the hatchery, the brown fish blended so well with the water, I couldn't discern that anything was down there at all. I saw mostly my reflection and the sky behind me. The fish saw me, of course, and were waiting for their food. And I used to wonder what I looked like to them. Did they think I swam in the light on the other side of the water? If I waited long enough, one of the fish would try to dive at me, and the surface would break into a thousand ripples; and in between the shattered pieces of light I would see them all swaying in harmony down below. I would have to throw them their food then, because they had revealed themselves.

I heard a motor. "Taxi's coming."

Inside the car, in the stuffy air which open windows didn't seem to help, I told him for the first time how I had hated him for his unfaithfulness. Sometimes I had hated him so much I *had* wished him dead and that was what I was remembering in the ambulance. But I hadn't been glad when it looked like it was truly happening. Then Clara seemed insignificant in the scope of his whole life. I remembered the crowd of doctors at the Institute nattering him with questions. I saw him once again locked in awesome concentration over his microscope. The way it had been before Clara.

The taxi passed along the same route the ambulance had taken. My father leaned forward and spoke through the dingy partition at the driver's ear to give directions to our house. Soon the taxi turned into our dirt road. Sunlight flashed through the trees; the jouncing car sent up graceful plumes of dust in its wake. As we climbed the hill, my father said that in the ambulance a picture had come to his mind of a crab apple tree in his mother's garden that blew over one spring. It had never bloomed more profusely; its brilliance took your breath away, and it seemed that that day the color was at its peak. "It was windy," he said, "and my mother and I were eating a lunch of buttered potatoes in the kitchen. We saw it topple. She stood up and screamed, 'It can't be!' She had shown far less emotion when my father died.

"So I was glad to see your worried face in the ambulance, Elizabeth." The taxi stopped with a jolt. He paid the driver, and we walked across the tall grass toward the front door. A rabbit skittered for the woods.

The air always smelled good here in summer, with the sun on the dry grass and a salty breeze blowing up from the water. Why hadn't we ever spread out our lunch here? Or my father practiced his saxophone and sent the rabbits running? Maybe it would have made things too heavenly, to tap the beauty here, and we would have fallen like the crab apple from the weight of too many blooms.

"I'm going to go upstairs to change," he said, "then try to pull the day together at the lab." Pull the day together. That was what you did. When the water's surface broke and gave you glimpses of the harmony below, of how we could all have gently swum together like a school of fish, it only made you realize such beauty wasn't in you. It might have been beautiful if I had run up the stairs after him, butted my head under his chin, and we had held each other close. The inspiration did set my foot on the stair, forgiveness was in my heart, and if he had turned around to look at me, some speck of loveliness inside would have set me free. But I stopped on the second step. Sometime later. Let me pull my day together first. At some other time I'll tell him I love him.

So I got a spatula and rubber gloves and walked to the cove. All afternoon until high tide, I chipped and scraped at the barnacles on the bottom of my boat. The ambulance and my father's stone-cold cheeks on the stretcher all seemed to have happened years ago. My jeans were slick and green with algae. Flies crawled among the ruined barnacles all afternoon. When my gloves became cut in too many places and began to tear, I left the boat beached and walked up to the lab.

Through the window I saw my father injecting eggs. It sounded like Bartók on the radio, but I could hear it only faintly. Leaf shadows played over the film of dirt on the window and made it hard to distinguish much else besides his silhouette as he held each egg up to the tensor lamp like a jeweler looking for flaws.

Judging from the row of eggs in front of him, he still had a lot of work to do, so I left and walked to the house for a shower.

Out front in a lawn chair, in the din of the crickets, I picked at a cold breast of chicken. The sky was wild and red, but it was one of those summer nights that portended autumn in the chill as soon as the sun went down. I set my iced tea in the grass and warmed my fingers inside my shirt. And then tires rumbled as a car entered our driveway. I saw headlights clear the hill and bounce as the car strained to keep up its speed over the ruts. Her left parking light was out. She drove halfway up the lawn when the drive ended, got out and stood against the car. I put my plate in the grass and stood, too, looking away where the drive became a scrappy path to his lab, where I could just make out a light in his window, as if my father could know she were here and come help me explain.

"Dad's all right. I guess you know by now," I said trying to sound breezy. "I guess we forgot to call you back."

"I checked with my answering service when he didn't show up for lunch," my mother said. "They told me you sounded upset, but no word about ambulances. No explanation. If I'd been given a hint, I could have called Dad's doctor and found out what happened."

For the first time I noticed she wasn't wearing polyester pants, but a skirt and blouse, a bit tight across the bosom, but a pretty blue silk with a bow at the neck. When she was piqued, her chin and cheeks burned. It looked better than makeup. "It turned out to be only palpitations. They did some tests. He was fine," I said.

"Oh I know . . . now. His doctor kindly phoned me this afternoon. I'd been trying to reach you for hours."

"I'm sorry. I just wasn't thinking. I got really involved scraping the boat."

She didn't seem to hear me. She bent at her reflection in the car window and retied her bow. "The Expressway was hell tonight. I *did* look a little crisper at lunchtime."

I tried to smile, but inside I was bucking against being blamed. It wasn't all my fault. He was her husband, and he could have remembered to phone.

Then she looked over the roof of her car at his light in the woods. "Maybe I'll just walk down and surprise him," she said. Fireflies flickered in her wake as she plowed through the grass toward his path.

# A Visit to the Master

I have come up to Holland to visit the famous sculptor, van Kralingen. At least I am certain he will be famous some day. In other words, I have come to have a talk with that friend of my youth, Old Yopple, or, when relations were formal, Jehan Petrus, or, sometimes, just plain Yop. I am enormously fond of him, and he, I think, of me. I doubt that we exchange a letter once a year. But because I *am* fond of him, I think about him a lot, usually at unexpected moments.

One of the most enlightening of these moments was two or three years ago, on a rainy afternoon in Berlin, during a visit to the Atelier-Museum of the German sculptor, Georg Kolbe.

The studio is a large modern structure built of red brick in that Bauhaus but warmer style pioneered by the Dutch during the 1920's. It is surrounded by a well-planted evergreen garden. The curator is Kolbe's niece, and it is she who opens the door into this shrine where nothing has been moved since the Master's death.

She is a bony woman of middle age and looks devout. I follow her inside. On the far wall are two inept Renoir watercolors, which look even worse in this critical North European light than they would in Paris or Pasadena. Even in the entrance hall, perhaps particularly in the entrance hall, the air is clogged blue with reverence as palpable as lazy layers of tobacco smoke. Full-length windows allow one to see the rain falling in the courtyard on the left, where life-size bronze men and women glisten sleekly in the wet.

We go into the main room, which towers with sculpture. Beyond this, to the one side, are a couple of sitting rooms, to the other, more workrooms. On a table in the visible sitting room stands a record player. In the main room, near the archway to the hall, is a desk of the museum-lobby sort, where postcards are for sale.

"Everything is just as He left it," says the niece, and blinks. "Is there any particular music you would like to view the Master by?"

This kind of hokum always cheers me up enormously, if only because it is only half hokum. The light spring rain gives me an idea.

"Why yes, as a matter of fact, there is Prokofieff's 2nd Piano Concerto. If you have it."

She is not displeased. Most people request Wagner. And she does have it. So after a stage wait, the music begins, cool, aloof, playful, and crisp as celery. Though Kolbe was a German, he was not ponderous. This elegant music suits the wiry disdain of his brave and sometimes touching sculpture excellently well. I circumambulate.

The Master was a sensuous man, successful enough to figure forth his tastes. There are good Persian rugs on the floors, the sofas and chairs are handsome, and so is his own art collection. On one wall is an oil painting he did as a young man. It depicts some crewmen or oarsmen, and looks like a Marees, both in color and composition. There is a first-rate Schmidt-Rottloff and an even better Kirchner. There are South Indian bronzes, Pre-Columbian artifacts, some blue-green Persian pots, maquettes of his own statues, and the library seems to consist chiefly of ethnic and theological books dealing with Southwest Asia. Nothing, not so much as an ash tray, has been moved since his death. Equally, everything portable has been screwed or clamped down to the exact place where he left it. The larger sculpture, including The Work He Had Not Time to Complete, stands in the high-ceilinged atelier beyond. There are more full-length windows to the garden and the rain. In a small room, beyond a gallery, are shelves and shelves of plaster arms, hands, feet, torsos, heads, each ticketed. The effect is that of an anatomical baggage room, or, for that matter, the horse knacker's yard at Auschwitz, esthetically recomposed.

As I move about, the Prokofieff concerto takes its inevitable, preoccupied course. Three more pilgrims come in, two teenagers in lederhosen, which would have cheered the Master enormously, and, despite the rain, a plump middle-aged man with a damp moustache. We do not speak. One does not speak in church.

The main room is occupied by single statues anywhere from six to ten feet high, the original maquettes, in white gypsum. Despite, or perhaps because of, the Prokofieff, there is a motionless bachelor silence about these rooms, an almost naval neatness, celibate, but not in the least monkish.

Beside the entrance desk, pinned to the wall, are large glossy photographs of the studio as it looked just after the liberation of Berlin. The studio was reduced to rubble, by comb concussion, but for some reason the statues were unscathed, and stand up to their waists in the débris, calm, definitive, and intolerable. The effect is impressive, and I remember that most of these statues were designed for a memorial, never built, to no one knows quite what. Kolbe was unquestionably Nordic, but not particularly co-operative, and it was by means of the excuse of this never-finished memorial, that he managed to equivocate with the Nazi régime, until the régime itself was finished, though the memorial was not. This is the sort of cleverness I admire, the cleverness of people who have their own work to do, and so put first things first.

It was a war memorial, I suppose.

The cult of the Master has, to an American, its hilarious moments. Or perhaps it is merely that the Protestant mind is not unduly susceptible to shrines. The studio has several of these. In the larger living room there is the chair the Master last sat in. Beside it, rests his cane. On the obviously down cushion on which the Inspired Bottom once rested somewhat heavily, there now rests lightly a glass dish containing pale red roses. They must be gathered from the garden every day, for the dew is still fresh on them.

In the main room, on a work table, where His tools were Last Laid Down, there are, apart from another bowl of flowers, some very odd objects indeed: snapshots of admirers, some of them old, some crisp as yesterday, a telegram or two "In Memoriam. The Master's Birthday, 1959" (he died in 1945). A seashell. A small plaster finger, broken off between the first and second joint. It is an ex-voto.

Like most sculptors, Kolbe was a narcissist. That is to say, he modeled his own body over and over again, but with different heads, and probably without realizing it. It is a body of odd proportion, long-waisted, narrow-hipped, a body more Western American than North European, one would think. It is the proportion of my own body, and of Yop's. Besides, one of the Master's works, Thus Spake Zarathustra, is enough like Yop to be his spitting image. So it is natural enough that I should fall to thinking of him, as I leave the studio, for he too aspires to be a Master. Or rather, he has no doubt that he is one, and is only watchfully waiting for his abilities to catch up with what he knows he can do, for to be a master, in this bland, inflexible, inexorable European sense, it is necessary to start young.

How is he getting on? I wonder.

Ten years ago, when we were all nobody much, and so easier of access, we lived together, by happenstance, in the same small French hill village in the Alpes Maritîmes, Yopple, Denise, some others, and myself. It was not a springtime for us, exactly, but it was most certainly a summer, drowsy, dusty, in old stone houses high above the olive trees. In the evenings, coming back from the farmhouse where we sometimes took an outdoor dinner, we walked in fireflies up to our waists. We had so much time on our hands that sometimes there was nothing to do all day long except to sit in high white rooms, blazing with sunlight, and listen to the river run, a hundred feet below. It was probably bohemian and untidy, but looked back on now, it seems to have been a period of equable contentment. There was time for work. There was time for ease. There was time for friendship.

Yop was then in his late thirties. I have a picture somewhere. He was handsome in a brooding blond Dutch way, even-tempered but severe, and had a face of refinement and the pale blue eyes of the Ancient Mariner. He was self-willed, charming, stubborn, and the closest thing to a genius I have ever met.

When he was about twenty-six, and working for a photographer, a sculptor brought a piece of sculpture in to be photographed. Yop had never really looked at a piece of sculpture before. He took the photograph, handed in his resignation, enrolled at the Royal Academy of Arts, and has never looked back since. He makes excellent tomato soup. He also has the self-protective guile of all innately innocent people.

Denise is harder to explain. She was born near Liège, and always reminded me, she and her sister both, of that famous late medieval statue, Les Dames de Hainault. As a matter of fact, she and her sister are known as Les Dames de Hainault. It is a work clumsy with hauteur. The family vice is insanity, pyromania until 1916, schizophrenia after the first world war. Pyromania is a forthright affliction, easy to detect and clinical to prevent, but schizophrenia has unexpected surprises.

One day I was walking with Denise and her sister Chantal over a little railroad bridge near Liège. Chantal is not talkative. When she does speak, you usually wish she had not. Over the hump of the bridge toddled towards us a pickaninny, authentic to the red ribbons in her hair.

"You see that. *You* made that," snapped Chantal, who took the Allied Occupation seriously, and scarcely knew where to deposit the blame.

"I most certainly did not," I said, being Southerner by sympathy, though never by act.

"Oh yes you did. The Occupation was terrible," said Chantal, and burst into tears.

By the time we had crossed the bridge, she had forgotten about it. However, sentences beginning, "After grandmother burned the children," were not particularly reassuring either.

Denise is the sane member of the family. Being too tall and bigboned to cuddle up to a Belgian husband, she has remained a single woman. She is hieratic, perplexed, handsome, cheerful, and a formal poet of great excellence, with an eerie command of the seventeenth-century French alexandrine. To celebrate the end of the Occupation, she illuminated a missal for the Bishop of Boston. It took her ten years. She has a childlike wistfulness. The best way to define her is in terms of her own language. Where anybody else would say, "Je m'assied," she says, "je me pose sur le fauteuil." She has a mild crush on all of us. She falls in love with one unsuitable person every ten years, never tells him so, and so remains a spinster by default. Vehemence and resignation are making lines around her mouth. I have lost touch with her.

Before she left our village, she bought from Yop one of his better things, "La Reine," a foot and a half of fired terracotta, the epitome

of autocratic scorn, regal and unassuming. This she referred to as
her "unengagement gift, you see, my English is improving."
   Then she went away.

   Between them, Denise and Chantal are the best-known illustra-
tors of children's books and greeting cards in Europe. Chantal has a
talent for Disneyesque faces, which get cuter every year, which is
why the books sell, but can draw nothing else. Denise has an exact
sense of design, a pressed-flower talent for vines and foliage and
animals and old buildings, and intricate, illuminated conceits. Unfortunately, the family is not only batty, but shrewd, and has signed
Denise to an airtight contract, whereby all monies are paid directly
to them, rather than to her. Out of these monies, which are large,
they make her a pitiably small allowance. She has tried to escape
several times, but the style is unmistakable, and they own the
name, and besides, the one cannot work without the other, so they
always starve her out and haul her back. She is the fun-loving,
irresponsible one, they say, whereas Chantal is the one with talent.
Chantal is always enough cute faces ahead, so that even is she has
to spend a year under restraint, there is still enough raw material
for Denise to work with. It is very Belgian, this arrangement, or to
be accurate, most Walloon.
   In the dentist's office, in Paris, I picked up a Belgian woman's
magazine which had a two-page color spread on both of them. They
live now in Bruges, so it seems, in a pleasant seventeenth-century
house on one of the minor canals. They are inseparable and deeply
devoted, says the letter press. They are known as Les Dames de
Hainault. There is a photograph of Denise at market, shopping with
a basket over her arm. She looks gravely older, but she is smiling.
There is a photograph of Chantal, virtuously busy at her art, though
the picture is so taken that you cannot see the board on which she is
working. On a table beside her is a copy of "Le Képi" by Colette.
   It is Christmas in Paris, and in all the shops on the Avenue are to
be seen Christmas cards by both of them. Since Denise is now
allowed to use her name, she must have wrangled some freedom
from the family contract. The article informed me that they own
not only the house in Bruges, but three more in what was once our
village. This is clear from the cards. The Holy Family tries to take
refuge in what looks very much like the garden entrance to my old

house there, on the way into Egypt. St. Joseph is my next-door neighbor of that time, the ex-Procurator General of Holland. The Magi turn out to be Sam Atyeo, an Australian diplomat who lived on a farm outside the village, Gordon Craig, who lives nearby at Vence, and the Negro one is a pickaninny. The Christ Child I do not recognize, but it has the approved Disney leer. The donkey I do recognize. It is Alceste, our common beast of burden.

The effect is jarring, but since it is snowing in Paris, I remember the warmth of those Southern summers in our village with more than nostalgia. In particular I remember one St. Martin's Eve, just before we went our separate ways for the year, when the gigolo of the owner of the hotel (a raddled old blond skinflint who kept him on too short a leash) dragged all the summer wicker furniture out onto the bonfire in the square, and then went drunkenly through the upper floors of the inn, throwing down chairs from the windows, while his mistress shrieked for her rents.

Augmented, the fire leapt up, until it cast reflections across the stone church tower on the other side of the square and made your face hot. The wicker caught instantly, presenting you with the angry red ghost of a chair, before it crumbled. It is a legend, that if you join hands with someone and jump through a St. Martin's bonfire, lovers or friends, you will then be inseparable. Partings are full of sentiment. Denise waited for Yop. Instead he grabbed me out of my chair.

"Come, David," he said, in a mood most unlike him, but perhaps he did not like the thought of being alone here all winter, "we jump now."

So, taking a running start, we closed our eyes, at least I closed my eyes, and we jumped. Our bottoms got warm, there was an acrid odor in the nostrils, and there we were on the other side. Yop laughed and looked abashed.

"It is better than blood brothers in a cheap novel," he said. "A novel for boys. But we are not boys."

Madam of the hotel was not pleased. She was fifty-five, she could not go without her cheap Corsican playboy, but she had just realized about the furniture.

Yop, I remember, has very dry hands.

I have lost track of him, so I write to Denise for the address. When last I saw her, on the iced pier at Ostend, eight years ago, where I had gone to catch a boat, there were words. She had come to the end of one of her silent ten-year broods. But all is forgiven, and she sends me Yop's address, though for some reason she seems not to wish to discuss him. She writes about other things, and tells me he lives in Leiden.

I intend to visit both of them, but because it is easier to go to Holland from Paris, than to get to Bruges, which requires an overnight stop in Brussels, which is a detestable place, I go to Amsterdam first, and from there drop Yop a card.

He refuses to meet me in Leiden, he says it is not possible. Many things are not possible for Yop, deliberately so. That phrase is his equivalent of disconnecting the telephone. He will meet me in Amsterdam instead. Characteristically, he has forgotten to mail the card in time, so I have only half an hour in which to get to the station. This makes me doubly nervous. Will I be able to recognize him? Can I still pick him out of a crowd? It has been eight years, and I had not realized until this moment how incredibly fond of him I am. It is a fondness based on admiration, the sort of fondness a German student feels for his old professor, full of weltschmerz and clumsiness and apprehension, and the impatience of the young grown older, but it is real, all right.

But there he is, and no, he has not changed. Being Dutch, he has grown stolid, he is surrounded by a beautiful silence, which he carries about with him, as is the way of the authentic Master, but he still has that quick, darting air of the clean, towheaded boy, the art of rushing slowly, with some pomp. He has that manner of being both uncle and nephew to himself and others which men of this type so often have, which Kolbe seems to have had.

Needless to say, since they have much in common, he is not unduly taken with the works of Kolbe, artists, like religious sects, differing the more, the less the differences are between them, in a stubborn fight to maintain their own identity, their own sense of being chosen.

"David, my dear David," he says. "It is so nice. I am so happy. I see nobody, absolutely nobody, but here we are again. So now I think we go to breakfast. But speak slow. I read English, it is my fourth language, but I do not hear it good." He is entirely affable. It is not his best mood. Like a bear, he invites trespass only to punish it. Yet trespass I suppose I shall. I usually manage to.

I lead the way to an outdoor café I like.

"No," he says. "It is too much food, it is too much tourist. We will go elsewhere, to a place where the service is slow, like a fishtank, and the waiter has good bones. You will see. And the food it is not bad."

We go into a tiled Gothic nineteenth-century palace of a place, where small businessmen are having long sad meals, and sit in the window to watch the people go by. The waiter has good bones, as promised, but almost no flesh. We eat something.

Yopple is happy. When he is happy he sits quietly, with his hands dangling between his knees, like a schoolchild waiting in the cloakroom on a bench. I am aware, however, that I am undergoing a detailed inspection. This will continue for the length of the visit. It always does. I am being inspected *to see if I have lowered my standards.* I am used to this, and do not mind, but it cannot be denied that the process has an almost military exactitude, and leaves one with an unforgivably comic desire to faint.

I ask about Denise. He clouds up at once. There is a long pause.

I say I have seen her cards in Paris, and am on my way to see her, perhaps.

"If you are popular, it eats you up," says Yop, and looks annoyed. "I have not seen her. It is not necessary. Come, we will take a walk now."

We take a walk now. I am aware that I have displeased him. But apparently *I have not lowered my standards,* for at the station, before leaving, he asks me to Leiden for lunch, to see the studio.

If you are fond of people, these mannerisms do not signify, in fact, they become endearing, because familiar, so off to Leiden next day I go. This time, it is his turn to meet me at the station. It is an efficient modern station, with automatic turnstiles. Yopple appears wheeling an outsize bicycle. It will not go through the turnstiles, and he looks vaguely disappointed about this. I have never been to Leiden before, and hope to see it, but apparently Leiden is irrelevant.

"Do you remember the bonfire?" he asks. Time for him is not a sequence but a pouch. In conversation, he just reaches in and takes out whatever happens to come to his hand first.

I say yes, and he looks pleased. I have the impression that he is lonely, and terrier eager to show off. He gets on the bicycle and gyres round me in slow coasting motion, like a seagull come to greet a boat. All the same, he is preoccupied.

In this manner, we weave through the crowds and several streets, until we hit, literally, a cobbled square too bumpy for bicycle gyring. He descends from the bicycle, and we walk with it between us, each of us guiding a handlebar, while we talk. On the far side of the square is a low building, a series of connected cottages actually, with an arched passageway as its entrance. Inside there is a small and charming garden, decorated with sculpture, none of it his, and crowded with vivid nineteenth-century flowers. The place was an almshouse, he explains, now converted into studios. He takes out an enormous rusted key and lets me in.

A sculptor's studio is apt to be a disappointment at first, for you expect more work than there ever is, but if the work be good, that makes no difference. The work, I am relieved to see, is very good indeed.

Probably creative people have no more respect for critics and collectors than a chemist has for litmus paper. Nonetheless, for the moment I have been promoted from defendant to judge. The rôle of prosecutor Yop has reserved for himself. He always does. It is best suited, he seems to feel, to his abilities. He takes a squint at the lighting and begins to move things about. He is putting the exhibits in order. I offer to help, but he is strong as an ox, just as stubborn, and needs none. He shows me several things.

There is an incredibly suave adolescent flute player, a maquette in terracotta, the equivalent in its own sex to Denise's "La Reine" in hers, but even more refined. I admire it. He is not altogether pleased. He is not yet old enough to have developed a resigned fondness for his earlier works. He says it is too refined, and that he has outgrown all that. He finds it too easy.

I look around me. On a shelf stands a mask of vaguely pre-Columbian cast, which I remember from the village. It has been shattered since then, however, and put together again with white plaster in the cracks, like an artifact from a long-dead culture. The effect is oddly pleasing, but disturbing, too.

I ask about a block of Irish marble I gave him once, the color of creamed spinach, with mica grits in it. I do not see it here.

"It was a rabbit," he says. "I've never done a rabbit before. It is in

Paris now, in a private collection. But it is very well lit, and they are good collectors." He sounds as though he were patting a small dog. Then he chuckles. "They keep a spare bedroom for me, but of course I never go. Unfortunately they have a Chagall. They are people of taste, how *could* they have a Chagall? It is in the bathroom. It is incomprehensible."

They are Dutch, too, I gather. Most of his collectors are. He appeals more to the North European than to the Frenchified taste, though there are some of his things in collections in New England.

Turning to pleasanter things, he shows me a sort of idol in terracotta, which, with the best will in the world, I find altogether hideous. Nor can I hide my feelings about it, for artists, confronted with the mere connoisseur, have the paranormal powers of family dogs.

Though *I have not lowered my standards,* plainly I don't come up to his, either. Yop gives me the beady, triumphant look of a school examiner who has at last discovered an irremediable flaw. "Ah well, perhaps in a year or two, when you are ready," he says kindly. He looks impish, for he has just won the hundred yard dash, he is still *ahead,* he is still incomprehensible to the laity, and this makes him feel that he is on the right track, and winning. The litmus-paper test never fails. Since he has some respect for my judgment, otherwise I would not be here, he feels confirmed. Dragging out a still more recent piece, he tries again, and asks me what it *is.*

I am cautious. He is so offhand that I know I must get it right this time. It is a gypsum model, about life-size, of a man on his hands and knees, blindly struggling to rise. Like most of Yop's better work, it looks matter of fact at first, but the longer you look the bigger it gets, until soon enough, it is bigger than you are, it surrounds you, you can move about in it quite easily.

"Someone who has been flung down or beaten, probably by himself, is rising again. He has been defeated but he is not defeated," I say, as though spelling it out, and concentrating hard.

The statue is surrounded by silence. It begins to take over the space around it, the room, and, ultimately, the spectator. The effect is inevitable, and explains why the young woman from Los Angeles, who once borrowed some of his works, found she couldn't sleep at night in the same house with them, and so had to return them. She said she kept waking up, and there they were, staring at her. It cannot be denied. There is no room in his work for the militant. One feels at ease with it only if one is relaxed.

"It is Adam, after the expulsion. It is Cain, realizing what he has done. It is near enough," says Yopple, smiles wryly, and gives a grunt. "I have learned a lot from doing it."

In the centre of the room, on a revolving plinth, is a life-size bundle, shrouded like a corpse, with rags, or perhaps like an insane person, since they are wet rags. These he begins to unwrap with surgical anxiety. I have passed. I am to be shown the work in progress.

All this time it has been standing there, purposely neglected, but difficult to ignore, for it dominates the room.

The heavy rags accumulate on the floor. For some reason, I am sure this is something I would rather not see, but it becomes visible anyway.

The bandages come off the head last, as though he were reluctant to reveal that. The statue is a larger version of "La Reine" life-size, and ten years older. And the head is Denise's head.

And yet I doubt very much if he realizes this, for he is not good at facial likenesses, they do not interest him. He is interested in something which people embody, not in individual people as such, he says, which no doubt explains the religious streak in and meditative nature of his work. Nonetheless, this is Denise's face, with all the life drained abruptly out of it, sad, immobile, passive, withdrawn. Though the torso is finished, the arms are not. Their armatures stick out through the clay, where the hands should be.

"It is the biggest thing I have tried to do," he says. "Oh, it is very difficult. I have been at work on it since," and he switches sentences, "since a year." His smile is a happy one. His hesitation is slight. Lovingly he shrouds the thing up again, from the head down, making sure the rags are damp enough. Then we leave the studio, and wheel the bicycle out onto the main street, where we wait for a trolley. The trolley, which is crowded, stops with an audible electric sigh, as though it wanted no more. There is certainly no room for more. Yopple drags his bicycle aboard. Several passengers seem to know him, and make room in a hostile manner, sullen and bovine as cows driven to take the higher ground.

Yop nods happily. "It is forbidden, but I am Town Sculptor, you know, so they let me do it," he says.

No, I did not know. Yet I am pleased to see this new benignity springs from success, and not, as it usually does, from something withdrawn, like a secret lever. The trolley clangs away through the breakneck streets, until we reach Plantsoen, which is where he lives.

It is very Dutch, Plantsoen. There is an unruffled pond, an equally unruffled swan, green banks, green shrubbery, some carefully thinned trees, some public-garden flowers, and not so much as a twig or a piece of string to litter anything. This park is surrounded by stolid, well-padded nineteenth-century neo-classical buildings, painted the color of clotted cream.

"It was once a monastery. It is suitable. It is a university now."

I agree that it is suitable, and get quite an odd look, by way of reply. We go up the steps into what turns out to be the administration building. The offices smell of chalk and too much work done slowly, but there is a bowl of daffodils on top of a steel filing cabinet, and the windows are wide to admit the sun. The Town Council has allowed him to live here, on the top, or mansard, floor.

At the end of the uncarpeted hall, a wide wooden stair leads upward. The treads all list inward, the wood is grey with use, but it seems firm. Yop leaps up the stairs in his usual springbok manner. Two years ago he walked to Greece, on impulse, as a Moslem would start out for Mecca in the morning, because it was time, and he has no patience with weaklings from the elevator age.

The second floor is given over to offices, so is the third, but on the fourth the walls begin to bloom with pictures. In Paris, this many floors up, there hangs always the inevitable and precisely dated Cocteau drawing, harbinger of still sleazier things to come. I find its absence here reassuring. Talk though they will, the French these days seem to view the fine arts as a branch of the perfume industry, but the Dutch are made of sterner and more cheerful stuff, they are more interested in quality than fashion, and therefore they are a good deal more nearly permanent to talk to.

But though we have come out onto the topmost landing, the climb has left me puffing. I have no breath to talk, so I look around me instead. What looks like a Khmer head stands on a black plinth.

Opposite it is a polished paneled oak door. He unlocks this and we go inside. The rooms remind me of something, though I cannot remember what. Perhaps it is merely that the fastidious artist anywhere has been making himself the same sort of house now for well over thirty years. The walls are white, the ceilings high, and everything is both deliberately underfurnished and specifically arranged; the pictures and sculpture, though few, are placed exactly right. On the wall is what looks to be a Feininger.

"It is not a Feininger. It is a me. I needed one," Yop says brusquely. "It is my best oil. But you are right, he is a clean painter."

No critical term in his lexicon is more favorable. He walks out and leaves me alone, while he fetches sherry, a drink he can't stand himself, but keeps for visitors the way a bourbon drinker keeps soda pop for the neighbors' kids. Having pretended to himself for a lifetime that he is always at his ease, whether he is or not, Yop, though not a teetotaler, scorns artificial aids.

I am aware that something is bothering him, though I do not know what. I am equally aware that something is bothering me, though I do not know what. The room where the Feininger hangs is a general living room, with walls about thirty feet long. Spaced along them are life-size statues of the same woman, suppliant, immobile, at first glance alike, but at second subtly dissimilar. One or the other arm of each is imperceptibly raised, less in a gesture of offering something, than of holding back, in one case a bunch of marble grapes, in another, a pomegranate. I have never seen anything quite like them, by him or by anybody else.

"I got the idea from watching Denise," he says, coming back. "She stands like that sometimes. Don't you agree?" It is the first time he has mentioned her. Apparently it is also to be the last. But he has great plans for these statues. He has been at work on them for years, and there are to be twelve of them. He is trying to talk the Town Council into having them cast and set up in a semicircle in the shrubbery of some public park. "It is my war memorial," he says. "They are like mothers."

They look more like spinsters to me, but I know better than to say so, and besides, he darts away again, to prepare lunch. Not wanting to confront the statues, I wander round the room instead. On a low table are two nephrite water buffalo I have never seen before. They are not very well done, but the curve of their horns is charming, and that, I suppose, is why he has bought them. On the bookcase is a small bronze from the Eumorfopoulos collection. He has always had it, but how he got it I do not know. Like a great many seemingly frank people, Yop leaves a good deal out. Eumorfopoulos has been dead a good deal longer than Yop has been a sculptor, but the only explanation offered is, "I liked it, so he gave it me."

Somewhat unwillingly, I find myself looking at the ladies along the wall again. They are sad and minatory, like everything else he does. It has not occurred to me before, but yes, Denise *is* a Yop. She has the same bearing, the same gravity, the same elliptical quietness, though she is *sans amertume,* a favorite phrase of his, or at least she used to be, a phrase popular among French intellectuals of the generation before this one. She even has, what is more startling, the same blind, perceptive, inexorable, defeated eyes as his statues have. It is just that when she smiles, which is the expression of hers I chiefly remember, her eyes light up with something childlike which hides for an instant that unflinching gaze into nothingness.

Yop comes back, bringing broth with fresh chopped cress in it, a salad, milk, and then excellent coffee. He is a good frugal cook, much concerned with textures and flavors. The Town Council, he says, are about to make him curator of the local historic windmill. He will have more room there to work. He adds that he is happy here; a few years ago there was a small difficulty, but he conquered it, so now he is content. He has much to do. He tells me about some of it. But he does not seem easy. Towards evening he walks me back to the station, through the jostling streets of the slow old town. He asks me where I am going next. I tell him that I had planned to pay a visit to Denise, at Bruges.

"She will not speak to me these days, I don't know why," he says shortly, and abruptly points out some antique glass in a shop window. He seems to be tugging at some kind of spiritual leash, I cannot control him, so off we go, like a small man with a large hound. The result of this is that we get to the station too early, and therefore have fifteen awkward minutes to get through. Though he plans well, he has walked too fast. Beside us is a magazine kiosk in six languages. Yop makes his choice. He has something he wants to get rid of, and I am just the person to cart it away, it seems.

"Look, I will tell you a story," he says. "Two years ago everything was wrong. I could not work. It was terrible. It was before I began my war memorial. I felt I was going mad. I had no serenity. I did not want to go on. My talent deserted me. I decided I might as well destroy myself, which was wicked, so"———and at last he pulls the rabbit alive and kicking from the hat, there is a breathless pause, he is a magician surprised by his own tricks———"so I *proposed to Denise.*" He takes a professional look at my astonishment, gauges it neatly, and goes on. "Naturally, she accepted. It was only a marriage of convenience, but I was terrified, terrified. The week before the wedding, I went down to Bruges. I did not have the time, I had begun my war memorial. It was big, big, I hated to leave it. But I went. Women have no right to interrupt, but she had asked me to. Well, you know Bruges. It is very pretty. It is too pretty. Also, it was raining. Then, as I was walking over one of the bridges, the sun came out for a moment. I stopped where I was. I took decision. I put my hand on the balustrade of the bridge, and I said, "Yop, this is not *necessary.*" He is trying to make vivid the temptation of St. Antony, he wants to get it right, he rummages in three languages, to find the right words, and gives up. There are no right words.

"And then?" I ask.

"And then?" He looks astonished. "Why, I came back, of course, on the next train. I was working again. There was no problem."

I cannot help it. It strikes me as incredibly funny, for though I can see Denise's face, pressed up against a rain-splattered window pane, I can also see the expression with which seriously, and little boy confessing, he confronts me, and so I double up and laugh until I cry.

"Oh Yopple, Yopple," I say.

He backs off critically. At first he is puzzled. Then he seems relieved. But he does not see what is so funny.

"I like you better now," he says. "Now you are the way you used to be, whereas today you have been *stiff.*"

I take out my handkerchief to dry my eyes. Yes, perhaps I have been stiff.

"But why is she put out?" he demands. "I told her it was no longer necessary. I even *thanked* her. I sent her pictures of the new work, and you know, I never do that until something is truly finished. But she has never written to me since."

He glares at me, half humorously, poking fun at himself as though he were poking a possum with a stick, and then, since the train has come in, he turns and strides off, confident, alone, back to his clay ladies wrapped in wet cloth, untroubled by their resemblance to what he has done.

I get aboard, but, watching the low fields slip by, as the train gathers speed, I decide not to go to see Denise after all, and besides, I remember something the woman said at Kolbe's studio, when I was trying to pump her for anecdotes of the Master.

"I was never allowed in here as a child," she said. "He never let any of us into the studio." And looking round at it, her mouth became a tight, bitter, reminiscent line. Following her glance, I see that the two studios are the same room. Do what we will, it is always the same room.

# Dean of Men

I am not unsympathetic, Jack, to your views on the War. I am not unsympathetic to your views on the state of the world in general. From the way you wear your hair and from the way you dress I do find it difficult to decide whether you or that young girl you say you are about to marry is going to play the male rôle in your marriage—or the female rôle. But even that I don't find offensive. And I am not trying to make crude jokes at your expense. You must pardon me, though, if my remarks seem too personal. I confess I don't know you as well as a father *ought* to know his son, and I may seem to take liberties.

However, Jack, I do believe that I understand the direction in which you—all of you—think you are going. I have not observed college students during the past thirty years for nothing. And I must try to warn you that I don't think even *your* wonderful generation will succeed in going very far along the road you are on. In this connection, Jack, I want to tell you a story. I can tell you this story because even its most recent chapters took place a very long time ago and because the events of the story don't matter to anybody any more—neither to me nor even to your mother. When you see your mother next, and if you repeat what I am about to tell you, she may give you a somewhat different version. But that doesn't matter. It is not really a story about your mother and me or about our divorce. Perhaps it is a story about you and me—about men.

I think I know the very moment to begin: I was fitting the key into the lock of my office door on a Sunday morning. I was in such a temper I could hardly get the key into the keyhole or turn the lock after it was in. There had been a scene at our breakfast table at home; I had left the house. It was a strangely upsetting scene for me, though commonplace enough on the surface. Your sister Susie, who was no more than nine or ten then—she couldn't have been more since *you* were still in a high chair, Jack—Susie had interrupted what I was saying across my Sunday morning grapefruit to your mother. And I had fired away at her, "Don't interrupt grown-up talk, Susie!"

That sounds commonplace enough, I know. But Susie persisted. "Why don't you go up to the Trustees, Daddy," said she, advising me on how to behave in the professional crisis I was then in and which I had been discoursing upon across my grapefruit, "why don't you go up to them and tell them how the President of the College is being unfair to you?"

Somehow I found her little remark enraging. I fairly shouted across the table, "For God's sake, Susie, shut up. Don't try to talk about things you don't understand or know a damned thing about!"

I blush now to think that I ever spoke so to a child, but I remember it too well to try to deny it. You see, Jack, I had actually already resigned my appointment at that college where I was then teaching, which was the very college where, a dozen years before, I had been an undergraduate. I had resigned just three weeks before in protest against an injustice done me, and I had not yet received a definite commitment from the place where I was going next year. (I did receive the commitment the following day, as I recall, but that is not really significant.) Anyhow, I was feeling like a fool, I suppose, to have brought into the world three children for whom I might not be able to provide—only two children, actually, though little Maisie was on the way by then. And I was feeling like a fool, I suppose, to have risked their welfare—*your* welfare, if you please—over a principle of honest administration in a small Mid-Western college. I was a very unhappy man, Jack, and there before me was my little ten year old daughter seeming to reproach me for my foolishness. . . . At any rate, after my second blast at her, Susie had burst into tears and had run from the dining room and out into the yard. Your mother got up from her chair at the end of the table and said to me, "I would be ashamed of myself if I were you."

I made no reply except to say through my teeth: "This is too much."

Your mother's words were still in my ears when I shoved open the door to my office at the college (Marie's words have a way of lingering in your ears for a very long time, Jack.) Anyhow, I had left the table without finishing breakfast, and left the dining room without any idea of where I was going. And then suddenly I had known. What drove me from the table, of course, were those words of Marie's that were still in my ears. For, Jack, those were the very words I had once heard my mother speak to my father, and, moreover, had heard her speak to Father at a Sunday breakfast table when *he* had teased my own sister Margaret till she cried and left the room. "I would be ashamed of myself if I were you," my mother had said, rising from the table in just the same way that my own wife was destined to do twenty years later. My father bolted from the table, left the house, and went downtown to his office, where he spent the whole of that Sunday. It seemed almost impossible that the incident should be repeating itself in my life. And yet to a remarkable degree it was so, and the memory of where it was my father had taken himself off to told me to what place I must take myself that Sunday morning.

It struck me, just as the door to my office came open, that I had never before seen my office at that early hour on Sunday. I had never, in fact, been in that building where my office was on a Sunday morning—or on the College campus itself, for that matter. It was a lovely campus, on a hill and with trees and with a little river at the foot of the hill, and it was a quite handsome neo-Gothic building I was in. I altogether liked that place, I can assure you. And in addition to my liking the other people on the faculty there, I had my old associations with the place from my undergraduate days. The truth is I had thought I would settle down there for life, to do my teaching and my writing. It was the third teaching appointment I had had, but in my profession many people have to move around even more than I before they find a congenial spot, Jack. I was not yet thirty-five. I had considered myself lucky to find an agreeable place so early in my career, a small college where I had memories of my youth and where I would be allowed to do my mature work in peace.

But I knew by that Sunday morning that I was going to move on. I knew that by the next fall I would be in some other, almost identical office on some other campus and that your mother and I, with our three children, would be established in another house in another college town somewhere. But when I shoved open my office door, somehow it was not as though it were the door to just any little cubby hole of an office. It was as if it were the door to my ancestral keep—my castle, so to speak; and I burst in upon my papers, my books, my pictures that morning as if expecting to catch them, my kinsmen—my cousins germane—in some conspiratorial act against me—yes, as though it were my books, my papers, my pictures who had betrayed me. But of course the room was just as I had left it. It was the same, and yet at that hour on Sunday morning it did seem different, too.

I can see myself there now, especially as I was during the first quarter hour of that long day. I didn't knock things about or tear up the place as it was my first impulse to do. Instead, after I had slammed the door and latched it, the first thing I did was to go quickly to my desk and turn down the photographs of your mother and Susie and even the one of yourself, Jack. I took the pages of my manuscript and of my typescript, which had been in little stacks all over my desk top, and quietly stuffed them inside the desk drawers. The books I had been reading recently—my own and those from the library—I removed from the table by my leather chair, putting them out of sight or at least placing them where they would not catch my eye on the lowest shelf of my book case. Then I took down from the walls the four or five prints that hung there, reproductions I had brought back from my Fulbright in Italy, and I set them on the floor with their faces against the wall. If I handled these familiar objects gently, I believe it was just because I had not, after all, found them in active conspiracy against me.

There was no conspiracy among my books and papers and pictures; but what was perhaps worse, I seemingly had found them all dead—murdered. I felt they were strewn about the room like corpses in the last scene of an Elizabethan tragedy. Dead and murdered, that is, so far as I was concerned. Dead and wanting

burial. And so, bending over them, I tenderly tucked them away as
if to their last rest. Then I went and half-sat, half-leaned against
the sill of the room's only window. The venetian blind there was
lowered and the louvres were only half open. I leaned against the
sill with my arms folded on my chest and observed the crepuscular
light in the room, and I was aware of the Sunday morning stillness.
Once again I heard Marie's voice, and after a moment once again
heard my mother's voice. Presently I recalled my father's voice too,
speaking not through his teeth as I had done that morning, but
growling out of one corner of his mouth. I remembered how, as a
younger man, I would sometimes wonder about that outburst of
Father's temper on that other Sunday morning. It had seemed to me
so unlike him. I used to speculate even, in the most literal minded
way, on how he had managed to occupy himself during the long
hours he had spent alone in *his* office on that Sunday. The scene he
had made at his breakfast table—or that my sister Margaret, or my
mother had made—suddenly now became very easy for me to
understand. Everything fell so easily into place that I felt I had
always understood it. My father was a lawyer and a business man
who had lost most of what he had as a consequence of the '29 Crash.
My sister Margaret was already a young lady at the time. She was
no little girl like Susie when she sat down to breakfast with Father
that other Sunday. She was a good-looking blonde girl with wide
green eyes, and she had a lovely disposition. She was always cheerful, always saying something clever or making you feel that you had
said something clever. Margaret was the oldest child in the family,
and I the youngest. But we were very close to each other, and I
believe she confided her most serious thoughts to me more often
than to anyone else, though surely it was Father she loved best.
There was frequently a great deal of banter between her and Father
at the table. She was such a well-behaved girl, so puritanical really,
that Father would tease her sometimes about leading a wild life and
keeping late hours. Mother would say she thought it in bad taste for
Father to tease his own daughter about such things and that perhaps he would be putting ideas into her head. But Margaret would
laugh at Mother and say that Father's evil mind made it all the more
fun to deceive him. Then she and Father would laugh together in a
sort of duet of laughter.

Margaret was popular with boys and always had a number of

serious admirers. But the more serious the admirers were, the more she and Father seemed to delight in making fun of them. I don't believe Margaret ever imagined she was in love with any of those young men until the time when Paul Kirkpatrick came along. Paul's family was one that nearly everybody knew about. They were such very rich people that even the Crash and the Depression hardly affected them at all. But it worried Margaret how rich the Kirkpatrick family was. It worried her, that is, that Paul would some day be rich, that she knew he would be rich, and that he was the only young man she found herself able to love. "I know I really love him for himself," she would say to me when we were walking in the Park together or if we were in her room with the door shut, "but sometimes there seems to be an ugly, suspicious side of me— another person (old nasty-minded Mag, I call her)—who laughs and cackles at me like a witch and says, '*I* know why you love him so, dear Miss Margaret! You don't deceive me!'" Then Margaret and I would laugh together, rather the way she and Father did. But she was serious, and was worried.

Perhaps Father worried about it too—more than I guessed, more than Margaret guessed. Naturally he would have liked for her to marry a rich man, but there had been so much talk at our house about how hard times were for us that Father may have been afraid Margaret was going to marry into a rich family for *his* sake. At any rate, he was harder on Paul Kirkpatrick in his fun making than he had been on any of the other young men. And Margaret went right along with him. They made fun of Paul's teeth—Margaret called them stalactites and stalagmites—made fun of his too lofty way of speaking, of the way he walked—they said he waddled—even made fun of his baby-smooth complexion.

Yet after one of those sessions with Father, when she and I were alone, Margaret smiled at me and said. "You know something? I really think Paul's very good looking, don't you?"

I told her that yes, I did think so. And it was true. Paul Kirkpatrick was quite handsome. He was an attractive and intelligent young man. But Margaret and Father kept on telling each other how ridiculous he was. It was the summer of 1930. Father was under great tension that summer. It was a year when he suffered one financial blow after another. And he never seemed more tense than when he and Margaret got on the subject of Paul. Sometimes it was very clear that he was prodding and trying to make her come to Paul's defense. But she never gave an inch. I was certain sometimes, however, from the way she sat smiling at Father that she was on the verge of blurting out that she loved Paul and was going to marry him. For I think my sister Margaret intended to marry Paul Kirkpatrick and would have done so had it not been for the family scene that Sunday morning. I had witnessed Paul's and Margaret's embraces and kisses at the side door more than once that summer. And once I saw—or just possibly imagined I saw—a ring with a large stone in Margaret's purse. Anyway, I remember she came down to breakfast later than the rest of us on that Sunday, and she was fully dressed, which was unusual for anyone at our breakfast table on Sunday. It seems to me that Father had not spoken at the table—he was often silent and abstracted then, though it was not in his nature to be so—he had not spoken until he looked up and saw Margaret sitting, fully dressed, at her place. "Well, you must have a church date with our toothy young friend," he said to her.

"He's coming over this morning," Margaret said with a smile. "I don't know about church." I am quite sure now that she was trying to prepare Father, and that Paul was going to "speak" to him that day.

I saw Mother look at Father, and it seems to me that I heard him swallow, though his mouth and throat were empty. Then, lifting a fork heaped with scrambled eggs, he said, "Why not? It's just as easy to love a rich one as a poor one, isn't it, Margaret?"

I saw the first patches of red appear under Margaret's ears and then the same red suffuse her entire face. And I saw the tears fill her eyes before the first sob came. When she pushed herself back from the table, Father was still holding the fork with the eggs on it. He put his fork down on his plate without spilling a morsel. But he was as white as the big napkin which his left hand then drew from his lap and threw out upon the table. "My God. My God," he growled from the corner of his mouth as Margaret ran, weeping aloud, through the living room and then through the hall and on upstairs. And my mother rose at her place and said, "I would be ashamed of myself if I were you."

How Father occupied himself and what he thought about when he reached his office that Sunday were questions that occurred to me during the very hours he was there, occurred to me even though I was just a boy of twelve at the time. My father was known as "a devoted family man," he almost never went to his office at night, and if some piece of business called him there on a Saturday afternoon or a Sunday, he groaned and complained endlessly. We knew he had gone to his office that morning, however, because Mother telephoned him after about an hour, to make sure he was all right. She knew about the money worries he had then, of course, and so she was quick to blame his behavior on that. In fact, she went to Margaret's room and reminded her of "the tensions Father was under" and told her that *she* must forgive him, too. I suspect that Margaret had already forgiven him. I know that she had telephoned Paul Kirkpatrick and told him not to come that day. Her romance with Paul did not last long after that. The next year she married a "struggling young lawyer" and with him, as my mother would have said, "she has had a good life."

No doubt my father wrote a few letters at his office desk, as I did during the course of my Sunday at my office. But probably it wasn't easy for him to concentrate on letters. I recall that even while I remained leaning against the sill of my office window it came to me that what my father might have thought about in his office, twenty years before, was his own father. For yes, there *was* a story in the family about a scene that my grandfather had made at *his* breakfast table, too. I cannot give so many details about it, though possibly my father could have. There are many obscurities about the old story that I can't possibly clear up and won't try to. In fact, I don't know anything definite about the immediate circumstances that led to the scene. Perhaps I never knew them. People in my grandfather's day disliked admitting they did wretched things to each other at home or that there *were* family scenes in their families. All of the incident that has come down is that my grandfather, no longer a young man—a man past middle age, standing in the doorway to his dining room with his broad brimmed felt hat on, hurled a silver dollar at my grandmother, who was still seated at the breakfast table, and that the silver dollar landed in the sugar bowl. There is just the additional detail that my grandmother would allow no one to remove the coin and that that sugar bowl, with the silver dollar buried in the sugar, remained on her pantry shelf as long as the old lady lived.

I have always imagined that there had been a quarrel between my grandparents about housekeeping money; perhaps my grandfather, who was not much of a family man in the beginning and who lived a big part of his life away from home, among men, and who was known by all men for his quick temper, perhaps he lost his head momentarily. He forgot he was not among men, and he hurled the piece of money at his wife as he would have at some man to whom he had lost a bet. He and my grandmother may have had other difficulties between them over money or over other matters. Perhaps it was really a symbolic gesture on his part, as refusing to remove the coin was on hers. He was not a rich man, but then he was certainly not a poor man either, and actually in his day he was quite a well-known public figure. He was in politics, as his father and his father's father before him were. . . . I must tell you something about their politics. They were not exactly small-time politicians. Each one of them, at one time or another during his lifetime, represented our district in Congress. For nearly a hundred years "we" more or less occupied that seat in Congress. But my grandfather was the most successful and best known of the line and in middle age was elected to the United States Senate to complete the unexpired term of an incumbent who had died in office.

Probably my grandfather brought the special type of politician they all three were to its highest possible point of development, a kind of frontiersman-gentleman politician with just the right mixture of realism and idealism to appeal to their constituents. Today people would no doubt call him a pragmatist. He was known for his elegant oratory on the platform and in public debate and known also for the coarseness of his speech in private debate or in private confrontation with his opponents. (My grandfather's grandfather had once horsewhipped an opponent on the public square, and his own father had fought a duel.) It was Grandfather's beautiful oratory and his beautiful voice that got him elected to the Senate. People didn't care what his stand on tariff or on the silver or gold issue was. They believed he was an honest man and they knew he was a spellbinder. He too believed he was an honest man and he didn't understand the new kind of urban politician that was coming to power in our state at the time. It may be he was actually betrayed and ruined by the new politicians simply because they were "low-born rascals." Or it may be he was inevitably betrayed and ruined by them because once a human type is perfected—or almost per-

fected—it immediately becomes an anachronism and has no place
in society. Who can say? He was, at any rate, betrayed and ruined
by a lowborn man named Lon Lucas, and he never held political
office again after that brief term in the Senate.

And now, Jack, I come to the part of the story that I believe it is
essential for you to hear. If you have not understood why I have told
you all that went before, you will, anyhow, understand why I wish
to recount the three episodes that follow.

What happened to my grandfather's political career can be briefly
summarized. The unexpired term in the Senate, which he was
filling out, lasted but two years. When the time came for him to
make his race for a full term, he was persuaded by Lon Lucas and
others that, instead of making that race, it was his duty to his party
to come home and run for governor of the State. The Lucas faction
comprised a group of young men whom my grandfather considered
more or less his protégés. In earlier days they had asked countless
small favors of him, and no doubt they had done so in order to create
that relationship to him. Now they pointed out to him that from
another faction in the party there was a man who, though loathsome to them all, was a strong candidate for the Party's nomination
for governor, and pointed out that only he, my grandfather, could
block the nomination and the election of that man. It would be a
disgrace to the State and to the Party to have such a man in the
governor's chair, they said. Yet the Senator could easily come home
and win the nomination and the election for himself and could just
as easily regain his seat in the Senate at a later time.

You may well wonder that an experienced politician could be so
naïve as to accept that line of reasoning or to trust his fate in the
hands of those ambitious younger men. Neither his father or his
grandfather would surely, under any circumstances, have relin-
quished that prize of prizes for a politician, a seat in the United
States Senate. I cannot pretend to explain it. I knew my grandfather only as an embittered old man who didn't care to have
children crawling all over him. But I have to tell you that within a
few weeks after he came home and began his campaign for governor, Lon Lucas and his faction turned on him. Some sort of deal was
made with the other faction. No doubt the deal was made long
beforehand. Lucas came out in support of the "loathsome man" for
governor, and one of the Lucas faction was put up for the seat in the

Senate. Very likely there were other considerations also, remunera-
tive to Lon Lucas and company if not to the candidates themselves.
Such details are not important here, and I never knew them,
anyway. But my grandfather was defeated, and he retired from
public life to the bosom of his family, where, alas, I cannot say he
was greatly loved and cherished.

He withdrew almost entirely from all male company, seeing men
only as his rather limited law practice required him to do. He lived
out his life in a household of women and children, a household
consisting for many years of his wife, his wife's mother and maiden
aunt, his own mother, who lived to be ninety-seven, five daughters
and three sons. He never allowed himself to be addressed as Senator
and forbade all political talk in his presence. The members of his
household were destined to retain in their minds and to hand down
to future generations their picture of him not as a statesman of high
principle or even as a silver-tongued orator but as the coarse-
tongued old tyrant of their little world. His three sons always feared
him mightily and took from his life only the one lesson: an anathema
on politics. My father was the only son who would consent to study
law and become a member of the old gentleman's firm, but even he
made it clear from the outset that he would not let his profession
lead him astray, made it clear to everyone that his interest was not
in government but solely in corporation law.

My father's guiding principle in life was that he must at all costs
avoid the terrible pitfall of politics. He gave himself to making
money and to becoming the family man his father had never been.
What finally happened to him I must present in a more dramatic
form than the summary I have given of Grandfather's affairs. It
would be as difficult for me to summarize the story of Father's
betrayal as it would have been for me to imagine and recreate the
precise circumstances under which Grandfather first learned of
Lon Lucas's double dealing.

When I had opened the venetian blind at my office window that
Sunday morning, I stared out at May's fresh green grass on the
Campus for a while and down at the small river, swollen by spring
rains, at the bottom of the hill. Then I went to my desk and
managed to write two letters to men who had published books on
the subject—in "the field"—I was doing my work in. They were

perfunctory, polite letters, requesting permission to quote from the work of those men in my own book. When I had sealed and stamped those two letters, I took out another sheet of Departmental paper; but it lay on my desk untouched for I don't know how long, a blinding white sheet at which I sat staring impatiently as one does at a movie screen before the film begins. Finally I put away my pen but left the piece of paper lying there as if meaning to project upon it the images taking shape in my mind. I saw my father stepping out of the family limousine in front of the Union Station in bright winter sunlight. My mother and I were already out of the car and waiting under the canopy. The Negro chauffeur stood holding the car door open, and listening to some piece of instruction Father gave him in passing. Since this was in the earliest days of the Depression, we still lived in the world of limousines and chauffeurs, a world that my father's business career had lifted us into. A number of years before this he had ceased altogether to practice law, in order to accept the presidency of a large, "nationally known" insurance company for which he had formerly been the chief attorney and which maintained its head office locally. The insurance company was now in serious difficulties, however. The company's investments were under question. It began to appear that funds had been invested in various business enterprises that seemed hardly to have existed except on paper. Many of these investments had been made before my father's incumbency, but not all of them. Anyway, the man who had most influenced the Company's investment of funds was a stock holder in the Company and a member of the board of directors, Mr. Lewis Barksdale. He was an old school friend of my father's and had of course been instrumental in electing my father president of the Company. It was he alone who would be able to explain the seemingly fraudulent use of moneys—explain it, that is, to the other members of the board—and he alone who could straighten out the snarl which the Company's affairs seemed to be in. And it was this Lewis Barksdale whom we had come to the Union Station to meet at four o'clock on a remarkably bright winter afternoon.

The Negro chauffeur threw back his head and laughed at something my father said to him, and then Father advanced toward us wearing a pleased smile. I remember remarking to Mother at just that moment on what a fine day it was and reproaching her for having made me wear my heavy coat, in which I was uncomfortably warm. The truth was, I was still irked by Father's having made me leave a game with a group of boys to come with them to meet Mr. Barksdale's train, and I was taking out my resentment on Mother. Without looking at me, she replied that it was due to turn colder very shortly and, squeezing my hand, she said, "Why can't you have an agreeable disposition like your father's? Don't be an old sour puss like me." Father was still smiling when he came up to us, and Mother asked him, "What is it that's so funny?"

"Oh," he explained, taking Mother's elbow and escorting us on into the lobby of the Station, "when I just now told Irwin not to come inside and fetch Lewis's bag but to wait right there with the car, he said he couldn't keep the car in that spot but fifteen minutes and that he was afraid the train might be late. I said to him that if he knew Lewis Barksdale as well as I do, he'd know that the engineer and the fireman would somehow understand that they *had* to get Lewis's train out here on time."

In the lobby, Father read the track number off the board and then marched us confidently down the concourse to the great iron gate at Track Number 6. Just as he predicted, the train rolled in on time. Father spoke to the uniformed gatekeeper, who let us go through the gateway along with the redcaps, so we could see Mr. Barksdale when he stepped off the train. Father trotted along ahead of us, peering up into the windows of the observation car and then into the windows of the next Pullman. Mother called after him that he had better wait there beside the first Pullman or we might miss Mr. Barksdale. And Father did stop there. But he told me to run on ahead and see if I could get a glimpse of him in the entry of any of the other cars. I said I was not certain I would recognize Mr. Barksdale, but Father said, "You can know him by his derby. Besides, *he'll* recognize *you.*"

I did run on ahead, looking up into the cars, watching the people that came down the steps from each car to the metal stool which the porter had set out for them. Mr. Barksdale, being a man who had no children of his own, was said to be extremely fond of all his friends' children. That was why, as the youngest child in the family—and the only boy—I was taken along to meet the train that day. I could vaguely recall earlier visits he had made to us and seemed to remember a sense of his paying special attention to me. Momentarily I was persuaded that I *would* remember him if we came face to face. But no man wearing a derby got off the train, and I made out no remotely familiar face in the cars or in the crowded entry ways. Moreover, no passenger climbing down off that train showed any sign of recognizing me.

When I followed the crowd of passengers and redcaps back toward the iron gate, I found Mother still standing beside the observation car. She said that Father had climbed aboard and was going through all the cars in search of Mr. Barksdale. At last we saw Father step off the first of the day coaches, away down the track. He looked very small down there, and when he waved to us and climbed back on the train, I felt a sudden ache in the pit of my stomach. "Mr. Barksdale's not on the train," I said to Mother.

"No, I guess not," she said. "I was afraid he mightn't be."

Finally Father reappeared in the entry between the observation car and the next Pullman. "Lewis must have missed the train somehow," he said as he came down the steps and swung out onto the platform. "Let's go inside the Station. I'm going to telephone New York and see if he's still there."

We found a telephone booth on the concourse just beyond Gate Number 6, but Father had to go inside the Station lobby to get enough change to make the call. Mother and I stood beside the booth a long time. "He ought to have waited till we got home to make the call," she said at last. "I suppose, though, he couldn't bear to wait." She and I had just agreed to go into the lobby and look for him when we saw him coming toward us. He was all smiles and was holding up two fist-fulls of coins.

"I got enough quarters to call China," he said and seemed to be elated by the feel of the coins in his hands. When he stepped into the booth to make his call, Mother and I moved away some twenty or thirty feet. He must have talked for ten minutes or more. When he came out again, his smile was bigger than before, and he began calling out as he hurried toward us, "Lewis *did* miss the train! And it was so busy in New York today he couldn't get a line to call me. He's coming on an earlier train tonight and will be here by noon tomorrow!"

By noon of the next day, which was Saturday, it was very much colder, and so I didn't complain about having to wear my coat. I did complain somewhat, however, about having to give up several hours of a Saturday to meeting Mr. Barksdale's train. Father seemed to understand and was not so insistent upon my going, but in private Mother was insistent and said it was little enough for me to do if it was what my father wished. As we were leaving the house, Father stopped a moment to telephone the Station and ask if the train were going to be on time. He had heard a report on the radio that the weather up East had turned bad. But the dispatcher's office reported that the train was scheduled to arrive exactly on time. In the car, Father said he hoped the dispatcher's office knew what it was talking about. "Trains on the week end are often late," he said suspiciously. When we got to the Station he told Irwin that since the train might, after all, be late, he had better take the car to the parking lot, and that we would come and find him there.

As we were passing through the lobby we all three read the gate number aloud from the blackboard, and we laughed at ourselves for it—rather nervously, I suppose. Father had kept silent most of the way down to the Station in the car and had left the talking mostly to Mother and me. He began to look more cheerful once we were in the big lobby, and as we passed out onto the concourse he said to Mother under his breath, "Keep your fingers crossed." As soon as we came out onto the concourse we could see that the train was already backing up to the gate. "Thar she be!" Father exclaimed with sudden gaiety, and he put an arm around each of us to hurry us along. But at the gate he didn't ask the gatekeeper to let us go beyond. We waited outside, and through the bars of the grating we watched the passengers stepping down onto the platform. After a few minutes Father said, "I won't be surprised if Lewis is the last to get off. He hates crowds." We kept watching until it was obvious that no more passengers were going to leave the train and come through the gate. In what was almost a whisper Father said to Mother, "He didn't come. What do you suppose could have happened?" And as we were passing the telephone booth on the way out, he said, "I'll call him from home."

We had been at home about half an hour when I heard him speaking to Mother from the foot of the stairs. She was leaning over the banisters in the upstairs hall. "There have been a lot of complications. Lewis has been getting together papers to bring with him. He says he can clear everything up. He's coming in on the same train tomorrow."

"Wonderful," Mother said.

"But I'm not going to ask you all to traipse down to the depot again."

"Nonsense. The third time's the charm," said my mother.

At about eleven the next morning Father telephoned the Station to ask if the train were scheduled to come in on time. He was told that it would be three hours late. There were heavy snow storms all over the East now. When Mother came into the big sun room where my sister Margaret and my two other sisters and I were all reading the Sunday paper and told us that snow had delayed Mr. Barksdale's train for three hours, she glanced out the sun room windows at the darkly overcast sky and said, "There will be snow here before night, I think." None of my sisters even looked up from the paper. I imagine I looked up from the funnypaper only because I wished to know whether or not I was going to be taken to the Station again. Mother saw me look up and said, "Father says you needn't go with us today, and I suppose he's right."

"I'll go," I said. It had occurred to me suddenly that the snow might be falling by that time and that I would like to see how the old grey stone Union Station looked with snow on all of its turrets and crenelations and how the train would look backing into Gate Number 6 with snow it brought in from the East piled all over its top.

"Well, we'll see," Mother said.

Sometime after two, Mother and Father were in the front hall getting into their coats. I was there too, still undecided as to whether or not I would go along. No snow had begun to fall yet. Father seemed unconcerned about my going or not going. When Mother asked him if he thought he might call the Station again, he replied casually that he already had, that the train would arrive as predicted, at three o'clock. He had already buttoned up his heavy, double-breasted overcoat when he added suddenly, "But there's another call I believe I'll make before we set out. It might take a few minutes. . . . You had better take off your coat," he said to Mother.

When he was gone, I asked, "Who do you think he's calling?"

"I imagine he's calling Mr. Barksdale in New York," Mother said. She didn't remove her coat, though. She and I said nothing more. We went and looked out at the sky through the sidelights at the front door. After a few minutes we heard Father's footsteps. When we turned around, he was standing there in the hall, smiling wearily, and beginning to unbutton his coat.

"Lewis is still in New York," he said.

"Why in the world?" Mother exclaimed. "What in the world did he say this time?" she asked.

"He didn't say anything. I didn't give him a chance to. As soon as I definitely heard his voice on the wire I put down the receiver."

"What are you going to do?" Mother asked him.

"There's nothing I can do. He's not coming, that's all. I'll just have to take it however it turns out now."

We didn't go to the Station, of course. And Father didn't go off to his room to be by himself, either, as one might have expected. He spent the rest of the afternoon with the family in the sun room, reading the paper, listening to the radio, and playing cards. The way he was with us that afternoon you wouldn't have suspected anything was wrong. At just about twilight it began to snow outside. And we all went about from window to window with a certain relief, I suppose, watching the big flakes come down and, from the snug safety of our sun room, watching the outside world change.

Father didn't telephone Mr. Barksdale again. They had been close friends since boyhood, but I believe they didn't communicate again for more than twenty-five years. When they were very old men and most of their other contemporaries were dead, Mr. Barksdale took to calling Father over long distance and they would sometimes talk for an hour at a time about their boyhood friends or about business friends they had had when they were starting out in business. We were glad whenever Mr. Barksdale called Father, because it cheered him and made him seem livelier than anything else did during those last years. He often seemed very lonely during those years, though he continued to have a reasonably cheerful disposition. After the legal difficulties and the embarrassing publicity that followed his being abandoned by his trusted friend, Father led a quiet, uneventful life. He returned to his law practice, and he was a respected member of his firm. But he made no real life for himself in his practice—that is, he seldom saw other members of the firm away from the office, and I don't remember his ever mentioning the name of a client at home. His real life was all at home, where, as he would point out, it had always been. He and Mother sometimes played bridge with neighbors, and whatever other social life they had was there in the neighborhood where we lived after we lost the old house and could no longer afford a staff of servants. He was an affectionate father, and I rarely saw him in what I would call depressed spirits. Yet how often one had the feeling that he was lonely and bored. I remember sometimes, even when the family was on a vacation together—when we had taken a cottage at the shore or were camping and fishing in the mountains—the look would come in his eye. And one was tempted to ask one's self, What's wrong? What's missing?

I don't honestly know when I decided to go into college teaching, Jack. I considered doing other things—a career in the army or the navy. Yes, I might have gone to Annapolis or West Point. Those appointments were much to be desired in the Depression years, and my family did still have a few political connections. One thing was certain, though. Business was just as much out of the question for me as politics had been for my father. An honest man, I was to understand, had too much to suffer there. Yes, considering our family history, an ivory tower didn't sound like a bad thing at all for an honest man and a serious man. . . . A dozen years after graduation I found myself back teaching in that college where I had been an undergraduate. Physically it was a beautiful spot, and, as I have already said, I thought I would settle down there for life, to do my teaching and my writing.

After my second year of teaching there I was awarded a research Fulbright to Italy, and so was on leave for a year. You were a babe in arms that year, Jack. I saw the Ancient World for the first time with you on my shoulder, and with your mother usually following behind, leading Susie by the hand. Well, while we were in Italy, the old president of the College died of a stroke. He had been president of the College when I was an undergraduate, and I suppose it was he, most of all, who made me feel that my talents were appreciated there. By the time I returned to the Campus from Italy, the following fall, the Dean of Men had been made acting president. Your mother and I smiled over the appointment but made no comment on it to anyone—not even to each other. You see, Jack, although Marie and I still thought of ourselves as being ideally suited to each other then, and still believed ourselves to be very happy together, there were already subjects she and I had had to agree to keep off. One of these—and by far the most important—was my professional career itself, including how I conducted my classes, my rôle in the Department, my stand on various academic questions, and even my possible advancement in rank. We had been in graduate school together—your mother and I—and during the first years of our marriage, before Susie was born, we both had taught at the same institution. It was understandably difficult for her to refrain from advising and criticizing me in matters she considered she knew as much about as I did. When I first began ruling out that subject as a topic for discussion, she became emotional about it. She had wanted to have a career herself, and she had had to give it up temporarily. I had not realized how much her plans for a career had meant to her. But now she accused me of being an anti-feminist, accused me of trying to isolate her in the kitchen, even of trying to cut her off from all intellectual life. In time, however, she came to see the matter differently—or seemed to. I think perhaps she tired of hearing other faculty wives talk about their husband's professional problems and didn't want to be like them. At any rate, she and I merely smiled over the news of the Dean's promotion to Acting President. His qualifications for such a high place seemed hardly to exist. He was formerly the Chairman of the Department of Athletics—that is, the College's head coach.

But since I knew that certain trustees and certain senior members of the faculty were on a committee to select a permanent president, I was careful to mention my amusement to no one. When a group of younger members of the faculty came to me, however, and told me that it was generally understood that the Committee was going to recommend that the Dean be made permanent president, I could not keep myself from bursting into laughter.

It was on an evening in the middle of the week that that group of young professors came to my house for the very purpose of reporting the information to me. How well I can see them on my front porch, in the bright porch light I had switched on. They were a very attractive and intelligent looking bunch of men. With their bright, intelligent eyes, with their pipes and tweed jackets, and with a neatly trimmed moustache or two among them, they gave one a feeling that here were men one would gladly and proudly be associated with, the feeling that one had found the right niche in life, that one had made the right choice of career. I remember that before they came inside, two of them—there were six in the party—stepped back and knocked the ashes out of their pipes on the porch banisters and that they looked with interest at the porch banisters and then looked up and noticed what the porch pillars were like. As a matter of fact, as they trooped into the hallway and then over into my study, they all of them were making comments of one kind or another on the house. . . . This was not so rude of them as it might seem, or I thought it wasn't. You see, they had telephoned me in advance that they wished to come over and talk to me about a matter. And I understood, of course, that they were too polite and too civilized to come to my house and dive right into a matter of business without making some small talk first. That was not their style, not their tone. Moreover, talk about people's houses used to be a fair and favorite topic at such a college as that one was, because there one didn't really own—or even rent—one's house. All houses occupied by the faculty belonged to the College. The good thing about the system was that the house was provided in addition to your salary, and so one didn't have to pay income tax on that portion of one's income. But by and large it was an invidious arrangement. The elderly professors, when they retired, often had no place to go. Further, since the senior professors and the administrators naturally occupied the best houses and one's rank could generally be deduced from the quality of one's house, the younger men (and their wives) eyed the houses of their seniors and thought of the circumstances that would make them available. When someone near the top died or retired, practically the entire faculty would move up a house.

My house was not of course one of the best houses. I was still an assistant professor, whereas most of those young professors who had come to see me were a grade above me in rank. My house, when we moved into it, had in fact been one of the most ramshackly looking places in the village—one that nobody else would have. I had spent a lot of time and work putting it into the reasonably good condition it was now in. It was upon this fact that my guests were commenting as they came in from the porch that night. And when we had seated ourselves in my study and I had started the coffee brewing, they went on to say that it had been a real advantage to me to have been an undergraduate there, that I had joined the faculty with a knowledge of which houses were basically good houses, that I *knew* (what no one else could have guessed) how recently the run-down looking house I moved into had been in relatively good condition. There was some truth in what they said, but they were not of course really serious about it. And I saw of course that they were teasing. I replied that my disadvantage was that the old president knew me and knew I was the only person on the staff who was fool enough to accept such a house.

They went on from that to speak of how I had known the late president longer and better than they had and to ask if it were not true that the newest and youngest member of the Board of Trustees had once been a classmate and a rather good friend of mine. They were speaking of Morgan Heartwell, who had been the richest boy in my graduating class, and who had during the brief years since our graduation gone on to add several million to the millions he inherited. Though I had seen him only two or three times since college, we had become rather good friends during the last term of our senior year and we still exchanged Christmas cards and even brief letters now and then when there was special occasion. Morgan had been elected to the Board during the previous year, when I was in Italy. I had written him one of those brief letters, from Florence, saying that I wished to congratulate the other members of the Board on the wisdom of their choice. And Morgan had replied briefly that he looked forward to our spending some time together whenever the Trustees met at the College.

The young professors who came to see me were overjoyed when I confirmed the rumor that Morgan Heartwell and I were friends. They immediately revealed the purport of their visit. There was a certain amount of caution in the way they brought forth the information about the Dean's candidacy, but after my explosive fit of laughter they threw caution to the wind. Morgan Heartwell was on the Committee. They wanted me to speak to him. They wanted me to let him know that only the handful of aging, senior professors on the Committee thought the Dean a possible candidate, that those men thought so primarily because they were conservative men getting along in years and because the Dean represented to them a known quantity, that except for them the entire faculty regarded his proposed candidacy as a piece of lunacy. They insisted at once that I was the only feasible channel they had to the Trustees, that if I could let Morgan Heartwell know unofficially how the overwhelming majority of the faculty felt, then the Trustees would come to see for themselves what the situation was. As a result, there would be no ugly rift and contest between the older and the younger members of the faculty. They were thinking of the good of the College. They did not believe that under such a man as the former head coach the College could maintain its academic excellence. They were taking the only course that their collective conscience and that professional ethics permitted them to take.

Here was precisely the sort of meddling, the sort of involvement, I had long since determined to avoid. I had even managed to keep out of most committee work, on the grounds that it interfered with the more serious work I had to do and on the very legitimate grounds that there were people aplenty who liked nothing better than committee work. I used to say that when I received more than one notice of committee meetings in the morning mail, I had heard the sound of my neighbor's ax, and that it was time for me to move on. My first impulse was to laugh as heartily at the rôle they were now asking me to play as I had at the notion of the Dean's being a college president. And yet, with their talk of academic excellence and professional ethics, they really left me no choice. I agreed on the spot to perform the mission.

And it turned out just as they predicted. Morgan Heartwell had entertained doubts even before I came to him, and so had the other Trustees he subsequently spoke to. The night that the group of young professors came to my house was in November. By March another man had been chosen for the presidency. The Acting President would serve till the end of the current academic year, and then the new president would take office.

But by March of that year there had been other developments. One of the senior professors in the College had died. The faculty was once again playing a game of musical chairs with houses. There were days when the community held its breath, waiting to know whether or not Professor So-and-so was going to take such-and-such a house. By March also, Marie had learned definitely that she was pregnant once again. (Maisie was born the following November.) Marie began to think that with the new baby, the inconveniences of the old house we were in would become quite intolerable.

Moreover, I had come to realize that upon the arrival of the baby, my study would have to be converted into a nursery. And so we began to take an interest in the houses which, one after another, became available.

The rule was that each house, as it became available, was offered first to the senior member of the faculty—no matter if he had moved the month before, no matter if the house had five bedrooms and he was childless or even wifeless—and then, if it were refused, the house was offered down through the ranks till it found a taker. We could hardly believe our luck—Marie and I—when no full professor and no associate professor spoke for the Dodson house, which was offered around during the first two weeks of March. It was a charming house with four bedrooms, a modern kitchen, a study. We knew that I stood first on the list of assistant professors. We waited for the customary mimeographed notice to appear in my mail box at the College.

Days passed. Two weeks passed. Still no notice. On the first of April I went to the office of the Acting President and made enquiry. I was told by the Acting President's secretary, Mrs. Eason, that the Acting President had decided that since no full or associate professor had taken the Dodson house, it would be removed from the list and offered to the new chaplain, who was scheduled to be appointed within the next two years. Meanwhile, the house would stand empty. Meanwhile, Marie would continue to scrub our splintery old floors and would wash diapers in a tub in the cellar. Meanwhile, I would give up my study to the new baby. . . . I lost my temper. I went to my office and wrote a letter to the Acting President, saying that I wished my present house to be put on the available list and that I expected to be offered the Dodson house. I received no reply to my letter. But two days later my house was offered to another assistant professor and was accepted. After another two days, I did receive a reply to my letter. The Acting President had consulted the members of his Committee on Houses (whose membership coincided precisely with that of the now defunct Faculty Committee for Selecting a President) and they agreed with him that the Dodson house should not at this time be offered to anyone below the rank of associate professor.

Fortunately—or so I thought of it at the time—I had in my possession a letter from the late President, written to me in Italy

only a few days before his stroke, promising that I would be promoted to the rank of associate professor on my return. Marie had
urged me to present that letter to the administration as soon as we
got home, but I felt certain that a copy of the letter was in the
President's files and that some action would be taken on it in due
time. It seemed unbecoming of me to go at once on my return and
demand that action be taken on my dead benefactor's promise. And
after I had waited six months, I felt that I hardly knew how best to
introduce the subject. But now I did bring forth the letter from my
file. If I were entitled to promotion, then we were entitled to have
the Dodson house. And only by presenting my just claims to the
faculty would I be able to determine for certain whether or not the
Dean, having heard of my rôle in checking his ambitions, had taken
his personal revenge upon me.

With my letter in my pocket, I went to call on all six of the young
professors who had sent me on my mission to Morgan Heartwell. I
pointed out to them, one by one, just how the business about the
house had developed, and I received the impression from each of
them that he was already well aware of the developments. With
each of them, I then brought out my letter from the late President
and insisted upon his reading it. And finally I asked each one of
them if he would be willing to present my case, in its entirety, at the
next faculty meeting. There was not one of them who did not
indicate that he was convinced the Acting President knew of the
part I had played in blocking his permanent appointment. There
was not one of them who expressed any doubt that the removal of
the Dodson house from the list had been an act of reprisal against
me. But they were a very responsible, discreet, and judicious group
of young men. Each of them asserted that he was thoroughly
sympathetic to my claim but asked to be allowed to give the matter
more thought before deciding what action ought to be taken. My
supposition was that there would be a general consultation among
the six of them and that some sort of presentation would be made at
the April meeting.

I shall never forget walking alone from my house to the Administration Building for that April meeting—at four o'clock in the
afternoon, on the first Monday in the month. I arrived earlier than I
usually did at those meetings, and so was able to choose a seat at the
back of the President's Assembly Room. Faculty meetings there, as

in most places, usually filled the room from the rear forward, in just
the same way that students ordinarily fill a college classroom. I sat
in the next to last row and watched my colleagues strolling in from
their afternoon classes, some in earnest conversation, others making jokes and tapping each other firmly on the forearm or even
patting each other on the back, and some few peering into notes on
reports they would give that afternoon. I kept my eye out, of course,
for the arrival of my six friends. Unconsciously I had invented an
image of their arriving as a group, perhaps still consulting among
themselves in whispers, and taking their places together on the first
row squarely in front of the President's lectern. Instead, I saw them
arrive one by one, seemingly unaware of my presence and certainly
unaware of one another's. Before the meeting began, all six had
arrived, but they were scattered over the room. I watched them in
their tweed jackets and blue or striped shirts chatting casually and
amiably with various black-suited, bow-tied senior members of the
faculty. At the moment when the meeting was called to order, I was
struck suddenly by the notion that I had not taken those men's
character and style into account. They would never be so obvious as
my fantasy had suggested. They *would* enter the room separately,
having decided earlier on the strategy. One of them would rise at
the proper time and bring up the question of the Dodson house.
And then, with seeming spontaneity and from all corners of the
room, the others would join in the attack, one of them finally—if
the chair adamantly refused to offer the Dodson house to the lower
rank—one of them finally making direct reference to the promise of
promotion made me by the revered late President.

Following the minutes from the last meeting, pieces of old business occupied the first half hour of the meeting. I sat through the
minutes and through the old business with patience, anticipating
what I believed was to follow. When the question "Any new business?" came, I closed my eyes and listened for the familiar voice.
Unless my ears deceived me, it was the young biologist in my group
who was speaking. He was one of those with a neat little moustache
on his upper lip. With my eyes closed, I could see him, could see
him self-consciously patting the bowl of his pipe on the palm of his
left hand as he began to speak. "Mr. President—." I opened my
eyes, and then for a moment I was convinced my ears did deceive
me. It was the young biologist all right, standing near the front of

the room and patting the bowl of his dark pipe on the palm of his left hand, but the piece of new business he was introducing was a matter of next year's curriculum. I sat through his remarks and through other remarks that followed on the subject. In fact, I sat through two other new pieces of business, even through a count of hands on one piece that came to a motion and a vote. But when a fourth piece, relating to the awarding of honorary degrees was introduced, I rose from my chair, moved down the row I was sitting in, saying, "Excuse me. Excuse me. Excuse me," marched down the center aisle and out of the meeting.

I went home, and behind the closed door of my study I began composing my letter of resignation. Marie, who was in the kitchen, had heard me come in. But she waited fifteen minutes or so before she came and knocked on my door.

When I opened the door, she looked at me questioningly. She was white with anger. "He refused to offer us the house?" she said.

"Not exactly," I replied. "The subject was not introduced. The six of them came to the meeting and spoke at length—about other things."

Her face turned from white to crimson. Her eyes, still on me, melted. She burst into tears and threw herself into my arms. Or, rather, she drew me into her arms, for as she wept I felt her two arms go around me and felt her hands patting me consolingly high on the back between the shoulder blades. As she held me there, it was all I could do to keep from weeping, myself. And somehow, for all her tenderness at that moment and despite all the need I had of it, it came over me that this was the beginning of the end for us, that our marriage would not survive it. Perhaps that was nonsense. The thoughts that cross one's mind at such times cannot always be accounted for. But the life we had lived since graduate school— beginning in graduate school—was the life most couples live who take refuge in the Groves of Academe. We had lived with each other, had lived *together* in the most literal sense. We had shared intellectual interests, had shared domestic duties, had breakfasted together, lunched together, dined together. We had slept together, too, but that had come to seem only one, not too significant facet of our—our "togetherness." I had no right to complain against this life, because this life was the life I had chosen. But I could see that the future would mean a narrowing of my activities among my colleagues wherever I might go, and that things relating to my profession, which had for some time been ruled out of our talk at home, must now inevitably become the very center of it.

When, after dinner that night, I received a telephone call from my friend the biologist, saying that he and one other of the group would like to come by and talk to me, Marie, who was sitting close by my side with her arm about my waist, indicated with a shake of her head that I should not let them come. But I was not yet ready for that. I told them to come ahead, and then I went and switched on the front porch light.

When they arrived, I led them to my study, and we sat down on three straight chairs in a triangle, facing each other. They told me that, before that afternoon's meeting, there *had* been a general consultation among the six men I went to see and that they had decided that to bring up my "problem" at this meeting would not be a wise move, could, in fact, create a very bad situation. "It would be most impolitic," one of them said. "Strategically speaking, it would be a very bad move," said the other. "It would be a bad business." And they proceeded to explain to me that though the Dean would no longer be Acting President, he would continue to be a very important part of the College's administration. A head-on collision with him just before the arrival of the new President might be a very disruptive thing for the College. After all, we were all going to have to continue to live with the Dean. "Even you are," they said to me. And all of this was said with the same voice that had said we must avoid any ugly rift and contest with the senior members of the faculty. Before they finished speaking, I saw once and for all what a foolish man I had been. But I did not make myself a bigger fool by losing my temper and telling them that I saw what a fool they had made of me. As we went to the front door, I agreed with them that probably my house could be reassigned to me—as no doubt it could have been—especially if one of them went to the Dean and explained that I had written my letter to him in a moment of anger and that I now wished to remain where I was. But when they were gone, I put out the porch light, went back to my study, and typed up the final version of my letter of resignation.

Marie and I were in perfect agreement about the resignation. During the months that followed, which was naturally a very trying period, her understanding, her sympathy, her tenderness—her indulgence, really—were my great support. When I returned from my office late that Sunday afternoon, depressed and with a crick in my neck after a long sleep in my leather chair (I have since decided that that was most probably the way my father had spent *his* Sunday in *his* office) Marie greeted me cheerfully, and little Susie almost smothered me with kisses. But somehow the vision I had had of our future, after the fateful faculty meeting, stuck with me. I never for a moment believed our marriage could weather this new turn my life had taken. I don't know why. As my mother would have said, the Old Nick himself seemed to have got in me. I *wouldn't* be consoled, I *wouldn't* be comforted, though I consistently made an effort to seem so. I had never before been so much help in a move as I was in packing up our possessions and unpacking them again when we arrived at our new place. My new appointment was at an enormous state university, situated in a middle-sized, Middle-Western city. I felt it would be possible to pass unnoticed for years, in the University and in the city. I met my classes, I attended Department meetings, I made revisions on the galley sheets of my book. It seems to me I spent a large part of every day taking Susie back and forth to school on the bus. And I spent hours in the Park with you, Jack. I don't suppose you remember the little boy there who kept purposely interfering with your play on the jungle-gym until one day I caught him and spanked him. His mother threatened to call the police. I'll never forget the satisfaction I took in laughing in her face and threatening to give her the same spanking I had given her little boy. And little Maisie, of course, was born in November after we arrived there. I never changed so many diapers for you and Susie put together as I did for Maisie, or gave so many bottles at pre-dawn hours. . . . No, I did not become the tyrant of my household, and I did not, like my father, disturb my wife with long looks and long silences. But I began to feel that with my talk about my book and my talk about the courses I was teaching I was almost intentionally boring Marie to death, boring my students to death, boring myself to death. Before the first semester was half over Marie was helping me grade my papers and was reading all the books I had to read for my courses. By the time the second semester came round she had made application to the Department and was taken on as a part-time instructor.

It was almost a year to the day after my difficulties about the

Dodson house began that two letters, which would altogether change everything for me, were put into my mail box at the University. One letter came from my predecessor at the college where I have since made my most important contribution to the education of American youth. This letter stated that they were looking for a new Dean of Men at that college and asked if I would be willing to come and be interviewed for the appointment. The other letter was from Morgan Heartwell. It was he who had recommended me for the appointment, and he wrote me that he had been able to do so because he had observed that I behaved with such discretion in my altercation with the Acting President, putting the welfare of that institution above my personal interests. He also urged me to accept the new appointment, saying that this was a college that had recently been given a handsome endowment, a college with a growing academic reputation. He was not, himself, on the Board of Trustees there, but close associates of his were and they had happened to mention the opening there.

When Marie read the first letter, she broke into laughter. Then, giving me a serious glance, she read through Morgan's letter. "How dare Morgan Heartwell write you such a letter!" she said. "How dare he suggest such an appointment for you!" She and I were facing each other across the little carrel that we shared in the University Library. When I remained silent, she put the letters down on the table and asked, "You are not seriously thinking of going for that interview?"

"I am going to take the job," I said, "if it's offered me."

Folding the letters and replacing them in their envelopes, she said, "Well, you may take it. But I'm staying on here."

"It has already occurred to me that you might say that," I told her directly. "I am not entirely surprised." She sat with her eyes lowered and she blushed so deeply that a new thought now occurred to me. "Is there someone else?" I asked.

"No, I don't think so," she said, looking up at me. "Is there for you?"

"I don't think so," I said.

Of course, the fact is we were both married again within two years to persons we did already know at that state university. But still, it is true that neither of us had been having a real love affair. Perhaps the persons we married, the persons we very soon afterward allowed ourselves to fall in love with, represented for us the only possibilities of happiness either of us had been able to imagine during that bleak year. I suppose it's significant that we both married people who shared none of our professional interests.

After I had been Dean of Men for two years, I was made Academic Dean of the College. In two more years I was President of the College. Even with as little time as you have spent with me through the years, Jack, you have seen what a successful marriage my second marriage has been, and what a happy, active life I have had. One sacrifices something. One sacrifices, for instance, the books one might have written after that first one. More important, one may sacrifice the love, even the acquaintance, of one's children. One loses something of one's self even. But at least I am not tyrannizing over old women and small children. At least I don't sit gazing into space while my wife or perhaps some kindly neighbor woman waits patiently to see whether or not I will risk a two heart bid. A man must somehow go on living among men, Jack. A part of him must. It is important to broaden one's humanity, but it is important to remain a mere man, too. But it is a strange world, Jack, in which an old man must tell a young man this.

# TED WALKER

# *The Peace Rose*

As I guessed he would, my father-in-law came outside to watch while I planted his rosebush this morning. He'd have heard the barrow rattling with tools as I wheeled it past his window, and I daresay he observed me taking out the first spadefuls of earth while he put on his hat and coat and found his walking-stick. He's old and infirm, but nothing much escapes him. Aware that he was shuffling very slowly toward me over the drenched lawn, I thrust the spade into the ground and leaned on it, waiting for him. He caught my eye, grinned, and then began again to win each painful and unsteady step of the distance between us.

He'd been looking forward to this. Five weeks ago, at the beginning of October, he and my mother-in-law had moved down from London into the annex of our house. I'd been busy since then. This was the first chance I'd had to attend to the rosebush he'd insisted on my digging up from his small, meticulous garden and bringing with the rest of their belongings. The Saturday they arrived, well after dark, I removed all the leaves from the bush, lightly pruned it, and heeled it temporarily into some moist compost in the shelter of the garden wall. If necessary, it could have stayed there until the spring; but on several occasions he'd asked obliquely when I thought I could get around to putting it into its permanent station. "Fair planting weather," he'd said, on a couple of consecutive evenings, as I garaged the car after work; and "Early autumn's the favorite time for getting off to a good start," he'd said yesterday, while I was clearing the leaves from their back path.

"The soil still looks warm from summer," he said to me now. "The roots can get a fair grip before the first bad frost sets in."

He was right enough. A good fortnight before their move down here I'd prepared the new, trapezium-shaped bed, and I'd shifted into it two dozen or so of my own Queen Elizabeths, framing a generous space in the centre for this huge old Peace Rose of his. The Elizabeths had already settled in well, and some of them had even made a little new growth during the Indian summer.

"Are you going to be all right there?" I asked him, once he'd steadied himself against the laburnum tree. The muscles in his legs are wasting; after the effort of his walking so far unaided, I was afraid he might slip and fall. "Take no notice of me," he said. "I'll just have a bit of a smoke and watch you get on with it."

There had been a heavy shower since dawn. When he fumbled to light his cigarette, he jolted back against the trunk of the tree and a spray of raindrops spattered down on him. "No, no—it's all right, I can manage," he said, as I took a pace toward him; but he knew I'd seen the cigarette disintegrate through his clumsy fingers, and the shreds of tobacco and sodden paper falling between his feet. "Too soon in the day, in any case," he said. "It'd only make me cough." And so I nodded, took hold of the fork, and made a show of loosening the subsoil I'd already loosened at the bottom of the hole.

He can't bear to have anybody help him. What he needs, times like this, is a short spell on his own to get things done the way he knows how. If he has a minute or two, unflustered, he can perfectly well extract the tin from his jacket pocket and prize open the lid with the second joint of his forefinger; then, if there's nobody too close to see him do it, he can easily hold the tin to his lips, like a Chinaman with a rice-bowl, and flip up a cigarette it took him ten minutes to roll after breakfast. Over the years, on the sly, I've noticed these special skills of his developing. He has his own kind of high-tariff dexterity with his Zippo lighter, too. He'll cradle it in the palm of his right hand, snap back the top with a brusque movement of the left wrist, rub the wheel along the ball of his rigid left thumb. I reckon that if he could guarantee being left alone a long while in a well-lit room he could still find the means, through his unyielding hands and fingers, of repairing the most delicate watch. Had this been his garden, not mine, he'd have had the rosebush planted a month ago. It would have taken him the best part of a whole day, but he'd have completed the job—and well—bit by bit.

"You're making a right meal out of loosening up that bottom," he said. "But I now what it's like, trying to get something done with someone breathing down your neck. I'll go back indoors."

"It's not that," I said. "I've just been thinking. I ought to make up some planting mixture to scatter round the roots. Should've done it before I got started. Won't be long." And I strode away before he could argue about it. He probably guessed that I'd dug in plenty of good compost when I'd got the bed ready and that I simply wanted to give him the opportunity of enjoying his first smoke of the day.

After mixing peat and bone meal together in a pail, I looked at him from the shed window. He was prodding the ground with his stick, testing for firmness. His cigarette was lit by now, and a ragged streamer of smoke was rising through the bare twigs of the laburnum. He looked frail but obdurate, a waif in some old-fashioned, sentimental movie. I was glad to see him there. When the fine weather came round again, he would become a familiar figure in my garden. He's in his mid-seventies; I wondered how many years he had left to enjoy it before he had to be confined to the house. I felt fond of him, protective towards him. Maybe he ought to be offered a plot of his own to look after, I thought—some easily manageable, compact bed it would please him to tend. He'd be able to push a light Dutch hoe between some vegetables, or keep the hose running during dry spells. These days it's possible to buy all manner of tools and gadgets specially adapted for the disabled. He'd be glad to feel he was being useful. However, there were months to go before any such idea could be entertained. First, he had what promised to be a severe winter to get through; frost, snow, and ice couldn't be far away now. In March I'd take the garden furniture outside again. He could sit at a table by the laburnum tree while I pruned the roses. Probably he'd try to cut back his Peace Rose himself. I hoped it would flourish for him. I threw an extra handful of bonemeal into the pail and stirred it in.

"That looks like a bit of good, rich stuff," he said, when I put down the pail in front of him. "What are those white flecks—hoof and horn?"

"Bone meal," I said. "Hoof and horn's a thing of the past."

"Hoof and horn. Bagged it up by the ton when I was a kid. Of course, that's going back 60-odd years. Came from the slaughterhouse into the crusher. Stank to high heaven."

I dropped four or five double handfuls of the planting mixture into the hole and then raised it into a mound for the roots and stock of the bush to rest on.

"And Irish moss peat," I said. "Best there is."

"Fancy having to import stuff like that. Fancy having to buy it. Leaf mold, I always swore by. You'd tie an orange box on the back of your bike, take the coal shovel with you out of the hearth, cycle up to the woods. Lovely, that mold. Soft as a woman's glove when you sank your hand in it. All those trees got felled, though, when they built the housing estates."

"Which trees?"

"Beeches. Long time before you were born. All part of Greater London now. We did our courting up in those beechwoods. You'd say you were going to get leaf mold for your father's roses, but really you were going to have a few hours with your girl."

I held the bush by the tallest stem, placed it on the mound, and kicked in enough loose soil to hold it in place. "Think it's going to look all right here?" I asked him.

"My old man knew what I was up to. He never said anything, but I know he knew. He had his leaf mold, he was happy. Yes—the bush'll look fine as it is. Just needs treading in. It'll do. By God, though, that's turning cold all of a sudden."

"We'll go inside for a cup of tea," I said. "I can finish this off later. Don't want you taking a chill."

I persuaded him to place his right hand on my shoulder, so that I could steady him over the grass to our back door and into the kitchen. My wife was rolling out pastry. "Your dad's pinched with cold," I said to her. "Put the kettle on, will you?"

Jane filled the kettle and plugged it in as we sat down. "Your mum might fancy a cup, too," I said. "Shall I go and fetch her round?"

My father-in-law shook his head. "I shouldn't bother, if I were you," he said.

"It's no trouble."

"A fool's errand," he said. "She's probably not out of bed yet."

"But it's gone eleven," said Jane. "Not like her."

"Well, it is Sunday, after all," I said. "She's having a lie-in. And why not?"

"It isn't that," he said. "She never gets up at the right time these days. If I didn't keep on at her, she'd stay put until the afternoon."

"I don't like the sound of that," said Jane. "Something's the matter. Maybe she ought to see the doctor."

"No. There's nothing untoward the matter with her. Only the sulks and general cussedness. I don't know what anybody can do about it. She didn't want to move down here, and staying in bed is her way of paying me out. I expect she'll get used to it. Just got to come to terms. Take no notice."

Jane sighed. "It's so silly," she said. "You're so much better off here. Country air. Out of that damp old house which was falling down round your ears. Away from all that noise and dirt. The planes taking off and landing every few seconds at Heathrow."

"You don't have to tell me all that," he said. "Of course we're better off. Every way, we're better off. Try telling her that, though."

Embarrassed for him, I got up and fetched the cups and saucers, sugar and milk, spoons, biscuits, plates. There'd been something of angry desperation in his voice. Ever since I bought this house— more than ten years ago—the annex has been set aside for their use. Each Easter and Christmas, a fortnight every summer, they've spent their holidays in it. It has always been understood between us that the annex was for them to live in permanently when they became old and in need of looking after. There are no stairs to climb; it's compact and snug, self-contained. The old man had been delighted to come—he would have come down as soon as he retired, if he'd had his way—but from the moment they arrived with their furniture and packing cases, my mother-in-law had been withdrawn and grim.

"I expect she's still missing her friends," I heard Jane say. "She'll be all right as soon as she's made some new ones."

"Friends? What friends? She hadn't got any friends up there. All her friends had long since gone. They'd died or been rehoused in those highrise flats the other side of the borough. They'd gone away to live with their children, else, or in one of those old folks' homes, the back of beyond. *I* had friends—one or two. There was old Charlie in the corner shop, and Smithy, that I worked with years ago. But I was stuck in the house all day long, wasn't I? I never got to see my two or three friends. She wouldn't let me out in case I fell down. Four walls was all I ever saw. Your mother went out of the house, went downtown for a bit of shopping, but she had nobody to talk to except the girl at the checkout."

"The neighbors, then."

"You're joking! Wouldn't so much as go out into the yard if she saw any of the neighbors in theirs. Fell out with the whole bunch of them, one time and another."

I made the tea and carried it to the table.

"It's bound to be difficult," I said, "learning to adjust to a new place. All the upheaval of moving."

"I've lost count of the number of times we've moved since we were married. And that's not including being bombed out during the Blitz. God knows, she ought to be used to packing and unpacking. It's something else."

"Prices are higher round here," Jane said. "No big supermarkets. A penny on this, a penny on that. It must be a worry." She poured the tea.

"Not that, either. Our pensions are more than enough for our needs. I can't remember when we were better off. We don't have to be all that careful with money."

With the palms of his hands he lifted his cup. "It's something else," he said. "Something else. I know what it is, too, but she'd dig up anything to moan about sooner than admit it. Nothing's right for her. Doesn't like cooking with electricity instead of gas, doesn't like a shower instead of a bath. Says the bus fares are expensive. 'Up in London,' she says, 'you can travel free if you're an old-age pensioner. You can sit on a bus all day long and not part with a penny piece. You can go right into the city, up the West End, go and look at Buckingham Palace.' And she's dead right, of course, no denying it. But what she'll not tell you is that she's not gone a hundred yards on a bus these last five years to my certain knowledge. That's not what's bothering her, either."

I drank my tea as quickly as I could. Jane and her father would have to sort out the problem between them, whatever it was. I got up and made for the door.

"It seems so ungrateful," he said to me. "I'm thankful to be here,

though. You know that, don't you? You shouldn't have had to sweep
those leaves from our path yesterday. Difficult job for me to do, the
way I'm fixed, but she could have done that."

"It was no bother. I'd just been sweeping our path."

"But it's all part of the same thing. She's not unpacked our
pictures yet. I'd do it, but I'd be afraid of dropping them and
smashing the glass. She's not got around to fixing the curtains
properly. I wouldn't know how to do a job like sewing curtains.
They look stupid, hanging down much too far. Five weeks, we've
been here. Five weeks and a day. Still those curtains with frayed
edges."

"It'll all work out," I said. "Now I must go and finish that
planting."

Five minutes later, when I'd trodden the ground firm, I took the
tools back to the shed. I'd spend twenty minutes more, I thought,
before going back to them in the kitchen—time enough for them to
talk things over. I had some tidying-up to do, and the lawn mower
needed greasing over if it wasn't to rust through winter. Jane would
pour a second cup for them both and then get on with her baking. A
gentle rain began to fall, which would save me the bother of
watering in the Peace Rose.

It was I who bought that rosebush originally. Twenty years ago,
that was, at the end of the fifties. Three shillings and sixpence, I
paid for it. I remember counting out the coppers and small silver
into the nurseryman's hand, knowing that it was about to rain and
that I hadn't the fourpence left for the bus fare home. It was a
spindly-looking plant, I recall; two weak stems and a rootstock like a
ball of fluff. Had I known then what I know about roses now, I
wouldn't have dreamed of paying good money for it. It was wrapped
in a *Daily Express,* and when I stuffed it into my mackintosh pocket
I pricked my thumb on a thorn. What possessed me to buy a
rosebush, that autumn afternoon on my way home from work, I
simply can't remember. At twenty-four, I had no interest in gardening. The plot of ground in front of the house I'd rented was still
full of decaying rubbish abandoned by the previous tenants. I had
no tools—not even a spade—with which to tidy what remained of
the sour and long-neglected flower beds I would be obliged, under
the terms of my lease, to keep in good order. Maybe the purchase

was simply a romantic and rhetorical gesture on my part. I might
have been attracted by the name. *Peace, 3/6,* I'd read from the chalk
scrawl at the nursery gate. Those were uneasy times. During the
years I lived in that house, I was to see, successive Easters, the
vastly long processions of the C.N.D. marchers passing our front
window with their banners aloft; some of them—usually young
mothers with children in push-chairs—would accept a cup of tea
and drink it without a word, resting against our wall. It was always
the Easter Sunday when they reached us, having been on the road
from Aldermaston since Good Friday. On the Monday they completed the few miles into central London for the mass rally in
Trafalgar Square. And there was to be a day, after I bought the rose,
when I kissed my wife and children goodbye in the morning and
went to work as usual, trying not to show the anxiety I felt about the
American warships which would be closing upon Russian vessels
off Cuba about the time I'd be breaking for coffee. Yes—I may have
bought the rose for its name. Peace was something worth paying the
price of a couple of beers for. In middle age I find it difficult to
reassemble the feelings of the young man I was, but I think it quite
likely that I intended the straggly bush to grow in my derelict
garden as a kind of charm or talisman. Three years before, soon
after our marriage, I'd sworn that I'd go to prison rather than fight
Anthony Eden's war with Nasser over Suez. Now, so soon after, I
was the father of three babies, poor, sharing a damp and decrepit
house with my in-laws, with few prospects of ever getting out. My
wife looked worn out, the children suffered from the smoggy climate of the Thames valley; it could be that the rose had more to do
with my inner turmoil and despair than the world's. When I got
home, I left it in its newspaper in the porch. I felt ridiculous and
embarrassed about it, I suppose, because I didn't mention it to
anyone, or do anything about getting it into the ground. It stayed
where it was, next to the milk-bottle crate, for the rest of that week
and all the next.

My father-in-law planted it. While I was out with the children
on the Saturday, he borrowed a trowel from a neighbour and cleared
away enough rubbish to make room for it. When I got home, I
noticed it at once as I pushed the three babies in their pram up the
path to the front door. No comment was passed by any of us. It
wasn't until the bush bloomed the following summer that it caught

my attention again. Two yellow, pink-edged flowers opened, so
heavy they bowed their stems almost to the ground. The plant sent
up new stems from the base, and the next summer there were to be
getting on for a dozen blooms. By then my father-in-law had made
the whole plot sweet and trim. Slowly we had begun to be on good
terms. I learned from him some of the basic skills of gardening; how
to dig, rake the soil to a fine tilth, how to sow seeds and how to thin
them, how to transplant. He showed me how to prune a rosebush,
cutting to an outward-facing bud with a clean, sharp knife. "As
soon as you can, you want to get away and start again," he said.
"Save up the deposit for a house. A couple of hundred pounds
should be enough. Young people shouldn't live with their parents or
in-laws. I ought to know—it's what I did, and it's a miserable
business. I know you were glad to have us move in with you when
you took on this house—help with the rent money and Jane's
mother to give a hand with the babies—but you'd be better off on
your own. I'll take the lease off your hands. It'll be no trouble
finding tenants for your part of the place, if needs be."

Another two years elapsed before I moved my family down to the
coast. I saved what I could, month by month, but the money
accrued very slowly. I kept up the Saturday ritual of taking the
children for long outings in their pram. It gave Jane a rest from
them, and I used to love going to the river, or to the great parks and
estates that were just within walking distance. Often we'd go to
Kew Gardens, having crossed the bridge at Richmond and followed
the Thames down past the Old Deer Park and Isleworth Eyot.
Sometimes we went as far as Richmond Park, looking out for the
wandering herds of deer, seeing the dome of St Paul's in the hazy
distance when we reached the bandstand. More often than not,
though, we went to the grounds of Osterley House. To get there, we
had to cross a busy road—The Great West Road—which connected
Heathrow airport with central London. There would be crowds
gathering along the road, sometimes, to catch a glimpse of some
celebrity who had just flown in. Crossing that road on the way to
and from work each day, I often saw famous people being driven
past, Eisenhower, I saw, and de Gaulle, and Harold MacMillan,
and J. F. Kennedy, and Yuri Gagarin in his officer's uniform, standing up in his open car to wave to us. Up in Osterley Park, though it
was surrounded by trunk roads, factories, housing estates, it was

like an idyllic, pastoral landscape out of classical literature. There was a formal pond, full of carp and golden rudd, its surface almost entirely covered by waterlily pads and exotic waterfowl. There were vistas of greensward, avenues of mature trees, dark thickets of rhododendron, a field or two of cows. The warden, a former police-man called Sergeant Guthrie, showed us birds' nests full of eggs: a mallard's and a barn owl's only feet apart in a hollow oak, a gold-crest's, exquisite and delicately woven into the hanging fronds of a cedar. I learned much of my natural history during those walks. "One of these days," I used to tell the children, "we'll live in a place where you can see birds and fish and trees all the time. You'll not have to walk far to see them. You'll just look out of your window, and there they'll all be." But the truth was, I didn't believe we ever would. I used to push them home before it got dark, before the fogs began to assemble in the streets. By the time we reached the front gate, they would be fast asleep, crammed together like dolls in the pram that was getting too small for them. It wasn't until our doctor told me, of my eldest, the boy, "This child has bronchial pneu-monia, you must remove him from this house, this area, if you want him to survive," that I began to believe there had to be a life for us elsewhere. I got myself a job in a nondescript seaside town, raked together what little money I had, borrowed 50 pounds off my mother. In July, we packed our possessions into a small, rented van, drove out of the Thames valley, across the North and South Downs, and moved into a small, raw, brand-new box of a house which still smelt of plaster and fresh paint. There, for about three years, we lived frugally until, like an unexpectedly early spring, prosperity arrived to amaze us. We bought this house, cash down, guessing that the annex would always be useful for visitors, or for our parents when they grew old.

When I went back into the house, I found Jane on her own. She was sitting at the kitchen table, reading the *Sunday Times*. I couldn't be sure, but I guessed she'd been crying.

"Your dad's gone back next door, then?" I said.

"Yes. He got upset. Didn't want you to see him in a state."

"I've got his rosebush well and truly into the ground. That'll please him."

"Yes."

"I've been thinking about old times, how he planted that bush after I'd brought it home and dumped it in the porch. Remember?"

"I remember."

"That's probably why he wanted to bring it down here. Still thinks of it as being mine, even though he's looked after it for twenty years. I like your old man. He's one of the best."

Jane folded the newspaper carefully into its creases, smoothing the wrinkled front page.

"We'll have to think of a way to jolly your mother along," I said. "We'll take them out somewhere, get them to join the Darby and Joan Club or something. She likes a game of cards. You could take her to a whist drive. She'll soon forget that slum of a place they've come from."

"It's where they lived."

"That's a strange thing to say. It was in ruins, nearly. Ought to have been condemned and pulled down. You heard what your dad said. There was simply nothing left for them up there."

"But it's where they lived. They lived in that house much longer than they'd lived anywhere else. You know how superstitious my mother can be."

I knew well enough. She observes all the conventional superstitions and is forever surprising me with irrational notions I've never heard of. On the day they arrived here, when I helped to arrange their furniture in the rooms, she wouldn't hear of the beds being placed across the line of the floorboards. The bedroom is a long, narrow room; the divans would have been much more conveniently situated, had she allowed them to stay where I'd put them. "It's bad luck like that," was all she'd say. "Bad luck to cross the lines."

"I'll tell you why she won't get up of a morning," Jane said. "And I'll tell you why she's not bothering to unpack the pictures and alter the curtains. She's convinced that they're going to die, now they've moved here. It's not worth doing anything that's lasting. She's got it into her head that they should have stayed where they were. Where they *lived*. As though by coming here they're giving in. Dad's just been telling me."

"Oh, Christ."

"Her first words when they came. 'This is where we're going to die.' What can any of us do to talk her out of that?"

"I don't know. I really don't know. The trouble is, she's right. But not yet, for God's sake. Not for a long while, yet. Your dad's not as sprightly as he used to be, but she's in perfect health."

"That's exactly what he said."

"Don't let it upset you, love. It would have been worse, if we'd let them stay up there—another of those damp winters."

"I asked him if that's why he brought his rosebush with him. To show her that he was thinking of the future. Something to look forward to, I mean."

"And what did he say?"

"He said it was nothing of the sort. It hadn't crossed his mind. And I don't believe he thinks of it as your rose still. He brought it because he's fond of it. No other reason. He said that since it's so old, it might not survive being uprooted, but it was worth giving it a try. You know my dad—there's nothing soft about him. If the damn thing dies of the frost, as it well might, he's not going to read any stupid symbolism into it. He doesn't think like that. Never has done." She started to gather up the cups and saucers. "All the same," she said, "I hope you've made as good a job of planting it as you can. He said to say thanks for taking the trouble."

We left it at that. After dinner, Jane went round to spend an hour with them. I expect she found the right words to say; common-sensical things about what her plans were for the next few days, when she'd be driving into town, how she's thinking of preparations for Christmas. She won't have said anything about death or getting old, and she won't have done any false jollying. Jane's very like her father. When she'd been gone about half an hour, I went out into the garden for a breath of fresh air. A touch of frost was crisping the grass, and the sky was clear. For a few minutes I watched them from the far side of the lawn. Light was blazing from the living-room window. I saw Jane get up and walk towards the window, stand on a chair, undo the curtain-hooks, slowly. By this time tomorrow, I guess, she'll have fixed those frayed hems.

# Faith

I was christened Faith Marie after my mother's favorite sister, who died of Parkinson's disease the week before her eighteenth birthday, and whose memory has been preserved with stories of her courage and kindness that always inspired me as a girl. "The good die young," my mother used to sigh, whenever she mentioned Auntie Fay, and the saying always worried me. I wanted to be good. It was the one success I could imagine. While I was young, I tried to be as good as I could be, and for as long as my father lived, I gave him little trouble. I was his pride, my mother used to say. If he hadn't died of a stroke in his sleep that Sunday afternoon ten years ago, my life would never have taken the turn it did.

Were father and mother alive today, I know we'd be living just the same as always. We'd be rising at six and retiring at eleven seven days a week. Father would be winning at checkers, gin rummy, and hearts, and mother and I would still be trying to beat him. On Thursday nights we'd eat out at one of the same three restaurants we always went to, and father would be manager of Loudon Bank and Trust, where he hardly missed a day for thirty years. Wherever he went, he'd be making a grand impression with the profound conviction of his voice and the power of his penetrating eyes, which could see right into a man. And all the anger in him, which he rarely expressed, would still be stored at the back of his eyes or in the edge of his voice, so that even when he laughed you'd know he wasn't relaxed. He never was relaxed, no matter how he tried. I know I'd be dressed like a proper school girl, conservative and neat in cotton or wool dresses, never pants, my long hair pinned at the sides and rippling down my back or tied up in a braid for church or holidays or dinners out, but never short and boyish the way I wear it now. I'd be odorless and immaculate as ever, without an inkling of a body. And people would still be saying what a graceful girl I was. The way I moved was more like floating. The way I'd walk across our lawn, carrying a frosted glass of mother's minted tea out to the hammock where father read his evening paper in the summer before dinner. Sipping his drink and surveying the mowed yard and trimmed bushes and ever blooming flowers (which were my mother's work), he'd tousle my hair and sigh, "Now this is the life," as if he nearly believed it. Listening to him, I know I'd be as pale as ever with the face of a girl who lives as much in books as in the world. And I'd feel as far removed from father and that yard as if each page of history or poetry I'd ever read were another mile I'd walked away from home, and each word I learned another door that closed behind me. Though I'd know, no matter what I read, that my mind would never countermand my conscience or overrule my heart. Looking at me, my father's eyes would turn as warm as ever, the way they only seemed to do when he looked at me. Not even at my mother, whose whole mind and heart had been amended, geared to please him, would he ever look that way without a trace of anger or suspicion. But when he'd look at me I'd see the love he'd never put in words and the faith I'd never disappoint him. I hoped I never would. To keep the peace, his, my mother's, and my own, was such a need I had that had they lived I'm sure the three of us would have passed from Christmas to Christmas, through the dips and peaks of every year, like a ship that's traveling the same circle where the view is always familiar.

I remember one Sunday father and I were walking home from church all finely dressed and fit to impress whomever we passed. We crossed the green at the center of town and were approached by a pretty girl no more than 20, who was singing at the top of her voice. She smiled at us as she went by, leaving a strong soprano trill in our ears. I wasn't surprised when father turned to look at her, outraged. "Now that's the kind of bitch I'd like to see run out of town," he said. I knew he'd say the same to mother or me if we ever crossed or disappointed him. Because he couldn't tolerate the slightest deviation from his rules. He loved me with all of his heart on the condition that I please him.

Poor mother couldn't live without father. He'd been the center of her life for thirty years. Unlike father, whose beliefs were sacred to him, she had no strong opinions of her own. When he died, she wept with fear as much as grief, as if his death had been a shattering explosion that left our house and town in ruins. She sat all day in his easy chair and couldn't be moved, as if all of her habits as well as her heart were permanently broken. My words and tears never touched her. Exactly like the garden flowers she used to cut to decorate the house, she faded a little more each day. And it was only two months after father was gone that she was laid beside him. She was buried in June, the week before our high school graduation.

Compton people who wouldn't speak to me today were concerned and kind when mother died. There were several families that offered me a home. But I was eighteen, old enough to be on my own, and more at ease in the drawing rooms of novels than I'd ever be in any Compton house. Today there are many in town who believe it was a great mistake, letting me live alone. But I was adamant about it, and I appeared to be as responsible and as mature as any valedictorian of her class is expected to be.

I was as shaken by my parents' death as if the colors of the world had all been changed. Having adjusted myself to my father's wishes for so many years, I had no other inclination. After he was gone, I continued to live exactly as he would have liked me to. If anything, I was more careful not to hurt him than before, as if in death his feelings had become more sensitive than ever and the burden of his happiness was entirely left to me. After mother's death and the end of school, I took the first available job in town at Compton library. I was grateful that the work suited me, because I would have taken any job to keep me busy.

Our town of Compton is a tourist town. For three months out of every year the population triples, and Decatur Street is a slow parade of bodies and cars that doesn't end for ninety days. At the end of June, the summer people come. In their enormous yachts and their flashy cars, they arrive. Every year it is a relief to see them come and then a relief to see them go. They are so different from us.

Compton people are short on words. Even in private with their closest kin, the talk is sparse and actions have more meaning.

Whenever father was troubled, mother made him a squash pie or one of his other favorites to indicate her sympathy or support. She never asked him to explain. If a man in Compton is well-liked, he'll never have to buy himself a drink at the taverns. By the little favors, by the number of nods he receives on the street, or by the way he is ignored as much as if he were dead, he'll know exactly what his measure is with people. And by the silences, by whether there is comfort or communion in the long pauses between sentences, he'll know exactly how close he is to an acquaintance. I've always known that Compton people were unique. Our women never chattered the way the summer women do, as if there were no end to what they'd say. I've seen the summer people's children awed and muted by the grave reserve and the repressed emotion of a Compton child. And I've seen the staring fascination of all Compton with the open manner of the summer people, who wander through the streets at noon, baring their wrinkled thighs, their cleavage and their bulges to the sun for everyone to see—a people whose feelings flash across their faces as obvious and naked as if they had no secrets. As a child, I used to wander down to watch them at the docks. They seemed as alien and entertaining as a circus troupe. At five o'clock, from boat to boat, there was the sound of ice and glasses, the smell of tonic water, shaving lotion, lipstick, and perfume. For evening the women dressed in shocking pink and turquoise, colors bright enough to make a Compton woman blush. There was always laughter interwoven with their conversation, and the liquor made the laughter louder and the talk still freer until the people were leaning into each other's faces or falling into embraces with little cries of "darling" or "my dear." And as I watched them, the gaiety, the confidence, and the warmth of these people always inspired me with affection and yearning for the closeness and the freedom that they knew. It wasn't till I was older I realized that all of their words and embraces brought them no closer to each other than Compton people are—that the distances between them were just as painful and exactly as vast, in spite of the happy illusion they created.

The summer mother died, I walked to work through the crowds to the rhythm of the cash registers, which never stopped ringing till ten o'clock at night in the restaurants and gift shops all along Decatur Street. And all summer the library, which is a busy place in winter, was nearly empty. I sat at the front desk in the still, dark room, listening to the commotion of cars and voices in the streets. And through the windows I could tell the weather in the patch of sky above the heavy laden elms whose leaves were never still, but trembled, bobbed, and shuddered to every slightest nuance of the air. And seemed to capture and proclaim the whole vitality of every day more truly and completely than any self-afflicted human soul could ever hope to render it. I have no other memory of that summer, which disappeared as quickly as it came. But the end of every Compton summer is the same. Even the most greedy merchants are frazzled and fatigued by the daily noise and the rising exuberance of the tourists passing down the coast to home. By then, the beaches and the streets are strewn with cans and papers, as if the town had been a carnival or a zoo, and Compton is glad to see the last of the crowd, whose refuse is only further evidence of the corruption of their pleasure-happy souls.

My first winter alone there were many nights when I cried myself to sleep. I missed my mother's quiet presence in the house, and the smells which always rose from the warm, little kitchen where she baked or washed or sat across from me on winter afternoons when I came in from school. Even for a Compton woman she was more than usually quiet, so shy that she had no friends. She went to church on Sunday but the rest of the week she hardly left the yard. My father shopped for all of our food to save her the pain of going out in public. If she'd had her way, she'd never have eaten out with us on Thursday nights. But father insisted on it. "She needs the change," he used to say.

I don't remember mother ever raising her voice to me in anger. All discipline was left to father. She didn't often kiss or hug me either. But she used to brush my hair one hundred strokes a night, and I remember the gentle touch of her hands. There were times when her shyness made her seem as self-effacing as a nun, and times when I thought I must be living with a saint, the way she read her Bible daily and seemed to have no selfish desires or worldly needs. She dressed in greys and browns, and her dresses hung loose on her bony frame. Though her face was usually serious if not sad, I always believed she was happy in her life with father and me. She couldn't do enough for us, particularly father. About her past I only knew that she was born of alcoholic parents who were now both dead, that she'd worshipped her sister, Faith, and that she never corresponded with her older sister, Mary, who lived in California and was also alcoholic. Most often mother didn't like to reminisce. If I asked her a question she didn't like, she didn't answer it. There were some weeks when she spoke so little that if she hadn't read aloud to me, I hardly would have heard her voice. It was her reading aloud at night that I missed the most after she was gone. It was a habit we kept from before I could read to myself, when to hear her speak page after page was a luxury as soothing and as riveting as any mystery unravelling itself to revelation. It was through the sound of her voice speaking someone else's words that I knew my mother best.

Many nights I cried with all the fear and passion of the child I was and would ever have remained had I been given a choice. And, with a child's love, I saw the images of my father and mother rise up in the dark above my bed as clear and painfully defined as the impression they had left upon my heart. For the simplicity of my old life, I also cried. The simple life of a child who wants to please. For I recognized myself among the spinster women of our town, of whom there are many. Women who never leave the houses of their stern fathers and their silent, sacrificing mothers, houses of a kind so prevalent in Compton. Daughters with all of the rebellion driven out of them at an early age, all of the rudeness skimmed away, severely lashed and molded by the father's anger and the mother's fear of all the changing values in the sinful world. Many of our Compton spinsters are sensitive, high strung. You can see they were the children who avoided pain, preferred endearments and affection. They rarely gossip the way the married women do. To their mothers and their fathers they are faithful and devoted to the end, loyal to the present and the past, forgetful of the future. So much I see about them now that I didn't know when I counted myself one of them.

I had one friend from childhood, Mary Everly, who was studying to be a nurse in a city fifty miles away. Though she sometimes wrote to me, she never came home, finding Compton a "stifling" place. I was close to no one else in town. A few months after mother died, the invitations to supper and the concerned calls from neighbors stopped. Like my mother, I was shy. I had no skill at small talk and was relieved to be left in peace. But I analyzed myself the way a lonely person wonders why he is not loved. And I studied my life until I was as far removed from it as if I had been carved and lifted out of Compton and left to hover like a stranger over everything familiar.

Two times I went to visit Father Ardley in his blue-walled office at the vestry, and twice the touch of his thumb on my forehead, where he signed the cross, brought me to tears. I was drawn to the love of the church. I had an unexamined faith in God, but a fear that His demands would be crushing, were I to take them to heart. It was an irrational fear I tried to explain to Father Ardley, whose eyes were as cold as a winter sky while his voice was like the sun warming it. "You are still in mourning Faith," he said to me. "Such a loss as you've suffered can't be gotten over quickly. You must pray to God and keep yourself busy, child," he said, though I had never been idle in my life, not ever then or now.

For seven years I was as busy as I could be. My conscience kept me well supplied with tasks, and there is no end to what a person ought to do. I worked at the library. I lived in my father's house. I baked for the church bazaars. I visited Father Ardley. The summer people came and left as regular as the tides. I had as many warm acquaintances as ever, and I had no close friends. I still wrote letters to Mary Everly, who was now a nurse, married, and living in Cincinnati with her second baby on the way. Though the memory of my parents' love sustained me, and my father's wishes continued to guide me, time diluted their power to comfort me. Some mornings, walking through the sunny streets to work, the thought of death would take me by surprise, and I knew that mine would mean no more to anyone in town than the sudden disappearance of a picket fence on Elm Street or a missing bed of flowers in Gilbey Park.

I never went out with men. Not that I wasn't attractive. My father used to tell me I was pretty, and Mrs. Beggin at the library said I was a "lovely looking girl" and she couldn't see why I wasn't married yet. But Compton men knew different. Something they saw behind my shyness frightened them away. Something my mother and father had never seen. For beneath it all I wasn't a normal Compton woman, not typical no matter how I tried to be. Whether it was the influence of the summer people or the hours I had escaped in books, I was always "different" as far as Compton men could see, and they were just as strange to me.

It was the eighth summer after mother's death that I met Billy

Tober. I was just 26. William Tober IV, his family had named him. He was a summer boy, four years younger than I, a college student, though his eyes were the shallow blue of a flier or a sailor. I noticed him before he ever noticed me. I'd always see him with a different girl with the same smile on his lips. He began to come to the library many afternoons. He liked poetry and novels, and he'd ask me for suggestions. I was surprised when he began to appear at the end of the day to walk me home. It wasn't long before we began to meet in the evenings too.

I wish I could say that I remember Billy well, and I wish that I could describe him clearly. But I can't remember much that he ever said and barely how he looked. I only remember the effect he had upon me. As if I knew how it would end, I never invited him to my house, and I'd only allow him to walk me halfway home, which made him laugh at first. In the evening, I'd meet him at Gilbey Park, which is just outside the center of Compton. It is a pretty hill of bushes, trees, and flowers which overlooks the harbor. On a hidden bench we sat and sipped the wine that Billy always brought. Though I'd never tasted liquor or sat and talked with a young man, I was completely at ease. The wine and dusky out-of-doors loosened my tongue until my hidden thoughts rose up as urgently as if my life depended on telling them. It often surprised me what I said, because whenever I was with Billy I was a different woman, so unlike my usual self I'm sure no one in Compton would have recognized me. It was as natural as breathing, the way I'd change into a giddy girl whenever I was with him. I fed on his flattery and couldn't get enough of it. "Where did you ever get such hair?" he asked about the curls my mother never let me cut. After that, it was my eyes he noticed. My neck was regal as a queen's, he said. And there was pride as well as grace in the way I walked. My hands, the smallness of my waist, my legs, my voice he also praised. I couldn't hear enough. For the month of July, we saw each other every night. At home, I'd often stare for an hour at the stranger in the mirror, this woman with a body that a man desired.

Whatever it is that attracts a man to a woman I've too little experience to know. But I believe that for Billy every woman was a challenge. To win her heart as well as her body was his goal. He was as restless and driven a person as I've known. Obsession with a woman must have soothed him. He used to tell me that he loved me, but I'm sure that if he'd heard the same from me, his feelings would have died. If I had loved him, I would have told him. He begged me often enough to say it. But I never was able to. "We're too different," I insisted. "I'm not myself when I'm with you." But I gloried in the power he'd given me. I was in love with his desire, which singled me out from all the world and made the world a painless kingdom where I ruled the more he wanted me. We met most nights in August. We drove out to Haskall Beach to a private place I knew. By then we hardly spoke, and there were times, with his breath hot on my face and his voice crying my name, I felt I'd be more comforted and serene if I were sitting there alone and free of all the yearning human arms can cause.

All those nights we spent together, I never took precautions. "Is it safe?" he asked me many times. But I ignored the question, as if it would have been the crowning sin if I'd been careful to prevent any meaning or possibility of love to come out of the fire of vanity and ignited pride which burned between us. Driving back to town, the silence in the car was so oppressive that it taunted us.

The day that Billy left, I felt relieved, and in the weeks that followed, I didn't miss him once, which surprised me. We wrote no letters to each other. Life went back to normal, and the longer he was gone the more I began to hope I'd never see him again.

When Doctor Filser told me I was pregnant, I could see he was surprised the way all Compton would be. I saw the way he looked at me with new, appraising eyes, and I burned to think of all the other eyes that would be privy to scenes of Billy and me on Haskall Beach. For I knew they'd piece it all together down to every detail.

When I told Father Ardley the news, I aimed the words and threw them at him one by one like darts. But his tone was not what I expected. He wasn't angry with me. "I suppose it was that summer boy you were seeing," he sighed, and he knew enough not to suggest the marriage he'd have insisted upon had Billy Tober been a Compton boy. Instead, he gave me the name of Brighton Adoption Agency.

For all of the nine months, I carried the child as if it were a sin beyond forgiveness and there was no forgetting or ignoring it. I felt my father's wrath in every room of the house, and I never visited his or my mother's graves, knowing the affront it would be. As if they had died again, I felt bereft. I was sure they wanted no part of me now and that I could never turn to them again.

Compton people were not so harsh. One hundred years ago they might have stoned me or run me out of town. Now, as much as they disapproved, they also pitied me. No one tried to deprive me of my job. Though there were some who would no longer speak to me, there were more whose pity moved them to be kinder than before. My humiliation was enough for them and lesson enough for their children. When they saw that my cross was sufficiently heavy, they approved. Even today, times when my heart is light and I'm tempted to laugh in public, I check myself. I know I'll always be on good behavior in Compton, and the more abject I appear the better off I'll be.

It is two o'clock, the last day of May, a Saturday, and all of the windows in the house are open for the first time this season. There is a cold breeze coming off the harbor, running through the rooms in currents which break against the walls and boil the curtains halfway to the ceiling. Every year it is the same, the day of opening the windows. The sea wind scours every corner of the house until its heavy atmosphere is broken. All of the memories which hang in odors are borne away until the rooms are only rooms and this woman, dreaming at a littered kitchen table, is just as relieved as if she'd just received communion, left all of her habits at the altar rail, and returned to her pew with no identity but her joy.

It is so quiet. The baby is asleep upstairs under a pink quilt. When he wakes, he will have roses in his cheeks. He is so blonde, his hair is nearly white. He bears no likeness to my family, and yet the night he was born I knew he was mine as surely as these arms or thoughts belong to me. After the pain of labor, as if I had been delivered of all shame, I asked to see the child. When I saw two waving arms, a tiny head, my heart rose up, amazed. And when they put him in my arms, it was love I held, all warmly wrapped, alive.

So many tired-looking mothers you see in Compton. They hardly seem to care how they appear. Wearing shabby clothes, herding their little broods across the streets, worried and snapping orders at them. But a Compton woman never shows her deepest feelings to

336 *Ellen Wilbur*

the world. When Paul was first at home, I used to kiss his little face at least a hundred times a day. Who but an infant or God could stand so much affection? And all of those kisses were just the beginning of love, the first expression of my newly seeded heart which bloomed, expanded, and flowered with every kiss.

At five o'clock I'd pick the baby up from Mrs. Warren who cared for him the hours I worked. We'd ride home on a crowded bus of Compton women in their fifties, carefully dressed, who rested their heavy bodies behind a row of shopping bags. When they saw the child, their eyes grew soft and bright. "What a love," they'd say, all smiles, and they'd ask his name or age and touch the corner of his blanket so gingerly, with reverence, as if he were to them the fearful treasure he was to me, and they had forgotten all of the strain, the distraction, the heavy weight of care which had exalted them and only remembered how close they once had come to perfect love. I could see them in their kitchens years ago, bathing their babies in the little plastic tubs that Compton mothers use. I could imagine them, once so shy and bending to the will of the town, their fathers, and their husbands, becoming fierce and stubborn, demanding so much satisfaction, comfort, and such happiness for their little ones as they had never dreamed of for themselves.

By now I ought to have the kitchen clean, the wash brought in and folded, and the vegetables picked and washed. It is so rare I sit and dream that when I do the memories come fast and heavy as an avalanche. I've known some cynics who remember only pain and ugliness, as if the way a man remembers corresponds with what he hopes. When Paul was born, it changed my past as well as the future. Now, when I look back, I see beauty. The older the memory, the more beautiful it has become. Even moments of great pain or disappointment have been transformed, given an importance and a dignity they never had at the time, as if whatever happens and wherever I have failed may one day be redeemed in the far future. I pray it will be so.

# The Formula

The Passport Bureau in Wroclaw stands a block from Kosciuszko Square, near the SB headquarters, the city jail, the Court of Justice. Nina had been there more times than she could count. There was a second entrance now to ease the traffic, but before they opened it, the lines of people wanting to leave were as long as the lines for bananas.

This morning she chose the main door. Climbing the stairs, she sifted through her mind all of her transgressions. Her worst sins took place three years ago, and they were comparatively minor. She'd distributed leaflets, yelled "Gestapo" at the Zomos. She and her husband had also sheltered, for an evening, an underground activist, but he had left the country a long time ago. She knew that in all likelihood the note calling her to appear as a "witness" was somehow connected to her trip. In all likelihood, she was about to have an encounter with the Passport SB.

The second floor was empty except for an old man who sat in a chair reading *Slowo Polskie*. She scanned the numbers above the doors, walked the length of the hall twice, but she couldn't find 214. It was almost nine o'clock. You couldn't be late for an appointment like hers.

A big guy with a droopy moustache emerged from 211. His stylish jeans outfit made her think he worked here. At the SB headquarters, she recalled, everybody cultivated the student-intellectual look. As if they had just left a Solidarity rally.

"Excuse me," she said. "I'm supposed to report to room 214."

His gaze traversed her figure. The white missy dress, red purse, coral necklace, lipstick, and sunglasses puzzled. This wasn't a place you dressed up for.

Which was why she'd dressed up.

"Do you have a summons?"

If she didn't, she wouldn't have been here. She dug into her purse.

"Okay. And your ID?"

She pulled the green booklet from her wallet. He opened it, looked at the picture, at her, then at the picture again. Exactly like East German border officials.

He grinned. "You don't look the same as in the picture."

"I'm older now."

"You don't look older. Younger, I'd say. And prettier."

She grinned right back at him.

He led her to a door that had no number. It also had no doorknob. She should have known this was the one.

He pressed a button. She heard a thin ring. The door opened a few inches. "Tell Heniek he's got a guest," her guide said to someone she couldn't see.

The door closed. Her guide returned her ID and summons, nodded good-by. As he turned to go, she said, "You know, you remind me of someone. I can't think who."

He leered. "An old boyfriend, maybe?"

She snapped her fingers. "Walesa!" she cried. "You look like Walesa!"

"Please," he said, wincing. He hurried off down the hall.

A few minutes or so later, the door was reopened by a fit-looking man who wore a pair of black-rimmed glasses and had, Nina thought, the build of a cyclist. She handed him her note and her ID. He glanced at them, put them in his pocket, then gestured at a chair in the hall. "Why don't you take a seat," he said. "I'll be right with you."

The usual tactic: making you wait to show you who had the power. And if you got scared in the meantime, so much the better. She was familiar with the trick.

Two years ago she had received a similar summons, though it had called her not to the Passport Bureau but to SB headquarters.

At the reception desk an old SBek had examined her summons, her ID, and her face, which she tried to make blank, then had barked "Wait!" and disappeared behind a door. She waited half an hour, during which time all sorts of possibilities occurred to her. Perhaps they had arrested someone who worked with her, or perhaps they had photographed her at a demonstration. She always carried her toothbrush to demonstrations, and she wished she'd brought it now. Martial law was still *the* law, and she was no longer a passive antisocialist element.

That day another SBek had finally materialized and introduced himself as "Captain Poniatowski." In the elevator, on the way up to the sixth floor, he attempted small talk, asking her if she planned to attend the football match. She sensed that he was a dullard. She had a cousin, a likable fellow named Wladyslaw, who on even his brightest day remained a victim of a mental-energy shortage. He failed his college entrance exams, he mangled numerous engines when he attempted auto mechanics. Finally, one day at a family picnic, he let slip the fact that he had gone to work for "them." Her uncle Zenek, her cousins Krzysztof and Marek asked Wladyslaw to go behind some trees. They came back rubbing their knuckles. Wladyslaw slunk off and drove away.

Her interview with Poniatowski had taken place in a tiny office that contained a coffee table, two chairs, and a small desk. The room had a side door that had been left ajar. They sat down at the coffee table, and he offered her a cigarette. She declined.

"Good you don't smoke," he said, lighting up. "Pity to lose such an attractive woman to lung cancer."

She wondered where they learned their lines. A training film, probably, since reading would be too taxing.

"Mrs. Bober," he said puffing on his cigarette, "do you have a dog?"

She said she did. She would have lied if she thought he was really interested in her dog. But they always began by asking you about something that didn't really interest them.

"Could you describe this animal for me?"

"She's just a little brown dog. There's nothing really outstanding about her."

"Breed?"

"Cocker spaniel."

"You're sure?"

"Oh, yes," she said. "I have her registration and a picture too. I'll show you." She reached for her purse.

"Never mind," he said. "I was just asking about the dog because one of our officers was bitten on your street. But the dog that did that was a German Shepherd. You don't know anything about it, do you?"

"Was the officer trespassing?"

"Trespassing?" he said incredulously. "You must know that during the present state of affairs, it's impossible for an officer of the security service to trespass."

She knew it, but she bet the dog didn't. "Oh, that's right," she said.

"Oh, well," he said, "this business about the dog doesn't matter so much. Since you're here, though, perhaps we can discuss another little matter."

He said he had noticed that she planned to go to Mexico. That was a Western country, he informed her, one whose aims and goals were, quite frankly, opposed to those of Poland.

"You'll be on your own there," he said, "and you must be careful."

"Yes," she said, as innocently as she could, "I remember what happened to Trotsky."

"Trotsky? Who . . . oh, well, yes. But what I meant is that if, say, someone there asks you to do something contrary to the best interests of our state, you must refuse. More importantly, if someone here in Poland—banned Solidarity activists, you know—if they ask you to carry something out of the country—even if they say it's just a box of dried mushrooms for relatives in the West—you mustn't do it. Bring it to us."

It was time now to play stupid. She hoped he was smart enough to recognize stupidity when he saw it. "Would they do that?" she breathed.

"They very well might," he said grimly. "You can't put anything past them."

She had paid her Solidarity fees the previous day. "I'll certainly do that," she said.

"You're a responsible citizen," he said. "We appreciate your help. Perhaps I'll talk to you again when you've returned from your trip."

She never took that trip because the Mexican government refused her a visa. She never head from Poniatowski again, either, and for that she was infinitely grateful. Because she knew that she had been called there for a purpose that had nothing to do with packages or, for that matter, with the good of the country. And at some point in the interview, Poniatowski had judged her unfit.

Yesterday, when she received the new summons, her first thought was that perhaps they had changed their minds.

They had changed their minds about her before. Ten years ago, she had wanted to go to the Netherlands. When she went to the Passport Bureau, the official she had to deal with was a former classmate at the Romance Languages Department. She remembered him as a hippie intellectual. He used to serve as a guide for the Wroclaw Open Theatre Festival. He was fiercely avant-garde.

"Couldn't get a job as a French teacher in Wroclaw," he told her, "and you know, I've lived here all my life. Didn't see myself in a provincial school in some godforsaken little village. I'm not Doctor Judym. Here they at least pay you decently and I might get an apartment in a year or two. Marta's pregnant, you know. We can't stay in my parents' two rooms forever."

He shuffled papers. "You've come for your passport," he said. "You didn't get it."

"Why?" she asked cooly, as if it didn't matter, though it did— very much. "I got one last year. Everything was okay then."

He looked embarrassed. "I'm sorry, Nina," he said. "Really I am. But just between you and me, your chances don't look good. It says in your file that you got involved with the BBC and refused to offer an explanation."

She opened her eyes wide to show that the charge offended her.

The charge, of course, was true. She had taken part in a peace demonstration in London and been interviewed by the BBC. When she returned to Poland and handed in her passport, an official asked her if she had participated in any demonstrations.

Since they obviously already knew, she saw no point in discussing it. She said no. But their devotion to the confession was priestly, and because she refused to offer one, they kept her at home for two years.

The knobless door opened. The man called Heniek stepped out

and asked her to come with him. Behind the door there was a long corridor with three doors on each side. (These, she noticed, had knobs.) Heniek ushered her into the first room on the left.

Sunlight streamed through two big windows. A coffee table stood in the center of the room, an armchair parked on either side. There was also a side door. It had been left ajar.

"Sit down," Heniek told her.

When they were seated, he pulled out his cigarettes. "Care for one?"

"No," she said, "I'm too scared of getting lung cancer."

"That *would* be a shame," he said. "Especially since you're such an attractive woman." He lit his cigarette, drew deeply, and sighed. "Now then," he said. "I know who you are. I'm Captain Kalinowski"—another Polish aristocrat—"and I asked you here today because I wanted to talk to you about your travels. You've been to England, West Germany, several other countries as well, and I see that you're about to visit the United States on an exchange program. Tell me a bit about the places you've visited."

She had been right. This was the Passport SB. They wanted something—it would be a while before she knew just what—and to get it, they would try waving the passport in her face.

There were two ways to handle the situation. You could be tough, tell them right away to forget it, in which case you could forget the passport. Or you could play a fool, babbling nonsense and pretending you had no idea what was going on, keeping them from getting more than a word or two in; sooner or later, your interlocutor would tire, and at that point he would either openly propose "cooperation," or else give up and send you home—in which case you might still get the passport. She knew she ought to tell him to take the passport to hell. But she wanted to go. She hadn't left Poland since 1981, and she thought that if she didn't get out soon, she'd go crazy. Leaving the country for brief periods was her safety valve. She would go to the West, start hating it, and come back here purged.

If she hoped to wake up in Florida one morning and find that she had started missing Poland, she would have to be careful now. "Well," she began, "the first time I went abroad was during my second year at the University."

"England, right?"

"That's right. I spent two months there at an international

student camp. We all worked on a farm. It was fun. We hitchhiked to London one weekend and—"

"Did anything special happen during your stay there?"

"What do you mean?"

"Anything to do with, say, the police of that country?"

At the peace demonstration, everyone had been briefly under arrest. She knew he knew that, and she knew it didn't interest him. She felt herself warming to the game. "You know," she said, "I did have an encounter with the police. Nice guys they were. Big. Tall, like you. I was hitchhiking, and the woman who picked me up was so funny." She giggled. "This woman had a plastic box with jellied eel in it, and she was eating eel with her right hand while driving with her left. She offered me some, but I *do* hate eels. Of course, you can't buy them here these days.

"Anyway, she hit another car—dented its right side. You know how they drive on the left there. So the police came and took us to the police station, and I was a witness. They gave me coffee and crackers."

"Can you imagine our police doing that?" he said. His question seemed to tickle him. He laughed until his shoulders shook and tears appeared in his eyes. She felt unsavory in his presence. "My goodness," he said, wiping his eyes. "And so . . . nothing serious happened?"

"Where?"

"In England. You weren't approached by Polish immigration circles? No one offered you anything?"

"*You* know how it is in the West," she said, sure that he didn't—SBeks weren't allowed to visit Western countries. "No one offers you anything there. They want you to pay for everything. That's capitalism. It's not like here, where everyone shares."

"Oh, the West isn't so bad," he said. "For instance, there are no lines there."

"Lines aren't so bad," she said. "I met one of my closest friends in a line. It was one of those long lines—my husband and I needed a battery for our car—and this line lasted several weeks. The line committee assigned me Monday and Thursday, two until four, and it was while standing that I met Ewa. She operates some type of machine at the carriage factory. Where in the West could a college teacher meet and become close friends with a factory worker?"

"Ah," he said, "you're being facetious."

She showed him her *Who, me?* face.

"Let's forget about England and such places," he said, dismissing the whole of Western Europe with a wave of his hand, "and discuss this trip to America."

"What do you want to know?"

"To begin with, where is this university?"

"Florida. They say it's very hot there. I don't know how I'll stand the heat."

"It's hot in Mexico, isn't it? How did you stand it there?"

Either they'd done a lousy job on her file or he'd done a lousy job reading it. "Were you under the impression I'd been to Mexico?" she said. "Someone gave you the wrong information. I never got a visa."

He reddened. The myth of the omniscient SB was being debunked. "I knew that," he said. "I just forgot." He sat forward, all business, and told her he wanted to know what her duties in America would be, who her co-workers would be, what kind of students she would have, where she would travel in her free time, and what she would do when she got there.

She told him that she would teach French, that her co-workers would be other teachers of French, that her students would be mostly eighteen-year-old Floridians, that she might visit Miami in her free time, and that when she got there she would probably doze on a beach.

"Very good," he said. "Now. What is this university itself supposed to be like?"

She tapped her forehead with a finger. "I'm so silly," she said. "You know, I had a University of Florida catalogue and I loaned it to someone and never got it back. If I had it, it would tell you everything you need to know. But you know what? I'll have their admissions office send you one."

"That won't be necessary."

"It's no trouble."

"*Please,*" he said, as if already imagining the reception he would get at SB headquarters when they found out he was receiving fat envelopes from schools in the USA. "Please. Don't bother. How is it you chose this particular university?"

"Last year we had a visiting lecturer from the University of Florida. He suggested that—"

"Your department has many lecturers from abroad."

Now she thought she knew what he wanted. The visitors. They were always interested in Western guests. They wanted someone to inform on them.

"You get to know many of these visitors, I imagine?"

"Oh, no. *You* know how people from the West are—they don't really talk. Spend a year around one of them and all you ever get to know is 'Hi. How are you. Fine.'"

"You never serve as an interpreter?"

She often did. "Me? I'm too shy."

He said he hadn't noticed that.

"That's because I feel relaxed now," she said, smiling and looking him in the eye. "When I'm relaxed, I'm not shy."

"And you're never relaxed around Westerners?"

"Hardly."

"That's strange," he said. "Especially since you go there so often." He lit himself another cigarette. "You like to travel, don't you?"

A threat was sewn up in that question. "I've always enjoyed it," she said, "but I think I'm getting tired of it. I really do."

"Yet you're getting ready to leave again."

"Only for professional enrichment. I think that when I get back this time, I'll stay. Everything I care about is here."

"I see," he said. "We were talking about visitors to your department. Who spends the most time with them? What about Docent Talik?"

She remembered something. Three or four years ago, they had continually pestered one of her colleagues, calling her day and night, until finally she disconnected her phone. They had never, as far as anyone knew, been able to place an informer in the department. There weren't even any Party members there.

The picture became clear. It was the department itself that interested them. They wanted someone to report what people said at name-day parties, at dinner, on the way home from work. A remark passed over a plate of *bigos* might one day be used to blackmail.

"Docent Talik?" she said. "She's a marvelous lady. A fine scholar too. You aren't familiar, are you, with her study of the epistolary novel?"

"I haven't got around to that yet."

"She was my thesis advisor."

"I know."

"Whenever we had a seminar with her, she would bring us these wonderful cookies she'd baked. If it snowed, she would always remind us to put on our woolen caps. She said, 'A woolen cap can save your life.'"

"Yes," he persisted, "but what about Docent Talik and the visitors?"

"She brings them cookies. This Fulbright lecturer I was telling you about? He loved her cookies so much she gave him a whole big box when he left. And a recipe. You know how Americans eat everything out of packages, ready-made."

He leaned over and tapped ashes into the ashtray. "You know," he said mildly, "you haven't answered my question."

"What question?"

"What is the atmosphere in your department? What do people talk about?"

"You didn't ask me such a question. You asked me about Docent Talik and her cookies."

"I didn't ask about cookies. I asked about Docent Talik and the visitors. Now I'm asking about the department."

She made herself sound peevish. "If you had asked me before," she said, "I would have told you."

"That's quite all right. I'm asking you now."

"What do you want to know?"

His jaw stiffened. Maybe she was getting to him. If so, this wouldn't continue much longer. "What is the atmosphere in your department? What do people talk about?"

She said they talked about everything. She said that as for the atmosphere, it was very much familial. Everybody, she told him, looked out for everybody else. Last week they delivered cooking oil to her store, she said, and you could buy as many bottles as you wanted. So she bought one for everybody in the department, even though the other customers in the store were grumbling that she intended to hoard the cooking oil and resell it. She had to call her husband to come and pick her up, because she had more cooking oil than she could carry on the tram.

"That," she concluded, "ought to tell you something."

"That," he said, "does indeed tell me something." He leaned over and ground out his cigarette.

It was a get-down-to-business gesture. For the first time, she felt scared. Now he would propose a deal, and when she refused, he would tell her no passport. All this playing stupid would come to nothing.

"Mrs. Bober," he said, "the reason I asked you to come is that you made a mistake filling out your passport application. You gave me an incorrect ID number."

If there was one thing life in Poland had taught her, it was how to fill out a form. She would never have made such a mistake.

"And since I needed to see your ID to correct the mistake," he went on, pulling out the booklet, handing it to her, "I thought I would invite you in for a chat."

He sat back and eyed her. "You know what I don't understand?" he said. "I don't understand why your husband would agree to your going away. I wouldn't let such an attractive woman go away to America by herself. I would keep her at home."

"My husband is very liberated. Besides, I'll only be gone for six months." She decided to probe. "If I get a passport, that is."

"I don't see why you shouldn't. In fact, I'm sure you will."

When he said that, she thought *I'm really going to get out.* It was only then that she realized just how badly she wanted to be gone. She had never quite recovered from that Sunday morning when she woke to find the phone lines dead, the airwaves silent, soldiers in the street. Her husband strung wires in a web across the ceiling, but they'd jammed the BBC. The loud hopes of the past sixteen months died in silence that December.

Just as she began to relax, he said, "But before you go, I do have to make a request. After you come back from the U.S., could we meet somewhere, maybe in a cafe or a restaurant, and have another little talk? You'd give me a call and we'd arrange a meeting."

She started to tell him she couldn't do that because her husband was a jealous man. Then she remembered she'd just said her husband was liberated. She couldn't think of any more banter.

"No," she said.

"No?"

You must never agree to meet them anywhere except where they work. You mustn't even meet them there unless you have something in writing that you can show someone before you go. Just in case.

"No," she repeated. "If you want to see me, you'll have to send me another summons to appear as a witness."

"That's just the formula. Let's not be so formal."

"I won't do it."

"Very well," he said. "But I'll give you a little call when you get back."

Opening the door for her, he said. "Don't tell anyone about our talk."

She instinctively reverted to her earlier role. "Oh, I've already told someone," she said.

He slammed the door. "Who?" he cried.

"Only my husband."

"Oh, well. . . . Just tell him it was related to your passport application."

"But it said I was to be a witness."

"Just the formula. He'll understand. Now . . . give me your word you won't tell a soul about our talk."

His hand was on the doorknob. She knew the prudent thing to do was give him her word—she could still tell anybody she wanted to. But she couldn't resist trying to annoy him. It would make the experience less humiliating. "I'll try not to tell," she said. "But I'm a born blabbermouth. Things slip out."

The hand on the doorknob went white. Heniek's face turned beet red. "Stay here," he ordered.

He scurried through the side door. She heard paper tearing, angry whispers. He reappeared, slamming the door behind him.

He slapped a sheet of paper down on the coffee table. "Come here," he said.

On the way across the room, she saw the side door open a crack. Heniek handed her a pen. "Write," he commanded.

"Write what?"

"What I dictate."

"But what will that be?"

"If you'll shut up, I'll tell you."

He waited for her to shut up. Then he dictated. "*I, Nina Bober, do solemnly hereby declare that I will keep secret the fact that a conversation took place between me and a member of the security service.*"

She knew the statement wasn't legally binding. She signed it and handed it to him.

"Thank you," he said, tucking it away. "Now, goodbye." He led her to the outer door.

Within seconds she was down the stairs and out on the street.

To keep herself from hurrying, she concentrated on breathing deeply, sucking warm summer air into her lungs. As usual, the streets were full of people. That was one of the things she loved about Poland. The presence of people in the streets. They didn't try to drive themselves everywhere. But then few of them could afford cars.

She crossed over the old moat. On a bench beside a cobblestone square where children were playing, she sat down and let her body go limp. She closed her eyes. She listened to the sounds around her—the voices of children, the clatter of a tram. Somewhere someone gunned a motorcycle.

She was going to America. She thought maybe when she got there, she would eat some peanut butter. A friend who immigrated to Long Island had sent her two jars a couple of years ago, and though she knew it was junk she loved it. This same friend of hers had written, in a letter that took almost two months to reach her: "My mother came last December. I took her to a supermarket in Lindenhurst, and when she saw all those people, hundreds of them, grabbing steak and ham and cornflakes and coffee, just grabbing items off the shelves indiscriminately and tossing them into shopping carts that already looked like mountains on wheels, it upset her so much she started shaking and we had to go home without doing any shopping. She refused to go in another store the rest of the time she was here. She went back to Poland two weeks early."

Probably there would be such stores in Florida.

When she opened her eyes, she noticed a group of little girls playing hopscotch in the square. Nimbly they kicked the pebble and hopped from block to block. She remembered playing the game when she was a child, in the ruins across the street from her building.

She had played, it seemed to her now, with an unusual degree of agility.

# NOTES ON CONTRIBUTORS

ANN BEATTIE was born in Washington, D.C., and educated at American University and the University of Connecticut. She is the author of several collections of stories, including *Distortions, The Burning House, Secrets and Surprises,* and *Where You'll Find Me.* Her novels are *Chilly Scenes of Winter, Falling in Place,* and, most recently, *Picturing Will.*

HAL BENNETT was born in 1930 in Buckingham, Virginia, grew up in Newark and has lived in Mexico. One of the most respected artists writing out of African American experience, he is the author of several novels—*A Wilderness of Vines, Wait Until the Evening, The Black Wine, Lord of Dark Places,* and *Seventh Heaven.* He has also published *Insanity Runs In Our Family: Short Stories* and *The Mexico City Poems* and *House on Hay.*

KELLY CHERRY is a novelist, story writer, and poet. Educated at Mary Washington, the University of Virginia, and the University of North Carolina at Greensboro, she is now Professor of English at the University of Wisconsin—Madison. Her novels include *Sick and Full of Burning, Augusta Played, The Lost Traveller's Dream,* and *In the Wink of an Eye.* In 1989 she received the first Poetry Award given by the Fellowship of Southern Writers.

LAWRENCE DUNNING, who was educated at Southern Methodist University, served four years in the Army Air Force in the Second World War, after which he worked as a publicist for the Dutch government, lived a stint in Greenwich Village, and, aiming to go to San Francisco, got as far as Denver where he worked as editor for an oil publication and for a missile manufacturer.

ANNE HOBSON FREEMAN's book of biographies, *The Style of a Law Firm: Eight Gentlemen from Virginia,* was published by Algonquin Books. Her stories and poems have appeared in many places, including *McCall's, Cosmopolitan, The New Virginia Review,* and in *Prize Stories from Mademoiselle* and *Best American Short Stories.*

ALYSON CAROL HAGY grew up on a farm in Franklin County, Virginia. She is a graduate of Williams College (where she was an outstanding athlete) and received her M.F.A. at the University of Michigan. Her fiction has appeared in, among others, *The Sewanee Review, North American Review,* and *Michigan Quarterly Review* and in her first collection, *Madonna on Her Back* (1986). A new collection is scheduled to appear from Poseidon Press in 1990.

NANCY HALE (1908–88) produced an impressive body of major work—novels, collections of short stories, plays, biography and autobiography, criticism, and books for children—from 1932, when *The Young Die Good* appeared, until the 1980s. She was for many years Lecturer at the Bread Loaf Writer's Conference and had worked as an assistant editor at *Vogue* and *Vanity Fair.* She was a good friend and strong supporter of the *VQR.* Rest in peace.

WILLIAM HOFFMAN, a native of West Virginia, served in the Army in the Second World War, after which he studied at Hampden-Sydney, Washington and Lee, and the University of Iowa. He is the author of nine novels and two collections of short fiction—*Virginia Reels* and *By Land, by Sea.* He and his wife live in Charlotte County, Virginia.

WARD JUST is the author of eight novels, most recently *Jack Gance,* two collections of short stories, and two books of nonfiction. He and his wife, Sarah, live in Paris.

JOANN KOBIN has published her short fiction in a variety of literary magazines including *Ascent, The Remington Review, The Massachusetts Review,* and *Ploughshares.*

PETER LASALLE, who grew up in Rhode Island and graduated from Harvard, is author of the novel *Strange Sunlight* and a collection of stories—*The Graves of Famous Writers.* His stories have been published in many magazines and in *Best American Short Stories* and *Prize Stories: The O. Henry Awards.* He has taught at Harvard and in France, and is on the faculty of the University of Texas.

CLAYTON W. LEWIS served in the Marine Corps and holds degrees from Duke University and the University of Iowa. After a time spent working for an advertising agency, he became a teacher and has been teaching at the State University of New York at Geneseo.

JAMES LOTT is Professor of English and Dean of the College at Mary Baldwin College in Staunton, Virginia. His work has appeared in *The Southern Review, Mississippi Review, South Carolina Review,* and *The Southern Humanities Review.* His story, "The Janeites," was chosen for the 1987 *O. Henry Awards* anthology.

HILARY MASTERS has published six novels, including those in The Harlem Valley Trilogy—*Clemmons, Cooper,* and *Strickland.* His stories have appeared in many magazines and have been collected in *Hammertown Tales* (1986). His extended biographical essay, *Last Stands: Notes from Memory,* received extraordinary critical praise. He lives in Pittsburgh.

JACK MATTHEWS is a collector and dealer in old and rare books and is Distinguished Professor of English at Ohio University. He has published novels, collections of stories, poems, and essays. His most recent book is *Memoirs of a Bookman,* a collection of essays. "Chad Creek" was selected for inclusion in the 1972 edition of the *O. Henry Awards.*

WILLIAM MEREDITH won the Pulitzer Prize for poetry for *Partial Accounts* (1987). Born in New York City in 1919 and a graduate of Princeton (1940), he served as a naval aviator in the Second World War. His first book, *Love Letter from an Impossible Land* (1944), was selected by Archibald MacLeish for the Yale Series of Younger Poets. Since then he has published eight collections of poems as well as translations, opera libretti, and essays. He was Poetry Consultant, Library of Congress, 1978–80.

KENT NELSON has produced two novels, *Cold Wind River* and *All Around Me Peaceful,* as well as a collection of stories—*The Tennis Player.* He has published more than fifty stories in a variety of journals, and his work has twice been included in *Best American Short Stories.* He lives in Exeter, New Hampshire, with his wife, Laurie, and their daughter, Lanier.

WILLIAM PEDEN, Professor Emeritus at the University of Missouri, Columbia, is a short story writer and novelist as well as an editor, scholar, and critic of distinction. His collection of stories is *Night in Funland* and his most recent novel is *Twilight at Monticello.* Peden served as Director of the University of Missouri Press.

DEBORAH SEABROOKE graduated from Cornell with a B.A. in English in 1972. She studied with Fred Chappell at the University of North Carolina—Greensboro. Her stories have appeared widely in the magazines and in a number of anthologies. A native of Huntington, Long Island, she is married and lives in Greensboro. She is finishing a novel.

DAVID STACTON (1925–68) was born in Nevada, attended Stanford and the University of California, and lived, at one time or another, in every country in Europe. A highly idiosyncratic artist, he wrote twenty novels with an amazing range of setting and subject—from ancient Egypt and medieval Japan to the cult classic about a contemporary film festival, *Old Acquaintance*. A painter also, Stacton died suddenly in Denmark. His work calls for rediscovery and appraisal.

PETER TAYLOR is Professor Emeritus at the University of Virginia. Born in Tennessee and a graduate of Kenyon College, he is the author of two novels, four plays, and six collections of short stories. *The Old Forest and Other Stories* won the PEN/Faulkner Award for 1985, and his novel *A Summons to Memphis* won the Pulitzer Prize. He and his wife, poet and story writer Eleanor Ross Taylor, live in Charlottesville, Virginia.

TED WALKER, who was born in 1934, lives and teaches in Sussex. He is a poet, story writer, and playwright. His stories have appeared in *The New Yorker* and in several collections. His plays have been produced by the BBC for both radio and television. His *Selected Poems* was published in 1987.

ELLEN WILBUR attended Bennington College and now lives in Cambridge, Massachusetts, with her husband and son. Her first collection of stories, *Wind and Birds and Human Voices*, was published in 1985.

STEVE YARBROUGH is a native of Mississippi. He studied at the University of Arkansas with James Whitehead and William Harrison. His stories have been published in *The Southern Review, The Hudson Review, The Missouri Review,* and elsewhere. He teaches at Fresno State and is working on a novel set in Poland.

\*       \*

SHEILA MCMILLEN is a graduate of the Universities of Pennsylvania and New Hampshire and the Iowa Writers Workshop. Her stories have been published in a variety of magazines and she has, at this writing, just completed her first novel. Formerly Director of the Green

Mountain Writer's Conference in Johnson, Vermont, Ms. McMillen is Lecturer in Creative Writing at the University of Virginia.

GEORGE GARRETT is Henry Hoyns Professor of Creative Writing at the University of Virginia. He is the author of twenty-three books and editor of seventeen others. His forthcoming novel is *Entered from the Sun.*